A
Long
Shadow

Caroline Kington

Published by
Lightning Books Ltd
Imprint of EyeStorm Media
312 Uxbridge Road
Rickmansworth
Hertfordshire
WD3 8YL

www.lightning-books.com

First Edition 2019
Copyright © Caroline Kington
Cover design by Ifan Bates

British Library Cataloguing in Publication Data
A catalogue record for this book is available from the British Library

Printed by CPI Group (UK) Ltd, Croydon CR0 4YY

ISBN: 9781785631184

A
Long Shadow

For Miles,
whose encouragement and enthusiasm
for this novel kept me writing

1

Susan

1943

The light was switched off, the door firmly shut and the tap, tap, tap of Matron's shoes echoed down the stone corridor. The dormitory was pitch black; not a flicker of light. The blackout curtains blocked the world outside from seeping in, and fear of punishment as effectively extinguished any temptation by the occupants to break the lights-out rule.

The darkness was full of sounds: all little sounds, for the girls knew any disturbance loud enough to attract attention would bring punishment for the whole dormitory; a low mewling from one girl who was terrified of the dark and would whimper like this until exhaustion, or sleep, released her and her neighbours from her terror; muffled sobbing from the bed of another, and then another and another – they had all cried at some point and were likely to do so again. An occasional low whisper made comforting contact in the dark, and all night long the hard iron beds creaked as uncomfortable bodies sought in vain to find oblivion on the unforgiving mattresses.

Susan Norris lay on her narrow bed, her heart thumping so fast she could hardly breathe. She was not a brave girl, but desperation had led her to find a degree of courage and a determination that would have surprised her mother, had she been alive to care. Her body was treacherous with fatigue and she was afraid of falling asleep and, once asleep, not waking till the morning reveille. Inside her coat, she shivered with fear.

It was cold in the dormitory. The blankets on the beds were meagre and many of the girls disobeyed the rules and wore overcoats over the thin, regulation nightdresses. They were not afforded the luxury of dressing gowns but as a consequence of the night raids, their coats were hung next to the lockers in case they had to take refuge in the shelters.

Those lockers contained all the possessions they were allowed to bring to Exmoor House. These were minimal and included a change of clothing for their eventual release, a face flannel, a hairbrush, a purse, which was emptied when they arrived, and a family photograph, although photographs of single men were expressly forbidden.

Susan had already packed her possessions in a small bag and concealed it under her pillow. It was so pitiably little it didn't make much of a bulge, but Susan had her heart in her mouth when Matron made an inspection of the dormitory before bidding them good night. Susan was also fully dressed, but wrapping her coat tightly around her as she slipped from the lavatory to her bed, nobody had noticed.

As the minutes ticked slowly by and the room grew quieter, she prayed hard there would be no air raid that night. Not that she had any great faith in God. He hadn't listened to her when, at the age of seven, she had prayed that her mother wouldn't die, or at the age of nine when she had prayed for

8

her father not to marry the hard-faced woman he had brought in to replace her mother; nor had He heard her when the telegram came reporting her father missing in action; nor when Franklin's regiment left overnight; nor when her period hadn't come. If there were an air raid, it would be difficult for her to slip away as she intended. The girls would be counted in and counted out of the shelter and if she was not there, the hunt would begin immediately and she would be brought back and punished.

Exmoor House was originally a workhouse. Part of the old stone building was used to provide shelter for the elderly too poor or infirm to take care of themselves. Faced with increasing numbers of young, unmarried, pregnant girls, particularly since the stationing of US troops in the West Country, another wing had been opened and girls were referred there from all over the region.

As if to punish them for their transgression, life in the mother and baby hostel was one long ordeal. Kept there for the six weeks up to the birth of their children, the girls worked long, hard days, scrubbing floors and staircases, washing, ironing and cooking for themselves and for the old folk. There were few enough privileges, and these were removed at the slightest sign of insolence or misbehaviour. A pitiful wage was paid for the work they did but this was kept by the moral welfare worker responsible for them until their release, unless, of course, they lost it in fines in the interim.

After childbirth, their tasks become less onerous, being more related to the care and cleanliness of the nursery than the old folks. At six weeks, having loved, cared, and nurtured their little ones through the most vulnerable period of their lives, the girls were expected to hand the babies over for adoption.

It was this prospect that had driven Susan to plan her escape.

9

She knew she would be too weak to resist the authorities who asserted it was 'in her and her baby's best interest'. But she knew that if she did give them her baby, it would be the worst thing she could possibly do. As she scrubbed the stone staircase outside the reception room where the babies were handed over, the bitter, desperate wailing of a young mother had struck a corresponding chord in her heart. She had not lost faith in God sufficiently to believe Franklin would not get her letter and come to her aid. What would be his reaction if he discovered she had given their precious baby away?

So she lay in her bed, shivering with cold and fright, heart thumping, baby kicking, listening to the clock on the wall of the old workhouse marking time. The hour when the raids normally seemed to start came and went. She should make her move: if she delayed, she would not be far enough away by the time her absence was discovered.

Quietly she slipped out of her bed, felt for her bundle and balancing it on her distended body, wrapped her coat tightly around her. Holding her shoes in her other hand she tiptoed, in her bare feet, to the door. It was not locked, as the girls, thus far gone in their pregnancy, needed to make frequent visits to the lavatory, and although one member of the Board of Governors had suggested that the door be secured and the girls use chamber pots, his suggestion had been rejected.

Unchallenged, she crept the length of the long, dimly lit corridor till she reached the night superintendent's office. Here she paused a moment then crept past. Her knees wobbled so much she could hardly walk, and she dared not breathe; her breathing sounded so harsh and so loud to her she was terrified it would alert the superintendent.

She reached the staircase, clasped the cold stone banister and tiptoed down the stairs. For the first time in her life she

10

had reason to be thankful they were stone: the creaking of wood would have been too much for her overwrought state. Reaching the bottom she whisked round the ornate stone newel post, taking herself out of sight of the main hall, slipping through a swing door to a back passage. Here there was no light to guide her and she had to grope her way along the passageway until she felt the coal-cellar door. It opened and shut behind her with a quiet click that sounded as loud as gun-shot to her.

The blackness and the smell of the coal inside were smothering. There was no guard-rail on these steps and a fall could prove fatal. She could see nothing, eyes open or shut – it made no difference. Sitting on her backside, she slipped on her shoes and bumped herself to the bottom, felt down to her left and found the pair of galoshes she had concealed there days earlier. She put them on, and stumbling and sliding over the piles of coal, she eventually found the packing case that had first given her the idea escape was possible. Clumsily she climbed on top of it, raised her arms and pushed at the coalhole hatch.

The night air rushed in, cold, damp.

With great difficulty she levered her heavy body through the hole and then, panting with the exertion, sat for a moment on the edge and looked around at the world.

It was not welcoming. There was no moon, no stars. The sky was almost as black as the coal cellar, and the air was damp with a light drizzle. But she was, at least for the moment, free.

2

Kate

2001

Everyone had gone, the inquest and verdict having been exhaustively dissected. Kate Maddicott sat alone at her kitchen table, her arms resting on the scrubbed wood, her hands cradling the mug of tea her mother had pressed on her before she had, oh so tactfully, oh so thoughtfully, slipped out to head off the children.

Tactful.

Thoughtful.

Rattling around her brain, faster and faster, like stones in an empty vessel, the words acquired a greater and greater resonance.

Everyone was being *so* tactful, *so* thoughtful. Even Ted, even Ted. Direct, plain-speaking Ted... From the very first moment he'd brought her the news, he...everyone...groped for the *right* words. Antiseptic, soothing: the right words. Words that wouldn't cause too much collateral damage, but words that hurt, hurt so badly, hurt without ending – impossible they could be otherwise. The right thing to say… Nothing was right. Tactful, thoughtful – at best, at best, oh…just so inadequate…

A tune came floating from nowhere – 'So ta-ctful, so thought-ful dum dum… So ta-a-actful are they-ey to–oo-oo me-ee.'

She stopped abruptly. What was she doing? What was she thinking? What was she feeling?

'Nothing! 'She shouted aloud to the empty kitchen. 'I'm feeling…nothing. Dan's dead and I'm feeling *nothing*. Nothing! I've no feeling left. I'm dead, too.'

The electric clock ticked on quietly, unhurriedly; the Aga pop-popped and gurgled deep in its belly, as it always did; and the walls, that long ago she and Dan had painted a soft yellow, glowed like a slice of lemon meringue pie in the late afternoon sun. Quietly, inexorably, the warm, welcoming kitchen had an effect on her. It impinged on the numbness that had gripped her; filled the empty vessels of her body and her mind with what felt like cold, grey clay, banishing all feeling.

She put her head on her arms and wept.

At first the grieving was a gut-wrenching animal sorrow, without shape or thought, but as she continued to weep, like fingers tracing over fresh wounds, she relived the agonies of the last few weeks. Images, graphic and painful in their detail, painted her darkness.

Ted's face, agonised, his mouth forming and re-forming, trying to frame words that didn't want to be articulated… 'Girlie, I don't know how to tell you this…it's Dan. He's dead. It was an accident. It must have been…'

What had she said? She couldn't remember what she'd said. She had walked across the farmyard to greet Ted with some trivial quip about a date he'd had the night before. It

13

was a beautiful morning and the seductive murmurings of the collar doves filled the air. At the sight of his face, everything froze. Sound stopped, senses stopped, the colour of the world bleached away.

'It was an accident, it must have been.' Dr Johnson, a little while later as he sat with her at the kitchen table, his fingers nervelessly pulling at the cap of his pen, trying to keep his distress under wraps. He had been present at Dan's birth and then helped Kate give birth to Ben and to Rosie.

'It was an accident. Daddy's had a terrible accident.' She couldn't stop the awful hurt. She couldn't kiss this pain away. At eight and six they were old enough to sense the enormity of their loss but not know how to deal with it. In Kate's dreams, Ben's stricken look jostled alongside Dan's mutilated and bloodied face.

They hadn't let her see the body. She had rushed with Ted to the edge of Sparrow Woods where they had found him, but an ambulance and a police car were already there and at the insistence of someone, she couldn't remember who any more, she was led away and Ted went with Dan, to formally identify him, they said.

How had it happened? How? Why?

'Why?' Always she came back to the same point. If it was an accident, how did it happen? And if it wasn't, why should Dan do such a thing? Why?

She was aware, after the first outpouring of sympathy, that there was doubt in many people's minds. Great Missenwall, their village, was a small community, and along with the shock and the sympathy had come the gossip and the speculation. In open discussion the emphasis was on the word 'accident'. But Kate knew what was left unsaid – farmers aren't in the habit of climbing stiles with cocked twelve bores, and then to trip…

But the only other explanation was unthinkable.

'Believe me, Kate, Dan would never take his own life. Never. He loved you. And he'd never, ever, do such a thing to the children. He loved them too much. Suicide is selfish. Dan wasn't selfish. Whatever his faults, he wasn't selfish. You know that. You must know that!' Polly, Dan's mother, her eyes red and swollen, her face drawn, had turned fragile overnight.

Kate knew Polly was right. The Dan she knew would never inflict such pain. Never torture them in such a way. He loved them. Of course he did. And he knew how much they loved him. He did, didn't he?

But then she'd discovered that Watersmeet farm was struggling; that it had been for some time. She'd been aware things were getting difficult, but never…never had she imagined that Dan would have kept the extent of his debts from her.

He'd not told her.

Before the children were born, they'd shared everything. More recently he had become moody and distant, not inclined to talk about the farm. She, preoccupied with the children, had let that side of their relationship drift. Had she let it drift so much Dan had felt he could no longer confide in her? That he couldn't tell her just how bad things had become?

'You were not aware then that Dan had reached the limit of his overdraft? That he was looking for ways to offset his debts?' Mr Morgan, at the bank, was too polite to show surprise, but he was surprised nevertheless.

She had no tears left. Her eyes felt scratched and sore. She stared, without seeing, at her untouched mug of tea while her brain, refusing to rest, searched for answers, for explanations as it had done, unceasingly, since she woke from Dr Johnson's drug-induced sleep to face the consequences of the nightmare

15

into which Dan, by the manner of his death, had plunged her.

At first she had functioned in a trance and then she had raged. Raged against the horror of it all, the unfairness of it all; and then raged against Dan for inflicting such pain on her, on his children, on them all. Then she put herself in the dock and crippled with guilt and self-loathing for having failed Dan, she floundered in unimagined depths of misery. Failed him because he hadn't told her he had gone beyond the limits of his overdraft, that he was under instructions from the bank to offset his debts...

And because he hadn't told her about the life insurance.

Far from being a comfort, that had been a terrible shock, the most unwelcome piece of news she could possibly have received. After her interview with Mr Morgan, she'd assumed she would have to sell the farm. Then she discovered that shortly before his death he'd taken out a life insurance.

What was she to think? The inference was unavoidable. What had Dan been thinking of? Had he planned all this? Why hadn't he told her? How had she become so disconnected? Had he tried to talk to her and she'd not listened, or simply not understood what he was telling her?

The inescapable fact was the insurance would not only clear their debts, but leave Kate with some capital. So what conclusions were there left to draw?

No, she absolutely refused to believe it.

In the private opinion of everyone but those who knew him best, the news of the farm debt and of the life insurance settled the question.

The coroner was convinced otherwise and a verdict of accidental death was recorded.

Kate pushed the tea away and putting her head on her arms, closed her eyes. If only she could go to sleep and not wake

16

up... No, that wasn't the answer. If only she could wake up and see Dan sitting there, on the opposite side of the table, smiling at her, teasing, because she'd nodded off. If only...

The futility of 'if only'.

She sat up and opened her eyes.

He wasn't there.

Of course not.

The following morning, as the day was breaking, Kate climbed the hill that led out of the valley. At the brow, she stopped and turned to look back down on Watersmeet. She breathed in deeply, feeling as she did so that it was the first conscious breath she had taken for ages. The air was fresh and sweet, untainted by the accumulated smells of the day. The sun, low and young, rose behind her to light the honey-coloured stone of the house and turn the reddening leaves of the Virginia creeper ever more scarlet.

She loved this view of the house. She had fallen in love with it the first time Dan brought her here at much the same time of year, eleven years ago. The façade of the house was early Georgian, 'with plenty of alterations from less gentrified Maddicotts round the back.' Dan had grinned, obviously pleased by her reaction.

It was not a large or particularly grand house but it was elegant, warm and inviting. It sat in the bottom of a narrow valley, bordered on one side by a modest river and by a brook in the front that danced its way in the early sunlight down to the river. A yew hedge separated the riverbank from the garden and a crumbling stone wall, sprouting daisies, valerian and ivy-leaved toadflax, stood between the brook and the front garden. A flat stone bridged the stream to provide access to a pair of old iron gates, and the flagstone path to the front door of the

17

house was bordered with thick bushes of lavender.

To the left was the farm itself – a motley collection of stone buildings grouped around the yard, including barns, and a milking shed. Beyond the house and farm wound the river valley, and the rolling meadows where Dan's sheep and cows grazed…

'They've been doing that for hundreds of years, you know,' Dan had said. 'It's good pasture and the milk is rich and creamy. You can try some, later.' He had stood with his arm firmly round her shoulders. The first weekend she came down to Watersmeet, they'd scarcely let go of each other. 'Look over there, the grey roof – that's the cheese shed; Mum runs the cheese-making operation from there.' Dan had paused. 'My dad's death was sudden. It hit her very hard. Setting up the business sort of helped her cope, I suppose…'

It was easier for Polly, thought Kate. She'd had Dan to take over, Dan to see her through the dark times. But now Dan had gone and left Kate; left her alone with two small children and a farm to run. And this huge question mark. Dan's father died of a heart attack. No doubts attached to that…

'You can't see from here Kate, but beyond that valley we've the crop fields and more pasture, and another dairy unit. Believe it or not, we once had five tenant farms. But now, with one exception, they've all gone. It's a shame, but that's the way it is. Bigger fields, bigger yields, and it's still a struggle…'

But if life was a struggle for Dan, it didn't show that day. She closed her eyes and pictured him, young and tall, with white even teeth and strong features, his hair the colour of dark honey. His skin was clear and light gold and his eyes…his eyes were a melting brown, and so serious.

When he looked at his farm, as he had done the day he introduced her to it, he had become completely absorbed. It meant everything to him. She had realised that then, and had been entranced by it. And with a prescience, which quite unnerved her at the time, for she had never encountered anyone quite so wedded to a place, she knew if their relationship was going to go anywhere, it would be she who would have to make sacrifices.

Sacrifices.

She screwed her eyes tight shut, the longer to hold onto his image. But the image dissolved, grief took over, and alone on the hillside, looking down at Watersmeet, the home and lifeblood of generations of Maddicotts, she wept.

3

Dan

1990

At the end of a slow-moving queue, Dan Maddicott, his stomach grumbling plaintively, shuffled towards the tables laden with goodies. With one hand he gripped a glass of champagne precariously moored on the edge of a plastic plate, and with the other he helped himself to food. Cold meats, cold salmon, cold turkey, savoury rice, potato salad, green salad, tomato salad, creamy, glistening coleslaw… The wedding feast held no surprises, but he was hungry and before long a laden plate counter-balanced the anchorage of the full glass.

The noise in the marquee was deafening. Released from the sombre surroundings of the church, where the muted coughing, the whispering, and the tentative singing had reflected the awe and unease of a congregation on their best behaviour, the wedding guests chatted, laughed and shouted without inhibition.

It had been a typical June day: the early sunshine had given way to a succession of sharp showers so there was no prospect of going to sit on the grass outside. He looked around the marquee for somewhere to sit, but as he'd been slow joining the queue for food, most of the tables were occupied.

Clutching his plate and glass and weaving a precarious path through the tables, Dan flashed a smile at his mother, already seated and absorbed in conversation with one of her numerous sisters, avoided the eye of his Auntie Marilyn, who had an empty place beside her, and was rescued by a shout.

'Dan! Dan! Over here!'

Max, his cousin, was at a table with a group of people, about his age, in their early twenties he guessed, none of whom he recognised. He headed towards them.

'Coo-ee, Danny!' His Auntie Marilyn had spotted him.

He smiled at her and with an apologetic shrug, indicated with his full hand, the table waiting to make room for him. The casual gesture had disastrous consequences. The champagne glass slid out of its mooring and emptied into the lap of a blue silk dress worn by a bridesmaid sitting at the table. Amid her shrieks of outrage and the shouts of laughter, Dan failed to correct the sudden imbalance of his plate following the abrupt departure of the glass; in a trice it tilted and what had been his breakfast, lunch and supper splattered across the floor of the marquee.

Mortified, cursing under his breath, he grabbed a napkin and attempted to mop the champagne-saturated dress.

Max jumped to his feet, shouting with glee. 'Meet my cousin Dan Maddicott, everyone. He's a farmer, yer know, oop from Zomerzet. They farmers got a way wiv birds – they like to throw food at 'em!'

Dan was saved the bother of a suitable retort by a call to attention from the top table. His glass was rescued and re-filled

21

from a stack of bottles under the table and he sank into an empty chair next to his victim, whispering his embarrassed apologies. She had, he noticed for the first time, soft dark hair and round, twinkling eyes, the colour of forget-me-nots.

An only child himself, Dan had hordes of cousins, many of whom had spent part of their holidays 'keeping him company' as his mother put it, on the family farm in the soft, rolling, green hills of the West Country. His father had also been an only child. His mother, however, was one of seven, and the cousins kept on coming.

It was a cousin, Max's younger sister Mary, who was getting married on this day. Their father worked in the diplomatic service, so the brother and sister had been frequent visitors to the farm. From their early years they had hunted hens, dammed streams, leaped among the hay bales in the barn, spied on the farmhands, and with their hearts in their mouths, sneaked into the yard of Woodside Farm to look with fascination at old Jem Leach's collection of caged birds.

The Leaches had been tenants of the Maddicotts for as long as the Maddicotts had owned Watersmeet. There was little love lost between them. If the children were caught, they could expect a vicious clip round the ear followed by an angry telephone call and a ticking-off from whichever exasperated parent had been forced to collect them.

The last excursion they had ever made to Woodside was vividly imprinted on Dan's memory. As he watched the little bride smiling up at her new husband, Dan's thoughts wandered back to that time when he, Max and Mary – she was about ten – had slipped into the empty yard of Woodside and crept into the gloom of the big barn where old Jem kept the large cage…

A barn owl, a buzzard, two kestrels and a falcon, all fastened by short trusses to individual perches, stared at them with angry eyes.

'They shouldn't be in here,' Mary whispered. 'It's cruel. I can't bear it. We must do something!'

Max was all for instant action. 'Let's set them free. He's a bastard, keeping birds shut up like this. Dan, your clasp should break this lock… Now…while the coast's clear. Imagine old Jem's face when he discovers his birds have flown!'

Dan hesitated. As he did so there was a roar of anger from the barn door.

'What yer think yer doin? Getaway from they birds. Little varmin. Jest wait till Oi gets thee…' And he rushed forward. They were too quick for him.

Scattering to the left and right of the old man, they made for the door and the freedom of the yard. Out in the sunlight they pelted across its uneven, dried-mud surface, to the open gate and the safety of the woods beyond. Dan made the trees first, Max hard on his heels.

There was a cry and spinning round, Dan saw Mary stumble and trip. She had barely got to her feet when Jem, with a shout of triumph, grabbed hold of her. Max pulled Dan down into the undergrowth and, dismayed, they watched Jem march a weeping Mary across the yard back into the barn.

Moments later he appeared without her and, with a triumphant lift of his head in the direction of the woods, shouted 'Oi've got thee now my little varmin. Oi've got yer sister under lock and key. Give thyselves up and Oi'll let her go. No show an' her stays there. All noight if necessary. Geddit?'

The boys got it all right.

Max was furious with Mary and was all for leaving her to her fate. 'He won't keep her there all night. He wouldn't dare.

23

Bloody girl – typical! Fancy tripping like that. We should never have brought her. It's her own fault. Bloody, bloody girl.'

They looked on as Jem pulled up a small bale, sat down and lit a pipe. A high, thin wail came from the barn then cut off abruptly.

The sound of that wail unnerved Dan. 'We can't leave her there, Max,' he hissed. 'You were gonna rescue those birds. We can't just leave her locked up. We've got to get her out.'

It was a challenge and at the prospect of a rescue attempt, Max was immediately fired. They lay in the undergrowth arguing over first one plan, then another. And the foul old man sat there, smoking his pipe, casting looks in their direction and cackling.

'If only we could distract his attention,' said Dan, staring across at Jem. 'Then get into that barn, without him seeing us. He's probably pushed her into the old tool cupboard he keeps in the far corner. I'm sure my knife is strong enough to break the lock.'

'Unless he's put her in the birdcage,' said Max with ghoulish relish.

Dan shuddered. 'Christ, Max! We've got to get a move on. Look – you stay here. I'll creep round to the back of the yard and make it to the barn without old Jem spotting me. Watch me carefully. When I signal to you, you must stand up and shout, yell, distract his attention any way you can so I can slip inside the barn without him noticing.'

Not ready to relinquish his role as the leader, Max scowled. 'No, you stay here. She's my sister. I'll be the one to do the rescuing. Give me your knife.'

Furious, Dan turned on Max. 'Don't be so pathetic. I can run faster than you, and I know the layout of the yard and barn better.'

Max never backed down lightly and certainly not to Dan, his junior cousin, but faced with this rare explosion of anger, he immediately conceded. 'OK, OK. But no mistakes. We don't want you locked up an' all…'

A call for quiet from the top table brought Dan back to the present. He craned his head to get a better view of the bridegroom.

As a teenager, if he thought about it all, he'd imagined that one day maybe he would marry Mary. But after the events at Woodside that day, the three of them had drifted apart. Then Dan's father had died prematurely; Dan went to an agricultural college and took over the farm, and in London, Mary and Max had become absorbed in their own circles of friends. Max had moved easily from university into the financial market and was, the aunts whispered, 'making more money than was good for him'. Mary had gone on to get a degree in business studies and found a job she loved with a PR firm.

And so now here she was marrying someone else.

Shortly after she'd announced her engagement, Mary had brought him down on a brief visit to Watersmeet. Clive was a wine taster for some prestigious company, and exuded ambition.

'Clive'! I ask you…what sort of name is Clive?' Dan had snorted after they'd left.

'You're just jealous,' laughed his mother. 'I thought he was very agreeable and Mary is clearly very happy.'

And indeed she was. The trouble was Dan could not find Clive 'agreeable' in the way his mother did. In Dan's opinion, he was just a little too smooth and a little too self-confident, and Dan did not like him. But he was on his own.

Clive stood up to make a speech. He was a good-looking

fellow, Dan had to admit, the cut of his morning suit emphasising an athletic physique, not tall (but then Mary was petite), with a thick head of dark hair swept back from a high forehead. He was smiling down at Mary and taking her hand, he addressed the guests.

Dan helped himself to some more champagne. It was hot in the marquee. The champagne was going to his head. He was hungry. He shifted in his chair and glanced surreptitiously under the table to see if he could retrieve any of his lost food. Two feet, his own, sat squarely in a mushy pile. He groaned.

'What's wrong?' The girl with forget-me-not eyes whispered. 'Are you unwell?'

'No, just hungry.' Dan whispered back. 'I haven't eaten anything today and I've been up since five. If I don't have something soon, I shall pass out when we stand to toast the happy couple.'

The girl smiled. A smile that lit up her face, her eyes, her mouth, every muscle; a smile like the early morning sun, slowly, steadily, rising, illuminating everything with liquid gold. Dan had never seen such a smile.

He melted.

By the evening, the formality of the wedding had given way to the obligatory drinking and dancing bash. Dan stuck with Max's group, hoping to spend as much time as he could with the girl he'd drenched in champagne. Her name, he learned, was Kate Dinsdale; her mother called her Katherine; her friends called her Katie; she preferred to be called Kate. She told him she was an old school friend of Mary's and she had known both Mary and Max since she was thirteen.

'So, you're Dan,' she smiled. 'I meet you at long last. Mary used to boast about you and Watersmeet...'

26

Dan found Kate entrancing. Tall and slender, her face illuminated when she talked, and her eyes – he'd never seen eyes so blue – were bright and intelligent. Under her questioning, he told her a little about Watersmeet and his life there and she, in turn, told him about herself.

She worked in television as a researcher, with aspirations to be a documentary producer. At that moment she was working on a series of 'Writers and Their Writings' and was terribly excited about a planned interview with some novelist or other. She was about to regale the bemused and bewitched Dan with the plot when they were interrupted.

Max, as Dan would have expected, was the epicentre of his coterie of friends and had flitted around the reception flirting with every eligible girl. His attentions were now on Kate.

'Darling,' his arm slipped round her waist. 'Dan's hogged you long enough. It's my turn. Come on, I want to dance.'

Kate playfully attempted to disengage herself. 'Later, Max, I'm talking to Dan about *Puffball*. It's set near where he lives, and I want to find out how...'

'The only puffball Dan knows about is the sort you eat! Contemporary female writers are not his forte. But I tell you what, if you want to find out what it's like living in the depths of nowhere, we'll go and visit Dan one weekend. Bring a little excitement into his dull old life, down on t' farm! But now, sweetheart, it's time to boogie.' And he steered her purposefully away.

Dan stared after them, feeling irrationally disappointed. He found Mary by his side. 'I didn't realise Kate was Max's girlfriend?' It was more of a groan than he'd intended.

Mary laughed. 'She probably doesn't see it that way. Max is determined they should be, and what Max wants, Max normally gets. But she's holding out. Brave girl. He's not used to being resistable.' She looked at Dan. 'Don't tell me you're smitten too? I thought you were devoted to me, only me, my darling Dan?'

'And so I am,' he looked down at his little cousin. Her heart-shaped face was flushed and her grey eyes were bright with excitement and laughter. 'Completely devoted,' he lifted her hand and kissed it with mock formality. 'But you have married another, and unless I am to spend the rest of my natural as a bitter and twisted bachelor…'

She laughed. 'Impossible. But I don't suppose there are too many matrimonial prospects in Great Missenwall. You'd better get in there, Dan. Don't worry about Max's feelings. After all, he'd have no hesitation in walking all over yours…'

By the end of the evening, emboldened by Mary's words, he had exchanged telephone numbers with Kate and elicited a promise that she would have dinner with him next time he was in the city.

But that was the sticking point. She lived in London; he lived in the heart of rural England. He was a farmer, a twenty-four-hour occupation; she was a television researcher with as little time to spare, it seemed, as he. A casual acquaintance was never going to be on the cards.

4

Susan

1943

At dawn, a grey, reluctant affair unremarked even by the birds, the drizzle had given way to rain. The road was a filthy combination of mulched leaves and mud. A slight wind drove the rain into Susan's face. Every now and then, overhanging branches of trees that might have offered her some protection against the weather deposited large drops of water on her head. These trickled straight down her neck and back, soaking her inside as well as out. Her thin coat was no protection against either wind or rain. Worse, the sodden, freezing fabric added to her discomfiture and, flapping sullenly around her body, slowed her progress. Rivulets of water ran down her coal-grimed legs and into her galoshes. The fine fair hair Franklin had loved to twist in his fingers now hung in darkened, dripping tails, plastering her small pale face.

She passed a herd of cows squelching in the mud around their feeder. They lowed a mournful protest at the sight of her.

They should have been snug in their winter quarters, not out in the mud and wind like her. Their barn had been blown to smithereens by a stray bomb, dropped after a night raid on Bristol. But they, at least, had someone to care about their plight and they had been given plenty of hay to eat.

As she passed the entrance of a farmyard a dog rushed out, barking ferociously. His unexpected and aggressive appearance badly shook her. She hurried on, trembling with fright in case he followed. Having seen her off, however, he lost all interest, and she trudged on, her trembling slowly subsiding.

The occasional rook eyed her askance through the rain.

Otherwise, there was nothing and nobody about.

Faint and hungry as she was, she was relieved. She knew her appearance would attract attention and she wanted to get as far away from Exmoor House as she could before she encountered anyone.

When she had first started to plan her escape, she had asked one of the girls in which direction Bristol lay, and so it was in that direction, without gaslight or starlight to guide her, she had started out.

In the blackness of the night it had been impossible to check her direction by any signpost, but at dawn she chanced on a milestone and was both encouraged and dismayed by the information that she had walked eight miles but that Bristol was still some thirty-five miles away. She was on the right road, but oh, how her feet ached, her body ached, her baby kicked, and how sick she felt.

There was an animal trough beside the stone milestone, fed by a bubbling spring. In the stone basin she washed her face and hands clean of coal dust, drying herself on the hem of her smock; then she drank the icy water. A hedge bordered a small orchard and she was able to reach the odd apple withering on the boughs. Thus fortified, she again set off.

She had decided, once she got to Bristol, she would try to find her Auntie May, her mother's sister. When her dad had re-married, her stepmother had quarrelled with her auntie and the family broke off all contact. Her dad removed his family to Shepton Mallet and the rest of her relatives had remained in the city. Susan could not remember much of Auntie May, but she did have vague memories of a plump, smiling face and of being fed warm, crumbly, ginger biscuits. On such sketchy evidence she had convinced herself she would not be turned away.

Progress was slow. As the day lengthened, the traffic on the road increased. Not a great deal, and mainly local delivery vans, tractors, carts and an occasional car, but Susan was all quivering antennae and at the first sound of a vehicle she would conceal herself in the nearest field or ditch until the danger had passed. Nobody spotted her, or if they did, they paid her no attention. It was a cold, wet day and people were more concerned in sorting their business and getting back to the comfort of their homes.

By early afternoon she was exhausted and thoroughly dispirited. For the umpteenth time she had dragged herself out of a ditch where she had taken quick refuge at the unheralded appearance of a tractor. Nettles had viciously stung her legs and a stray briar had lashed out, drawing a thin scarlet line across her cheek.

For the first time since she had set out, she gave way to loud unchecked sobs. So wrapped up was she in her misery, she didn't notice a ramshackle van coming round the bend behind her.

31

5

Kate

2001

As the number of days after the inquest lengthened, the pressure on Kate to make a decision about the farm's future grew.

The family and the community had rallied round, and the funeral, so dreaded by her, actually helped them all.

Her mother returned home. Before she left, she tried hard to make Kate go with her, but Kate resisted. She knew that both Ben and Rosie couldn't really believe their father was dead. And in her heart, too, there was denial, a refusal to believe she'd never see him again. Those feelings were made worse by thinking she'd seen him – in the street, in a shop, in a passing car. Each false sighting left her bruised and bleeding afresh.

In the meantime the whole legal business of the estate was being processed; the farm was ticking over, and she knew they were all waiting for her to tell them what should happen next. It was Polly, her much-loved mother-in-law, who finally stirred her to action.

'I know, Kate, that you still haven't made up your mind about…well, about your plans yet,' she began. 'But I think it only fair to tell you, I've decided to give up cheese-making.'

Polly Maddicott had always seemed ageless to Kate. She was neat and elegant, her skin smooth, her eyes clear and her cropped hair shiny. But today, Kate noticed as Polly sat, nursing a mug of tea in an old Windsor chair, a ray of sunlight falling across her face highlighted lines that had not been there before and silver hairs glinted among the auburn.

'I suspect,' Polly continued, betraying no emotion, 'in the end you'll feel the wisest course is to sell the farm. Your mother said you've more or less decided to…'

Kate was irritated. 'Mum's leaping to conclusions, Polly. You know what she's like… I haven't decided anything yet. Besides you know I'll tell you first.'

'That's as maybe. But I've been thinking a great deal about my future as well as yours. I really don't want to pressurise you, you've got enough to contend with as it is, but…well, if you sell, I think I'd like to move.'

'Away from here?' Kate was startled. Polly was so much part of Watersmeet it seemed inconceivable she should even think of leaving. 'Away from Watersmeet? But you've spent most of your life here. You've so many friends here. Where would you go?'

'Oh, I don't suppose I'd go very far. But Kate, my cottage is so close, every time I open a window or step out of my door, I look down on Watersmeet. If you were to sell… No, of course I wouldn't go far away. You're right, I do have some very good friends here. But also because Ben and Rosie have their roots here and I hope they would come and stay with me, often.'

When Polly had left, Kate cleared the tea things, turning

over and over in her mind the seemingly insoluble question: if she sold the farm, where would she go?

Her mother wanted her to move back to Canterbury permanently. Before she left, she had launched into a jumbled outpouring of thoughts and opinions. Her eyes bright with determination, scarcely pausing to draw breath, allowing no interruption, no discussion, no opposition.

'It would be lovely to have you closer to us, darling. We've seen so little of you since you got married. Great Missenwall is so far away and now your father's getting on, he doesn't like to drive too far… Not that he'd be able to leave his bookshop for long. You could help him with the books, just like you used to… It doesn't seem so long ago you and Emily were still living at home, your hair in pigtails…well Emily's was, you always insisted on having your hair cut. Not that it didn't suit you… you've always had such pretty curls. Doesn't Rosie take after you? Not quite the same colouring, of course, she must get that from Polly… And Ben is *so* like poor Dan…'

'Mum, please…'

'Darling, they're growing up *so* quickly, we're missing out on their childhoods… And of course, there's *such* a wide choice of schools in Canterbury. You've *so* few suitable schools around you and you've got to think of these things. After all, if you sold Watersmeet, they could both go to a good prep school and then go to King's. It's co-ed now, you know, and still so well thought of… They couldn't have a better start… Then if you choose to start your career again, we could look after them. You know how much they've enjoyed coming to stay… Your father and I have talked it over and we both agree Ben is too young to feel he should follow in Dan's footsteps. And anyway, farming is so terrible these days. Foot and Mouth, BSE. The poor farmers seem to stagger from one crisis to another…'

She finally ran out of steam and choked. 'Would you want to burden little Ben with all that?'

No, whatever else, Kate couldn't face the thought of moving back to Canterbury.

But London was different.

Max had come to stay the previous weekend; a breath of air from another life.

While she was preparing supper, he took the children off for a romp in the garden. Kate could hear them shouting and laughing in a way they'd not done since Dan's death.

She tried to express her gratitude when he left.

'Poor little buggers,' he said, giving her a hug. 'This valley is still frozen with shock. You can almost touch it. They need to get out and feel something else apart from all this grief. And so do you, Kate. You're drowning. Why don't you cut and run? Nothing you can do will bring Dan back. You're not a farmer; you've not a drop of farming blood in your veins. You're a city girl and in London there are loads of Dan's aunties and cousins, all of whom would love to make a fuss of you and the children. You need to build a life for yourself, not throw it away, keeping a farm going for Ben or Rosie, which they might not want anyway.'

It was tempting. Life in London seemed so remote it was almost exotic. But if she did go back, she'd have to start a career all over again. The TV industry, her industry, had moved on, as had most of her contacts. There would be a lot of catching up to do.

But she was barely in her mid-thirties. There were years ahead of her. She was a creative, energetic person. Starting afresh would help her...would help her deal with her grief. Working in a different world would mean not being confronted with her loss every day. And Ben and Rosie, surely it would be the same for them? And wouldn't it be better for them if, away from the shadow of the tragedy that engulfed them, she were to have a more fulfilled life?

Max was right: at heart she was a city person. She'd loved the little flat she'd had in Ealing, with all the buzz and instant accessibility of theatres, exhibitions, concerts. She acknowledged she'd given it all up without a backward glance, but that was because of Dan, and now…

The anonymity of the city was also attractive. The dramatic nature of Dan's death, it seemed to her, had made her and the children the centre of too much unhealthy attention and speculation. Yes, definitely, a fresh start would be beneficial all round…

'No,' said Ben. 'I don't want to, ever! London stinks!'

Rosie burst into tears.

The phone rang. It was a local farmer, William Etheridge, a family friend.

Faced with her tear-stained, angry children, Kate hardly listened to him.

'Hope this is not a bad time to call, Kate, but there is something I'd like to discuss with you. A proposal that you…'

'Sorry William,' Kate interrupted, 'but now is not a good time. I've upset the children and I need to…'

'Good God, Kate, I didn't mean right now. I am slap-bang in the middle of harvest, but if the weather holds I should finish combining Thursday. Are you free Friday evening, at about 6.30?'

Putting the phone down, Kate turned her attention back to her children. Ben was sat at the table, his arms folded, a look of cold stubbornness so reminiscent of Dan on his face. Rosie had hidden her face in her hands. She crouched down between them and put her arms around them both.

'I'm just trying to work out what's best for us,' she said softly. 'You've always loved your visits to London. We've so many friends and family there. If we stayed here, I'd have to decide what to do about the farm. Farms need a farmer and I'm not one.'

'You could be. You could learn. Ted 'ud help you 'til I was old enough. Rosie and me have already learned loads helpin' him, so I don't see why you shouldn't.'

'Ben, it's not that simple…'

'Yes it is. If you wanted to, you would. You would! You wouldn't want to leave home. Well I'm not leavin' here and you can't make me and nor is Rosie, are you Rosie?'

But the only reply the little girl made was a muffled, 'I want my daddy.'

Much later, tossing sleeplessly in her bed, she remembered her arrangement with William Etheridge. She puzzled over the call.

The Etheridges had been farming locally since the beginning of the last century. They were very successful and ran a large pedigree beef herd, the envy of the farming community. Muriel, William's wife, had developed a racehorse stud on the farm and this had considerably added to their wealth. Kate and Dan had been on good terms with them, although William was older than Dan by about seven years so they were not childhood friends. Muriel and Kate had met at a party about a year before she married Dan. The two women couldn't have been more different but they got along exceedingly well and had become firm friends. Then Muriel had died suddenly of cancer two years ago. After that Kate had hardly seen William.

The last time was at Dan's funeral.

Sadly she remembered how awfully inadequate she'd felt at

Muriel's funeral. Looking at William's grim face, the heartfelt sentiments she'd been going to express had felt mawkish, inadequate, and died on her lips. And it had seemed somehow indecent to try and say anything to their two children who, at thirteen and ten, looked so vulnerable and lonely. Very different from the loud, confident children who'd filled the house with their noise.

It must have been the same for people at Dan's funeral. Afraid to say anything to her in case she burst into tears. Afraid to touch the children in case they broke.

How badly we manage death, she thought.

Finally she fell asleep, wondering whether she should cook supper for William. Whether, indeed, she could be bothered.

The following morning she mentioned the call to Ted.

'He said he has a proposal to discuss with me, Ted. Have you any idea what that might be?'

Ted, looking even more impassive than usual, was silent for some time before he replied, 'I've not heard anything in particular Kate, but maybe he is going to make you an offer.'

'An offer? For Watersmeet?

'I doubt for the whole of the place. He's a businessman. He'd have no use for all of it. I wouldn't be surprised if he didn't make you an offer for a substantial part of the land, and for the herds. I know he's a beef man, but we've a good reputation. He might want to expand into the dairy market – quicker returns than beef. All the beauty of diversification without having to start from scratch.'

Kate stared at him, suddenly feeling very sick. 'But that would leave just the sheep, and a few fields of cash crops. Watersmeet farm wouldn't be viable any more.'

'That's true, but at least you'd be able to carry on living here, without the worry of the farm.' Ted's voice was impassive. 'You

38

could let out the land he doesn't want. Keep hold of Woodside Farm, if you want to, and that will supplement your income. In your position it makes sense.' He looked at her sideways. 'That is, if you want to stay. This is only speculation, mind; he might come with a completely different proposal. He doesn't give a lot away, not even to his manager.'

'Ted…' It was a question they both knew Kate would ask, would have to ask, both dreading the asking, both dreading the answer. 'What would *you* do if I sold the farm?'

Like Polly, Kate thought, as she waited for his reply, Ted had aged. He moved stiffly, without vigour. His black hair was shot with grey. The lines around his mouth and eyes had deepened into gorges and his face was leaner and more cadaverous than ever.

'Well, that depends, Kate, on who bought it, what their plans for the farm might be, whether they wanted a farm manager, and whether they wanted to work with me and my old-fashioned ways…'

'Old-fashioned? You? What are you talking about? I've never heard such rubbish…'

At her indignant tone, a smile flitted across his face. 'But times are changing that quickly, Kate. For one thing I never had a college education. All I know I learned here, on the farm. Dan's father taught me and then I made it my business to carry on learning when young Dan had to take over. My knowledge of modern technology is limited, to say the least, and farming is now dependent on that technology. Mebbe the time has come for me to hang up my overalls.'

'And Ben said I could learn to be a farmer!'

'Well, happen he's right. For farming to be successful these days, you know, it has to be run, well, like any other business.' Ted sighed. 'The managing director of a shoe company don't sit at a bench and stitch the leather; he don't even design the shoes. No, he employs people who know what they're doing and he manages 'em. *He* don't get his hands dirty.'

'But Dan was totally hands-on, you know he was. He'd be horrified to hear you talk like this. How can you compare a farm with a shoe shop? And anyway, I know labour costs are a permanent headache. So how can any farm afford to have someone running it who doesn't get their hands dirty?'

'Look how much time Dan spent on that computer of yours. Sure he was a hands-on farmer, but if Watersmeet is to survive the twenty-first century it means, for the boss at least, less and less time spent doing the actual farming, and more and more pushing paper.

Kate stared miserably at her boots. 'Yes, you're right,' she said sadly. 'And it made him very depressed.'

And they relapsed into mournful silence.

But it was very important for Kate to know that whatever she did, Ted would be all right. Dan would expect nothing less.

So she rallied, and gave Ted a direct look. 'You still haven't answered my question, Ted. If I sold the farm and you, for whatever reason, couldn't stay on, what would you do?'

There was only the slightest hesitation. 'I'd move on, Kate. Change direction. Finish with the land as I finished with the sea before I came here. An old friend of mine's running a garden centre, up near Lacock. He always said he'd take me on if I was minded to leave the farm. We have to adapt to survive. And I'm a survivor.'

'A garden centre! But you don't like flowers. That's no solution. Oh, why can't we get rid of Frank Leach, then you could take over Woodside Farm? He's ruining that place… I hate him being there.'

'So you might, but Woodside is as much Frank's as

Watersmeet was Dan's. You know the way it is, Kate, his family have farmed it for as long as there have been Maddicotts at Watersmeet. He's entitled to be there.

A few days later, William Etheridge, invited by Kate for supper, arrived just as the children were finishing their food. Hearing they were to have a visitor, Ben became prickly and morose and Rosie acquired an unaccustomed shyness. Both children melted, however, when they saw that William had brought with him a bundle of brown and white energy in the form of a Springer spaniel pup.

Muriel had bred Springers and William had held on to her favourite bitch, breeding the occasional litter.

'I hope you don't mind,' he apologised as the two children and the puppy tore outside in a confusion of barks, shrieks and laughter. 'The little blighter shows no interest in playing with his sisters and follows me everywhere. I thought Ben and Rosie might like to play with him for a bit. Wear him out if they can.'

She smiled at him. 'It was a good idea. They were feeling particularly gloomy before you arrived.'

'They'll be finding it difficult, and making it more difficult for you, I expect.'

She nodded ruefully. 'The last few weeks have been the worst I've ever...' She shook her head. 'It's been truly awful, I don't need to tell you, William, and I can't wait to get my life kick-started again. I'm drifting around in a sort of limbo. There's so much to be sorted out and so much to be taken into account. And I know I've got to make a decision about the farm – soon. It's not fair on the kids. That's partly why they're so moody. They're in even more of a vacuum than I am.' She sighed. 'They're due back at school in two weeks' time and they don't even know whether they're still going to be there,

41

or here, for that matter, at Christmas. And they miss Dan so much. So much.'

She stopped, her throat so constricted it hurt to breathe, let alone speak. She was furious with herself. She'd resolved to keep her feelings under tight control, to maintain a dignified, composed exterior and try to enjoy the evening. She didn't count William as the sort of friend she could really relax with, or have a riotous time with, or conversely, blub in front of. Being so much older he had always seemed rather remote. And now all she wanted to do was howl her eyes out…

He made no attempt to console her but sat quietly while she struggled to regain her composure.

Then he got up. 'Where do you keep your corkscrew? I think it's time we tackled this bottle of wine.'

Kate watched him as he pulled the cork and poured the wine. Although she had known him for some ten years, she realised she had never really *looked* at him. He was Muriel's husband, a friend of the family, part of the furniture…

In his early forties, he was a good-looking man. Not as tall as Dan, his general build was stockier, his hair was brown, thick and wavy, his eyes were grey and quite deep set, and his nose somewhat Roman. In repose, his face had a reserved, almost stern look.

He'd always seemed a kind, capable, strong person. She knew he was respected by his farming neighbours; described as arrogant by those who didn't really know him and reserved by those who did. Muriel had always been the sociable one. When she had died, invitations to Highclere, the Etheridge's home, had died with her.

'Here,' he said passing her the glass and giving her a slight smile. 'Shall we talk business now, or would you rather wait till after supper?'

'Now, I think. The children are having great fun with the puppy and I want to hear what it is you're proposing.'

He took a sip of wine put his glass down and looked at her calmly. 'I want to make you an offer, an offer for Watersmeet farm.'

Kate felt as if she'd been punched in the solar plexus 'An offer? For Watersmeet?' she managed to croak.

The punch was followed by a whole battery. By the time he'd finished, she was reeling.

'For the farm, Kate. I don't want your tenant's place and I'm not interested in the house or yard, or the immediate outbuildings. I know there's money to be made by turning barns and things into holiday cottages, but personally, I'm not interested in that sort of business. Mind you, it's something you might consider doing in the future – it would make sense if you wanted to boost your income...'

The kitchen door burst open and the appearance of Ben and Rosie was a welcome diversion, giving Kate a chance to recover and to delay her reply.

The children were transformed. Eyes bright, cheeks flushed, and worn out with chasing the puppy around the garden, they were despatched to bath and bed with a promise from William that they could choose a name for the puppy and pay him a visit as soon as they had picked one.

It was an interlude she needed. Although Ted had alerted her about William's likely intentions, and she had put herself through numerous dry-runs, testing her response, imagining how she'd feel; when he *actually* said the words 'make you an offer'... She felt sick. She wanted to weep. She wanted to howl. It was all loss. She'd lost Dan – and was she about to lose his farm, the farm he, and she, had held so dear...?

'Dan!' she silently screamed. 'How could you put me through

this? How could you!'

But by the time she'd kissed the children goodnight, she'd sufficiently marshalled her thoughts to resume the conversation, calmer and more collected, and with only the trace of a wobble.

'So you are proposing to buy *everything* except the house, the immediate farmyard and outbuildings, and Woodside Farm?'

He gave her a slight, encouraging smile. 'That's right. I'd want to rent the milking parlour from you for the home herd, till I get one of my own built, but I don't want the cheese shed, as I don't plan to continue with cheese production. I know Polly's worked hard to build up its reputation, but it's too small-scale to make it worth my while. Dan's done well with his herds and I'd like to build on that.'

'And the sheep?'

'I'll sell them. I am not interested in diversifying that much, and these days, unless we're talking about rare breeds, which are more trouble than they are worth, there's little to be made out of sheep. The extra acreage means I'll be able to expand.'

'But you don't want Woodside?'

'No. Quite frankly Kate, I don't want to be bothered. You've an awkward tenant there and his land is in a poor state. No, I wouldn't want Woodside.'

'What about my workforce?'

'Your dairymen I'd like to keep. They're good and I would hate to see them go. Josh, I could probably find work for, but not the people you employ in the cheese shed."

'And Ted?'

'Not Ted. I'm sorry. He's a good man, but I've no reason to replace Jim Evans and even with the enlarged operation, I don't need two managers.'

She was silent, she could feel the tears well up and slide

44

down her face and there was little she could do to stop them.

'Think it over, Kate,' he said gently. 'I know how important Watersmeet is to the Maddicotts. This way, at least you, and more particularly the children, would be able to stay on in the house.'

Early the following morning, she slipped out of the house. The sky was pearly grey and the morning chorus was in full throttle. She paddled through the dewy grass and made for the corner in the garden where the brook bubbled into the river. Dan used to come here when he needed to be alone. She stood now in the same spot, willing his spirit to give her guidance.

Could Watersmeet be the same without its farm? Would it not become a genteel ghost of its former self, its raison d'être removed? Like the thousands of converted farmhouses and renovated barns dotting the countryside, cut off from their fiefdoms by aggressive boundary fences, emasculated with picture windows, lacy curtains, gravel drives, flower tubs and hanging baskets. With no animals in the yard and no other activity to justify their existence, how long would it be before Watersmeet's lovely old farm buildings became victims of economic pressures to be converted into holiday cottages?

William Etheridge had hinted as much. Hinted that managing holiday cottages might be within her capabilities, whereas managing a farm…

A clear image of Dan's face as he looked down on Watersmeet eleven years ago, floated before her eyes.

The decision was not so difficult after all.

6

Dan

1990

For a week after the wedding, Dan plotted and fretted. It had been difficult enough to arrange his cover for Mary's wedding. To try to fix it up again so soon…and all because he'd taken a fancy to a girl who might, or might not, be interested in seeing him again. Never before had the rhythms and demands of the farm seemed so constricting.

There was nothing for it – he would have to throw himself on Ted's mercy.

Dan was just nineteen when his father had died so unexpectedly. Ted had taken over running the whole farm, enabling Dan to go to agricultural college. An austere, silent man, then in his early forties, he had worked on the farm since he had left the Merchant Navy.

Dan had been no more than four when Ted joined as a labourer. The young Dan had been entranced by the whiff of other worlds about Ted and, with dogged persistence, drew from him tales of odd and exotic places, tales that coloured his childhood and that, in the quiet telling, had drawn the man and boy together.

An only child with a widowed mother, Ted had joined the Merchant Navy when he was sixteen. His first ship was gone for over a year, working from port to port along the entire east coast of the Americas. Ted described the terrible, icebound weeks trapped in the Hudson river; he told Dan of the moose he had shot and of the antlers he had struggled to take home; of how, in some broad stretch of an unidentified South American river, four of his mates, desperate to feel dry land after months at sea, had hired a native dugout to take them to the shore and were held to ransom in the alligator-infested waters.

He recounted tales of the sultry bleak ports of the Gulf; the dirt and the smells of Calcutta; the colour and excitement of Hong Kong; and of Shanghai, which felt to him the most dangerous place in the world and where, as a homesick boy, he had been initiated into manhood with his first tattoo.

He showed Dan the small green snake curling round a stick on his forearm. Dan, then aged about six, thought it the coolest thing he had ever seen and vowed to have one of his own as soon as he was old enough.

Dan loved Ted with all the unaffected ardour of a small boy. As he grew older the hero worship gave place to respect and trust. The bond between them was very deep, and deepened still more after the death of Dan's father.

So Dan told Ted about Kate, and Ted agreed to stand in for Dan's share of the milking the following weekend.

It had to be that weekend, for the first cut of silage had been finished and with the long spell of fine weather, it looked as if the barley would be ready for harvesting the following week.

Once they started the cutting, Dan could not be spared.

Dialling Kate's number with nervous fingers, his throat dry, Dan wondered at himself. He'd never been short of girlfriends, why was it all such a big deal? But when his call was answered by Kate's recorded voice, he felt as if the proverbial rug had been pulled from under him and he slammed down the phone. Then he dialled again and left a message saying he had to make a trip to London that coming weekend and asking if she would be free for dinner.

That was on Monday.

By the time Thursday arrived, Dan was in a deep gloom. There had been no word from Kate.

That evening he was helping John Potter, the dairyman, with the milking when he found Ted at his elbow.

'What's with this weekend then, Dan? D'ye want me to do your shifts?'

Dan sighed. He'd been waiting for Ted to ask this question and was in a whorl of indecision. How much longer should he give her to phone? Should he go to London anyway; look her up; take a chance on her changing her mind if she saw him again; sweep her off her feet? Mary was probably wrong. Kate was Max's girlfriend and didn't need Dan hassling her…

He could take a chance but free days were a precious commodity. Dan was responsible for the weekend milking because John Potter had a young family. If Ted covered him this time, he couldn't ask him again for quite a while, particularly with an early harvest in the offing.

He pulled a wry face. 'Maybe I'll take a rain-check, if it's all the same to you, Ted. I…'

Just then his mother called from the kitchen door. 'Dan… phone!'

Ted took over the Saturday morning milking and Dan headed for London on what felt like the longest train journey of his life. He hadn't even worked out where he was going to stay – there hadn't been time. Max was out of the question. He wasn't sure if Mary was back from her honeymoon, but he did have his mother's sisters to fall back on. The trouble was they were all so nosey. On matchmaking-heat since Mary had married, they would instantly subject anything he did or said to long speculative discussions. It had been for that reason he'd been vague telling his mother about his motives, movement, and destination that weekend.

To his great relief, Mary picked up her phone. She was excited to hear from him, would make up a bed for him, and promised to show him a pile of photos of exotic lands and wedded bliss.

Kate lived near Ealing Broadway, in West London. They'd agreed, when they'd talked, that Dan should make his way there and then they would go on to a restaurant.

Arriving in London with a couple of hours to spare, Dan took himself off to Mary's little house in Barnes.

Clive opened the door to him. 'Ah, the country cousin… Come in. Come in. We're through here, watching the cricket.'

Dan was marshalled into a tiny sitting room full to bursting with braying, post-adolescent males in various states of excitement, drinking cans of beer, their eyes glued to the screen.

'We've sent Mary out for some more supplies. She'll be back in a minute. Find somewhere to perch. I think you must have met most people here at the wedding.'

For one nerve-splitting moment Dan thought Max might be among them. Common sense came to his aid. Max was not a particular crony of Clive and nor did he like cricket enough to spend an afternoon crouched in front of a television.

Clive pushed a can into Dan's hand and raised his voice above the level of the cricket commentary. 'This is Dan, guys, Mary's super hero. If they hadn't have been cousins, she'd've married him. Would've saved me a lot of trouble!'

'Slimey bastard,' thought Dan, cracking the can and keeping one ear open for the door. He didn't want to spend precious time watching the telly with a load of prats.

He sipped his beer and considered Clive's comment. The guy had been married for less than a month. It seemed a bit premature to strike that sort of attitude about his wife, even if they were all 'being lads' together.

Dan felt his protective hackles rising. He couldn't bear the thought of Mary being hurt. He knew she'd taken a long time to get over the Woodside episode. Waking night after night, in the grip of terrible nightmares, she refused ever to go out again with him and Max if they went off into the countryside.

He rarely thought about that afternoon but as he stood there, brooding about his cousin, he recalled the panic of indecision as he and Max had fought to agree on how best to rescue Mary and he'd undertaken to get into that barn. His skin prickled as he remembered the extreme fear he'd felt when he left the shadow of the trees…

He'd slipped round the back of the barn and finding no way in, crept, his heart thumping, to the front of the barn behind old Jem, from where he signalled to Max.

Instantly Max leapt into action, jumping up and down in the undergrowth and hurling foul curses at the old man.

Jem did not stir from his position but was sufficiently distracted by the stream of invective not to notice Dan slip into the darkness of the barn.

50

Even though it was what he'd half-expected, Dan was shocked to find Mary in the birdcage. Her face was white, frozen with terror. Seeing him, she whispered desperately, 'Dan, Dan, help me, please. Get me out of here, please.'

'I will, don't worry, Mary, don't cry. Hold tight.' He pulled out the big clasp knife Ted had given him and struggled with the lock.

Desperate.

In vain.

Hopeless.

Helpless.

The lock would not budge nor break.

He abandoned the effort. He would have to get the key from Jem…or better still, somehow, get Jem to unlock the door for him.

He touched the little girl on the shoulder; her body was trembling violently. 'Mary,' he whispered, 'you've got to do exactly as I say. I'll get you out, but you must do exactly as I say. Do you understand?'

She nodded.

'I'm going to hide. When I signal, you must give a really loud, terrible scream, then lie on the floor as if you've fainted, but be ready to run when I say run. Got it?'

She nodded again.

He crept into the shadow of a tractor by the entrance. Then he signalled to her. Her scream was bloodcurdling.

On cue the old man came into the barn. 'You, gerl, stop that screamin', you little varmint. They birds 'ull…'

He stopped when he saw the huddled form at the edge of the cage, hurried forward, produced a key from his pocket and unlocked the padlock. As soon as the gate was open, Dan rushed forward, hit the old man full in the back, pitching him headlong into the cage.

'Run!' he shouted to Mary. 'Run, Mary, run!'

As soon as she was clear of the cage he turned the key in the lock, trapping the stunned man. The commotion from the angry birds was vicious and violent, but Dan, spurred by an anger of his own, did not look back.

'Dan, fantastic! How lovely to see you. How long have you been here?' A tanned Mary flung her arms round his neck.

In the kitchen he helped her unpack her shopping and listened to her chatter about the honeymoon. They'd gone to South Africa, 'as Clive is very interested in developing his company's range of South African wines,' and had spent half of their time visiting the vineyards of the Cape.

'I didn't think you were particularly interested in wine, Mary. You hardly drink at all. Don't tell me you spent your honeymoon sniffing corks, swilling and spitting?'

Mary laughed. 'That was a bit dull, but it was only part of it, and it was worth it 'cos the growers were really impressed with how much Clive knew. And we got to visit some amazing farms. Oh, Dan, you should go there…such beautiful houses, with white curly facades in the middle of these lush green vineyards, mountains behind, and a blue, blue sky above. It was stunning.'

Dan grinned at her. 'And you used to be so fired up about apartheid. I remember you demanding to know whether Mum had bought South African fruit. There were Granny Smiths in the fruit bowl and you put them in the bin… Did you go and see how the other half live?'

Mary blushed. 'Everyone says it's getting better now De Klerk is in charge, and yes, I did. We passed near one or two townships: ugly, awful places. Really, I'd like to have spent some time there, you know, not just driving past. But, as Clive said, we were on our honeymoon, with a lot to do in a short time, and we did do such a lot! As well as the vineyards, we visited a beautiful game park where we saw loads of elephants. We had a bungalow in the reserve and, oh Dan, it was fantastic seeing them wander past, practically right under our window. Then we stayed in a lovely little town, right on the coast; I've never seen such silver beaches. It was a real shame it was too cold to go swimming. Clive says the surf there is the best he's ever seen and we are going to go back when they have their summer.'

'I didn't know you liked surfing?'

'Clive's going to teach me. He's really good. Oh Dan, it's such fun being married!'

She positively sparkled, and Dan relaxed. Whatever he thought about Clive, she was obviously very happy.

'Now, Dan, its your turn. What are you doing here?' She laughed up at him. 'I'm not so naive as to think you'd tear yourself away from Watersmeet just to pay us a social call. I know Max is away and I can't think of any reason for your coming up to London and at such short notice. Unless…' She gave him a shrewd look. 'What are you doing this evening, Dan Maddicott?'

Dan was prepared for this, 'I am taking Kate Dinsdale out to dinner,' he replied calmly. But he was not prepared for Mary's shriek of triumph.

'Brilliant! I knew you were smitten. I was right! But I didn't expect you to move so quickly; this is serious…'

Dan cut across her stream of euphoria.

'Mary, don't be daft – I've only met Kate once. I'm taking her out to dinner. That's all. Who knows, she might be deadly boring… She might find me deadly boring. But…' he frowned, 'the only thing is, I feel a bit well, awkward, about muscling in on Max's scene.'

'Max's scene? What do you mean?'

'I got the distinct impression at your wedding Max is pretty keen on Kate. But it wasn't clear to me whether they're an item. I mean, why should she agree to see me if they are? What's the score? I don't want to screw things up, for him or me. She's your friend, Mary. Is there anything I should know?'

'I've known Kate since I was eleven. She's my oldest and best friend and a total darling. She's known Max for years, but it wasn't until he bumped into her again, a couple of years back, that he fancied her. I was dating Clive by then, so we four would go out together.' Mary shook her head. 'You know Max, Dan. He's always been a terrible flirt – one girlfriend after another. Girls find him attractive, and he's never had any trouble going out with whoever he wants. Until, that is, he wanted Kate. She doesn't dislike him; far from it. We always have jolly fab times together, but she keeps him at arm's length: friends, but no more than that. It drives Max wild. He can't understand it, and the more full on he becomes, the more detached she is. I've told him to cool it for a bit. He's not going to get anywhere the way he's carrying on.'

'So where do I come in? Why did you tell me to pitch in?'

'Because I really don't think Max is going to get anywhere. Honestly Dan, I think Kate knows him too well. When we were spotty little adolescents, she had this huge crush on my brother…' Mary chuckled. 'That was when I'd planned to marry you, Dan. I carried a grubby snapshot of you standing in front of Watersmeet and I used to show it to my mates. They were very impressed!'

Dan laughed. 'I'm very flattered, Mary.'

She dimpled. 'Truthfully, I think it was more the house they

54

were impressed by... Anyway, Kate and I used to fantasise about her and Max coming to stay with us at Watersmeet, after I'd married you. Unfortunately, Max was in another hemisphere altogether and could scarcely bring himself to notice her, let alone be polite. She learned the error of her ways. And, actually, having seen, firsthand, the way he treats women, I think she's decided he's not for her. Besides, I really don't think she and Max are particularly suited. She's quite serious, you know, and rather more sensitive than one might think.'

'Whereas Max...'

'Exactly. I love my brother but, for the moment anyway, making lots of money quickly and spending it having a good time is what drives him. If Kate did decide to become his girlfriend, she'd end up getting hurt and I'd hate Max for that. So go for it, Dan. For what it's worth, I think you'll get on brilliantly. My best friend with the man I love best in the world, next to Clive and Max, of course! How cool is that...'

And, much to the amusement of Clive who walked into the kitchen, she flung her arms round Dan and kissed him resoundingly.

So Dan found himself at the entrance to Ealing Broadway station, scrutinising his A to Z, trying to work out the direction. Kate had told him on the phone, but he'd been so pleased she'd called he hadn't properly listened, and now he was late.

He plunged over the road and across the Green. Madeley Road was in front of him and reaching it, he felt he'd crossed an invisible border into another country. The hot, grey city gave way to soft, green suburbs; chestnut, lime and laburnum jostled for space; small frothy hedges enclosed small frothy gardens of fuchsia, roses, chrysanthemum and daisies and the miniscule grassy patches that only the English would call lawns.

The whole effect was pleasing, marred only by the intrusion of dark patches of tarmac where the gardens had been sacrificed to provide parking space, and resembled nothing so much, he thought, as missing teeth in an otherwise perfect, smiling picture of des. res. suburbia.

Dan hoped Kate didn't live in a tarmac-fronted house. Why it should matter, he didn't know. The sun was setting, sending long slanting rays down the street. He perspired slightly, anxious not to be late. If only he wasn't late.

He hated being late. It came with the job, drummed into him long ago by his father. 'Animals don't understand apologies, Dan. Being late is not an option for farmers.'

Max and Mary had teased him when he would break off from whatever they were doing to tear back to help milk the cows or feed the pigs, or became anxious because they were going to be late for supper.

As he grew older, he came to appreciate that town and country folk had different priorities. Kate's life would be so very different from his... With a tinge of trepidation he wondered whether he was wasting his time, this relationship could go nowhere, their lifestyles being so different.

He stopped.

There was the house. And there was the frothy garden and little lawn, the hydrangea bush and laburnum tree. And there was Kate, the low rays of the evening sun catching her face in a warm peach glow...

The brush of the soft lips on his cheek, the gentle tickle of a dark curl, the seductive whiff of a sweet fragrance and Dan realised that nothing mattered, except that he was glad to be there and that she was glad to see him.

'Up the stairs. It's the first floor flat. We're lucky my flatmate has had to go out. She was hanging on, hoping to catch a glimpse of you before she went…'

'I am really sorry I'm late. I…'

'No, don't be. We've been spared. Louise's great, but she is very inquisitive. I'm surprised she hasn't given me a questionnaire for you to fill out.'

There was no awkwardness. No embarrassing silence. They drank wine in Kate's flat till it grew quite dark, and talked and talked. They cancelled the restaurant booking Kate had made in Soho and went instead to an Italian in Ealing Broadway, and talked and talked.

They then went back to Kate's flat for coffee and then the talking stopped.

7

Susan

1943

One hand on the wheel, the other clasping a flagon of cider, Jem Leach was in rare high spirits. He had, that morning, disposed of four barren ewes in a livestock market where his reputation was not known. It had taken him some time to get there, depleting his valuable hoard of petrol, but it had been worth it and periodically he chuckled aloud at the success of his venture. Cheating those fool farmers at Devizes was, in his twisted logic, a small notch in the score he held against the damn Maddicotts.

The regular swigs of cider also contributed to his good humour, and perhaps it was the combination of these two circumstances that led him to behave the way he did. Looking back later, he could find no other reason, for the milk of human kindness did not flow thick in his veins. It was a state he relished. He had no time for the rest of the human race. Animals and especially birds, with which he had a particular affinity, he understood and liked better, and now, at forty-four, he had as little to do with the rest of the world as he could manage.

'Nobody does nothin' for Oi' he shouted periodically as he bumped along the almost deserted road, 'An Oi does nothin' for nobody!'

He should have put that on his dad's grave, the old man said it often enough. Jem cackled at the thought. Twenty years ago now, he'd died, leaving Jem sole heir to the tenancy of Woodside Farm. Both of Jem's older brothers had been killed in the First World War, but Jem seldom thought of them with anything more than a grim satisfaction that the cuffs and blows he'd suffered at their hands were as nothing to the violence of their endings.

A sneer spread across his face. He would, he thought, be hard put to remember their names now...

'Good riddance to bad rubbish!' he shouted, lifting the flagon to his mouth once more. So now there was just Jem and his mother. It was hard work keeping Woodside Farm going; the hired help had drifted away before the present war and had not been replaced. But Jem didn't mind. What he minded, more than anything in the world, and what drove him in all his dealings with that world, was the fact that the farm was tenanted, part of the Maddicott estate.

'Maddicott!' Jem spat the name and took another swig.

It was a story often told within the Leach family, and one that had grown with the telling, how in the previous century, his family had wanted to buy the farm and just when it seemed to be within their grasp, they'd been cheated. The Leaches nurtured their resentment, and what made Jem particularly bitter was that he – the thought choked him – that he would be the one who'd give Woodside Farm back to the Maddicotts. If he died without an heir…

He finished the cider, threw the flagon over his shoulder into the back of the van, thought of the wad of notes tucked in his belt and felt better.

Ahead of him on a particularly desolate stretch of the road, he saw a small stout figure. It was a woman. He slowed down and peered at her through the rain streaming down his windscreen. She appeared to be rubbing her legs in a frantic sort of way.

He drew alongside. The woman was much younger than he'd first thought and was heavy with pregnancy. He wound down his window. The startled face of a young girl, her eyes full of tears, looked fearfully up at him. She had big round eyes and with rain-plastered hair clinging to a heart-shaped face, she reminded him of a half-drowned young barn owl he had rescued from the river years ago.

And maybe it was that memory which caused him to act so out of character and offer the unknown, waterlogged waif, a lift.

They talked little, but from her inarticulate replies to his limited questioning, Jem realised that Susan was on a hopeless mission. Even if he left her well on the way to Bristol, she would not reach it before nightfall and probably not even the next day. It was also clear that, once in the city, she'd no idea how she would set about finding the aunt. The problem was not his, but as she perched, in her dripping clothes, on a box in his cab, like a trapped bird, frightened and helpless, he thought of his mother's reaction to the wild and broken birds he had bought home in the past. It brought a gleam to his eye.

'You'se not gonna make Bristle, ternight, gel. Us farm aint so far. Best stay wiv Oi.'

She looked at him, panic in her eyes.

'There's nobody there thou need fear. Me mam is there. She's old 'n' lame, and thou needs have no fear of Oi. Oi'd not touch soiled goods.'

8

Kate

2001

Polly burst into tears when Kate told her she was going to keep the farm. When Kate had calmed her down, she went in search of Ted. She found him with his head inside the engine of one of the tractors.

She felt suddenly quite diffident. Her proposal was Herculean and knowing how indispensable he was, she viewed his bent figure with nervous trepidation.

Ted straightened up, wiped his greasy hands on a cloth and gave her a searching look.

'What's up, Girlie?'

'I've come to a decision, Ted and, er…I wanted to run it past you because… I've told Polly and she's all in favour, but I need…' She took a deep breath. 'Ted, I've decided to keep the farm.'

He did not so much as twitch a muscle and, unnerved, she rushed on, 'I know everyone thinks I should sell. That, or take

William Etheridge's offer, but honestly, I don't think I could live with that…decision. I know it'd be the easy way out and it's probably the most sensible. But I'd feel as if I was selling everything Dan loved and worked for. He'd have fought tooth and nail to keep this place together.' She faltered. 'His death means, financially at least, we have a chance of survival.'

Ted's expression was hard to fathom.

'The thing is, Ted, I can't do it alone. I need you. If you want to leave…you know, make a clean break, then, of course, I'd understand… I would.' She cleared her throat and gave a shaky laugh. 'I know the idea of working for someone with absolutely no experience at all, and a woman at that, wouldn't be the first choice for many farm managers, but…'

'What would you do, Kate, if I decided to go?'

She struggled not to burst into tears. 'I suppose I'd ask you to stay long enough to help me find someone to replace you.'

'Do you want me to stay?'

He gave her a long searching look.

'I can't think of anything I want more, Ted.'

'Good. As it happens, that's my way of thinking too, Kate.' And he smiled – the first time, she realised, with a pang, that he had done so since Dan had died.

Ben and Rosie had been persuaded to go and play with friends after lunch so in the glowing afternoon sunshine, Ted, Kate and Polly pushed papers, charts and accounts round the kitchen table and made decisions.

They had just finished when the yard-door opened and Ben came in. He stopped and frowned, seeing the three adults at the table.

'You've been having a meeting?'

'Yes, darling. We've been talking about the farm.'

Ben went quite white and Kate hurried to reassure him. 'Don't worry Ben, it's good news. Where's Rosie? I want to tell you both together.'

'She's getting out of the Fosters' car. She's so slow. I'll go and get her.'

And he turned and whisked out through the door. They could hear him yelling across the yard. 'Rosie! Rosie! Come quick. They've been having a meetin'. We're gonna keep the farm!'

And as the news had been so well broadcast, Kate felt it was imperative to tell the rest of the workforce as soon as possible.

She found it impossible to sleep that night. What was she taking on? There was still time to change her mind, wasn't there? Was she up to it? Stepping into Dan's shoes like this... She wasn't cut out to be a farmer. Her talents lay in other directions. If she was going to re-start a career, surely it should be doing something she knew she could do. Oh, if only she could be sure she was doing the right thing...

The moonlight shone with silvery brilliance through a crack in the curtains, casting a trail across her bed. She got up and pulled back the curtain. The garden was bathed in a luminous light. Swathed in silver and deep black shadow, the shrubs, trees, flowers and grass had transformed into a strange and unfamiliar landscape. Staring out at the moon world, she remembered a conversation of a few years back, with Maggie, wife of the head herdsman, John Potter, who had become her good friend and confidante.

Maggie, Kate recalled, had just told her she was going back to work as a hairdresser. It wasn't just to boost the family finances – she missed the whole thing of earning money independently; of using her skills, and of having a life and relationships outside her family.

Kate had felt a sharp pang of envy. She knew that she'd had a career that had given her status in the eyes of her friends and family, something she admitted, that mattered. And suddenly she had really minded not having that any more.

She'd been quite down about it. She couldn't confide in Dan, as she knew he'd worried when she'd given up her work. For a few days afterwards she found fault with everything – grumbled at the children for the perpetual mess they seemed to leave behind; moaned at Dan for the unsociably long hours he worked; slammed and banged her way through the housework; finally picking a quarrel with Dan for leaving a pair of muddy overalls on the kitchen floor.

'Poor Dan, he didn't know what was going on,' she'd confessed to Maggie. 'And then, because he was tired, he started shouting back, and accused me of being an irritable old bag.'

'Well from the sound of it, you are!' Maggie grinned. 'So, Kate, what are you going to do about your frustrated talents? We can't have you and Dan rowing. We regard you as icons of perfect wedded bliss!'

'Oh I don't know, Maggie. Is it just *me*? You've found a solution. Muriel's got her stables and the dogs. *And* her house always looks immaculate, and she entertains all the time… All I seem to do is dissipate my energies looking after the babies and the housework. If only there was something else I could do…'

'Be realistic, Kate,' Maggie was practical. 'With both children so small, you're not going to have time for anything else. Wait until they are a bit older; something will occur to you. After all, Muriel packed her two off to school practically as soon as they could walk. You don't want to do that, but once they start school, perhaps you could do what Polly does and make cheese, or work with Dan on the farm?'

'Me? Work on the farm? Don't be daft, Maggie. I can't tell spinach from dock, or a heifer from a bullock…'

The meeting was fixed for mid-morning. The cheese processing would be finished and the sluicing of the equipment could wait. The two dairymen would have had breakfast, and Josh, in the middle of ploughing, could take an early lunch, bringing his sandwiches with him. Everyone had gathered in the repairs barn, used for weekly farm meetings and for the farm-workers to take their breaks.

Walking across the yard, Kate thought about her workforce and how they would react to her news.

With Ted on her side, a major hurdle had been overcome, but she knew she really needed the support of the other five. She could, she thought, work out those who would be supportive and those who'd be more wary.

John Potter, the dairyman in charge of the home herd, she was sure of. Known always as John Potter, he was only a few years older than Dan, and Kate liked him. He was the antithesis of the earthy and irrepressibly bubbly Maggie. Devoted to her and to his sons, he was sparing of speech, gentle, with a ready laugh and infinite patience.

Matt Freeman, the other dairyman, manager of the High Acre herd (so called because the number two milking parlour was attached to the old High Acre Farm) was a different matter. He bitterly resented, Kate knew, the fact that the Potters and not he and his family, occupied the High Acre farmhouse.

Polly had filled her in on the story. Years ago, when Matt first came to the farm, Sammy Godwin, who then ran the home herd, occupied High Acre with his wife. Matt was given one of the tied cottages in the village to accommodate him, his pregnant wife, Lizzie, and their little daughter, Brenda, then aged two.

When Sammy Godwin retired and John Potter was hired to replace him, the Godwins retired to a modern bungalow on the outskirts of the village. Polly told Kate it was she who advised Dan to give the Potters the vacated High Acre farmhouse. It was attractive and roomy, farm wages were not high, and John Potter came highly recommended.

Matt was furious.

'He came storming up to Watersmeet shortly after everything was settled,' Polly told her, 'demanding his rights. He'd always wanted to live at High Acre and he'd convinced himself that there'd been an unwritten agreement between him and Dan's father that High Acre house would be his when the Godwins retired.'

'So how did you deal with him? What did Dan say?'

'Oh, Dan was all ready to give way and make re-arrangements. The Potters, after all, hadn't moved in. But I insisted he stood firm. Lizzie told me she wanted to stay in the village. The kids could walk to school, she loved having neighbours around her, and as the bus to Summerbridge stops in the village, she was not dependent on Matt giving her a lift every time she wanted to go to town. And she definitely didn't want to move into a draughty old farmhouse, miles away from anywhere. But Matt brushed all that aside. It was a status thing. With Sammy gone, he was now the senior stockman and so he should have the bigger house – so typical of Matt. I told him Jack, Dan's father, hadn't mentioned any such arrangement to me. And furthermore, I reminded him, when Jack decided to establish two herds, he said they should run independently of each other and there should be no hierarchy between the stockmen. Matt didn't like it one bit and left, blaming me for interfering. I don't think he's forgiven me yet!'

Of all of them, Kate reflected, Matt, most probably, would have cheered had she sold to William Etheridge. The same was true of his sidekick, Mike Rosewarm, their relief dairyman. He was not in today so would not be at the meeting.

'But I've no doubt Matt'll be on the phone to him as soon as we've finished,' Ted had commented, dryly. 'And it'll be round the village and half way round Somerset before opening time.'

Josh Trubody, the farmhand, would put up no resistance to Kate. She knew, however, his support could not be relied upon, as he would always go along with whoever shouted the loudest.

Josh! Kate smiled. At thirty, he was still unmarried and living with his mum, the baby of a family with five daughters. He had no strong opinions about anything and no ambitions, content to work on the farm where his father, who'd died shortly after his longed-for son was born, had worked as gamekeeper.

The two employees from the cheese shed, Colin Rowe and Brenda, Matt's daughter, were part of Polly's domain. They knew if the farm were sold, Polly would retire. Their livelihoods, even more so than the farm workers, stood in the balance.

Kate liked Colin. He shared Polly's enthusiasm for the business and cared very much about losing his job, particularly as he was saving up to get married. Brenda was a different matter, constantly railing against the restrictions of living 'in a poxy little village', working in a 'poxy dairy'.

Temperamentally she was like her father, but she had inherited her mother's fair good looks and slender figure. Despising Lizzie for being meek, careworn and downtrodden, she treated her with casual contempt. As a little girl, Brenda had adored Dan and although she was only twelve when Kate entered his life, she had viewed Kate as a rival.

Kate knew she could only count on Brenda's support if it suited Brenda.

'Well I don't care,' Kate heard her announce as she entered the barn. 'And I don't see why you should. It's a godforsaken dump, Josh. Get a life.'

She was sitting on a battered sofa, her legs dangling over the arms, her white dairy cap on the floor, her fair hair tumbling round her shoulders, drawing hungrily on a cigarette.

Josh was placidly munching his way through a pile of cheese and chutney sandwiches; Colin was at the kettle, pouring water into an assortment of mugs; Matt, a picture of gloom, sat at the other end of the sofa, smoking, and John Potter was talking to Ted.

At her entrance, conversation stopped.

Speculation about the tragedy and the fate of the farm had been almost the sole topics of conversation since Dan's death.

The atmosphere was sharp with expectation.

The corrugated roof rattled gently in the wind, the kettle quietly exhaled, a chair creaked, and there was silence.

All eyes were on her.

Her throat felt dry and scratchy. She coughed, took a deep breath and then sounding, to her surprise, quite normal, she began to tell them of her plans for the future of the farm, their future.

'I will understand if you decide you'd rather not stay,' she said finally. 'Obviously I'll be sorry to see any of you go, but if you do stay, I'd like to think I have your support, absolutely, one hundred per cent, because that's what I'm going to need...'

After what felt like the longest silence in her life, John Potter spoke up, simply and warmly, 'Well, you've got one hundred per cent from me, Kate.'

'And from me,' said Colin. 'Christ, I admire your guts. It's a macho world you're taking on. Rather you than me!'

She smiled, grateful for his support, and turned to other the three.

Josh, slowly chewing his sandwich, eyed Kate then Ted.

'So, what's going to change? As far as I'm concerned, that is. Who'll I take my orders from?'

'From Ted, as you've always done, Josh. I'm not going to interfere as long as things are running smoothly.'

'Does that include the dairy herd? You're not going to come round the milking shed, fussing?' enquired Matt.

'No, I won't fuss, Matt, as long as the work is done properly.' Kate tried to sound firm. 'You've the expertise and the experience. I know Dan thought highly of you. And that applies to all of you. Which is why I hope you'll all stay. But,' a new note, a note of steel, entered her voice and with it her relationship with them changed, irrevocably. 'I'll be keeping the books, looking after the balance sheets, and looking at productivity. So if things do go amiss, I'll be aware of them and will make a fuss. As, indeed, Dan would've done.'

'Well, I'm glad you are staying,' said Josh, with unexpected resolution. 'No point in changing things if you don't have to, that's what I always says.'

'Well, that's that, then.' Brenda, who'd got considerable mileage at Kate's expense from gossiping, to those who would listen, about the real reason Dan had died, gave a short laugh. 'Life goes on as before, except the farmer's wife rules the roost. Hurrah for female bosses! You'll like that, Dad. You're all for women's lib.'

Kate felt a stab of irritation. 'If the arrangement doesn't suit you, Brenda…'

Brenda dismissed the suggestion with an airy wave of her

hand and got to her feet. 'No, no. It makes no difference to me. Oh well, excitement over, back to sluicing. What fun!'

Kate turned and looked at Matt.

'What happened to this idea of William Etheridge, then?' he demanded. 'I thought he was going to take over the dairy. Made a lot of sense to me.'

'If I wanted to give up the farm but keep Watersmeet, then yes. But that's not what I want, nor what Dan would've wanted. I don't have to tell you that this farm meant everything to him.' She looked at him, head cocked, eyebrows slightly raised. 'So, do I have your support, Matt?'

There was an awkward pause. Brenda turned and looked at her Dad with a sardonic grin.

Matt flushed, aware that everyone was waiting for his reply. 'Don't see I've got much option,' he finally muttered. 'I'll give it a go.'

'Thank you, Matt.'

Kate relaxed and smiled. 'And thank you, all of you. I'll do my level best to make sure you don't regret your decision. The last couple of months have been awful. For all of us. Dan's death wasn't just my loss, I realise that, and I can't tell you how much I've…well…really appreciated your support.' She sighed, suddenly wanting the meeting to be at an end, needing to be on her own, feeling her energy fading rapidly. 'I think it's time to move on now, though, don't you? And I, for one, aim to make this farm as successful as Dan would've wanted.'

Walking back to the farmhouse, Kate was trembling so much she had trouble putting one foot in front of the other. 'I feel as if I've just climbed a bloody mountain,' she thought, feeling both elated and scared.

She, Kate Maddicott, had just committed herself to…well, certainly to the equivalent of climbing a bloody mountain.

'Oh my God!' she groaned. 'What a fraud! What am I doing setting myself at the head of these people? They know far more about farming than I do. I can call myself the boss, but it's another thing to be it…and I've so much to learn…'

And she thought of Dan, who had always conducted himself with such quiet authority she'd taken his role for granted. As his wife, as the farmer's wife, she'd shared some of that authority, but that had been the extent of her influence.

And now she was stepping into Dan's shoes. Still unable to distinguish a heifer from a bullock, she was becoming a farmer. She was taking on a role that would have been unimaginable to the ambitious Arts graduate, intent on conquering the media world, thirteen years previously.

No wonder she had quaked when she'd asked for the support of the workforce.

No wonder she felt overwhelmed that they'd given it.

9

Dan
1991

The first time Dan showed Kate Watersmeet house, glowing a soft gold in the early evening light, he knew she was captivated. He was normally reserved, but there was something about Kate: the way she listened with her head half-cocked and with a hint of laughter lurking in her blue, blue eyes, that made him bubble over, wanting to impress her, to please her, to show her everything.

Over Sunday lunch, his mother was driven to protest, 'Dan, Dan, hush for a moment… Eat your food before it gets cold.'

Dan laughed and stabbed at a roast potato. Hard and unyielding, it skidded across his plate, scooping up gravy as it went, before landing in his lap.

Polly smiled at Kate. 'Well dear, what do you think of our home? Very different from London, isn't it?'

'It certainly is,' Kate, trying to cut a lump of lamb, gave up and smiled back. 'I've never been on a farm before, even though Canterbury, where I grew up, is surrounded by orchards and fields. The truth is I'm a townie. The closest I ever get to a cow is the picture on my milk carton. I can't believe how early Dan gets up; I couldn't get out of bed at that hour… I'd rather go without milk. Oops!' She had tried to slice a well-roasted parsnip, but it skeetered across her plate, sending a fine gravy-brown spray onto the tablecloth.

Polly appeared unconcerned. 'Don't worry, that cloth needs washing, anyway. Some more vegetables?'

Biting back a giggle, Kate shook her head. 'No, thank you, this is lovely.'

'Most people who live in the country don't spend time on farms, either,' Dan pushed his plate to one side and smiled at her. 'They're as likely as you to buy stuff without knowing, or caring, how it gets on the shelves, and grumble about the cost.'

'Yes, but we all grumble about the cost of things, don't we?' Kate persisted. 'What's struck me is that life here is more, well…it's so much more different than I'd imagined. I mean, Great Missenwall is very picturesque, but it's a bit of a haul from here, isn't it? And you have to admit, one village shop doesn't offer much in the way of choice, does it? Even something as simple as going to the pub like we did last night, to meet your friends, was an effort.'

Polly placed a large apple pie on the table.

'Which is why,' said Dan, 'every time fuel prices go up, we complain. That pie looks lovely, Mum. Any custard?'

Polly poured a vivid yellow, thick sauce from a spitting saucepan into a jug. 'It's burnt a bit on the bottom; never mind.'

She brought the jug to the table. 'You're right, Kate, of course you are, but we're used to it. It's the way we live. As it happens, I wasn't born on a farm. I was probably even more of a 'townie' than you. My family lived in London and I had five sisters. Our lives were caught up in a social whirl, and we were so competitive in our ambitions… I wanted to be a writer. But then I met and married Jack and became a farmer's wife.' She looked wistful. 'Believe me, I hated it to begin with. If it hadn't been for Jack, I'd have gone straight back to London.'

She cut into the pie.

'I hope you like apple pie. It's one of Dan's favourites.' She served Kate with a large slice. 'However,' she continued, gesticulating with the pie knife and scattering globules of pastry over the table, 'it cannot be denied that life can be much harder in the country. I'd much rather be poor in the city, if I had the choice. But we're the lucky ones; we can choose how we live. Dan might say he can't, that farming is in his blood and that Watersmeet must come first. His father certainly thought that. Rose had done a good job on him. For her, duty came before everything…'

'Rose?'

'Dan's grandmother. She was 'the farmer's wife' when I married Jack. She was a tiny woman, but an absolute tyrant. Jack and his Dad, hulking great men both, were terrified of her temper, and she bullied me unmercifully.' She gave a faint smile. 'Anyway, my point is Dan doesn't *have* to be a farmer. If some catastrophe were to overtake the farm, Dan would survive… You haven't started your pie, dear. Eat up.'

Kate looked down at her large slice of apple pie with dismay. The apples were still hard, sitting in water speckled with granules of sugar and topped by an almost uncooked pastry crust. She struggled with the urge to giggle.

Dan, taking a large bite, glanced at Kate, her face alight with suppressed laughter. It couldn't be better – his mother and Kate liked each other.

Life, he knew, hadn't been easy for his mum. She'd given

up a lot, marrying his dad. When he was young, she'd spend hours sitting at the kitchen table writing stories on her old portable typewriter, or reading, or listening to music, and Dan realised that tensions would arise because the house was often untidy and things would be lost or bills mislaid. After his father's death, she'd put away her typewriter and thrown all her energies into the farm.

She'd always been pleasant to his girlfriends, but with Kate, she was the most relaxed he'd seen her.

'Mary often spoke of you when she stayed with us. So you lived in Canterbury?' Polly asked.

'Yes, in a house that once belonged to my mother's parents. It's a rambling old townhouse with a bit of history and too many bedrooms for us, so my mother runs it as a B&B. My dad has a secondhand bookshop in one of those narrow streets behind the cathedral.'

'Do you have any brothers and sisters?'

'One sister, Emily. She's two years younger than me and not at all like me.' Kate laughed. There was a brittle edge to that laugh that made Dan look up, but not noticing, she carried on. 'My dad says Emily's principal role in life is to stop the Dinsdales becoming too staid and conventional. She's full of ideas and passions, which burn out pretty quickly. She's dropped out of art school but she tells us she's going to be a professional artist. Who knows?' Kate shrugged. 'Emily usually gets what she wants. She lives in a commune in Hackney and has a baby girl. She's nearly six months old now. She's lovely. Emily calls her Flick.'

Kate's visits to Watersmeet became a regular fixture. Mary was delighted. She even managed to drag a reluctant Clive down one weekend.

76

It wasn't a great success. In early December the weather had turned nasty. Following a high wind the day before, Dan and Ted had to do emergency repairs on one of the cowsheds. It rained constantly and the yard was slippery with mud and slurry. The girls made the best of it, taking over the cooking from Polly, lighting and tending fires in the bedrooms and the sitting room, mulling wine and roasting chestnuts and making a huge fuss of Dan every time he appeared, wet through and filthy from his labours.

Clive wore a permanent I-told-you-so-what-on-earth-are-we-doing-here? expression, and complained bitterly about the weather, about the mud, about boredom, about the 'piss-poor' wine in the local pub, and at the level of conversation both there and at Watersmeet.

No cajoling from Mary eased his sulky mood and the visit finished with an icy marital row that escaped nobody's attention.

Shortly after that visit, Dan became aware that something was upsetting his cousin. He'd phoned her for advice on what to buy Kate for Christmas and Mary was crying so hard she didn't attempt to conceal it. Quite what the trouble was, she wouldn't say, only that she'd had an argument with Clive and it was just 'one of Clive's rages'.

'What do you mean, "rages"?'

Mary sniffed. 'It's hard to explain, Dan. I don't think it's me he's really angry with. He does love me. He always tells me so afterwards. It's just he gets frustrated with things... Work...or whatever. He hates stupidity, of any sort, and if I...well...make a mistake, then its sets him off. He doesn't mean it, Dan. He really doesn't... It's stupid of me to get so upset, which I do, and so then, of course, he gets even crosser.'

'He doesn't hit you, does he?'

Sniff. 'No, of course not. He doesn't shout at me either. He's just, well, icy, and sarcastic. He wasn't like this before we got married, and I don't know what to do, I really don't. I love him so much. I'm terrified one day I'll do something stupid and he'll leave.'

'Have you spoken to Max, or to your mum?'

'Mum's in Hong Kong, with Dad. I daren't tell Max. He'd be straight round, and that would only make things worse. Please help me, Dan, I don't know who else to turn to…'

'Have you tried talking to Kate?'

'No, and I don't want you to tell her either. She hides it, but I know she doesn't really like Clive.'

Dan digested this in silence.

'She wasn't keen on my marrying him. In fact, she tried to persuade me not to… She said I didn't really know him… I was rushing things. Dan, don't you see, it would be awful if she were proved right. And if you *did* tell her and then it all blew over, it would be difficult for us to remain friends, 'cos I know she'd always be on her guard with Clive.'

Her voice faltered. 'I love Clive. I couldn't bear it if my friends and family took against him. You mustn't tell anyone. Promise. It's not too much to ask. It's teething problems, and if I can talk to you from time to time, I'm sure we'll get through it.'

'You can talk to me as much as you like, you know that. But honestly, sweetheart, I'm not too sure how much use I'd be. This is all a bit beyond me. Look, if you really don't want Kate to know, then I won't tell her, but I think Mum should know what's going on. If you're in trouble, she's the best person to turn to. But listen: you must promise, if things get bad, you'll come to me for help. Will you?'

'I will, Dan, I promise.'

At first it appeared Mary had been right: that it was teething problems, and apart from a tearful conversation on Boxing Day, very little was heard from her.

Polly made discreet enquiries of her sisters, all inveterate gossips and better-placed than she to assess the state of Mary's marriage. They were unanimous in the opinion that not only was all well in the little house in Barnes, but that Clive was 'charming and affectionate', and that Mary had 'done very well for herself.'

As the months passed, Dan's own relationship with Kate blossomed. He couldn't remember a time when he felt so happy. He just loved being with her, loved talking to her, loved making love with her. His sadness on Sunday night, when she had to return to London, was always tempered by the thought he would talk to her soon, see her again soon, and that one day, although neither of them had broached the subject, she would not go back to London.

Then in August, a year after they met, Kate had a series of weekend studio recordings; the harvest started in earnest and it became impossible to meet. The last weekend in August arrived and Kate tried very hard to persuade Dan to go to stay with her. Her series was finishing and she might be able to get away early enough for them to spend Saturday night and the whole of Sunday together.

Dan stood firm. Throughout the year everyone else had bent over backwards to give him as much free time as they could. This was one of their busiest periods. Kate had to understand.

Then Mary phoned.

It was early on Sunday morning and Polly took the call. When Dan returned from milking, she was fully dressed and cooking his breakfast, which took him by surprise. His father had established a ritual that on Sunday mornings, his mother would have a 'lie in' and after the morning milking he'd take her a cup of tea, then cook breakfast. Dan had continued with this tradition.

Polly came straight to the point. 'Dan, as soon as you've eaten, you must get washed and changed. There's a train to London at quarter to nine. I know you're harvesting but it can't be helped. I daresay Ted will find someone to cover for you, and if you're not back in time for the afternoon milking, then I'll call on old Sammy Godwin and help him myself.'

Dan was confused. 'But Mum, Kate knows I can't come up this weekend. She knows I've got a hell of a lot on. I'm seeing her next weekend. It's all arranged.'

'Not Kate, darling, Mary. She phoned half an hour ago and she sounds terrible. She and Clive have had another row, worse, Mary says, than anything so far. It apparently started on Friday night. She sounds hysterical, Dan. Clive left yesterday and she's no idea where he might be...'

'Another row? But she hasn't told us of anything since last Christmas...'

'She says there've been many. But she thought she could cope; she didn't want to bother us! But now, it seems, it's all too much for her. I've told her you'll go up to London today and bring her back here for a few days.'

'Is that a good idea? If she and Clive have problems, running away is not going to help, surely?'

'From the little Mary said, a breath of fresh air and some space between them might be very helpful.' Polly hesitated, troubled. 'I don't know, Dan. I don't like it. He sounds so... well...violent.'

'What, physically violent?'

Polly rescued the toast burning under the grill. 'No, not as far as I can tell. But violence, you know, takes many different

80

forms… I'd like her here. She sounds lonely and frightened.' Polly frowned at the toast she was scraping. 'She's obviously cut herself off from people who care about her… So the fact that she's phoned us is a measure of her desperation. You must go, Dan. She won't have the courage to come away by herself.'

Dan sighed. 'Of course. I'll go.'

On the train to London, he leant his head against the window and gazed out at the woods, fields, rivers and hills slipping past. His mind drifted back to the other time he'd gone to his cousin's rescue.

'Run Mary, run!'

She ran.

Dan flung the key into the dark recesses of a corner of the barn and streaked after her. He caught her hand as they reached the barn's entrance and they ran out together, into the blinding brightness of the yard. They were just in time to see Max collide with Frank Leach, Jem's son, who had appeared from the direction of the chicken huts, carrying a pail. He dropped it as soon as he caught sight of Max, grabbed his wrist and twisted his arm in a tight lock.

Dan dropped Mary's hand. 'Run Mary, run. Get help. Find Ted. Get Ted!'

And Mary, sobbing bitterly, ran out of the yard and up the lane, out of sight through the woods.

Dan turned to Frank, shouting, 'Let him go. Let him go!' and punching the arm gripping Max as hard as he could.

Frank sneered. 'Oh, it's young Master Maddicott. Let him go? Is you givin' Oi orders? Not bloody likely. Yer's trespassin' and Oi'd like to know what's goin' on here. Where's me Dad? Him wouldn't like to think we had Maddicotts sneakin' over our land.'

With that he gave a savage tweak to Max's arm. Max screamed with pain. Dan, beside himself with fury, picked up Frank's pail and threw the contents at his head. The whole slimy, stinky, grey scrapings of a hen house floor hit Frank full in the face. With a savage roar, he released his hold on Max and turned on Dan.

'Oi'll kill yer, yer little bastard. Oi'll fuckin' kill yer!' Furiously wiping the muck from his eyes with his sleeve, he made a grab for Dan's throat.

'OK, Frank, that will do.'

Never, in Dan's entire life, had Ted's quiet, cold tones been so welcome. He turned and saw Ted climb down from the Land Rover. Mary sat in the front seat, her head buried in her hands.

Her head in her hands she sat in front of him now. 'I don't know Dan. Supposing he comes back and 'cos I'm not here, he decides to leave for good. I couldn't bear it.'

'You say he's always sorry when he calms down. You say he loves you. If that's true, he'll understand you're not running away; all you're doing is giving yourself a bit of breathing space. And maybe he might realise he risks losing you. *And*, Mary, that you've a mind of your own. He can't carry on with you like this. You know that. Look at you. It's years since I've seen you in such a state.'

She took some cajoling, but making it clear she would not go if Clive returned before they'd left, she wrote a note and packed a bag.

It was quite late in the day by the time they got to Paddington. Dan sat Mary on a bench and went and got her a ticket. He returned to find her on her feet, panic-stricken.

'Dan. Dan. I must go back. I forgot... He's got a really important meeting tomorrow. He needs me at home. I can't leave now. It's not fair of me. I'll come down later in the week. I promise. I…'

Dan put his arms around her, soothing, consoling, holding her close until she started to relax.

'Aren't you missing the evening's milking, Dan?'

Dan spun round.

Kate.

Standing there.

Staring at them.

Seeing…thinking…what?

Startled, he blurted, 'Kate! What are you doing here?'

'Seeing off my producer. Since I was free today, we decided to press on with editing. I could ask the same of you… You obviously had a change of plan. Funny…the way you painted it, I had the impression you were enslaved to the harvest. Hello Mary.'

As Dan attempted to explain, Mary pulled herself away from him and making an effort to regain her composure, went and kissed her friend. Kate barely responded but Mary didn't notice. Her troubled horizons being no wider than her relationship with Clive, she over-compensated in her efforts to appear normal. Dan could see the wedge of misunderstanding between him and Kate hammered home with every word, but was powerless to stop the flow.

'Oh hello, Kate. Isn't it sweet of Dan? He came up to have lunch with me, saw I wasn't well and since Clive is away, insisted I pack my bags and go and stay with him and Aunt Polly.'

Every subsequent question from Kate and answer from Mary compounded the rift. When Kate brought the conversation to an abrupt halt with some excuse and hurried off, a stricken look on her face, Dan could do nothing but call after her,

'Kate…wait… I'll phone you tonight.'

But she hadn't looked back.

He phoned her that night, but her answer phone was on and she didn't return his call. It was the same the following night and the one after that.

With Mary in such a fragile state, he tried to maintain a cheerful air but, like an invisible cancer, his unhappiness took over and away from the house he became taciturn and short-tempered.

For the first twenty-four hours, Mary was in a state of high anxiety and Polly had her work cut out to stop her from jumping on the next train, phoning Clive, or collapsing into hysterical self-recrimination.

Clive phoned on Monday evening. Polly took the call. He was charm personified. 'Polly, I can't thank you enough for looking after Mary. Poor little thing, she took my bad temper to heart. Entirely my fault. It's been critical at work and I took my tensions home. Unforgiveable. Fresh country air is what she needs. She's been very tired recently. Honestly, Polly, I've been quite worried… I'm planning to whisk her away, in the near future, on a second honeymoon, not work-related this time but for two weeks in the Seychelles…'

Passed on to Mary he told her he loved her; that he understood why she needed a few days away; that she was very lucky to have such relatives and please could she be back on Thursday as his boss had invited them over to dinner, which might lead to his promotion. He apologised for upsetting her, but said, 'Honestly, you should know by now, darling, I was just letting off steam…'

After the call, which left Polly half-won over and Dan snorting with scepticism, Mary was blissfully happy, so two more restorative days were spent at Watersmeet, aided by further affectionate calls from Clive. When she finally boarded the train home, she hugged Polly and Dan, long and hard in turn.

'Thank you. Thank you both for being so right. Coming here was the best thing I could have done. Everything is going to be all right now, I know it. Dan, give my love to Kate. She's so lucky to have you.'

The stab of pain, a searing, intense pain, was so unexpected it took Dan a few seconds to recover. Mary, turning to climb into the train, didn't notice but Polly did, and the small furrow, which had appeared in her brow earlier in the week, deepened.

It was Ted who'd told her something was troubling Dan. 'Like a bear with a sore head he is, Polly. Never known him to be so short-tempered with the men before.'

'Has he said what the trouble is, Ted? He's said nothing to me.'

'Nope. And when I asked him, he fair bit my head off. As good as told me to mind my own business. Not like Dan at all, Polly, which was why I thought I'd mention it... See if you can shed some light...'

But she couldn't. She could see he was making an effort to be cheerful around Mary and she noticed the long evening phone calls to Kate seemed to have stopped, but she knew Kate was busy with her work and did not immediately make any connection. Then she saw Dan's reaction to Mary's throwaway remark and knew immediately where the trouble lay.

She waited for him to break his silence.

Dan waited for Kate to call him back.

Then she did, the night Mary left.

Polly had gone to bed early and Dan, slumped in front on the television, had just decided drearily there was no point in waiting any longer for a call that wasn't going to come that night either, when the phone rang.

The loving, reassuring words he wanted to say, that he'd been rehearsing all week, went unsaid and before he had got anywhere at all, she'd rung off saying, 'I'm busy this weekend. I'll ring you next week sometime. Bye.'

The awfulness of: 'I'll ring you sometime'; the emptiness of it; the power of it to hurt, and carry on hurting.

He'd rung her back, but she'd put the answer-phone on again. He'd left her a message all the same, pleading with her to phone him back.

Then he took himself up to bed. The night was black and sultry, and far off he could hear faint rumbles of thunder. He lay, sleepless and tormented, half-listening to the advent of a storm.

10

Susan

1943

Susan woke with a frightened start at the sound of hammering on the rough wooden door of the tiny bedroom. It was still very early and there was no light visible through the dust-grimed window. She panicked. Had that man, Jem, told them where she was? Was she going to be taken back to Exmoor Lodge and punished? After everything she'd gone through that whole awful day, was she going to lose her baby?

'Who is it?' she quavered, pulling the damp scratchy blanket tightly around her. 'What do you want?'

''Tis time ye were up gel, bebbe or no. There's work to be done so get thee bones down to kitchen.'

It was the man's mother.

It had been dark by the time they had bumped their way down the long track to Jem Leach's farm. Susan was dimly aware of deep, dripping woods, of a darkness she had never experienced before. With drooping spirits, she felt she'd entered a different world, a world over which, she sensed, she'd have even less control than the one she had left.

Jem climbed out of the van, collected one or two packages and with a curt summons to follow, disappeared round the side of a low building, barely visible in the black night. Moments later a gleam of light spilled across the yard. She climbed stiffly out of the van only to find her way barred by a dog hurling against its chain, barking ferociously. Susan was terrified. Slowly, trembling, she edged past him and stumbled into the path of light.

The hostility of the dog's welcome was as nothing to the reception awaiting her from the man's mother.

In the gloomy light of a low-ceilinged, shabby kitchen, by the embers of the kitchen stove sat an elderly woman in black, nursing a stout stick. She was listening to her son's curt explanation. A basilisk stare turned on the poor girl dripping and shivering by the door.

'I've told ye before about bringin' stray critturs into my house, Frank.' There was no warmth in her voice. 'An ye knows what I would 'ave ye do with 'em.' She banged her stick on the hearth.

'Yes, yes, Ma. In the meantime, her stays.'

'Just for the night, if you don't mind, ma'am,' stammered Susan, her heart sinking. The thought of going back out into the cold wet night was almost too much to bear. But they ignored her, and bending forward, Jem whispered something into his mother's ear, which Susan could not hear. Mrs Leach again subjected her to a cold, searching look.

After a silence that seemed to Susan to stretch on forever, and during which the groaning of wind-whipped branches and the rushing, gushing rain outside the house grew stronger and noisier than the crack of the fire and the hiss of the gas-lamp inside, Mrs Leach gave a small sharp nod. 'There be a room, top of they stairs. Blankets, but no sheets, mind. In the chest thee'll find some dry clothes. They were my sister's. She were a stout biddy so they should cover thy shame. Come down sharpish if thou's wantin' supper.'

Supper was simple fare; a hotpot of pig's knuckle and root vegetables with potatoes and cabbage, but having been half-starved most of her life, it was the best meal Susan had ever remembered eating. The food, the warmth of the cumbersome clothes she'd put on, the lack of sleep, and extreme exertion of that never-ending day began to take its toll and her poor body longed for sleep. The old lady had other ideas. The hospitality was to be paid for.

The rap of the stick on the hearth accompanied a series of curt instructions, and the weary girl was set to work. She was sent into the yard to fill a heavy kettle from a standpipe by the back door and told to place it on the stove and stoke the embers. Then she was set to clear the table and with the hot water from the kettle had to wash not only the dishes from supper, but what seemed an interminable pile of cold, greasy, blackened pots, pans and plates.

When this was done she was still not allowed to go to bed but subjected to a rigorous and minute interrogation from the old lady. Jem, in a wooden armchair on the other side of the hearth, listened in silence, drawing on an evil-smelling pipe.

So great was her fatigue, the questions and her answers were a blur, but later, when she had time to think it over, Susan suspected she had probably told the old lady very much more than she meant to, much more than her instinct told her was wise, but the desperate, overriding need to be released to sleep threw caution out with the wind and rain.

As her leaden limbs finally mounted the stairs to bed, she heard mother and son in a low animated conversation, the first time they had really talked to each other that long, long evening.

Waking abruptly to the old lady's summons, Susan hastily climbed out of bed and put on the borrowed clothing, her own being still too wet, thinking, hoping all the while that, before long, she would be on her way.

But when she reached the kitchen, she was again set to work by the old lady, whose eyes seemed to be everywhere, and who expressed each dissatisfaction with an alarming thump of her stick.

Susan cleaned the hearth, lay and lit the stove, scrubbed the table and swept the floor. As dawn crept through the grimy kitchen window, tentatively illuminating the corners of the room, Susan could tell it had not been cleaned for a long time. Grey dusty cobwebs trailed from the blackened beams. Pots and pans hanging from their hooks, and the crockery on a large old dresser, were all tarnished with grease. The floor, covered with flagstones and oil rugs, was so discoloured with tramped-in dried mud there was little to differentiate the floor from the yard. Her sweeping raised clouds of dried dirt that settled on everything in the room. Grumbling vigorously, the old lady directed her to scrub.

She was half way through this thankless task when the door opened and a grey wet day followed Jem Leach into the house. He barely glanced in Susan's direction, grunted at his mother, then having washed his hands in a chipped enamel bowl set by the fire, sat at the table and demanded tea. A pan was placed onto the fire into which the old lady threw thick rashers of bacon cut from a haunch hanging in the smoke above the hearth.

Then, and only then, Susan was allowed to sit and was given a cup of weak tea and a bowl of bread and milk. From her end of the table she nervously eyed Jem sitting, ignoring her, his large red hands nursing a steaming cup. It was time to say something. If she didn't go soon half the day would be lost, and now she had no idea how far she was away from Bristol.

She tried to convey as much in a few faltering sentences.

'Um…it's bin very kind of you, but…well, I really ought to be on my way. I'll just change out of these things, and…well, I'll be off…'

It was as if she hadn't spoken. The bacon was placed in front of him and he started to devour his breakfast with ravenous speed.

Susan repeated her attempts to extricate herself and stood up to emphasise her intention of departing as soon as possible. 'Thing is, I wants to get to Bristle afore it gets dark… So I really must go… You've bin very kind, but…'

Jem paused in his munching to look at his mother. She nodded slightly, a silent response to an unspoken question.

Darting a look at Susan, he addressed his mother, 'Takin' cows back to pasture up the top road, Ma, met some bodies lookin' fur someone. Asked Oi if Oi see'd some girl or other… runaway, they said.'

Susan sank back on her stool. 'What…what did you say?' she asked, her heart thumping.

Jem gave a mirthless laugh. 'Oi told they the last runaway Oi see'd was a young pig who tried t'escape the knife.' He speared a piece of bacon and waved it in front of his face. 'Foolish pig, should've knowed better.' He put the bacon in his mouth and chewed slowly, looking at Susan. 'They bodies moved off, but they's out there, my gurll. If Ma, there, is agreeable, best lie low

91

'ere for a few days. Make thyself useful round the house. Ma could do with a helping hand.'

Ma Leach looked far from agreeable, but she nodded assent, making it quite clear to Susan that making herself useful would be the least she would expect in return. 'We've nowt to spare. Times is hard. Thy keep can be worked fur, else thee can go back from whence thee came…'

Susan could only stammer her gratitude for the sanctuary temporarily offered, but deep in her heart she felt, somehow, she had escaped from one prison only to walk into another.

And she made a vow to herself and to her unborn child that it would be only for a few days; until she felt safe. Then she would move on, with or without their help.

11

Kate

2001

Kate woke early. The first rays of the sun filtered through cracks in the curtains and fell across her bed, but it wasn't the light that had disturbed her. It was the sound of footsteps coming up the stairs. Not loud and heavy, but soft, very slow and deliberate.

Kate lay there, her heart thumping, her breath fast and shallow. She had locked the doors last night, hadn't she? How could anyone have got in? Who could it be? What should she do… Get up and confront whoever it was? Lie still and pretend to be asleep? The children…supposing they went into the children's room?

Every nerve in her body screamed: 'Dan what should I do? Why aren't you here…?'

There was a little giggle outside the door. Rosie?

Followed immediately by a stern 'Sssh!' Unmistakably Ben.

Weak with relief, she fell back onto the pillows and waited.

There came a soft knock on the door.

'Louder,' hissed Ben.

Another knock: louder.

'Come in.' Kate feigned sleepiness as the door opened and the two children entered the room. Ben was carefully carrying a mug.

'It's your tea,' he said gruffly.

For a fraction of a second she froze. Ben had taken on Dan's Sunday morning tea-in-bed ritual. Suppressing the urge to burst into tears, she took the cup. The tea was grey and tiny puddles of dust and grease floated across the surface.

'I made it, for you.'

'I helped,' piped Rosie.

'Drink it,' urged Ben.

Cautiously she sipped the brew. It was almost cold.

'What a lovely surprise,' she said.

'Good. We'll go and get breakfast now. Only…' He hesitated. 'Daddy always cooked bacon and things and I'm not sure how to do that. I guessed at the tea; that was easy. But…you'll have to show me how to do eggs and stuff.'

Kate struggled with the impulse to leap out of bed and cuddle her two children, but she stayed put and let them relish their newfound dignity.

'If you lay the table and put out cereal, milk and sugar, I'll be down shortly and see to the rest. Thank you for my tea.'

'Is it alright?'

'It's the best cup of tea I've ever had.'

And she showered and wept, before going to the kitchen to show Ben and Rosie how to grill bacon, and to discard the remnants of the tea which, she discovered, had been made in the kettle.

It was the last week of the summer holidays. Time, which had felt as if it would stand still forever, suddenly seemed to kick into action and everywhere, not just in Great Missenwall, there was a flurry of activity, a sense of things to do, people to see, decisions to be made. It was a time of moving forward and starting afresh, and Kate, for her part, was ready to do so.

But she fretted about her children. Although they seemed more settled, they appeared to have no appetite for school or being with their friends again. Kate wished she could wrap them up in the loving cocoon of Watersmeet and hold them there until they were stronger.

'I think that would make things harder for them when they did go back, Kate,' said Polly. 'It would just be putting things off…and if they did start late, it would make them objects of curiosity, even more. You know how critical the start of the school year is for children. That's when they learn the school routines, get their timetables, meet their teacher, decide where to sit and who their friends are…'

Kate sighed. Polly was right. 'But children can be so cruel. Rosie's still very tearful, and Ben, while he's seemed more cheerful of late, all too easily retreats into himself and pushes me away.'

'It's early days yet. In the long run the children will come to terms with Dan's death better than you or I. But it's a bitter passage.' And she looked so sad Kate's heart went out to her. Poor, poor Polly, her suffering was as great as theirs.

She put her arms around her and hugged her.

Polly sniffed, then rallied with a shaky laugh. 'Ben's been a lot more cheerful since you decided to keep Watersmeet.'

'Yes he has,' Kate grinned. 'And he's become positively bossy. He's decided as I'm to be the farmer, I've to learn as much as I can and *he's* going to teach me. He insisted on dragging me into both milking parlours and told Matt and John Potter they had to show me what to do "'cos", he said, I was "gonna take over the milking at weekends…" I must say he has amazing faith in my abilities. Imagine me, milking! You should have seen Matt's face – no way would he let me near his precious cows!'

'So what role has Ben assigned for himself?'

'Oh, chief overseer and tractor driver. And as a truly liberated male, he told Rosie she can look after the hens and maybe help with the lambing.'

Polly laughed. 'How very magnanimous.'

Knowing the wildfire nature of local gossip, Kate felt it was important to see William Etheridge as soon as she could.

When they discovered where she was going, the two children demanded to go with her.

Kate was taken aback. 'Why on earth do you want to come? You've never wanted to before, not even when Tilly offered to give you rides on her new pony.'

'We want to see Splash.'

'Splash?'

'Mr Etheridge's puppy,' Ben explained. 'You remember, he said we could give him a name. We're gonna to call him Splash, 'cos those brown patches looks like he's been splashed with mud.'

'I wanted to call him Spot,' said Rosie. 'But Ben said that was babyish and that he don't look like Spot.'

'Doesn't he, a bit?'

'Spot's not a Springer for a start,' snorted Ben. 'And Springers love splashin' about. Don't you think Splash is a good name, Mum?'

Kate smiled. 'I don't think I have ever met a dog called

Splash before. He certainly suits the name. But he is Mr Etheridge's pup, so it's his decision. However, you two, I do have business to discuss with Mr Etheridge, so if I take you, you must be good and entertain yourselves.'

'Splash,' said William Etheridge thoughtfully. 'It's certainly not a name the Kennel Club would warm to. They would come up with something like Sandy Lane Lord.'

Ben looked appalled.

Rosie giggled.

'But I see no reason why he shouldn't have two names. Splash it is. You'll find him in the kitchen, with his mum. His brothers and sisters have all gone off to their new homes. Why don't you take him out to the yard? Tilly's there, grooming her pony.' As the children shot off, he turned to Kate. 'Do sit down, Kate. I'm about to pour myself a drink. May I get you one?'

He had shown her into what Muriel used to call the little sitting room.

Nothing about it had changed since Kate had last been there. It was the epitome of what Kate had always felt to be Muriel's effortless good taste. This did not accommodate dogs, children or any evidence of the farmyard: deep, comfortable, sofas, a thick-pile Kashmir carpet, elegant, silvery-grey striped drapes, a vast display of white lilies in the empty fireplace, and a discreet Georgian pendulum clock ticking quietly on the mantelpiece in front of an elaborate gilt-edged mirror.

And there was the one difference: no invitations – 'stiffies' Muriel called them - stuck into the frame of the glass.

Kate watched him as he mixed her a gin and tonic.

The evening he'd come to Watersmeet with his proposal was the first time they'd ever been alone with each other for more than five minutes. It had been a surprise to discover how relaxed she'd felt, how easy it was to talk to him.

She knew he was a successful businessman and she'd no idea how he'd react to being turned down. She'd be sorry if he took it badly and the fact that she cared at all surprised her.

'You're very quiet, Kate,' he smiled. 'Do you have a decision for me?'

'Yes I do, William.' That came out more assertively than she'd meant, but having begun she rushed on. 'The offer was tempting. I've thought very hard about it, but I'm afraid I'm not going to accept. For all sorts of reasons you'd probably think mawkish or sentimental, I want to keep Watersmeet together. I'm going to run the farm myself, with Polly and Ted.

If he was disappointed he gave no sign.

'Would you like to tell me your plans?'

He paid close attention as Kate sketched out the gist of her meeting with Polly and Ted, and then he asked a number of searching questions.

'He's giving me the third degree, but in the nicest possible way,' she thought, without any twinge of resentment.

'Well,' he said finally, sitting back in his chair with a smile. 'I've finished my cross-examination. If you're determined to go ahead, I see no reason why it shouldn't work out. And don't forget, if, for any reason, you ever need help or advice, on anything at all, then please ask. But with Ted Jordan at your elbow, I don't suppose the need will arise.' He lifted his glass. 'Good luck, Kate. Here's to your success.'

On impulse, Kate found herself inviting him to join Polly and herself for supper one evening.

'I have to go to Canterbury at the end of the week – I must tell my parents face to face. But when I'm back it would be lovely if you could come. And bring Tilly and Edward – if they'd like to, that is. They don't go back to school as early as my two, do they?'

As she was about to go and round up Ben and Rosie, William stopped her, looking unusually awkward.

'The pup. I was wondering…thing is, I've grown rather fond of him, but I haven't got time to train a dog, and anyway I've got quite enough littering the place. Bit of an encumbrance I know, but would you consider letting Ben and Rosie take him on?'

Kate gasped.

William hurried on. 'I quite understand if you don't want the bother. Springers think they're a branch of the human race. As gun dogs, they are superb. As pets they can be a bloody nuisance. It'd be like having another child in the house.'

Kate was touched. 'William, that's so kind of you. Thank you, very much. I'll talk it over with the children, but I think I know exactly what their reaction will be…'

At supper, she discussed his offer with Polly. 'I think it'll be good for them. They're a bit young to take complete care of him, and we'll have to train him. But honestly, Polly, I think having the puppy will help them. I'll check with Ted, and if he's OK about it, then I'll accept William's offer.'

Polly was enthusiastic. 'I like dogs around the house. Jack disliked pets and insisted that his dogs earned their keep, although in the end, Fern, the last one, spent more time in front of the fire than she ever did out in the field.'

Kate fixed a date for the promised dinner with William Etheridge. It coincided with Max phoning to suggest he might come down for the weekend and she'd readily agreed. He had an easy-going charm that made him popular with both men and women. She knew the children would be excited,

Polly was always pleased to see him, and Kate still had a great affection for him. His lazy, laid-back manner belied a restless energy, which as a boy had got him into endless escapades, and as an adult made him the natural leader of a bunch of fun-loving, fast-living, high earners who worked in the City.

He had not married, much to the despair of his mother, Polly's eldest sister, but seemed to flit from one girl to another. After Kate's marriage to Dan, his overseas assignment had been extended and they saw little of him until after Ben was born, when he came back to London. Thereafter he had paid them the occasional flying visit, laughing at their rural domesticity, a Sophie, or a Claudia, or an Emma on his arm, and rarely staying more than twenty-four hours.

This time he came alone, and for the whole weekend.

As he helped Kate lay the table for dinner, he started quizzing her about William.

'Who is this guy?' he grumbled. 'I thought we were going to have a quiet evening together and you were going to tell me about these plans you have for Watersmeet.'

'We've got the whole weekend to talk about that, Max. And if you think you can persuade me to change my mind about the farm, don't even try. William Etheridge is a neighbour. He is a farmer, a widower, with two children: Tilly who's twelve and Edward who's now fifteen. Their mother died two years ago. She was a good friend of mine.'

'How very neat!' Max sneered. 'Lonely widower, two children, seeks attractive widow with two of the same.'

Kate stared at him. 'That's really horrible of you, Max. Why are you being so cynical? As it happens, it's nothing like that at all. If you must know, he offered to buy me out and the reason I invited him here is because he was very nice about it when I turned him down.'

100

She was cross with him and when he made no attempt to make amends, her irritation grew. He played with the children as Polly helped Kate prepare the supper, only rejoining them in the sitting room when William arrived. He took control of the drinks, assuming a proprietorial role, which led him, during the course of the evening, to cross-examine William in what seemed to Kate to be an increasingly aggressive manner.

He then changed tack, and tried to enlist William's support in ridiculing the idea that Kate could run the farm.

'I understood, William, farming is something you're born and bred to. It's not a learned skill, but an instinct. So how can Kate, here, bright as she is, hope to make a go of it? Particularly in these hard times?'

'I think you've a rather a conventional idea of farming, if you don't mind me saying so.' William's tone was polite but not warm. 'Isn't it regarded, nowadays, as a business, like any other? The days of the straw-chewing countryman, happier communing with his animals than with humans, has gone. Instinct certainly helps, but a successful farm, these days, needs good business acumen as much as anything else. It's as important, if not more so, than knowing how to operate a crop sprayer, or how to put on milking clusters. With a decent workforce in place, there's no reason why Kate shouldn't make a good farmer, if she's a mind to it.'

Kate nodded. 'And I've got Ted.'

Max poured himself another glass of wine and persisted. 'But surely you've just had the worst decade in farming, ever. Kate, be realistic. Are you, an inexperienced newcomer, going to buck the trend? Dan had Ted. He worked his socks off for Watersmeet, and it damn near went to the wall.' He shrugged his shoulders. 'But maybe we've all been misled. Maybe BSE, and Swine Fever, and Foot and Mouth, and floods, and all the other disasters, have been exaggerated. Farmers realising that whinging about milk quotas and lost subsidies doesn't win them the punter's vote, whereas the sight of a little white calf, or poor, muddy little lambikin, condemned to death, does.'

Kate refused to rise to the bantering note in his voice. 'It hasn't been exaggerated, Max… Come on, you know how the media exploit a situation. Tackling the bigger issues doesn't sell papers. Heart-warming pictures of lambs always will. Its always easier to pluck heartstrings than engage in intelligent debate.'

'Then why are you going into it if it's bad as you say? Sell to Mr William Whatsit, big-in-beef, over there. Do yourself a favour, come back to London.'

William made his excuses shortly after, ending the evening earlier than Kate had envisaged, and for that, she blamed Max.

12

Dan

1991

The storm broke shortly before three in the morning. In the dark silence that preceded it, the night creatures stopped hunting and being hunted and fled for whatever nest, perch, hole or hide would provide them with shelter. A violent crack of thunder heralded the deluge and a fierce wind tossed and turned the trees, pushing them this way and that in a wild contorted dance.

Autumnal leaves, brutally and prematurely forced to release their tenuous hold on life, whirled into the wind; branches whipped off, lashing and slashing a destructive descent. Throughout the wood, paths were transformed into fast-running, mud-laden streams. Even the reeds in the river bent under the onslaught and the river ran faster and fuller.

A great willow, upstream from Woodside farm, groaned, cracked and fell. One half of the trunk crashed into the river and, carried along by the fuming torrent, wedged against the arch of a small road bridge. Foaming with spume and debris, the rushing water hurled against the impromptu dam. Upstream, where the bank was less steep, and bordered on one side by fields, the river rose. Slow, watery fingers seeped, trickled, and ran into the meadow.

At the edge of the river a herd of cows had huddled for protection under a huge ash tree. As the water swirled around them, they crowded up onto the remains of an old levee. This rapidly became a small island with the bubbling, racing water on one side and a lake slowly, inexorably, spreading out on the other. Thus stranded and sensing their danger, the matriarch began to bellow.

Dan lay in bed, listening to the storm. Having drifted into a doze, he awoke at the first crack of thunder. Storms had always been a source of secret excitement for him. He loved the fireworks, the drama, the over-the-top displays of wind and rain, the unpredictable nature of it all. But much as he might thrill to the thunder and lightening, he was alert to potential danger and damage.

Yet thoughts of the storm or its aftermath, were not uppermost in his mind as the rain lashed against the window, and the wind rattled the sashes and howled down the chimney.

If he could put the clock back, would he have behaved differently? Maybe he should have taken Kate into his confidence. But it was Mary's decision not his, and Kate should have trusted him. Dan struggled. He loved Kate; he would never consciously cause her any unhappiness. She must know that… She must! He loved Mary too, he did, but in a very different way. Mary was the sister he'd never had. Kate must see that… If Mary was in trouble and turned to him, then he had to do something. But if he was going to lose Kate as a consequence…

He groaned aloud. Last night's telephone call had been awful. Kate had been so polite, so cold. For the umpteenth time he ran over it, searching for some comfort, something he might have overlooked to tell him things weren't as bad as they seemed.

'Is Mary still with you?'

'No. She went back to London today... Kate, I don't know what you're thinking, but things aren't what they might seem. I went to London to... I didn't lie to you, I *was* working, but Mary needed my help; I couldn't *not* go.'

'No, obviously not. I know you have this 'special relationship'; she's told me about it often enough.'

Silence.

'Kate...

'Yes?

'Will you...can you make it down here this weekend? We need to talk, properly, not like this...'

'I'm busy this weekend, Dan. I'll give you a ring next week sometime. Bye.'

And she had rung off, leaving Dan staring at the receiver in disbelief.

From their first date, they had never ended a telephone call without firmly establishing when the next call was to take place and who was to make it.

Dan got out of his bed and padded to the window. The storm was easing off. He could hear a distant grumble, a faint bellyache of thunder; the wind had dropped, and the rain, while still falling steadily, sounded less dramatic in its intensity. It was dark, but the night sky was changing colour and it would not be long until dawn.

'Time enough to face the day,' Dan sighed, and went back to try and grab some elusive sleep.

Grey tendrils of light were spreading across his bedcovers when he was woken from an uneasy doze by the sound of the telephone.

'Kate?'

It was his neighbour, William Etheridge.

The gamekeeper had been out early, checking pheasant covers after the storm, and had spotted a group of Dan's heifers in trouble. The water was still rising and the levee, on which they were marooned, was slowly disappearing under the flood.

'He crossed the river by the bridge below Woodside Farm and said the water level there is nearly over the road; the arch appears to be blocked by a tree or large branch and a pile of debris.'

Dan, cursing, swung into action. He roused Ted and Josh from their respective houses, loaded the Land Rover with a bale of hay, a long length of stout rope and the power saw, then sped across the fields up the valley, along the track skirting the edge of the woods on the opposite side of the river from Woodside Farm, and arrived at the edge of a lake that had materialised overnight.

Alarmed by their sudden arrival, a large grey heron flapped an ungainly departure, tucking up its long gangling legs and uttering a short rude curse. The early rays of the autumnal dawn reflected off the two hundred yards or so of lapping brown water that separated them from the mournful group of cows gathered on the river's edge.

'I think we might need to get Matt up here, Dan. This could be trickier than we thought. They're his heifers and he'll calm them. It's lucky there are cows with them, that's why they are not panicking.'

106

'Not yet. Wait till the aunties start to freak…' Dan frowned. 'Matt's going to be slap-bang in the middle of his milking, Ted. Let's see what we can do first. If we have no success, then I'll go and take over from him.'

The three men set to. The hay was strewn tantalisingly on the dry ground, and with shouts of encouragement they tried to persuade the cows to brave the floodwaters.

Dan tied the rope around his waist and headed into the flood to establish how deep it was. As if apologising for the aberrant behaviour of the storm, the sun rose, golden, beautiful, dispersing the remnants of the grey dawn and setting fire to the leaves of the trees on the opposite bank in a dizzying display of copper, yellow, green and red.

But Dan, cold, wet, anxious and sick at heart, had eyes only for his animals. His venture into the flood established it wasn't too deep for them. If only one of the cows, preferably the most mature, could be persuaded to move, the heifers would follow. The group had stopped its keening and was gazing across the watery waste at the men, and more particularly at the hay.

Dan stood, thigh deep, halfway across calling, clucking, encouraging. He could feel the force of the water between his legs and knew the water was still rising. 'Come on. Come on!!'

It was only a matter of time before the levee crumbled under the force of the water and the weight of the animals.

Suddenly a cow moved. She plunged into the water, splashing, running, forging a straight line, past Dan, to dry land and the hay. He recognised her as she lumbered past – an excellent milker, nearly four years old, out with the heifers, having a breather between one set of calves and the next. She saved the herd, for they all followed her example, one after the other, running, jumping, splashing and lowing through the flood to the safety of the higher ground and the hay.

Apart from a brief stop to change his saturated clothing, Dan did not return to the farmhouse until the evening, spending the day cutting and clearing the undergrowth to gain access to the bridge, and removing as much of the dam of logs and branches as possible until, with a sudden rush, the impatient, swollen river swirled under the arch of the bridge, taking a substantial amount of the debris with it. Early evening was spent in the flooded meadow, clearing the drainage ditches and digging fresh outlets for the water to escape back to the river.

So it was a very tired, wet and muddy Dan who entered the kitchen of Watersmeet. The last rays of the sun glanced low through the windows, deepening the shadows, catching shapes and forming fantastical silhouettes on the walls and furniture.

His mother had gone out for the evening and he knew he would find food waiting for him in the bottom oven of the Aga. He had just filled the kettle and pushed it on the hot plate when he heard the distant beep-beep of the answer machine.

Kate!

Maybe it was a message from Kate.

Trembling, he pressed the replay button.

It was.

'Dan. Please, please don't leave me any more messages. Every time I hear your voice, I… I think it's best if we…if we don't see each other any more.' She paused, and then continued in a lower voice, flat, almost devoid of emotion. 'I really thought you loved me…and Mary… Mary is – *was* – my best friend… I'm finding this so hard to deal with. I can't believe I was so mistaken… that I could be so wrong is… It's really hard… Dan. I don't know what you want to say to me, but I really don't want to hear any excuses, or apologies, or explanations. Please don't phone again. Bye.' And with her voice sunk almost to a whisper, the telephone clicked off.

108

Dan stood for a moment in a state of shock. Somehow he made his way out of the kitchen and, feeling his way, like a blind man, climbed the stairs to his room. He lay on the bed, gazing unseeing at the ceiling. This was worse than anything. He had lost her. He had lost her and the enormity of his loss drove out all rational thought, all action, all feeling.

The dusk deepened around him. The telephone rang again but Dan did not stir.

At about nine o clock Polly returned home.

The house was in darkness so she assumed that Dan was out. As she entered the kitchen, an acrid smell assailed her nostrils. The kettle had boiled dry. Tutting with annoyance at her son's carelessness, she carried the kettle out to the yard to cool off. When she returned to the kitchen, she simultaneously registered the beeping of the answer phone and the fact that the cutlery set for Dan's evening meal had not been moved. A quick glance in the oven confirmed he had not eaten that evening, although his boots, by the door, and the dried-out kettle were testament to his return.

Puzzled, she went to listen to the message on the answer-phone.

'Hi Dan, its Joe here. I am at the Duck. It is now 8.30 and the lads want to go on into Summerbridge for an Indian. The place up Castle Hill, so, see you…' He was cut off. The tape was full.

Puzzled, Polly went into the hall. The house was dark and still. She climbed the stairs to Dan's room and listened at his door. Nothing, not a sound. She tapped lightly. Still no sound. She opened the door and looked in. Dan was lying on his bed, fully clothed, staring at the ceiling.

'Dan. Are you all right?'

His voice came back flat, totally devoid of any emotion.

'What? Oh, Mum. Yes, I'm all right. Just a bit tired. It hasn't been…a very good day.'

'Would you like me to run you a bath?'

'No, I'll do it myself, by and by.'

'Joe left a message on the answer phone for you. He says he and the others are off to Summerbridge if you want to join them.'

'Oh… I don't think so.'

'I'll bring you up a cup of tea.'

He made no reply and, troubled, she closed the door and returned to the kitchen.

Since the answer phone had been installed, Polly always ran through the messages when the tape was full to make a note of numbers or other vital bits of information.

Thus it was she heard Kate's message.

Thus it was the knot of misunderstanding started to unravel.

Some while later, she took Dan a cup of tea. He had not moved. Undeterred, she went and sat on his bed. Gently stroking his face, she told him she had heard Kate's message. A deep, agonised groan seemed to wrench his whole body.

'I've lost her Mum, I've lost her. I hurt so much. I love her, but it's no use. She won't listen to me. She doesn't want to hear from me ever again. There's nothing I can do.'

'Poor Kate. She sounded so unhappy. I think she must be in as bad a way as you. What happened? Can you tell me? Why does she mention Mary? What did you do?'

'I didn't *do* anything. Except to promise Mary not to tell Kate about Clive.'

And so he told his mother about the meeting at Paddington and how Kate had seen Mary in his arms.

'So not only does she think I lied to her about being too busy to see her, but she catches me in a fond embrace with her

110

best friend, in London of all places. And poor old Mary makes things much worse by pretending it was quite usual for me to 'pop' up and have lunch with her whenever I felt like it. The trouble is I can't see a way of explaining to Kate without telling her about Mary, and now, anyway, she doesn't want me or my explanations.'

'I don't think that's true at all, Dan.'

'You've heard the message.'

'Yes. And I heard a very unhappy girl trying to put a brave face on what must seem an appalling act of betrayal. If you love Kate, darling, then you've got to do something. She believes she doesn't mean that much to you, and worse, that her lover and her best friend have betrayed her. Can you imagine how she must feel? How bitter that would make her? You can't accept defeat so easily... For her sake as much for yours.'

Dan stirred. He felt awful, but that terrible blank numbness ebbed away. Polly's words affected him and roused him from his stupor. Polly ran him a bath and he peeled off his stinking muddy clothes and lay in the hot water, his tired brain going over and over the problem.

Polly re-assembled a late supper and waited.

It was well after eleven. Dan had just pushed aside a plate of food he'd been eating without enthusiasm when Polly heard the sound she'd been waiting for. Dan heard it too and looked up, puzzled.

'Who on earth can that be, at this time of night? Mum, I really can't face anyone...'

But Polly slipped out of the room as Kate came in from the yard.

Drops of rain sparkled in her dark curls and glistened on her cheeks. Her face was white, her voice tremulous. 'Dan... Dan, I'm sorry... I...'

111

He was at her side in a flash, his heart thumping with such joy and excitement, emotions unimaginable a few minutes ago. He folded her to him.

'Kate, my darling Kate. What have you got to be sorry about..? Why, why are you crying?' He tenderly kissed the tears on her cheeks.

'Because I was so stupid, because I should have realised…'

His mouth found hers and further speech was impossible. For a while they stood there, cleaving to each other, neither wanting to be the first to break away.

Dan finally drew back and stroking her hair, looked into her eyes, still full of unshed tears. 'Kate,' he said softly. 'I love you. I would never intentionally do anything to hurt you. You must know that?'

A slight blush brought colour to her cheeks. 'I realise that now. I should have let you explain, but I was so hurt, so devastated, I couldn't see how there could be any other explanation. Then, when Polly phoned…'

'Mum? When did she phone you?'

'This evening. She explained everything. I wanted to see you right away. I needed to see you, to touch you, to tell you I love you.'

Her hand softly caressed his cheek; a tremulous smile played over her lips then vanished as, looking deep into his eyes, she said slowly and with great gravity, 'I love you, Dan Maddicott.'

13

Susan

1943

Slash.

The eighteen-year-old elm quivered.

Slash…slash…slash…

The strokes were even and unhurried. With the slightest of groans, the tree toppled and joined the rising pile of trees, brambles, and creepers Jem Leach had chopped down. With reluctance and great resentment, he was obeying instructions from the local 'Ag' man and was clearing part of the woodland that made up the greater percentage of his farm.

A lot of the wood grew on the slopes of a steep valley that dropped down to the river, where large tracts of the land were boggy and unfit for agricultural use. The pastures he used for his cows and sheep were on the higher, drier reaches of the valley sides. Before the war, the woodland had provided good cover for birds as well as coppicing materials for him to use and to sell. The woods had also brought him a useful income from the local gentry who paid him for the privilege of rearing and shooting pheasants.

Pheasants were the one bird he had no time for. "Stupid bloody furrigners they!" But they had made him money in the past, and as soon as this war was ended, he expected his wealthy neighbours to resume their sport. In the meantime, when so much food was hard to come by officially, the birds were a useful supplement to the Leaches' diet as well as a valuable commodity for under-the-counter trade. He had only recently exchanged three brace for a tank of petrol and it had been this that had taken him to the distant market to sell his worthless ewes.

He'd not been at all happy, therefore, when he was instructed to put part of the woodland, as well as a meadow, under the plough and sow potatoes, but as his mother pointed out, the Government were prepared to pay him a good price for anything he produced and so, unlike most, they were better off now than they had ever been. They were even going to lend him one of those new-fangled tractors to dig out the tree roots and render the land fit for the first ploughing.

There had been pressure for him to take on extra labour, but he had seen them off. Even the most officious member of the local Agricultural Committee, or 'War Ags' as they were known, thought better of billeting an unwanted land girl on the Leaches, who made it clear they 'didn't want no strangers pokin' their noses in. Interferin' and takin' what's not theirs…' It was a constant refrain of Mrs Leach. Jem, working his land, tending his stock, talking to his birds, and scheming with his mother on how best to take advantage of the topsy-turvey world created by the war, saw no reason to disagree.

Woodside Farm was a good four miles from Great Missenwall, and the Leaches themselves were infamous for their hostility towards strangers, or visitors of any sort, and were not slow to protect their privacy with a shotgun; their neighbours had learned to keep their distance.

Their landlord, Samuel Maddicott, had as little to do with them as was possible. He was a member of the local War Ag, and the committee members had very quickly agreed, contrary to practice where tenancies were involved, that if the Leaches were to do their bit for the war effort then it shouldn't be a Maddicott who advised or supervised them. All business was conducted through his land agent whom, inevitably, the Leaches disliked almost as much as the Maddicotts.

Samuel Maddicott, a peaceful, hardworking man, had only been to Woodside Farm twice in his life – a matter of great triumph to the Leaches. It made no difference to them that his second visit, shortly after the outbreak of the war, brought the doctor to them when Edith Leach suffered a major stroke. The doctor was in time to save her life solely because Samuel had found him standing beside his car some two miles away from the farm. He'd had a puncture. Samuel had ignored Jem's vigorous protests that his mother 'would rather die than accept any favour from a Maddicott' and had helped the doctor deliver the unconscious Mrs Leach to hospital.

Crack!

A young oak shivered and fell.

Jem worked steadily on, slashing, hewing, and steaming in the raw November air, a rare smile flickering across his features as he thought of his mother.

The mother of three sons and a daughter, she had driven out the daughter she detested and then having lost both of her eldest boys in the first two years of the Great War, had manoeuvred and manipulated to prevent him, her baby, from being sucked into the maelstrom of the next.

Their life had always been one of hard work and deprivation, but she had a strong instinct for survival.

In the aftermath of the Great War, when agriculture went into an acute decline and their poverty was desperate, she held them together. In the early Thirties, when the bony fingers of unemployment and hunger touched every member of the working classes and it looked as if they might lose the farm, her refusal to give up kept them going. Her strength saw them through the unexpected death of her husband, Arthur, from blood poisoning, the consequence of an injury he'd refused to have treated. And then, against all odds, she survived the stroke that should have killed her.

Before that stroke, Edith had always kept their farmhouse meticulously clean, and had taken great pride in her cooking. If Fate had not introduced her to Arthur Leach, she would undoubtedly have gone on to become cook in one of the grander houses of the county. Jem's father had told him, when Jem was a child, that all his mother needed to make soup was a stone and a pot of boiling water, and it was true that the Leaches survived while others starved because of her ability to make something out of nothing.

Her stroke, however, had left her barely able to cook and clean. That affected her badly. When she returned from the hospital, lame and an invalid, she rejected all assistance from the outside world. Well-intentioned neighbours, who made the mistake of calling with offers of help or fresh produce, were unceremoniously shown the door. A widowed sister had come to stay, but Mrs Leach did not take kindly to her presence, or interference, as she saw it, and when the sister died, she struggled on alone, indomitable.

By nature a single-minded, vindictive woman, the hardships of her life embittered her, so she embraced the Leaches' hatred of the Maddicotts. Her son was tutored from an early age to view them as the enemy at the gate. The only story he ever heard at his mother's knee was the legend of how Jeremiah Leach, a hard-working, God-fearing tenant farmer in the 1830s, had been promised by a Maddicott that if he raised the necessary capital, in twelve months Woodside Farm would be his. That Maddicott, like all Maddicotts before and after, was a dissolute, drunken gambler who needed the capital to meet his creditors. On the appointed day Jeremiah, having raised the necessary sum, hurried to Watersmeet, only to learn an elderly Maddicott aunt had died, leaving her nephew his fortune. The deal was off. Jeremiah was unceremoniously shown the door, the yoke of tenancy firmly back in place.

The only redress they ever received for this injustice was the creation of an entail, which guaranteed the Leaches the right to pass on the tenancy of the farm from father to son in perpetuity. This small reparation in no way mollified them; if anything it made it worse. Generations of Leaches nurtured the resentment, and the story of the saintly Jeremiah and the wicked landlord grew with the telling.

And now, when it seemed inevitable the Maddicotts would eventually repossess the farm because Jem had failed to marry and produce an heir, Fate dropped a solution into their laps, and he, Jem Leach hadn't realised it.

His mother had, though. That very first night when he had delivered Susan Norris to her, dripping sorrowfully on his hearth, he thought he was delivering someone they could keep as an unpaid skivvy. His mother had seen further.

The whole of that night, long after she sent him to bed, she had schemed. Early the next day, when the girl was still asleep, she outlined her plan and had given Jem his instructions.

Jem laughed out loud. His axe flashed through the air and a slender birch fell to the ground.

Two days later, Edith Leach put her plan into action. Warning Susan that she should not venture out of the house, or answer the door to anyone, in case she should be discovered and returned to Exmoor Lodge, she had Jem drive her into Great Missenwall.

There she made three calls. The first to the doctor's surgery, the second to the police station and the third to the WVS centre, where the good matrons of the town dispensed tea, clothing and gossip.

A silence fell on the gathering as her dark, bulky body filled the doorway.

Cups of tea hovered mid-air, mouths stopped chewing, and hands, sorting through piles of clothing, were stilled. She was known only to a few present, but her reputation was such that she was disliked or feared by all. She knew this and was determined to take advantage of it.

A small pretty woman, unknown to Edith, was the first to break the silence.

'Mrs Leach. What a surprise. How nice to see you out and about. Do come and join us. Would you like a cup of tea?'

Her attempt to be welcoming was rewarded with something akin to a snarl.

'Tea's not what I'm after. I've no time to waste with the likes of ye. I've come to tell ye that us'll have need of they bebbe clothes, by and by.' She poked at a pile with her stick, then looked around at the mesmerised faces of the women, a hint of triumph in her sunken eyes. 'My son, Jem, has hisself a wife. Her bebbe is not long due...'

By the time she was ready for Jem to drive her home, Great Missenwall was buzzing with the news that not only had Jem Leach finally found someone to marry him, but that the poor girl was about to bear him a son and heir.

118

Such were Mrs Leach's powers of intimidation that no one, not even the doctor or the station sergeant to whom she had reported the loss of her daughter-in-law's documents and ration book, thought to question the truth of her story.

And all hearts went out to the unknown girl who found herself the pregnant bride of Jem Leach, and worse, at the mercy of her mother-in-law.

14

Kate

2001

The telephone rang.

Splash curled asleep in his basket by the stove, snored, occasionally giving little excited yelps as if he was chasing rabbits in his dreams.

The long clock in the hall struck two.

The phone stopped and then started ringing again. Kate sighed and looked up from her books. She had less than an hour to get through this paperwork before having to collect the children from school.

She'd not found it easy taking on her new role. There was so much for her to learn on the farm, as well as running the house and caring for the children, and there were times when she felt overwhelmed. When she fell into bed at night, she was usually asleep within seconds.

She preferred it that way. It gave her less opportunity to mourn, although her sleep was full of dreams of Dan.

Sometimes they were so real, and he so alive, she would wake in the dark and reach across to his side of the bed, hoping, against all reason, to find him there.

The telephone stopped and then rang a third time.

It was the headmistress of the children's school.

'Susan Bloomfield here. Sorry to disturb you, Mrs Maddicott, but…er…' The voice faltered.

Kate froze, panic alarms going off in her brain. Not again, please God, not again!

'What's wrong? Rosie, Ben? Are they all right?'

'It's nothing to worry about, I'm sure, Mrs Maddicott.' Her tone was measured, careful. 'It's just that Ben seems to have got into a fight with another boy, in the lunch break. His teacher says he's not turned up for afternoon school.'

Kate's legs buckled and she sat on the floor, gripping the phone to her ear, trying to make sense of what was being said.

'I just wanted to make sure he hadn't come home before I alert the authorities.'

Try as she would she couldn't keep the panic out of her voice. 'Mrs Bloomfield, Eastwood School is four miles away. Ben is eight years old. Even if he could find the way back, it would take him ages to get here.' She tried not to panic. 'When did he go missing? What happened? A fight? What sort of fight? That doesn't sound like Ben. Who was he fighting with? What about?'

'I've left Mrs Greenstock with the children to find out what happened. My priority is to find Ben. I've got to contact the police and the Education Authority. I'm so sorry Mrs Maddicott. It's awful for you. But, please, don't worry. We'll find him soon. Why don't you come out to the school. I'm sure we'll have him safe and sound by the time you get here.'

'But supposing he comes back and I'm not here?'

'Well, yes… Can someone watch out for him? I do think it would be better if you came here.'

'Does Rosie know what's going on?'

'Not yet. The infants have a different playtime, as you know. But we're a small school, and when anything happens it's hard to keep things quiet and in proportion.'

For some reason that phrase stuck in Kate's mind. When Mrs Bloomfield rang off she found herself repeating it over and over, like a mantra, in an effort to suppress the worst scenario her imagination was busily conjuring up.

She knew she'd find Polly in the cheese shed, and when she finally forced her trembling body across the yard, she got as far as saying, 'We must keep this in proportion…' before she burst into tears.

Shocked as she was, Polly took charge. Ted was summoned to alert everyone and to get up a search party and Polly agreed to stay in the farmhouse while Kate went to the school.

The whole way there, Kate drove very slowly, scrutinising every hedgerow, every field entrance, every gateway, every inch of the road, willing Ben to materialise. But there was no sign, and no news of him when she got to the school.

Mrs Bloomfield led her to the staff room. The fight, it transpired, had occurred shortly before lunch. Ben had shot off in the direction of the cloakroom and his absence wasn't noticed until a good half-hour later. He'd been missing for over an hour. The police had already been to the school and had gone again, apparently to make an initial search.

Mrs Bloomfield was clearly worried, and in trying to conceal her concern, was uncharacteristically formal. 'We've talked to Ben's classmates, and to his particular friend, Tommy Harrington. Apparently Ben got into an argument with one of the older boys. They were queuing for lunch and a group of lads barged in front of Ben and Tommy. He objected. There was some pushing. Something was said, which badly upset him. He ran off and that appears to be the last anyone saw of him.'

'What was said?'

Mrs Bloomfield hesitated. 'Children can be cruel, Mrs Maddicott. They lash out without thinking of the consequences. I'm sure that's what happened here. The lad didn't stop to think what he was saying.'

'What did he say?'

The Headmistress shifted uncomfortably. 'I'm not sure that…'

'What did he say?'

Mrs Bloomfield, embarrassed, looked away, 'Um… It was something to the effect that Ben's Dad was a coward… Everyone knew his death was no accident… He'd killed himself because he couldn't face up to, er…to losing his farm.'

Kate froze. She couldn't move. Icy trickles of shock ran down her spine. The words crashed around in her head. Coward? Dan? Is that what people thought? Is that what Ben now believed? His Dad had killed himself? The cruelty, the awful cruelty… How could anyone – anyone suggest that?

'Who was it? Who said it?'

Mrs Bloomfield looked even more uncomfortable. 'I'm not sure it will help…'

Kate snapped, 'I think that's for me to decide, don't you? I want to know who it was. Ben must be in an awful state. When we find him, I'm going to have to help him understand why anyone should say such…such a terrible thing. Besides, he'll tell me himself who it was.'

A treacherous voice whispered in her head. 'You might not find him. You might never see him again.'

Mrs Bloomfield sighed. 'Believe me, Mrs Maddicott, I am

not taking Harry's behaviour lightly. If that is what he said, then he'll be dealt with. But my first priority is to find Ben…'

The door to the staff room opened a crack, but Kate disregarded it. She was living her nightmares all over again, but it was not Dan but Ben this time, and she had to find him before he was lost to her, too…

'Harry who?'

There was an embarrassed cough and Kate turned to see Lizzie Freeman, Matt's wife, at the doorway. Her face was flushed bright red and she was close to tears. Not looking at Kate, she said apologetically to the headmistress, 'I'm so sorry Mrs Bloomfield. I came as soon as I could… Matt, my husband, he's having his afternoon nap between milkings, so I come alone… I'm sure, whatever he's done, Harry don't mean no harm.'

'Harry?' Shocked, Kate turned to the headmistress. 'Harry Freeman? I don't believe it!'

Lizzie Freeman burst into tears when she was told what Harry said to Ben. She'd looked after Ben and Rosie many times since they were little, and loved them. In Kate's opinion she was by far and away the nicest member of the Freeman household.

'Oh Kate, I'm really sorry… I'm sure he didn't mean it… Why should he say such a thing? He wouldn't make something like that up. He must've heard the talk… It's awful… I'm so ashamed… I'm really, really sorry, Kate. If Harry did say them things, he was just repeating common gossip… He didn't mean it.'

Kate, shocked, stared at her. 'Common gossip? What are you talking about? How could you allow anyone to talk that way, Lizzie, let alone in front of Harry? What were you thinking of? Not Ben or Rosie or Polly, or me. And certainly not Dan, who was one of the nicest, kindest, most loving people ever to walk on this earth!'

The afternoon dragged on interminably. Every time the telephone rang, her heart pumped so fast she could scarcely breathe.

The police returned emptyhanded and left again, putting on a good show, it seemed to her, of optimism and reassurance.

Unable to bear the enforced inactivity any longer she went to collect Rosie.

Rosie clung to her. 'Mummy, where's Ben? Why are we going home without him? Has he really run away? Will he come back? Is he dead, like Daddy? Where's he gone?'

Kate lifted the little girl in her arms. 'We'll find Ben. Don't you worry,' she said with a conviction she was far from feeling.

When they got home, she left Rosie with Polly and went to find Ted. He'd phoned to say he was coming back to drop off John Potter for the afternoon milking.

Splash followed, dancing at her heels, assuming he was about to be taken for a walk. Kate looked at the puppy Ben so adored and a tear trickled down her face.

'We've all been out, all afternoon.' Ted was tired, and showed it. 'John Potter's got his cows to see to, so if you want to take his place, Kate...? Though mebbe...' – he looked at her white, drained face – 'you should stay at home. Have a bit of a rest. You're all in.'

'I couldn't. I've got to be doing something. I've got to find him. Please God,' she murmured for the hundredth time, 'let me find him.'

Ted gave her the binoculars, and as she climbed into his Land Rover, Splash squeezed himself in between her legs. She took solace from his warm, round body and stroked his long velvety ears, trying hard not to cry remembering Ben that morning, curled up with Splash in his basket, his arm tightly round the puppy's neck, promising him he would be back from school soon.

As they drove off, Ted explained that the police had agreed he'd concentrate on an area about three to four miles wide that stretched from Watersmeet towards the school. Where their land bordered William Etheridge's, William himself had taken up the search with his men.

'Everyone is out looking, Kate, and we have several hours of daylight left, so don't despair.' He glanced at her. 'I know what you're thinking, it's only natural, but many kids run away from school. Sometimes it's the only way they can deal with things when they get out of hand. I must've run away six or seven times before I was Ben's age, I was that unhappy. He'll come to no harm, he's got his head screwed on, he has. Now, the first thing we have to do is to go to Woodside Farm.'

'He wouldn't go there!'

'I know. But if he got lost, he might stray further afield than we predict. Leach's land is on the perimeter of possibility, but the police think we should search everywhere, no matter how unlikely it might seem. They've already called in at Woodside but there was no sign of Frank. My guess is he hid when he saw their car. He's no love of authority, has Frank. You don't have to talk to him, Kate. I'll deal with him.'

Kate had never been to Woodside Farm before, nor had she ever spoken to Frank Leach. Dan had seen no reason to take her there, and since his death she'd been content to leave Ted to deal with their tenant. Frank's dislike of the Maddicotts was legendary, so the possibility that Ben might have wandered onto Leach land troubled her.

Some four miles from Watersmeet they pulled off the road

through a half-concealed entrance. The long, winding drive through the woods to the farm emphasised its isolation. The surface was pitted with ruts and holes half-heartedly filled with broken stone and brick. A recent rain disguised the depth of some of them and the Land Rover pitched and rolled in an uneven passage down the track.

As they lurched along, Kate scanned the dense undergrowth choked with fallen trunks of trees, moss-covered boughs and straggling bushes. Ferns hung, wilting with autumn, black with decay; the larches were an arid yellow, and the leaves of the sycamore were dotted with black spots like the plague, all bearing testament to the beginning of the dying season.

She shivered. 'These woods are so gloomy. Ben wouldn't have come here.'

'Mebbe not. But I did say to the police I'd call.'

The wood on one side gave way to meadow. It was separated from the track by a sagging line of barbed wire, from which dangled an occasional twist of orange baling twine.

'When Jem was alive, he kept sheep in there,' Ted nodded in the direction of the field full of rusty brown dock and thistle. Old pieces of decaying machinery added to the air of dereliction. In the centre of the meadow were three long, wooden huts, corrugated roofs, windowless, with hoppers at the end of each.

'When his Dad died, Frank got rid of all the stock and built those hen houses. He kept battery hens and sold the eggs on to some firm or other who'd market them as farm-fresh eggs.'

'They don't look as if they're in use now.' Kate gazed at the shabby, weather-beaten buildings with distaste.

'No, he gave up on that some time ago. It's a shame he's let this land go. In his father's day they'd some good grazing up here.'

The vehicle rounded a bend in the track leading directly into the farmyard. The big stone barn to the left was also showing signs of dereliction: its roof sagged, holes were apparent where the tiles had slipped off, and tufts of sedge weed and crowfoot grew out of the stonework.

The farmhouse in front of them had a similar air of neglect. It was a long, low, two-storied stone house, with a central porch. The peeling paint of the front door was obscured by the russet brown heads of long-dead buddleia that had taken possession of a corner of the porch. The windows were grimy and obscured by curtains pinned up in a haphazard fashion, effectively preventing a prying world from peering in. A missing pane or two had been patched with plywood. Weeds had replaced flowers in the borders skirting the front of the house.

Climbing out of the Land Rover, Ted looked around and frowned. 'We're going to have to get heavy with Master Leach. Part of his tenancy is due care and maintenance. I've let this slide since Dan… Dan said he was going to deal with this.'

The yard was absolutely silent apart from the raucous screech of a pheasant somewhere in the undergrowth. After a moment, Ted stretched back into the cab and sounded the horn. Its strident note rolled round the farmyard and was answered by the harsh cawing from a flock of surprised rooks. As the noise of the birds died away, the silence reasserted itself.

Kate climbed out of the Land Rover and joined Ted. The atmosphere unnerved her and when Splash jumped out and started sniffing around, she called to him urgently, 'Find Ben, Splash, there's a good dog. Where's Ben?'

Then gripped by a sudden fear, she walked swiftly across the yard into the barn, calling, 'Ben! Ben?'

But the barn was empty except for rusty bits of machinery,

stacks of poultry feed, drums of chemicals, boxes, scattered straw, a broken ladder to the loft, and dark, watchful shadows. It smelt dank and musty. A twisted skeleton of chicken wire and splintered wood was all that remained of the cage where Mary had once been imprisoned.

Kate returned to the yard in time to see a tall, heavily built man emerge from a side door of the house. He moved lightly on his feet for all that he was now in his late fifties. His hair was still black, and what remained of it was long and greasy, dripping on to the shoulders of his grimy collarless shirt. He was unshaven, and his skin underneath his thick black stubble, was pale and mottled. His eyes, narrowed now as he regarded them, were almost colourless; his nose was hooked and his mouth was thin-lipped and permanently drawn down at each corner, almost to his chin.

The spaniel pup started barking but Frank Leach disregarded him and snarled. 'What 'ave yer come 'ere for Mister? Why 'ave yer brought the widder? Oi'se ain't got nothin' to say to either of yer so yers can clear on out and take that nasty piece of yapping mongrel wiv' yer.'

Ted remained unruffled. 'We came at the request of the police, Frank. They called earlier, but couldn't find you…'

'Why should they? Oi'se got nothin' to say to they, and Oi'se got nothin' to say to ye, so clear off!'

'All in good time. We're looking for young Ben Maddicott. That's why the police were here. He's gone missing and we need everyone, everyone including you, Frank, to look out for him. You must let the police know at once if there is any sighting.'

'He ain't here. Did yer send the police snoopin' round sayin' Oi had 'im ?'

'No, Mr Leach, no.' Kate interjected. 'It's just that if there's a chance he strayed this far, we need to know if you've seen him. He's a little boy; he could've hurt himself, fallen in a ditch, or got completely lost and be badly frightened. We need all the help we can get to find him…'

Frank's sour expression almost imperceptibly lightened. He shrugged his shoulders and said nothing.

'If you find the boy, you'll ring the police, or me right away,' said Ted sharply. 'Or you'll be in real trouble. Make no mistake.'

'Oh, Oi'll make no mistake,' came the soft reply.

Kate climbed back into the Land Rover shaking all over. Ted scooped up the puppy and put him on her lap. She buried her face in his silky coat and prayed for this interminable nightmare to end.

'If it's any comfort, Kate,' said Ted, as they bumped off down the track, 'I really don't think Ben would get this far, even if he strayed completely in the wrong direction.'

'But supposing Frank goes looking for him? I don't trust that man one little bit, Ted, he's…evil!'

'You're overwrought. Frank's a recluse. I know he's difficult, but there is absolutely no reason to think he would ever harm anyone, let alone a child. He's not evil. Dan would've been the first to agree, however much he disliked him.'

'But he threatened Dan when he was a boy, you know that. When Mary was locked in the bird's cage, Frank threatened to kill him, you heard him yourself. Dan told me…'

'Because Dan had just thrown a bucket of chicken shit over him. Understandable in the circumstances, don't you think? Now, here's the road.' He glanced at her, hesitating. 'I suggest we take it as far as the church, check the churchyard and then go over to Rooks Spinney. Then, if you can face it, Sparrow's Wood. It may be that if Ben recognises where he's going, he might head for somewhere with strong connections to Dan.'

'Yes. Yes, I see.' Kate swallowed. She'd not been anywhere near Sparrow's Wood since they'd found Dan's body.

Ted drove slowly on and Kate resumed her scrutiny of the verges and the woods and fields beyond. Every now and then they would stop the vehicle and shout but there came no answering cry, save the plaintive mew of a pair of buzzards circling high over the trees.

The church stood alone on the side of a hill, a little distance from the village of Great Missenwall. It was a small Saxon building and Kate had fallen in love with it when she'd first seen it. Its simplicity, so different from the awesome grandeur of Canterbury Cathedral where her spiritual education had taken place, had touched her. Here she had married Dan; here the children had been christened, and here Dan had been buried.

She closed her eyes, and for the umpteenth time that afternoon, pleaded with God to deliver her Ben at Dan's graveside.

'Let him be there, and I promise you, I promise you I'll never doubt you again.' God couldn't ignore that, surely?

But when she got to the earthy mound, Ben wasn't there.

Ted went to look inside the church, Splash frisked around the gravestones, and Kate knelt at Dan's side, the tears slipping down her face. She fingered the bunch of roses she and the children had placed there last Sunday and whispered, 'Dan, Dan, help me find him. Help me.'

'This is consecrated ground. Dogs should be on the lead.' A voice spoke sharply.

She looked up.

The vicar, seeing her, was instantly contrite. 'Oh, Kate, I do apologise, I didn't realise it was you...that you were... It's just that the verger gets so cross if we don't enforce the rules.

I've just heard about Ben. I am so very sorry. You must be sick with worry. I was coming up here to offer up a prayer. Would you come and join me? Don't worry about the dog. He'll be all right here for a little while.'

Wearily, Kate stood up. 'I'm sorry Vicar, I don't know… We thought Ben might be here. Ted and I are out searching, and…'

'Five minutes won't make no odds, Kate,' said Ted, who'd re-appeared. 'I'll put Splash back in the Land Rover and wait for you there.'

She followed the vicar through the gravestones into the little church. They had just got inside the cool, musty interior, when the porch door opened with a bang. The evening sun streamed in past Ted, casting his face and body in complete shadow, but from his silhouette Kate could tell that a complete change had come over him.

'Kate. Come quick. He's been found. He's safe. He's all right!'

Kate let out a cry. Ted put his arm around her and she clung to him.

'William Etheridge found him. As I got back to the Land Rover, the mobile rang. He found Ben on the back road going to his place. He says that Ben had been trying to get back to Watersmeet, had got lost, vaguely recognised Sandy Road, so thought it might be the lane home. William says he's absolutely fine, but very tired and very much wants his mum.'

William appeared from the house as soon as their wheels scrunched on the gravel of his courtyard. In her haste, Kate tripped getting out of the car. William, helped her up and gave her a firm, reassuring hug.

'It's all right Kate. He really is quite safe. It's all over. I've notified the police; they've been in touch with the school and the other search teams.'

132

He led her into the house. 'He wouldn't have anything to eat or drink 'til he saw you. Tilly's looking after him, in here.'

He showed them into a small sitting room where she had never been before. It smelt of books, leather and tobacco, and in the corner of a battered sofa, watched over by Tilly, Ben was curled up, fast asleep. Choked, she went to him. Splash beat her to it. With a bark of joy, he leapt onto the sofa. The child woke instantly.

'Splash! Splash! Mum's brought Splash.' The puppy started licking his dirt-grimed cheek, and Kate was stricken at the pallor of his tear-streaked face.

'Ben,' she said softly.

He looked up. 'Mum,' he said, and lifted his arms to her in the way he'd done as a small child. She gathered him up and they clung to each other.

She was so overwhelmed, she was hardly aware of the others leaving the room. She sank weakly onto the sofa and held her little boy close, the horror of the last six hours unwinding like a spent coil. Tears ran silently down her face. She'd stood on the edge of a darkness far greater than she could ever have imagined, greater even than the despair she'd experienced after Dan's death. She'd lost Dan; she thought she had lost Ben, and now she was aware of the loss of something more intangible, something fundamental to her existence.

Her world, which she'd felt to be so light, so sunny, protected from anything *really* unpleasant, was no more. It had gone. Perhaps it never really existed, or if it had, then it had only been on borrowed time. It was as if a spell that allowed them to feel they lived a charmed life had been broken. Now she was in a place after the fairy tale had ended; the dream had been abruptly, violently, interrupted, and she was wide-awake in the real world, with pain and loss and fear for her companions.

133

She understood, with great clarity, for the first time since Dan's death, that she was truly alone.

Ben reached up a hand and touched her cheek. 'Why are you crying, Mum?'

She ruffled his hair and tried to smile, 'I thought I'd lost you, Ben.'

'But you haven't. I'm here, with you. So don't cry, Mum, please don't cry.'

He clung to her all the way home. As she carried him into the house, she turned to Ted. 'I don't know what to say, Ted. To you, to everyone who helped look for Ben.'

'Don't be so daft, girl,' he replied gruffly. 'It's the least anyone would do. Now get him in and put him to bed. He's all in, and so are you by the look of things.'

Later that evening she lay at Ben's side, stroking his hair, gently coaxing him to talk to her about what had caused him to run off. In a strained, tight voice, he told her.

'Harry said they all knew it wasn't an accident. He said everyone on the farm knew, everyone in the village knew, everyone in the school knew. *You* knew. I was the only one who didn't. He said I was thick. It was obvious. My dad killed himself. He said his dad said you don't have those sorts of accidents with a twelve-bore. He'd shot himself 'cos he was a coward. He was gonna lose the farm and he couldn't face it.'

Bitter tears racked his frame.

'Ben, listen to me. I promise you what Harry said is not true...'

'Then why did he say it?'

'He wanted to hurt you. When people want to hurt other people, they choose to attack where it will hurt the most. Harry knows how much we miss Dad, how much his death has hurt us. But Ben, you *know* it's not true. Dad loved the farm, yes, but he loved you more, much more. And he loved Rosie and me.'

Ben was silent.

'Harry is wrong about the gun, too. People do have accidents. Twelve-bores are powerful guns. Dad made a mistake and left the gun cocked as he climbed that stile. The coroner said so, Ben, and he wouldn't say that unless it were true.'

Wearily Ben replied, 'But he wasn't there, Mum. And they've been sayin' that Dad saved Watersmeet for us. They were sayin' the farm was doing badly, but now we don't have to leave 'cos Dad died. If that's true,' he struggled on, 'it *is* my fault, 'cos he was saving Watersmeet for me. He always said that Watersmeet would be mine one day, mine and Rosie's.'

Kate struggled to comfort her poor little boy. She boiled with anger at the thoughtless cruelty that had left him so burdened and hurting. If she didn't do something to help him, she knew this uncertainty over Dan's death would blight his life, as it was blighting hers. She, too, had to accept it was an accident: that Dan had not killed himself from some misguided belief it was the only way to preserve their life at Watersmeet.

And if that was the case, she had to understand why he hadn't taken her into his confidence, or whether he *had* reached out to her, but she'd not noticed. Not only did she have to *believe* it was an accident, she had to *know* and know convincingly. She needed, particularly, to assuage the surges of anger and resentment she felt whenever the treacherous little voice in her brain, which would not be silenced, held Dan accountable for his actions and all their subsequent suffering. If she did not resolve the issue, she knew the uncertainty would cast a shadow over their lives and undermine the whole bedrock of their love and life together.

She stroked his face.

'Ben, I want you to think about Daddy and all the times you had together. Think about them hard. Tell me about them if you want to. After a while, you'll find it'll be easier to know how much he loved you and would do *nothing* that would make you unhappy. Certainly not as unhappy as you have been since he died.'

She kissed him and said softly, 'And I am going to make you, and Rosie, too, a promise. Somehow, I am going to prove to you Daddy's death was a horrible, awful accident; that he didn't kill himself, so as well as believing it, you will *know* it.'

Ben turned on his pillow to look at her. 'You promise?'

'I promise.'

15

Dan

1992

'This is it,' said Kate, giving Dan a reassuring smile. 'Grey Lodge. Home of the Dinsdales for at least twenty years, and my mum's family for the last hundred.'

As she pulled the car into the side of the road, Dan peered up at the house. It was aptly named. A wide-terraced Georgian house with a smooth, plastered exterior painted a dark grey. A rather grand pillared front door, painted a much paler grey, added an elegant touch to its townhouse appearance. To one side of the door a discreet polished plaque, with many accreditations, claimed a superior B&B availability which was, according to a less superior cardboard sign in the window, not available at that particular moment.

Dan pointed this out to Kate as they climbed out of the car. 'Perhaps it wasn't a good weekend for us to come, Kate? They appear to have a full house.'

Kate shook her head. 'Mum always puts that sign up when

she wants a family weekend. Don't worry, you'll have a bed.'

'With you, preferably…' He was distracted by the twitch of a net curtain. 'I think we're being watched,' he whispered.

Kate grinned. 'That'll be Mum. When she's old and infirm she'll live in an armchair behind that net curtain.'

They had no sooner got through the front door than Mrs Dinsdale's voice could be heard, even before she'd opened the sitting room door.

'Katherine, darling. What a lovely surprise. I thought I heard a car. Did you hire one? How very sensible. I'm glad you don't keep a car in London. I wouldn't have a moment's peace, thinking of you driving in all that madness. You hear such terrible stories. How lovely and early you are, darling. Your father has just got in, so we must have some tea. I'm sure you are ready for something. I've made a Dorset apple cake. We have so many apples at the moment; quite a bumper year. You used to love my apple cake. I'm glad of the excuse to make it. Not that I need an excuse. You'd be surprised how many of my PGs ask for a slice with their tea… So this is Dan? I am so pleased to meet you at long last…'

'Yes, I'm…' It was as if he hadn't spoken.

'So unlike Ivan… Though why I thought you might be, I really don't know. Do you prefer Earl Grey, or Lapsang Souchong? Of course, I have got Indian if…'

Kate cut across the flow. 'Yes Mother, this is Dan.'

And a stunned Dan shook hands with a plump, middle-aged woman, a bit shorter than her daughter, her dark hair, streaked with grey, caught up in a bun with soft tendrils framing a high-cheeked face, slightly reminiscent of Kate. She had bright blue button eyes that peered at him intently over a pair of spectacles that slipped down a small, retroussé nose.

'How do you do, Mrs Dinsdale?'

138

She pressed his outstretched hand. 'Oh please, call me Margaret. Mrs Dinsdale sounds so formal, don't you think?'

'Well, yes. Tho...'

'My goodness, you look far too young to be a farmer... I'm sure you're hungry; all young men usually are...'

'Well, yes... I've not...'

'Supper will be at 7.30. Dear me, I totally forgot to ask Katherine whether you're a vegetarian, Dan. I do hope you are not...'

'Er, no, no, I'm...'

'Although of course, if you are, it's not a problem at all; although I have made a beef-in-beer casserole. It's quite a favourite with us, and such a useful dish when one doesn't quite know when one is going to eat...'

'Yes, I'm sure...'

'I suppose I assumed you would eat meat, being a farmer. But I realise that's a terrible assumption... It must be very hard to kill the animals you have raised, let alone eat them?'

'Er...'

They were ushered into the sitting room, where a tall grey man was waiting for them. Almost cadaverous in appearance, wearing a baggy grey woollen cardigan with leather-patched elbows, a loose black rollneck sweater and battered grey corduroy trousers, Roger Dinsdale was the modern embodiment of a grey friar. He shook hands warmly with Dan and welcomed him in a quiet, dry voice. As if to counter his wife's loquacity, Kate's father, as Dan discovered, was a man of dry wit and few words.

'It's as if,' Kate confided, when she showed him the attic room where he was to sleep, 'early in their relationship some casting agency tried them out for the parts of Mr and Mrs Bennett from *Pride and Prejudice* and they have been stuck in those roles ever since... They are not like the Bennetts, though. Mum, for a start, is much brighter than she seems. She might prattle on, but she doesn't miss much. It's as if she's articulating her thoughts as they arise, without any of the natural editing process. Whereas Dad...'

'Edits everything?'

'Exactly. The trouble is I think Mum's overeducated for the role she's ended up with. She and Dad were both students at Kent; she was doing languages, he, history. When they first got married, she worked full time as a translator. Then we came along, and then the house, and then the B&B business and so – the end of her career. She seems cheerful enough but...' Kate looked at Dan, earnestly, 'I don't want that to happen to me, Dan. If I ever get married and have babies, I would definitely find some way of carrying on with my career. I love my job. I don't want my brain to atrophy.'

'No chance of that!' Dan laughed, but he felt uneasy.

When she had arrived so unexpectedly that night, to pull him out of darkness, he had held her in his arms and whispered into her hair, 'I love you, I love you, Katie Dinsdale, and I'm not going to let you go...' and she had smothered him with kisses and loving, and he knew that he wanted to marry her more than anything he had wanted in his life. But he was a farmer, would always be a farmer, and he knew it was a lifestyle that was all-encompassing, took no hostages, demanded sacrifices. How could he ask Kate to marry him? But he couldn't bear the thought of a life without her...

She'd suggested this visit to her parents in Canterbury shortly after that, and it seemed to signal a significant movement forward in their relationship. It was her mother's birthday on the Sunday, and Kate had been very keen for Dan to accompany her and meet her parents.

'Who's Ivan?' he hissed, stretching out on the bed.

Her blue eyes twinkled. 'This is the first moment we've had to ourselves since we arrived, and rather than comment on my mum, who's on top twittering form, or on my dad, you pick up the reference to Ivan. Trust Mum to mention him. He was my boyfriend when I was at Sussex. He was a politics student, a rabid Marxist, and Mum loved him, or rather, everything he stood for. She thought he was so romantic.'

'What happened?'

'Oh, he dropped me when he graduated. I didn't fit in with his plans, and anyway, I was far too bourgeois for his image.'

'Did you mind?'

'At the time I minded very much. But I'll tell you all you want to know some other time. We must go down to supper.' She caressed his face, 'I love *you*, Dan. This is real. Ivan is history.'

They sat down to supper in a dining room crammed from floor to ceiling with books.

'Dad's stock,' said Kate. 'Every room not used by the PGs is crammed with books. Dad thinks by keeping them at home, he won't have to sell them. It breaks his heart every time anyone buys one. It's like parting with an old friend, isn't it Dad?"

Her father was clearly used to this line of teasing. He turned to Dan. 'Do you read much, Dan?'

Before he could reply, they were interrupted by noises from the kitchen.

Kate's mother leapt to her feet. 'It can't be… Roger, you didn't tell me! What a wonderful surprise… Now I *really* feel a birthday girl… Just in time for dinner, too. But she can't eat the casserole. Roger, you should have warned me. I could've made a cauliflower cheese, or something...' and so saying and still talking, she rushed out of the dining room.

Kate's father got to his feet, a look of bemused pleasure on his face. 'I think it must be Emily. No one else comes in through the scullery. Well, well. Excuse me for a moment.'

Dan looked at Kate for an explanation.

She shrugged. 'It seems my sister Emily has arrived for the weekend. You're going to meet my family in one whole dollop, Dan. I hope it's not going to be too indigestible.'

He felt surprise. 'Don't you like your sister? Both your parents seemed pleased.'

'They adore her...'

They were interrupted by the return of her parents and a slender girl, barely out of her teens. She had dark wavy hair, much like Kate's, but waist-length and tumbling loose over her shoulders. She was smaller than Kate, more petite, with softer, prettier features, and although her eyes were not so blue, they were larger and fringed with long dark lashes. On her hip she carried a tiny girl, the closest to a doll Dan had ever seen, with pale skin, soft, flushed cheeks, bright blue eyes and black curls.

Emily's arrival, Dan reflected later, changed the whole atmosphere. Not only did Mrs Dinsdale's volubility accelerate as she flustered about food, bedding and the baby, but he found himself ousted from the spacious attic room he'd hoped to share with Kate, and given a single room designed for a B&B guest. And as for Kate...yes, it was almost as if Kate had been demoted.

Dan did not doubt that her parents loved her. Between Kate and her father there seemed to be an easygoing, albeit conspiratorial, bonhomie. But both parents *worshipped* Emily. Margaret fluttered around her like a gigantic moth, and Roger positively glowed as he sat, gingerly holding the small child on his lap while Emily ravenously attacked a hastily assembled dish of pasta, fielding her mother's non-stop questioning.

Yes, she had decided to come down at the last moment. No, she didn't want to miss Mum's birthday. Yes, she knew Mum would love to see Flick. No, she didn't come by train – a friend had given her a lift. No, she wasn't sure how she would get back yet. No, she would have to go back on Sunday. Yes, it would be brilliant if Kate gave her a lift. Yes, she still lived in the squat. No, it was all kosher. Yes, she'd enough to live on, just. Yes, Flick's father was still in touch. Yes, he gave her a bit of money towards Flick's upkeep. No, they were not in a relationship. No, she didn't want to be. No, she saw no point in telling them who he was. No, she was not working, not in paid work, anyway. Yes, she was painting. And so forth…

All this was relayed so charmingly, with such vivacious good humour, Dan could quite understand why her parents were so captivated. He was, too. When the activity of the kitchen drew her mother away, Emily turned to him and questioned him about himself, and about Watersmeet.

'It does sound idyllic,' she said, finally. 'I'd love to go there. Would your mother mind if Flick and I turned up one weekend? We would be as good as gold and not get in your way, I promise. I could bring my paints.'

'Of course. You'd be very welcome. Any time you like. My mother would love to meet you, especially Flick.'

She smiled at him, warmly and sweetly. The smile reminded him of Kate.

Kate at his side. Silent.

She'd been silent, he realised, since Emily had danced in. And not only had she said nothing, nobody had spoken to her.

The child on Roger's lap started to whimper. Margaret bustled in.

'Emily, it is time that baby went to bed. The cot is up and waiting. Here, let me take her. I've made up her bottle. You relax, darling. You look worn out... Such bags under your eyes... You must be exhausted after that terrible journey. What did you say your friend was called? Stay and chat to Kate and Dan... You haven't seen Kate for simply ages... Roger, make a start on the washing up, would you? I'll be down to help as soon as I have got this little girl settled... And make some tea...or coffee, of course, if that's what's wanted...though I think it is a very bad idea to have coffee before going to bed... It's a modern habit, I know, and far be it from me to tell my grown-up daughters what they should drink before bedtime. Offer Dan a brandy or something, dear.' And she swept Flick, now protesting loudly, out of the room.

Dan rejected all offers of further alcohol. He was unused to wine at mealtimes; he had been up for milking at 5.30 and his eyelids prickled. His offer to help Roger clear away was firmly rejected.

'We've had our orders. Kate and Emily, take Dan into the sitting room. We'll join you there.'

Dan followed Kate into the sitting room; Emily stayed to wheedle a fresh bottle of wine out of her father. In the moment they were alone he seized her hand and turned her to face him.

'Kate, are you all right?'

'I'm fine...'

But she was not fine. He knew that. The light had gone from her eyes.

Sitting alone on his single bed, gloomily surveying the blank TV screen, the ubiquitous plastic kettle, teapot, packet of biscuits, teabags and chunky white china that managed to drain even the most characterful rooms of their identity, he worried about Kate.

144

Drained. That was it: that was how she appeared. He'd never seen her look so lifeless, and hated it. He wanted to hold her and tell her he loved her. Their time together was so limited, and now it seemed as if Emily would be travelling back to London with them, which meant there would be very little time for any intimacy.

His body ached for hers. The feel of his skin against her, the warmth and softness of her breasts, the silkiness of her pubic hair, the delicacy of her touch.

He shivered, and wished Emily fairly and squarely back in her squat in Hackney. He hadn't even had a chance to say goodnight to Kate to his satisfaction, as her mother had shown him to his room. He knew the family had rooms in the attic, but he was on the guest floor and he didn't fancy barging into the wrong one in search of her.

There was a soft knock. Dan leapt to the door. Kate stood there, a cream silk dressing gown wrapped tightly round her body.

'I've come to say goodnight...' but before she could say any more, Dan pulled her into the room.

Later, holding her in his arms, he asked her about her sister and her parents.

She sighed. 'It's as I said. I do love them. All of them. But it's always been the same, and it sounds so pathetic.'

'Playing second fiddle to Emily'

'You noticed. Yes, I suppose it must be obvious. She is, and always has been, the centre of attention. I don't mind that. She's lovely and great good fun.'

'Kate...'

She ignored his interruption. 'But it's more than that. It's as if she can't bear not to *be* the centre of attention. That sounds like I'm just being envious, but it's always been the same. If I threaten, in any way, to take centre-stage, even for a moment, she will intervene: do something, say something, *anything*, to divert attention back to her. And my parents seem to fall for it every time. Even Dad, who you would think would have more, well…perspicacity.' She bit her lip. 'And what's worse, I become sort of frozen in her presence. It's like she drains me of all energy, and anything I say or do feels dull and boring…'

He stroked her hair and held her close in the narrow bed.

'Being an only child, I've never had to share my parents, except with my cousins in the holidays. But that was different.'

'Oh it's not just with parents…with anyone who might have shown any interest in me when Emily was around. As I grew older, I learned not to bring friends home. Why do you think Emily turned up this weekend?'

'Your mother's birthday?'

'She hasn't bothered to come home for Mum's birthday for the last three years. No, it's because you're here. Because Mum told her you were coming here at last. Because they sense you're important to me. That's why Emily's here. She's scalp-hunting.

'You're exaggerating!'

'No, Dan, I'm not. Look back over this evening. You did find her fun…and attractive. I could see you were really tired, but you stayed up and helped her polish off that bottle of wine. You've even invited her and Flick down to Watersmeet, regardless of whether I'm there or not. Oh God! Now I sound like a jealous old cow. What must you think? First of all Mary, and now Emily…'

And she wept onto his chest, and he wiped her tears with the corner of the sheet, and made love to her, and vowed that nothing, and no one, would ever come between them.

The following morning Kate had planned to show him Canterbury. Emily challenged him to a game of tennis in the afternoon, but he sidestepped the offer. 'I've persuaded Kate to show me all her old haunts. When you come down to Watersmeet, you and Kate can challenge Joe, an old friend of mine, and me, to a doubles duel. We don't have time to play much these days, but he's got a mean serve and my backhand is not so bad.'

They had a wonderful day together. The weather was kind, and old Canterbury showed off her wares to mellow perfection. They explored the back streets of tight, terraced houses; wandered along the edge of the golden waters of the Stour; spotted speckled trout hanging suspended in the water's current, half-hidden by the streaming emerald weeds; climbed the smooth, grassy mound in the Dane John Gardens; walked the mile or so out to Kate's old school; drifted around the cool, grey, echoing cathedral; negotiated the crowds of tourists along the Burgate to have coffee in the café Kate and her cronies used as a meeting place after school, and went to visit Roger in his bookshop, in a narrow lane tucked away behind the High Street.

The next day, sitting alone in the garden and basking in the warm sun of late September, Dan heard a female voice drifting through the open kitchen window. He thought at first, from the timbre and flow, that it was Margaret talking.

It was Emily.

'A farmer! I ask you Mum, quite frankly, what's Kate doing with a farmer? I know he seems nice enough. He's quite good-looking, in a raw sort of way, but he's not exactly our Katie's type, is he? I mean if you compare him to Ivan... Ivan was an intellectual... He was exciting, really well-read. And what about that guy, Max? I thought Kate and he were well-suited. Dan might be very nice and kind to animals...although that doesn't necessarily follow, being a farmer... But he's certainly not an intellectual, is he? And what about Kate's job? I thought she was the ambitious one in our family? I thought we were going to see her name on the screen. You go on enough about how well she's doing, and how proud you are of her. Is she going to throw all that away to marry a farmer, or is he a temporary diversion?'

Dan sat rooted to his chair, self-conscious and very uncomfortable. Emily had unerringly articulated his fears.

He shared this, one evening a few days later, with Joe, his lifelong friend. They were the same age, lived in the same neighbourhood and shared a farming background, although Joe's father was very much alive.

Joe was the eldest of four, and worked alongside his father on their pig farm. He was shorter and stockier than Dan, with a freckled face and a shock of straw-coloured hair. He was easy-going and good-natured and had always been popular with their contemporaries. His current girlfriend, Susie Bancroft, the daughter of the landlord of their local, The Duck and Fox, was pulling pints behind the bar, and had supplied Dan and Joe with quite a few.

'It's a real problem, Dan,' Joe agreed, shaking his head over his beer. 'Unless you marry a female farmer, and let's face it, you could count the number of those on one hand and they're probably past it anyway; or marry a farmer's daughter, if you can find one still hanging around…you're condemned to live the life of a solitary bachelor.'

'It's odd, isn't it?' mourned Dan. 'Why's it changed so much for us lot? Our parents didn't think twice about marrying whoever they liked, and now…look at the Young Farmers: bunch of saddos, desperate for a bit of skirt. What's happened?'

'It's women's lib, that's what it is. Girls have their own careers and they can pick 'n' choose. They don't need us any more. Quite honestly if you were a girl, unless you were desperate, would you choose to hitch yourself to a fella that gets up at the crack of dawn every day of the bloomin' week, comes home from work smelling to high heaven, on call twenty-four hours, and for what? Escalating prices, diminishing returns and a lot of hassle.'

'You're right. No girl in her right mind wants that for herself. It's no good…' And on that cheerful note, they sighed heavily into their beers.

'What's all this?' Maggie Potter, who had just come into the pub with her husband, laughed down at them. 'Talk about doom-and-gloom merchants. What's up, boys?'

Before Dan could stop him, Joe said bluntly, 'Dan wants to ask Kate to marry him, but he can't.'

'Why not?' inquired Maggie, pulling up a chair.

''Cos I'm a farmer,' replied Dan heavily. 'Nobody wants to marry a farmer.'

'Unless they're mad,' added Joe. 'And Kate's not mad. Is she?'

'No, she certainly is not. She's beautiful, and intelligent, and clever, and ambitious, and…'

'Have you asked her?'

'What?'

'Have you asked her?' repeated Maggie patiently. 'Perhaps she has a view on the matter. Maybe she'd like to decide for herself. 'Am I mad enough to want to marry a farmer? Maybe I am, maybe I'm not. But maybe he should ask me'!'

Both men gaped at her for a moment, then Joe turned to Dan and grasped his arm. 'She's right, Danny. You should ask her.'

And he did.

Both Dan and Kate wanted the wedding to be at Great Missenwall; to be married in the little church where generations of Maddicotts were christened, married and buried; where Polly had married Jack, Dan's father, and where he was now buried. Polly, however, pointed out that they had to consult Kate's parents.

'It was different for me,' she told them. 'When I married, my father was dead and my mother lived in a small London flat. It was natural for us to be married from Watersmeet. Kate's parents probably have other ideas. They'll want to give her away from their family home, and you have to respect those wishes, however inconvenient it may be for you. I know it would be sad if John Potter, Maggie, and Ted, and half the county were not able to come, but we'll have to make do with a party here at Watersmeet, after you are married.'

Dan reluctantly acquiesced, but Kate would not give up on the idea, and Polly, worried about finding herself in the middle of a tug of wills, suggested they should go and discuss the wedding at Grey Lodge rather than invite the Dinsdales to Watersmeet.

'I don't want them to feel coerced in any way,' she explained. 'And I'm sure they will be much more comfortable meeting me on their home ground.'

In spite of Dan's attempts to prepare her, Polly was stunned by Margaret Dinsdale's welcome.

'So pleased to meet you Polly… May I call you Polly?'

'Yes, please do…Mar…'

'Welcome to Grey Lodge. It's not called Grey Lodge because of its colour, although of course that's what you might be forgiven for thinking…'

'No, of course…'

'No, it's all part of Greyfriars. Some parts of the house are very old. We believe it was a lodging house for the poor pilgrims who were tended to by the Friars…'

'Really. How…'

'So we could say that Grey Lodge has been in the B&B business for some six hundred years…except it hasn't been, of course.'

'No?'

'My grandmother would've been horrified at the thought of paying guests. But the way I like to see it is that our visitors are pilgrims too… Of a different sort, I grant you; by and large they don't come on foot, for one thing… Some of those pilgrims walked right across Britain, you know… Must have taken them months.'

'Goodness, yes. How…'

'Have you read *Canterbury Tales*? That's the first question my PGs ask me. I've had to become something of an expert. Do come and sit down. I'll make some tea. You must be very tired…'

'Well, no, not…'

'Have you had a terrible journey? All the way from the West Country…'

'Yes, but…' Polly caught Dan's eye. He'd warned her to expect monologues rather than conversation, and she'd accused him of exaggerating. He grinned at her and she accepted defeat.

Margaret Dinsdale swept on: 'Katherine tells me you live in a very beautiful place. I had a cousin who used to live down there… Somewhere close to you…near Salisbury. His family used to farm. You might know them… What was their name now? You must remember, Katherine? He stayed here once, on his way to Paris… With his wife, lovely girl, but dead now, alas. It's so sad, don't you think, Polly, when people die like

151

that, still in the bloom of youth?'

She was interrupted by the telephone ringing in the hall.

'I'll just get that, and then we can go and eat. Poor things, you must be so hungry. I do hope you like casserole. It's beef-in-beer… quite a family favourite. I wonder who that can be. It's very late for a PG enquiry. I certainly can't accommodate anybody else tonight…' And she bustled out of the room.

Over the rise and fall of Margaret's voice in the hall, Polly turned to Roger and asked about his bookshop.

Roger obviously took an instant liking to Polly, and began to talk with more animation than Dan had ever seen. When Margaret returned to interrupt them, Dan could swear a look of annoyance passed over his face.

'I'm afraid, my dears, we'll have to wait for supper just a little bit longer. What a lovely surprise…so exciting. I should have enough casserole… Katherine never eats much of it anyway and I am not particularly hungry myself. I can't believe it… After all this time! I thought we would never know. But I'd better go and put on some more potatoes…and defrost a cauliflower cheese. What a good thing, Roger, you bought me the microwave for Christmas. I wasn't at all sure at the time I'd have any use for it… I always thought they were rather nasty things… All those strange waves… I'd heard if you stand too close you can get cancer…but I'm sure that can't be true. Do you have a microwave, Polly? It's at times like this they truly come into their own, don't you think?'

Roger saved Polly the necessity of a reply. 'What, my dear, has put you in all of a twitter like this? You've never knowingly underfed anyone. Why do we need more food?'

Dan saw Kate stiffen at her mother's reply. 'Why, Emily of course. That was Emily on the phone. She's come down to Canterbury and is staying with friends because she knows we have a house full. So thoughtful…just like her…though goodness knows it wasn't necessary… When have we ever not been able to find Emily a bed…? And I so love Flick. She's my granddaughter, Polly. Such a pretty baby, although she is not really a baby any longer… She's nearly two-and-a-half… I can't believe how quickly she's grown…and she doesn't stop talking… She's so sweet, you'll love her. She takes after Emily… Emily was just like her when she was little…so pretty, so delicate. She was premature, you know, and Roger and I were terribly afraid that we would lose her… I used to lie awake at night listening to her breathing. We could've spoiled her, but she's such an enchanting girl, even if I say so myself. We just don't see enough of her… That happens, doesn't it, when your children grow up and leave home? Though it must be different when you live on a farm… Your home is your workplace, so your children don't leave home…at least, not all of them… If you have more than one that is, but you don't, Polly, do you?'

To which Polly replied gravely, 'No, I don't. And I think I'm very lucky Kate is going to come and join us. I'm sure you must miss both your daughters very much, and I want you to know you'll be welcome to come and stay whenever you wish.'

Margaret looked blank. 'Kate? Yes, of course. We'd love to come, although, of course, with the guesthouse and Roger's bookshop…we hardly ever get a weekend. Which is why we rely on the girls coming here, and Emily comes so rarely. She has such a busy life in London, you know, and her art is taking up so much time. She tells me she's been given a small exhibition of her own in a gallery off Tower Bridge… We really must go up to the opening, Roger… She's promised to let us know when it is. She tells us so little about her life, Polly… It's very hard at times. She wouldn't tell us who Flick's father is, even though he's been supporting her. Oh my goodness, Roger,

I haven't told you…'

'Told me what, my dear? You seem to have told us everything we need to know.'

'No, no… I haven't told you the reason, the *real* reason that Emily is coming to dinner tonight. Roger, at long last, she wants us to meet *him*.'

It was Roger's turn to look blank. 'Who?'

'Flick's father. Emily is bringing him to dinner tonight.'

The stunned silence that greeted that announcement was nothing compared to the shock waves created at Emily's arrival.

She was accompanied by a young man, about Dan's age, with mocking dark eyes and a shock of black curly hair that fell in an unruly fashion over a high, white brow. He carried Flick in his arms.

Margaret Dinsdale gasped. For once she was almost completely bereft of speech. 'Ivan!'

He grinned. 'Hello, Mrs D. Hello, Kate.'

16

Susan

1943

She screamed.

The scream filled the rafters of the house and reverberated around the walls. Even the rats in the roof and the mice under the floorboards paused momentarily with the horror of it. It filtered out through the ill-fitting window and echoed across the yard, causing the old Shire horse to stamp uneasily in her stall. It reached the tops of the naked poplars fringing the wood, sending a small flock of pigeons flapping nervously into the darkening sky.

Edith Leach, grumbling with the effort of carrying a can of hot water up the stairs, looked down at the contorted face of the girl with a mixture of irritation and concern. She was not concerned for the girl, not at all; what worried her was that the unforeseeable might happen and at the last moment her plans would be foiled.

Susan's mouth was dry. Her hair and face were soaked with tears, her skin felt hot and clammy. Exhausted by her labours she had lost track of time, now marked only by short periods of respite before her whole being was torn apart by the terrible convulsions that seemed to go on and on. No longer in charge of her body, she was racked by an internal pressure so great she felt she would burst. The overwhelming desire was to push and be rid of this nightmare, but she no longer had any strength to do so and with each contraction she thought she would die.

She had been removed, at Mrs Leach's insistence, from her own tiny room to Mrs Leach's and placed on the old lady's double bed. It was an untypical act of kindness, but Susan was too distressed to wonder at it. She had already been in labour for eleven hours and didn't notice Mrs Leach had brought in items of Jem's clothing, which she had draped around the room, and that one or two of Susan's own meagre possessions were placed on the chest of drawers.

After what seemed an eternity, Mrs Leach had told her she was sending Jem for the doctor. She had originally told Susan medical help would be an unnecessary expense. She, Mrs Leach, had given birth to four healthy children without any help, in much more difficult circumstances. Susan was young, fit, and well-fed, thanks to the Leaches, so she shouldn't have any difficulty with this birth and anyway, the fewer people who knew of the existence of Susan and the baby, the better.

She hadn't told Susan of her trip into Great Missenwall, or that the existence of Susan in her expectant state was not only a well-known fact in the local community, but the subject of much curiosity and speculation. The sad little girl had continued to be terrified at the prospect of discovery and hid herself from the sight of the outside world.

Mrs Leach's decision to send for the doctor, therefore, while seeming portentous to poor Susan, was also seen by her as an indication that perhaps the old woman wasn't totally without pity. There had been times, over the last few weeks, when she'd been in such despair she thought about jumping into the brown, swift-flowing waters of the river that formed one of the boundaries of the farm. It seemed the only escape from the tyranny of the old lady.

Susan's continuing hope during her enforced stay had been her aunt. Tentatively, she had mentioned her again to Jem, wondering if there was any way in which she could be traced and so arrange for Susan's removal. Jem had been surprisingly compliant and said he would make enquiries.

Days passed; he brought no news and a timid enquiry was met with a surly 'Don't pester Oi'.

In the meantime, under the strict tutelage of Mrs Leach, Susan learned how to bake bread, make pastry, dumplings, pies; how to roast, boil, mash and bake potatoes and other root vegetables; make stock, stews, soups, and how to cure meat, to pluck birds and to skin rabbits. All this, in addition to a rigorous cleaning of the house from top to bottom, left her too exhausted to venture far from the farmyard, and as her body got stiffer and more awkward, she knew she had left it too late to try and walk to Bristol.

One morning, a dark December day, Jem walked into the kitchen where Susan sat struggling with a pile of mending and darning. He threw a small pile of grimy newspapers down on the table in front of her.

'Got these fur ye. Oi've no news of yer aunt. If she'd survived they raids, she'd be lucky. 'Ain't no ways ter find her. You're on yer own, gurl.' And he walked out of the kitchen.

With trembling fingers, Susan turned page after page of

pictures of a burning city by night, of streets reduced to piles of rubble and skeletons of stone. She couldn't recognise the city of her childhood, but certainly some of the locations mentioned leapt out at her: Newtown, St Philip's Marsh, Old Market. It was here she had been born; here she had been convinced she would find her aunt; here she would find a sanctuary where Franklin could seek her out. Great sobs gathered within her and paying no heed to the old lady's scolding, she made her way blindly up the narrow wooden stairs and lay down on her bed, completely bereft.

It was then that her baby decided it was time to be born.

It was an hour since Jem had set off. The light in the sky had gone completely, and one or two bright stars glittered in the blackness. Mrs Leach lit a lamp in the bedroom and sighed with exasperation.

Susan scarcely heeded her. Barely conscious, she hallucinated in the shadows of her pain. The face of the unknown doctor who was to attend her became Franklin's. He had received her letter, found out where she was and had come not only to rescue her, but also to deliver his own child. Franklin was looking down at her with such care, stroking her hair, telling her she was going to be all right. He would look after her. He wouldn't let her suffer any more.

It was another hour at least before Mrs Leach heard the sound of Jem's van returning, followed by a second engine.

Susan's screams had given way to a thin, unearthly wailing that unnerved even Mrs Leach. She snapped at her son as he appeared. 'You took yer time, son. Let's hope it ain't be too late. Where's doctor?'

'The doctor's busy, Mrs Leach.' A brisk, middle-aged woman, a complete stranger to Mrs Leach, appeared at the door. 'It *is*

158

Christmas Eve and he's in the middle of a measles epidemic. I'm the relief midwife, on loan from another parish, so you'll just have to make do with me. Now, where's my patient?'

With a lot of tut-tutting and pursed lips, she set to work. Jem made to escape from this woman's world, back to the barn and his birds, but she called him back in no uncertain terms and set him to fetching and carrying and boiling endless pans of water. Mrs Leach, her lameness limiting her ability to assist, angrily found herself consigned to tearing up a perfectly good sheet for rags to staunch the bleeding.

Susan, coming round from one of her swoons, imperfectly registered the presence of the nurse and cried faintly, 'Frank, has he come yet...my baby?'

'Don't fret. He'll be here soon. Frank, that's a nice name you've chosen for him. Now be a good girl and do as I tell you.'

The midwife was efficient and very experienced. She might not have been grateful for it, but Susan owed the woman her life as well as that of the baby boy who finally emerged a little after midnight, blue in the face, with his umbilical cord round his neck.

Having made Susan as comfortable as she could, the midwife wrapped the baby, now bright red and crying lustily, in a piece of sheeting, and called Jem Leach into the room.

Susan looked on aghast as the nurse placed the baby in Jem's astonished arms and said brightly, 'There you are Mr Leach: a miracle. You're a lucky man. With God's good help, your wife has given you the most precious Christmas gift of all: a healthy son.'

Helpless tears rolled down Susan's cheeks.

And Jem, looking down at the tiny baby in his arms, experienced a rare moment of emotion.

He had an heir.

159

17

Dan

1992

'That young woman could do with a good spanking!'

Polly was uncharacteristically vehement as they drove home after their weekend in Canterbury.

'Talk about one-upmanship – it was dreadful. I'm sorry Dan, I know they're Kate's family…but that young lady… I'm surprised Kate hasn't strangled her!'

'Or her mother,' Dan added dryly.

Once the initial shock of Ivan's re-appearance in the Dinsdale household had been absorbed, the rest of the weekend had been spent in explanation and exclamation, which boiled down, as far as Dan was concerned, to Emily getting her way as usual.

Having taken Ivan off Kate and become pregnant, she'd decided she didn't want to settle down after all and tried to send Ivan packing. He, made of sterner stuff, stayed around, and when Kate announced her nuptials, young Emily thought she'd like to get married, too. So of course, Mr and Mrs Dinsdale were so over the moon, they couldn't think of anyone or anything else.

Kate had appeared unruffled by it all, but Dan was furious and said as much to his mother.

'I understand how you feel, Dan,' Polly replied. 'But Emily's attempt to upstage Kate has worked to our advantage. Margaret was so busy planning a summer wedding for Emily in Canterbury Cathedral, it clearly hadn't occurred to her they'd have a similar expense for Kate's wedding, in September.'

Dan growled. 'No. Kate and her plans, *our* plans, are no longer important. Mrs Dinsdale only has eyes for the star turn, and that is exactly what Miss Emily intended. Well, that bloke, Ivan, is welcome to her. I just hope she's still on her honeymoon on our wedding day, or she'll find some way of grabbing the limelight. But knowing Emily, she'll be taken hostage by some bloody terrorist before we can tie the knot.'

Polly laughed. 'I've no doubt you're right, dear. But I did say some good has come of this. I had a quiet word with Roger before we left and suggested, as he's going to have two weddings on his hands within a very short space of time, he and Margaret might consider letting us have your wedding at Watersmeet.'

Ivan and Emily came to stay at Watersmeet before their marriage. Kate was not enthusiastic, and nor was Dan, but Polly was firm.

'We cannot choose our relations, but we can make the best of them. If you can't become friends, at least you can be friendly. You never know when you might need each other.'

During the course of the weekend, much to his surprise, Dan discovered he liked Ivan. He was, Dan found, very different

161

from anyone he'd ever met.

After Ivan's shock appearance at the Dinsdales, he and Dan had kept their distance. Dan, furious with Emily, was deeply suspicious of him. He disliked the way Ivan referred to Kate's mother as 'Mrs D' and the way Mrs Dinsdale flapped and flirted with him. He particularly disliked Ivan's manner, which he perceived as mocking and supercilious.

However, when Ivan came to Watersmeet with Emily and Flick, Dan could see he was making a real effort to be good company and was genuinely interested in what he saw.

Emily made polite remarks about the house, the gardens, the river and surrounding countryside, but displayed little real enthusiasm for anything she saw. She shrieked with terror at coming face to face with the cows, was dismayed at the slurry in the farmyard, complained of the smells, and was fearful of the blackness of the night.

Ivan, freely admitting to knowing nothing of farming or the countryside, wanted to see everything, and bombarded Dan with endless questions.

Walking back with Dan to the field after the evening milking, he looked around with unaffected pleasure. 'It's beautiful here,' he said, gazing at the meadows glistening green with late spring grass, and at the hedgerows, bursting with the pink foliage and yellow fronds of sycamore flowers, bridal-white hawthorn blossom and the soft, green folds of young hazel leaves. The cows were moving slowly, taking advantage of the fresh grass fringing the track.

'I can see why Watersmeet means so much to you. But I don't think I could make such a sacrifice. Working ten hours a day, in all weathers. All that muck, all that graft...and presumably on call when you're not working. It's disproportionate.'

He dodged a freshly deposited cowpat and sighed, shaking

his head mournfully. 'Tell me why, Dan… You are an intelligent fellow. I'm an intelligent fellow… At least, I think I am. Tell me, why do you do it?'

Dan grinned, shrugged his shoulders and slapped a dawdling cow encouragingly on her rump. 'You're right. I must be mad. I guess I must represent everything you despise?'

'Because of my being a Marxist, you mean? It's true Karl would disapprove of you. You do represent everything he disliked: a bourgeois landowner, a farm labourer, and an entrenched traditionalist. I'm afraid, come the revolution you'll have to go.' Ivan laughed. 'The thing is, Dan, that in spite of the complete awfulness of your working life, you've stuff other people want and that makes you dangerous.'

'Oh?'

'It's people like your family who completely undermined the revolution.' Ivan shook his head.' You've worked hard, grafted even, and instead of being impoverished, dispossessed and alienated, you've got a nice house, plenty of land, a car, telly, washing machine and lovely bride-to-be. Now, the lumpen proleteriat, instead of despising you, seizing your goods and slitting your throats, decide they want some of the cake too… So instead of attacking the system that so exploits them, they join it, and in a while they all have cars and tellies, and if not Watersmeet exactly, they have a nice little house in the suburbs, a nice little wife and one point seven children; and they know if they keep their noses clean and work hard, one day they will be able to retire to the country, the place Marx despised above all else.'

Dan laughed. 'And the inevitable revolution is not longer so inevitable. So where does that leave you, Ivan? Sitting pretty, as far as I can make out. A job in Parliament; a flat in some poncey part of London, with a posh wedding in Canterbury

Cathedral in the offing… Who's remained truest to their roots, eh? What price the revolution?'

Ivan grinned. 'I give you the revolution, but that's all. On the question of roots: those I haven't strayed far from, more's the pity. My parents are both armchair revolutionaries: my Dad lectures in politics at the LSE and my mother writes academic books about the structure of society; the MP I work for is probably the most left-wing member of her party; my flat cannot accommodate Emily and Flick, so it will have to go, and there is no way that Mrs D will ever drag me into Canterbury Cathedral!'

The pasture was reached and the cows pushed and chivvied their way in. The two men then made their way back to the farm.

'I've just got to go and clean up the milking parlour, then I shall be ready for a pint.' Dan grinned. 'Are you up to meeting a few more peasants like me, Ivan?'

'I should be delighted, Dan. Oh, and Dan,' he hesitated, looking awkward. 'I just want to apologise to you, and to Kate, for crashing your scene in Canterbury. Emily suggested that weekend would be good because she knew you'd both be there. She hadn't twigged you were bringing your mother, and that we dropped our bombshell on a nuptial planning session.'

'As it happens, your bombshell made things easier for us. But…erm…what troubles Kate, I think, Ivan, is why on earth Emily didn't tell her before now that you were Flick's father? What was the point in keeping it a secret from her?'

Ivan looked uncomfortable. 'I've no good explanation. And I don't feel very comfortable about the way the news was delivered… Except Emily said Kate was head-over-heels in love with you and would take it in her stride. Which I think was the case, don't you?' He pulled a face, 'Emily's ability to maximise the dramatic potential of any scene is breathtaking. I sometimes feel she's wasting her talents devoting herself to painting.'

'You're right, she'd make a brilliant actress.'

'Except she couldn't bear to share the stage with anyone else; unless it was one of those old Buzby Berkeley musicals, with males-in-tails at her feet.'

Which was, without stretching the imagination too far, observed Dan, how it was when the four of them went to the pub later that evening.

Saturday night was always popular at the Duck and Fox. There the community of Great Missenwall, farm workers, town workers, retired folk and weekenders, united in breathing out and relaxing. The large and comfortable lounge bar, with its subdued red lighting, faded pictures of the past glories of the Great Missenwall cricket teams interspersed with prints of every variety of duck known to man, had not yet succumbed to the pressures of the restaurant trade, so tables of all sorts, with chairs of all sizes, were constantly being rearranged to accommodate the various demands of the bar's clientele.

Their arrival was greeted by a shout from Joe, who was sharing a table with John and Maggie Potter, and a couple of other friends.

It was clear to Dan that within seconds of introductions being made, seats being found and drinks sorted, Joe was completely smitten by Emily. Every time she spoke to him, his tongue appeared to play tricks in his mouth and his face changed colour, right up to the roots of his hair.

John Potter became unusually talkative too, and Dan's other two friends, who had intended to go off to a party in Summerbridge, showed absolutely no inclination to move, hanging on Emily's every word. And how she came to life in

165

the centre of this small but adoring crowd, how she sparkled.

Maggie Potter surveyed the effect of Emily on her husband and on the others, with great amusement and, sotto voce, conducted a running commentary for Kate as the men competed for Emily's attention. Kate laughed, relaxed, and for the first time in her life, sat back to enjoy her sister's performance.

Ivan, to Dan's relief, reacted to all of this with good humour.

Then Josh Trubody arrived and Emily's cup ran over.

Josh, at twenty-two, stood six-feet-three in his socks. His hair was the colour of honeysuckle, his eyes the violet blue of periwinkle. His skin, tanned and clear from a life spent outside, was blessed and not yet coarsened by the elements. His features regular, his teeth white, his shoulders broad; he was drop-dead-gorgeous.

Emily blinked. Then sparkled. She'd never encountered anyone so physically beautiful in her entire life. As for Josh, he seemed as bowled over by her.

Emily's magnetic powers to enslave ninety per cent of the people in her vicinity, regardless of their intellectual capabilities, had been one of the reasons Ivan had been so attracted to her, he told Dan, as they watched the romantic comedy being played out across the table.

'Coal miner, cabbie, professor, politician, they all fall in love with her. It's fascinating. She collects them without discrimination, poor sods. I tell you, Dan, she has a charisma politicians would die for. If she had stood up for Marx in Essex, and said, 'Follow me. Turn your back on your semis, your dishwashers, the roast-on-Sunday, and the Montego in the drive; spurn the mortgage, tear up the catalogues, spit on the never-never, reject the buy-now-pay-later culture, Britain would be halfway to being a healthy Marxist State.' He sighed. 'As it is, she has a power without direction or purpose. I see

166

that as a challenge: a force to be harnessed, if you like, because if it isn't, it could be very destructive. Maybe that's why her paintings are so intriguing. They convey something of the beauty and beast in her.'

Dan stared at him. 'I don't mean to offend you, Ivan, but you sound more like a lion tamer about to put his head in the mouth of a lioness with PMT, than a lover and prospective bridegroom.'

'Is there a difference?'

They were diverted by the return of Josh, who had been persuaded by Emily to join them. He'd grabbed a chair and was trying to squeeze it into a small gap between Emily and Joe. Joe shifted closer to Emily. Emily tried to move in the opposite direction to make room for Josh. Joe closed the gap again and told Josh to go and sit opposite.

'It's musical chairs!' chortled Maggie. 'The most determined wins, and my money is on Joe. I've never seen him so transfixed.'

'Not if Susie has anything to do with it,' remarked Dan, overhearing her. 'She's pissed off at not having seen him all night, and plans to come over and join us as soon as she can persuade someone to cover for her.' He stood up. 'Don't let anyone nick my chair. I'm off for a pee.'

'Ditto,' said Ivan, and the two pushed their way through to the public bar.

It was as crowded. A snug, old-fashioned bar, it was brightly lit and sawdust was liberally scattered over the wooden floor. Set in the wall opposite the entrance was a small cast iron fireplace, alive in the winter but currently unlit, the logs covered in cigarette packets, ash, and screwed up crisp packets thrown there by a public too unobservant to notice there was no fire, or too idle to dispose of their rubbish in any other way. A mangy stuffed fox hung above the fireplace, and to one side, next to the bar, was the battered door to the Gents.

On a Saturday night, the poaching fraternity gathered in this bar, along with the single fixtures. Occasionally speaking to each other, sometimes playing draughts, all listened to the wilder sounds of the bar next door and watched in silence as, with increasing frequency, individual after individual lurched through to the Gents.

Following in Dan's wake, Ivan squeezed past the drinkers standing at the bar. Jostled, he staggered sideways and knocked the arm of a man sitting at the side of the fireplace just as he was lifting his glass to his mouth. The drink splashed his face and spilled down his chest. He let out an angry shout. Dan turned to see Ivan confronted by Frank Leach.

''Ere what d'yer think yer doin', yer clumsy bastard?'

Ivan attempted to apologise but this appeared to make matters worse.

'Yer all the same, yer bloody townies. Yer come in 'ere, flashes yer money, thinks yer own the place, thinks yer can push us around. Well yer can't.' He grabbed Ivan's arm. 'Yer owe Oi a drink.'

An embarrassed silence settled on the bar. Dan intervened. 'No he doesn't, Frank. It was an accident. You heard him. He was pushed. I think you should take your hands off him.'

'Oh yer do, do yer?' Frank sneered, tightening his grip. 'And Oi suppose yer gonna make Oi. Yer'll keep yer bloody nose out of our business, Master Maddicott.' He turned to Ivan and thrust his face in his. 'A drink, mister, if yer please. Now.'

Ivan's normal pallor was tinged green. 'Yes, of course,' he stammered. 'I'm sorry. It was an accident. Er, what are you drinking?'

'A double scotch would suit Oi nicely.'

'I'm sure it would, but you're not getting it.' Dan pushed

his way to Ivan's side. 'Ivan, there is no way I would let you part with your money. Frank, take your hands off him. Jack Bancroft is just the other side of the bar and you know what he thinks about brawling. It's no skin off my nose if you get banned, but I don't want you involving my friends in one of your spats. If it's your drink you're really worried about,' he leant across to the bar and slapped a couple of coins down, 'that should replace the cider you lost.'

Out-manoeuvred, Frank dropped his hand and swung round to Dan. 'Yer can keep yer stinkin' money, Dan Maddicott. Oi might have known he was a friend of yourn. Yers all of a piece. Arrogant little shits. Thinks yer owns the world. Well yer don't, and yer don't own Oi.' With that, he spat into Dan's face, turned on his heel and pushed his way out.

Dan's shock gave way to rage. He was about to lunge at Frank's retreating back when he caught sight of Ivan staring at him, horrified. He stopped, gave a shaky laugh, and wiped his face with a napkin someone thrust into his hand.

Ivan nervously touched his arm. 'That was really horrible. I'm so sorry, Dan. I just knocked into him. He over-reacted. Perhaps he was drunk, but that was…he was…'

'There's no love lost between Frank Leach and Dan,' said a man at the bar. There was a chorus of agreement and some expression of sympathy towards Dan, and the atmosphere eased.

In the privacy of the Gents, Dan looked at Ivan, concerned. 'I'm sorry about that little scene. Are you all right? You looked, well, as if you were going to be sick.'

'I'm a total coward when it comes to physical violence; I turn to jelly. When I looked at your face,' Ivan gave a shaky laugh, 'I thought you were going to hit him. You were so angry… Why? Who is he?'

169

'It's all so much hot air, Ivan. He's my tenant and it's just unfortunate for us both that he is. Our two families have a history of rubbing each other up the wrong way. It's an old story to do with the tenancy of the land from way back when. Frank's particular dislike of me, however, was cemented by a bucket of chicken shit when I was twelve years old.'

'Oh?'

'His Dad had locked my cousin Mary in a cage with wild birds, after he'd caught us trespassing. Her brother Max and I had managed to get away. So, of course, we set about rescuing her, and just as we'd succeeded, we encountered Frank in the yard. He had a pail of chicken shit with him, which I tipped over his head.'

Even after all this time, the memory of Frank's reaction had the power to make Dan shiver...

'Oi'll kill yer, yer little bastard. Oi'll fuckin' kill yer!' Frank had screamed and, furiously wiping the muck from his eyes, he'd made a grab for Dan's throat.

'OK, Frank, that will do.' Never in Dan's entire life had Ted's quiet, cold tones been so welcome.

With a snarl, Frank made another grab at Dan, who dodged and darted behind Ted.

'Cut it out, Frank. Boys, I want an explanation,' said Ted, sternly.

'Mary was locked up in the bird-cage, Ted.' Max shouted. 'That old bastard caught her and locked her in the cage. We had to rescue her. She was terrified.'

'What bird-cage?'

'The one he keeps in the barn, the one with wild birds in it. He's got a buzzard, and an eagle owl in there. You should see their talons... And old Leach put Mary in there.'

'Where is Jem?'

'Yeah, where is he? What have yer done wiv me dad, yer murderous little bastards?'

Max shrugged his shoulders and looked nervously at Dan.

There was a moment's silence.

Dan didn't feel so brave any more. 'He's locked in the bird-cage. I got Mary to scream and then pretend to faint. He came to have a look, unlocked the door and I pushed him in. I've locked him in.'

Frank let out a yell.

'Oh brilliant, Danny!' Max shouted, exultantly. 'Give him a taste of his own medicine.'

'That will do. Get in the car. Dan, give Frank the key so he can let his father out.'

By this time they could hear low hoarse cries from the barn.

Frank was beside himself with fury; his face and clothes begrimed with the grey slimy muck, Dan thought he looked like something out of a zombie movie, and experienced a sharp twinge of fear.

'Er... I haven't got it.'

Frank started to roar obscenities as Dan explained, 'When Mary ran, I followed her and threw the key onto the floor.'

Frank, cursing, turned and ran to the barn. Ted followed him, ordering the boys to wait in the Land Rover with Mary.

After what seemed an age to Dan, he reappeared followed by Frank and Jem, none the worse for his adventure it seemed, judging from the level of invective directed at Ted and the three children.

Ted cut him short. 'Listen to me, Jem. I suggest you shut up and say no more about this. Make a fuss and you might find yourself charged with assault, kidnap, and worse. The police would take a dim view of you locking up the little girl. And you know it's illegal to keep wild birds captive; the RSPCA would be on your case like a ton of bricks. In the meantime, I suggest you and Frank go and sort out your sheep. They've broken through the fence in Rabbits Lane. I tried phoning you, but you were so busy playing bully-boy you didn't answer, which is why I called round. Just as well, in the circumstances.'

As Ted climbed into the driver's seat, Frank stuck his head through the passenger window and hissed at Dan, 'Don't think yer've got away with this, cos yer ain't. Oi'll not forget, don't yer worry. Oi'll pay yer back for this. That's a promise'...

Ivan shivered as Dan finished his story. 'Not an enemy I'd like to have. Has he paid you back, do you think?'

'The fact he's still my tenant is pay-back a hundred times over, but no, I don't think he's satisfied. He also holds me responsible because the RSPCA did find out about the birds, took them away and prosecuted. Jem got fined pretty heavily. He died shortly after that. I am not sure that Frank doesn't blame me for his father's death as well, though I would've thought that would have been a liberation for him; Jem was a vicious old slave-driver.'

Ivan and Emily had just left for London the following morning when there was a tap at the kitchen door.

Joe poked his head round it. Looking rather awkward, he accepted the offer of coffee and sat down.

'It's very quiet.' He cocked his head. 'Where is everyone?'
'Everyone?'
'Emily, and her fellah, whatsisname.'
'Ivan.'
'Yeah, him. I thought...well, I challenged Emily to a game of tennis, and as it's a nice morning, I thought...'

Dan grinned, but Kate felt sorry for him. 'They've gone, Joe.'

'What? But they can't have done… It's not even lunchtime. Why have they gone so early?'

'Ivan had a paper to write for his employer by tomorrow. They had to go back.'

'But Emily said…'

'Emily says lots of things she means at the time. She probably forgot. I'm sorry, Joe. There'll be other times.'

Joe fell into a gloomy silence and Dan was exasperated. 'I don't know why you're so upset, Joe. You can play tennis with anyone. And anyway, you can stop mooning over Emily. She's going to be married. She and Ivan are an item, so hands off.'

'Well they didn't look much like an item. He hardly spoke to her all evening. She's so lovely; if she was my fiancée, I wouldn't let anyone near her. He didn't seem to care a jot. What a cold fish.'

'Yeah, well, people have different ways of expressing themselves. He's a nice bloke, and I hope he and Emily will be very happy. And anyway, Joe, why are you so concerned? I thought you were meant to be having a thing with Susie?'

'I was. She's a nice girl. But next to Emily…' He gave a deep sigh. 'That's the trouble with living round here, we never get to meet anyone different. You're lucky, Dan; you met Kate, but you didn't meet her in Great Missenwall did you, or Summerbridge? And meeting Emily has made me realise what I might be missing… And she liked me, I know she did… Maybe they won't get married.'

But they did, in the Registry Office in Canterbury, on a warm July day, and Dan and Kate were there to throw confetti and drink their health in the garden of Grey House.

*

Dan and Kate's own wedding was planned for September. When the day dawned, Dan, unable to sleep, slipped out of the house. The sun rose golden on dew-soaked grass, and leaving bright green prints in his wake, he walked across the lawn, slipped through a gate in the yew hedge and followed the bank of the river to the little brook.

The grass was rough mown here; the delicate petals of fading Himalayan balsam and the seeded heads of the rose-bay-willow-herb quivered under the weight of the dew, and reed, rush, bramble and nettle fringed the bank. An old willow bent across the water, and in the crook of its branches grew a young oak and a vigorous rose briar, glistening with hips.

He'd been coming here ever since he was small and wanted to be on his own. The spot had a special significance for him. As a young boy, standing here, he'd realised he was watching something which happened every millisecond, not only of his life, but of hundreds of years before him: this was the point at which, after so many hours of existence and so many miles of travel, trickling, bubbling, dancing down from the hill way above the farm, the stream gave itself up to the mightier personality of the river.

It was a profound moment, a moment when his horizons opened and he realised that he, too, was part of something huge, something quite beyond his comprehension, too big for him to absorb, and very humbling.

He had never ceased to be fascinated by the merging of water into water. Watching the brook, always flowing, never stopping to change direction and never the same water, not in the brook, nor in the river; and the river itself, heedlessly slipping on, taking the contents of the stream and a million others like it onwards and downwards, ultimately to lose itself in the greater personality of the sea. All that energy in perpetual motion, that ineluctability…

Not by nature a spiritual person, he thought of this as his place, the place where the waters meet.

The air was full of birdsong.

Dan threw back his head and sang, too.

Later, in the church, with Joe at his side, Dan started to feel nervous. Talking, planning, attending to all the detail was one thing, but now the moment had arrived, the enormity of it all hit him. Marrying Kate was the culmination of his dreams. Everything about his life was going to alter, from now until he died. He breathed in deeply, tried to relax and listen to the sounds of the church steadily filling, the whispered greetings, the suppressed laughter, the growing excitement.

'Are you OK, Dan?' whispered Joe, 'You've gone very white.'

'I'm fine. What time is it?'

'Nearly two. She should be here soon.'

Mrs Goodstone, the organist, started to play. The vicar arrived and came over to chat to Dan and Joe. The dust motes danced in the coloured sunbeams and the heady sweet smells of the flowers filled the little church. The congregation was now completely assembled and waiting. The church clock chimed two o'clock. The organist finished her party pieces and waited to strike up the triumphant march.

She waited.

The congregation waited.

Dan waited.

Kate was late.

After five long minutes of coughs, whispers and nervous giggles, Dan began to feel rather sick.

'Why is she so late, Joe? Do you think something could have happened?'

'Don't worry Dan,' a worried Joe whispered back. 'She's only five minutes late. You know the bride never arrives on time. She'll be here any minute now, I bet.'

But the minutes ticked by, and still no Kate. The congregation started to become restless. Dan could detect the faint insistent tones of Kate's mother haranguing Ivan and anyone else in near reach. The vicar, frowning slightly, walked over to the organist and whispered to her. She nodded and began to play a random piece of music.

'Kate, Kate, please come,' whispered a desperate Dan.

A similar prayer was being offered up by the vicar, by Joe, by Polly, and by most of the congregation who were there because they cared about Dan or Kate.

After ten minutes, Ted detached himself from his pew and slipped outside. Dan, his mind in turmoil, his knees threatening to give way, sat down. Something must have happened to her; she wouldn't do this to him otherwise. She loved him; he was completely sure of that. Perhaps something had gone wrong with the pony and trap.

Muriel Etheridge had loaned the trap to bring the bride and her father to the church and to take Kate and Dan back to Watersmeet for the reception. Kate had been staying with her parents at Holly Cottage, the old lodge house Polly was planning to move into after the wedding, so Dan hadn't seen her that morning. But he'd spoken to her on the phone, and her excitement and happiness had been as palpable to him as his own.

The church clock struck the quarter. Dan groaned. The vicar came over to him and spoke softly. 'This must be awful for you, Dan. Do you have any idea why she might be so late?'

Dan shook his head.

'If she doesn't come soon...' The vicar left the sentence hanging on the air.

Joe leant across, 'I'll nip outside and see if I can find out what's going on. Don't worry, Danny.'

The congregation had fallen silent with the strain. Even Kate's mother was quiet. The organist was playing through all the hymns in her repertoire. Dan recognised them from his childhood at Sunday school.

She had just finished 'All Things Bright and Beautiful', when Tom returned. He went straight to the vicar and whispered to him, then turned and beamed at Dan. The vicar, signalling to the organist, stood, smoothed his vestments calmly as if he'd not experienced a moment's qualm in the preceding half hour and moved to his place. Dan, turning round, saw Ted slip back into his pew.

Ted smiled at him.

It was OK.

Ted rarely smiled and ever since he could remember, Dan knew when Ted smiled, whatever the circumstance, it was OK.

And there Kate was, smiling, tremulous, her vivid blue eyes brilliant with unshed tears; in Dan's eyes, the most beautiful girl he had ever seen. The organist struck up, and Kate moved down the aisle on Roger's arm to join Dan at the altar.

Later, when they had a chance to talk, he learned how the pony and trap had arrived at the cottage as planned and Kate and her father had set out. Climbing the long hill that led from Watersmeet to Great Missenwall, a tractor had appeared coming down the hill. Instead of slowing down at the sight of them, it appeared to go out of control, accelerated and veered towards the buggy.

The horse panicked, reared, and tried to bolt. It was only the expertise of the groom that prevented a terrible disaster, but as it was they ended up with the trap half in the hedgerow. They were unhurt but very much shaken, as was the horse.

The groom had unhitched the animal and decided it was not safe to continue until he had calmed the horse down, and so that was where Ted, having borrowed a car to find out why they were so delayed, found them and brought them to the church himself.

Dan shivered and put his arms around Kate. 'You could have been killed. Oh Kate... My darling, darling, Kate, I could have lost you. My life would have ended, just when I felt it was beginning.'

Once they had all got over their fright, the wedding day was glorious. A fresh pony had been delivered, and Kate and Dan, showered with confetti and flowers, were driven back in state to Watersmeet, followed on foot by the wedding party, except for the most elderly, and Mary, who was heavily pregnant.

Kate, slender in a buttoned, high-necked, silk gown, with dark glossy curls and forget-me-not-blue eyes, radiantly presided over the celebrations.

Dan's heart sang.

Everything about his life was now perfect.

It was only after they'd returned from their honeymoon, that Dan discovered the identity of the tractor driver.

Frank Leach.

18

Frank

She had made her nest in a dark corner of the disused hay-loft, behind a stack of boxes, well away from predatory eyes. She had scrabbled up the remnants of straw and old sacking and had settled down, as secure a farm cat ever is, to give birth to her litter.

He had been watching her over the last few days, noting the last slow movements of her pregnancy, noting her absence. Lying on her side, suckling her tiny, blind, offspring, she snarled and spat at him as he pushed away the boxes and seized each of her warm little babies. She scratched and screamed, but in vain. Ignoring the cat's desperate fight and the plaintive, squeaking mews of the kittens as he tore them from their mother's nipples, he thrust the tiny bodies into a sack.

Task completed, he twisted the mouth of the sack securing it with a piece of pink baler twine. Slinging it over his shoulder, he descended to the floor of the barn and made his way unhurriedly across the yard, down a track into the woods.

If he had looked behind him he would have seen the thin shape of the mother, exhausted from the effort of birth, milk streaming out of her dugs, following him. But he did not look behind and strode on till the track bent to the left and came to the river.

He stopped.

There was movement in the sack, despite the fact that the little bodies should, by now, have been crushed or suffocated by the stones he had put in there. Swinging the sack once, twice, he tossed it high into the centre of the river. For a few seconds the air within it kept it afloat and then, leaving behind a ring of bubbles on the surface of the water, it sank.

He grunted with satisfaction, turned and walked back the way he had come, not noticing the cat in the undergrowth.

19

Dan

1993

The study at Watersmeet was not just a study – it was a museum, an archaeological dig, a reference library, a family archive, an office, a storeroom, and an absolute mess.

When, at the age of 21, Dan had returned from college to take over, he resolved to sort it out and make a fresh start. But in the face of such an overwhelming mountain of farming history, he'd flapped a few documents, retrieved the catalogues he'd put in the bin (just in case they should prove useful), cleared a space on the huge old desk for a computer and proceeded to add a new generation of paper to the accumulated layers of his ancestors.

The study was at the rear of the house. A long window looked out onto the rose garden and lawns. The garden dipped down to a long privet hedge, dividing the lawn from the vegetable garden, and ending at another wall where a gate led to the meadows beyond. To the right, the river flashed silver through a yew hedge, and to the left, the back of an old barn separated the garden from the farmyard.

Dan loved this view. He understood why his father and grandfather had spent so much time closeted in this room. It was more than likely, he surmised, that they didn't tackle the paperwork any more diligently than he did, but like him, gazed out on the farm, the valley, and the hills beyond.

After all, he thought, after toiling for hours pushing paper, that view was an essential reminder of what it was they worked so hard for.

The bookcases lining the room were a testament not only to those labours, but to the industry of generations of Maddicott women who were largely responsible for the bound ledgers, files of receipts, household diaries, journals, and old photograph albums. These were all squashed next to crumbling bibles, hymn books, books of Common Prayer and ancient leather books that had been a fixture for so long that, not only were they not read, but no one even knew their titles or provenance.

The desk, almost the size of a billiard table, faced the window. A threadbare Persian rug covered the scuffed oak floor, an old wooden swivel-chair, the horsehair oozing from a split in the leather, and an equally ancient armchair with broken arms and sagging cushions, were the only other items of furniture. It was not designed to be a comfortable place. Jack Maddicott and his father before him had always made that clear to their family. It was the office.

As a child, Dan would tiptoe into the room in his father's absence and draw in deep breaths of the musty, dusty tobacco-infused air of his family's history. He especially liked the rosettes that decorated the shelves and walls, along with paintings and photographs of prize-winning stock.

As a rare treat, his grandmother, Rose, would draw down one of the albums and she would sit her grandson on, or rather in, her capacious lap. Nestling like a fledgling against her corseted bosom, Dan would gaze at portrait after portrait of the individuals who made up the history of Watersmeet, of whom he was now the sole descendant.

Rose herself had been a prolific diarist, keeping a journal for every year until her death. These had been bound and formed a tight row filling one of the long bookshelves.

'I suppose I should make an attempt to read them,' he said to Kate after they'd become engaged, and, full of future plans, were looking afresh at the house.

Kate was full of enthusiasm. 'Why don't you then? What an archive! A detailed record of life on a farm for the whole of the Second World War and after. Producers in my department would give their eye-teeth to get their hands on this stuff.'

'Hmm, I don't know. My grandmother was quite private. She'd not like her thoughts having a public airing.' Dan laughed. 'And she was very secretive about some of these journals; one or two were even kept hidden under the floorboards in her room. But I guess that was her generation…'

'So she wrote these journals, trusting they'd never be read by anyone?'

'Yes, except she wanted *me* to read them, God knows why.'

'How do you know that?'

'Well, she showed me where she'd hidden them, for a start. She made me promise not to tell anyone. I thought she was getting a bit soft in the head…as if anyone should care. But then she mentioned them again in her will. Not all of them – she was very specific about the ones I was to read.'

'So why didn't you?'

'Blimey, Kate, I was sixteen. Life was beckoning. Much as I loved her, attempting to decipher an old lady's handwriting was not high on my list of priorities…'

She laughed at him. 'I can see that. Maybe one day, you'll let me have a go?

He pulled her to him. 'Do you think, Mrs Maddicott-to-be, you will ever have the time?'

Daylight was fading and the grey rain-filled sky made it seem later than it really was. Weary, Dan rubbed his eyes and pushed the piles of paper away from him. He gazed gloomily at the screen of the computer for a second longer, then clicked 'save' then 'quit'.

'I quit,' he said aloud.

His chin on his hands, he gazed out of the window at the increasingly gloomy landscape and brooded. It seemed to him that there was more paperwork, reams more, than when he had taken over the farm from Ted's capable management.

That was the year, he recalled, when BSE had first reared its ugly head. Only six years ago, a nasty little ripple, a frisson of fear, an intimation of a nightmare that was not going to go away and was going to affect them all, because they were all involved, whether as consumers or suppliers, whether they liked it or not.

The first few months had been extraordinarily stressful: every time a cow or calf looked off-colour the tension in the farmyard notched up. The number of confirmed cases had steadily grown over the years. So far, they'd not been affected; the farm prospered and although the number of cases of BSE in the country had reached over 35,000, the feeling was that the numbers had peaked.

There was a great deal of animosity between the beef and dairy farmers: beef farmers seeing the bottom drop out of their market, blamed the dairy farmers for the crisis, and with some justification, Dan thought. He and William Etheridge remained on good terms, but in many respects, because of the quality of their herds and necessary emphasis on impeccable husbandry to maintain that distinction, the two farms had escaped the worst consequences of the disaster – so far.

There was a tap at the door and Mary came in with a steaming mug of tea.

'I thought you might like this. Supper will be in about half an hour.'

'You're a star, Mary. Is Kate lying down?'

'Yes, but she's determined to join us for supper. Polly's bathing Toby and I don't know who's having the greatest fun. She can't wait for your baby to arrive, Dan.'

'Nor can I, and nor can poor old Kate. Being ordered to bed for the last two weeks was the final straw.' He hesitated. 'I haven't really asked you, but are you sure Clive doesn't mind you and Toby being here?'

It was Mary's turn to hesitate before saying lightly, 'No, he doesn't mind. He can play at being a bachelor again: he needs to do that from time to time. Don't misunderstand me, Dan, he loves Toby and me; he was overjoyed when I became pregnant, and there can't be a prouder father; but I think, sometimes, he feels a bit crowded, so your plea for help was rather timely.'

Dan bit back the rude comment he wanted to make. He'd long since learned that at any criticism of Clive, Mary would immediately retreat into a protective shell.

He smiled at her. 'Well, we're really lucky to have you here. And I think young Master Toby is a lovely baby. It's great Mum's got him to practise on.'

'Yes, but I suppose if Emily's going to be here, you don't really need me?'

'Emily?' he looked at her blankly.

'Yes, she phoned this afternoon; said she was coming down to look after Kate; said she'd promised her mother since she couldn't come…'

In the face of Dan's continuing blank stare, Mary protested, 'I'm sorry Dan, I just assumed, from the way she spoke, that it had been arranged… They are sisters, after all…'

Emily had not been down since the wedding, although Ivan had appeared once or twice with Flick and the news that Emily needed time to herself to get ready for an exhibition.

Joe's crush had not abated, and he sought news of her whenever he saw Dan or Kate. He split up with Susie Bancroft, resigned as Social Secretary of the Young Farmers, and seemed to go into a listless decline that worried Dan, but which he was too busy to do much about.

Their first year of marriage year had sped by.

Mary had given birth to Toby shortly after Dan and Kate arrived home from their honeymoon. Clive had been as excited as any young father might be, and Mary had looked so relaxed and happy that the two of them concluded any problems between Mary and Clive had been resolved by the arrival of the baby.

Kate had tried to maintain a high profile in her job in London, but the stress of commuting that distance and the number of times she had to stay overnight, because of a late studio or an editing session, meant the early days of their marriage were not the idyll they had dreamed of.

The crunch had come shortly before their first Christmas together at Watersmeet. She had phoned him and asked him to meet her train a lot earlier than she'd originally planned. He could tell from her voice something was wrong, but she wouldn't be drawn.

When she arrived, she looked white and strained, and scarcely returned his embrace, responding monosyllabically to his questions. When they reached the top of the lane leading down to Watersmeet, he pulled the car over and stopped.

'OK, darling, what's wrong?'

Kate said nothing, at first, but stared ahead, not looking at him. He put his arm gently around her. 'Kate?'

At that she dissolved into tears, angry and miserable in equal measure. She was incoherent and Dan found it hard to establish what was wrong until, exhausted by her outpouring, she quietened sufficiently to explain.

'I so love you, Dan, and I know it's not been easy these last few months. I've been away so much and it's not what we wanted. Maybe I was being unrealistic, thinking I could maintain my work in London and live with you here, having the best of both worlds. I didn't appreciate how much I'd have to compromise, how much I was asking of you. I've not been the easiest person to live with, have I? Coming home, tired and ratty, feeding us on takeaways, falling asleep before you're even in bed. You must have wondered why on earth you married me?'

'I married you because I love you. These are teething problems...'

She shook her head. 'No. Because for all the sacrifices we've made to ensure the work I did was in no way affected by my marriage, those...' her voice shook, 'those...bastards are not putting forward any of my proposals for the next round of offers...'

Dan was aghast. 'But you worked so hard on them. Your boss...he said they were really good...'

'Yes, but he said that they can't take the risk of my not being around to see them through. He didn't make the mistake of saying it was because I was now married, or that I might

187

become pregnant, but suggested the distance I had to commute made me less flexible, and was putting too much of a strain on me. How dare he? Oh, he was sympathetic, but he said he was under pressure from other quarters to suggest I apply for a transfer. He said there was a post coming up in Bristol, after Christmas, and I should apply for it…'

'And if you don't want to do that?'

'Then it's likely my contract won't be renewed when it runs out.' She put her head in her hands. 'Oh Dan. It's so unfair. I tried so hard.'

Dan stroked her hair and consoled her as best he could. However the thought of having her working closer to home, of seeing more of her, made his heart leap. He knew better than to say this outright, hoping in time Kate would see this for herself.

His optimism was well-founded.

She hadn't moped for long. When she married Dan, she'd made the decision about priorities. The thought of spending more time with him helped soothe her hurt pride. In the end it was with a cheerful heart that she went for an interview in Bristol, and was genuinely delighted when she was offered a contract. And when, at more or less the same time, she found she was pregnant, she was overjoyed.

She coped with the early stages of her pregnancy well. She threw herself into her new job and directed her first documentary; her contract was extended and she was ambitious to do more. But at seven months, Dr Maryon had put his foot down. Her blood pressure was too high. She was forced to take sick leave, which would then run into maternity leave, but everyone suspected she would never return, although Kate retained the hope she might be able to find more freelance work when the baby was old enough.

Dan's cup overflowed having her at Watersmeet full time, but Kate found the life of a semi-invalid very frustrating. Then he suggested Mary might come down with baby Toby and keep her company; Mary had jumped at the invitation and the friendship between the two women, which had been on hold since Mary married Clive, blossomed.

Dan smiled at Mary. 'I'll give Emily a ring. She's not been near us for a year. I don't think it would be a good idea for her to come, just at this moment. Kate's too…'

'Fragile?'

'Yeah. I don't want Emily throwing any little bombshells at her. Thanks for the tea. I'll come through in a minute.'

Ivan answered the phone. He sounded tired. Emily was out, he was having trouble with getting Flick to bed and he had a pile of work to finish that night.

Dan was sympathetic and then explained the purpose of his call. Ivan was surprised. Emily hadn't mentioned any plans to go to Watersmeet, either before or after the baby was born.

'I expect she phoned on the spur of the moment after speaking to Mrs D. Of course I'll tell her to hang back. We can come and worship at the cradle when you are good and ready for us.' He hesitated. 'Actually, I'm glad you phoned, Dan. I was half thinking of ringing you…'

'Oh, what about?'

'Your friend, Joe. Did you know he's come to London several times to see Emily?'

'You're kidding?'

'No, I'm not. Emily seems to think it's totally coincidental – she bumps into him at a gallery, or at the entrance to a tube station, or he comes into a café where she's stopped for lunch… But I know how hard you guys work, and how difficult it is for you to get away, let alone come to London as often as Joe seems to do.' Ivan sounded embarrassed. 'I know he fell for Emily pretty hard. Do you think he might be…um…stalking her?'

'Christ… I hope not. Blimey, Ivan, I don't know what to say. I'll talk to Kate. She's fond of Joe. We'll see if we can find a way to tackle him about it.' It was Dan's turn to hesitate, 'And Emily really hasn't arranged anything, hasn't encouraged him?'

'She says not, but you know Emily.'

After Ivan rang off, Dan sat and thought about Joe. He'd neglected his friend. It was time to do something about it. He pushed back his chair, switched off the light and went in search of Kate.

As soon as he saw her, all thoughts of Joe and Emily went out of his mind.

The baby was on its way.

It was a long, anxious evening and night. Dr Maryon joined them at the hospital in the early hours of the morning and decided forceps would be a good idea. Dan was terrified. He'd delivered more calves than he could remember, intervening when necessary if the cow got into difficulties, but this was different. This was his beloved Kate. He held her hand, mopped her brow, whispering encouraging words, willing the baby to be born.

And then, suddenly, there he was – his firstborn, his son, mewing and kicking with outrage at having been so forcibly brought into the world.

Dan thought he would burst. Kissing Kate, then the baby, the baby and then Kate, he whispered, 'I must be the luckiest man in the world!'

20

Kate

2001

The day after Dan died, Kate shut the study door. The door had always been left open when he worked in there and she couldn't bear to pass the room and not see him at his desk. She'd not gone into the room since. Ted retrieved the papers for their farm meetings and she put all the information they needed on a new laptop, turning one end of the long kitchen table into a makeshift office.

A few days after her promise to Ben, Kate realised she would have to go into the study. There was so much of Dan in there, so much of *all* the Maddicotts, and she felt, instinctively, that in there, supported by the invisible Maddicott presence, she might find what she was looking for.

The children in bed, the paperwork brought up to date, Kate opened the door. The daylight was fading as the year was fading, so she switched on the light as she went into the room.

She stood there, momentarily paralysed.

It was as if Dan was there. Or rather, had just been there and was temporarily absent. The cushion in his battered old chair still bore the imprint of his body. His favourite coffee mug, a birthday present from Ben, sat on a shelf beside the desk, a thick layer of grey mould sealing the inside.

Above all, the air in the room held the smell of Dan.

Nothing had prepared her for the aftermath of death, and nothing so poignantly reminded her of her loss, as Dan's smell. It lingered in her bed until her mother washed the sheets; lingered in his clothes until she was encouraged to turn them out; lingered in the car till time and usage had blown it away. For that reason she had resisted his old Barbour being removed from its peg on the kitchen door, and for weeks after his death, when she was alone, she would bury her face in it.

Now, in the stale air of his study, this powerful reminder of the physical loss of him overwhelmed her.

She sank into his chair, put her arms on the desk, her body racked by deep sobs. She cried until she ran out of tears, then continued to sit, incapable of movement, her head resting on her arms, eyes shut, her brain dulled by the excess of emotion.

'I love you, Katie Dinsdale, and I am not going to let you go.' Dan's voice floated through her head. So clear, so confident, for a moment she thought his voice had come from the room.

Startled, she looked up, but she was alone with the dust and spiders, and with all those books and all those papers.

She recalled her words to Ben. Dan had loved them. It was true. He loved them, and would not have done anything to make them unhappy. And she, not just her children, had to have faith in that love…

She needed to get rid of all doubt. But oh, how? How? It was like entering a no-man's land, the way ahead riddled with emotional land mines… But there was no going back, the promise had been made. She had to have an answer, whatever that was. Until she knew for certain, one way or the other, their lives would be circumscribed by emotional shadows and fruitless conjecture. But where to begin, how to begin…

Kate had not told anyone of her promise to Ben, although she thought long and hard about doing so.

Polly was the obvious confidante. Not only would she have a different perspective, but she would give Kate much-needed emotional support. The trouble was Polly would not be impartial. Could not be, by the very fact Dan was the most precious thing in the world to her and any suggestion he might have deliberately taken his own life would be fiercely rejected. If Kate were to come to the conclusion Dan *had* committed suicide, she didn't think she could cope with the effect on Polly.

She didn't want to confide in Ted, although she knew she could. He was so busy picking up the pieces on the farm, steady and strong, she wanted him to stay that way and not add to his load.

She thought about Maggie Potter, but rejected her. Maggie was a terrific friend but she told John Potter everything, and this was one confidence Kate would not want shared.

Mary? Mary, though devastated in the immediate aftermath of Dan's death, had been very supportive. But she was sorting her own life out, and was happy at long last. She'd told Kate she was determined to put the past behind her and Kate didn't want to drag her down.

Emily was too preoccupied with her own life.

Ivan, she knew, had loved Dan, but he was an MP now, and almost inaccessible.

Which left Max. He and Dan had shared a childhood. As well as cousins, they'd always been good friends, even after she and Dan got together; and Max, she knew, had never told Dan how much he minded about their marriage.

She leaned back in the chair, remembering how he'd reacted when he heard the news.

He had phoned Kate and demanded they meet for a drink. He hadn't minced his words. 'What are you doing, Kate?'

'What precisely do you mean, Max?'

'I mean, Kate, I don't want you doing something you'll regret. You're ambitious; you're intelligent and creative; that's why you've been doing so well. Your bosses wouldn't have given you all that responsibility unless they believed in you. They obviously think you're going places.'

In truth, Max was only spelling out the internal dialogue Kate had been having with herself, but Max's tone made her defensive.

'There's no reason why I shouldn't continue after we're married. Lots of people commute up from the West Country, and if that doesn't work out, then Bristol has a flourishing media community. Lots of production houses have opened offices there, even if I can't get a transfer within the BBC.'

Max leant forward and said, with heat, 'You wouldn't be happy in some provincial little backwater, turning out tin-pot regional programmes. Think about it, Kate. You'd become frustrated and miserable. And how would Dan cope with that…if he even noticed? He works twenty-four-seven.'

'He loves me, Max. And I love him. We'll work it out. I guess I'll just have to compromise…'

'But you don't have to. Kate, all your friends are in London. Your life is in London.'

'What are you suggesting? That I haven't thought all this through? I've been over and over it all, from every angle.

You're right, there's an awful lot I'll miss, a lot of sacrifices I'll have to make. But weighing everything up, the overriding fact is I love Dan and I want to spend the rest of my life with him.'

Max slammed down his glass, spilling the wine and got to his feet. He seemed as much upset as angry. 'Well, if that's the way it is, there's nothing more to be said. Goodbye, Kate.'

'Max, please...' But Max had turned and stalked out of the wine bar, leaving a perplexed Kate staring after him.

She hadn't seen him again till well after their wedding. Dan had agonised over whether to ask Max or Joe as his best man. But then the problem had been resolved by the news that Max couldn't get out of an assignment that sent him overseas and so wouldn't be at the wedding. Now he was Ben's godfather and had been a great strength since Dan's death. But...

She suspected Max still had an agenda as far as she was concerned, even after all this time. His behaviour when William had come to supper had been odd to say the least.

No, not Max, she needed to keep him at a distance.

She sat up and rubbed her eyes. It was time to stop dithering and get on with it... But there was still the big, unanswered question: did she have the strength to trawl, alone, through the last months of Dan's life, to come up with...with what?

She took a deep breath. She needed to be systematic, not emotional. She should take the same approach as if she were doing research for a documentary... Except that it was Dan... Dan, whom she knew so well, or thought she did. And although there would be no shortage of people who knew him, they would all have a view about his actions and motives and would, she knew, tell her what they thought she wanted to hear.

Her tearstained reflection in the black, blank screen of the computer stared at her. In recent years Dan had spent so much time on this computer. Might it hold some clue? Might it contain information that would tell her whether there was something wrong, or shed light on the way he was thinking…?

Wiping her damp cheeks with the heel of her hand, she leaned forward to turn the computer on. As she did so, she brushed the keyboard. Instantly the screen sprang to life.

'Like Aladdin's genie,' she thought, 'it's been lying in wait.' So now she had to find the commands that would reveal its secrets.

After an hour spent among spreadsheets and business correspondence, her head spinning, but none the wiser, Kate sat back and looked around the study for a different line of inspiration. Her eye fell on the long line of journals written by his grandmother, crammed onto a shelf above the desk. Dan had never found the time to read them, not even the ones she remembered him telling her Rose had told him to read when she'd died.

'If only Dan had kept a journal like his grandmother,' Kate mused, 'then I probably wouldn't have needed to look further.'

But Dan had never been a great one for writing.

'The same applies to me, I don't write anything,' Kate sighed. 'Except the odd sick note for school, the occasional postcard or thank-you letter. I used to write to Dan all the time when I was working, so it's nothing to do with being too busy. Old Granny Rose puts me to shame. That's one tradition I can carry on.'

And so saying, she opened a new folder on the computer. 'I shall write a journal of this year, from Dan's death onwards.'

But as she started writing, her heart was so full of thoughts of Dan, remembering the letters she used to write, loving him and longing to be with him, she began her journal as a letter to him, pouring out her love for him and her need to understand what had happened.

She told him of the children, of Ben's distress and of her promise. She wrote about the farm, the small changes they had made, of her struggles to learn about farming. She described the books she was reading and how she'd rather read than watch television because she found that watching TV without him made her particularly sad. She was so absorbed that when the chimes from the hall clock struck eleven o'clock, she was startled.

'So much for my research, Dan,' she said to the empty study, switching off the light. But she felt better, stronger.

The following evening, she was about to resume her searches on the computer when Splash rushed, barking, to the back door.

It was William.

'Sorry to drop by unannounced, Kate. I just wanted to know how young Ben is after his ordeal, and to give him these.' And he thrust a cardboard box into Kate's hands. It was full of Spiderman figures. 'He told Kitty how much he loved Spiderman. Edward used to collect these but he outgrew them a long time ago. We thought Ben might like to have them, if it's all right with you. They're pretty ghastly.'

She laughed. 'They are, but Ben will love them. How kind. Thanks, William; and please tell Edward I really appreciate it.'

After a moment's awkwardness, she offered him a coffee and he accepted.

'So how's Ben?'

'He had a couple of days off school and it was good, for both of us, to have some time alone together. I've talked it over with Polly and Ted and we think the children should be encouraged to talk about Dan, without forcing it, of course. It's important they keep their memories of him alive, for them to remember how much he loved them. It's such a delicate process, and it's early days yet, but I think both children seem more settled.'

'I found it difficult to talk to Edward when Muriel died,' said William, with unusual candour. 'He would go to his room and very firmly shut the door. Didn't show me any emotion, although he certainly felt it. Kitty was easier. She cried a lot and let me cuddle her, and we would talk about her mummy. Funnily enough, it's much the same now they're older in that Kitty will mention her mother quite easily. Edward never does. I think his age has something to do with it, though.'

'Poor Edward, it's not easy losing a parent at any age and, I suspect for a teenager, it's particularly hard. You depend on your parents being there for you.'

'Hmm.' William grunted. 'You're probably right. Life's tough in different ways for us all. By the way, have you heard Pete Warren has put Ashcroft Farm up for sale?'

Kate was shocked. 'Joe's father? No I hadn't. Why? He's lived on that farm all his life...'

'Yes, but he's nearing retirement and, really, he's no interest in continuing; pig farming's in such a dicey state. It was bad enough with swine fever, but they've been in the front line with foot-and-mouth. With the all-clear still not given, he's decided to cut his losses, take the compensation, and quit.'

'Even so, it's drastic! Selling Ashcroft farm!' Kate felt shaken and upset. 'His family have been there for generations. I suppose losing all his pigs the way he did, must have affected him badly. I saw a bit of it on television. It was awful: the sows trying to protect their young from the gunmen; dead animals falling on top of live... And he had to stand by and witness the slaughter... Janet said he was heartbroken.'

'I'm sure he was, but I think it was the loss of Joe he minded more. Although he has those other two sons, it was always Joe

198

who was his right-hand, who was going to take on the farm when he retired.'

The loss of Joe.

How sad, how final those words sounded. It was, she realised, seven years since he'd sat where William sat now, his eyes red from crying.

It had all started with Emily.

Initially Joe's infatuation had been a joke among his friends, but it showed no signs of lessening with the passage of time.

Then one evening, shortly after Ben was born, he called round. Mary was with them, she recalled, and they'd just finished supper.

Dan greeted him with delight. 'Joe, at last! I'd been wondering where you were. I want to celebrate the birth of my son and heir with you, but you're very elusive.'

Kate thought Joe looked preoccupied, but he made all the right noises, congratulated her and Dan, drank the baby's health, chatted to Mary about London, answered Polly's questions about his family and ate the remains of their supper.

Finally he cleared his throat. 'Actually, I've got some news for you. It will be all over the neighbourhood pretty soon, but I wanted to tell you myself, first.'

'You're marrying Susie Bancroft. Making an honest woman of her!' interrupted Dan with glee.

Joe looked embarrassed. 'No, it's nothing like that. The thing is, I've decided to give up farming. There's no future in it. Not for me anyway. It's just that, well, I've been feeling more and more that…well, life is passing me by, down here. Outside the farm, there's nothing to really do, nothing worth talking about. And it's hard to meet anyone new. So I've decided to get out, start a new career for myself before it's too late.'

His announcement was greeted by a shocked silence.

Polly was the first to break it. 'How does your dad feel about this, Joe?'

Joe looked uncomfortable. 'Umm…he's upset. But I don't see why. He doesn't really need me, he's got Henry and George, both of whom would leap at the chance to take over when they finish college.'

'What are you planning to do?' Kate asked.

'I've been offered a job, in London; that's why you couldn't get hold of me, Dan. I've been up for various interviews. I didn't want to say anything 'til it was sorted.'

'London? You? That's ridiculous.' Dan was incredulous.

'I don't see what's ridiculous about it.' retorted Joe.

'Because you're like me. You're a farmer, whatever you say. You'd hate London. What on earth could you do there?'

'Make money, for a start, which is more than pigs are doing for us at the moment. I'm fed up with jumping to every whim of the market place. One minute we make money, and then we don't. We're in a no-win situation at the moment – can't do this, can't do that, but our soddin' European neighbours can and we can't compete. It's a mug's game, Dan, and I'm sick of it. It's all right for you, you've got a dairy herd that's the envy of half the county. And you're sitting pretty with the price of your milk and all those other subsidies dropping into your lap. Well, I'm fed up with grafting for nothing, so London, here I come.'

'What are you going to do?' Kate inquired. 'You said you'd been up for various interviews. Who with?'

'Funnily enough it's still in agriculture. I think that's why I got the job. I'm going to train as a salesman for an international agrochemical company. They specialise in crop protection and they've got branches all over the country.'

'Joe, you can't…I don't believe it,' protested Dan. 'Of all

the… You? The lectures you've given me about unthinkingly zapping the bugs and killing the land, and now you're going to sell the stuff? Why?'

'I've told you. I'm fed up with…'

'Is this anything to do with Emily?'

'What?'

The two friends glared at each other. The girls exchanged puzzled glances.

'What on earth has this to do with Emily, Dan?' Kate asked.

'Well, Joe, is it?' demanded Dan.

A slow flush suffused Joe's face. 'I don't know what you are talking about,' he said thickly.

Dan was relentless. 'The day Ben was born, I spoke to Ivan on the phone and he told me he thought you were following Emily, stalking her.'

'That's ridiculous,' spluttered Joe. 'I bumped into her in London a couple of times, when I was up there for these interviews. Then she invited me to a show in some gallery. My being in London had nothing to do with her. My God, Dan…'

Mary intervened, trying to ease the growing antagonism.

'Where are you going to live? London's an expensive place. Do you have any friends you can stay with?'

'I don't know yet. I might have to stay in a hostel till I find somewhere. I'll be all right.'

Mary had given him her telephone number and a half-promise of temporary accommodation, subject to Clive's agreement, and he'd left shortly after, with the women's good wishes for his new career partially salving his wounded pride.

Dan, in a rare ill humour, was persuaded to walk Polly home while Kate fed the baby and Mary cleared up.

'I've known Joe since I was a kid. Whatever he might think, he's a country boy,' Mary observed. 'He'll be lost in the city.

The glamour will wear off very quickly.' She paused, then added tentatively, 'Do you think there is any truth in the Emily business, Kate?'

Kate sighed. 'Probably. The awful thing is she doesn't mean anything by it. It's just that she collects admirers. You know Emily! She needs to be the centre of attention, always. She feeds off it. Her path is littered with men who've fallen under her spell and fondly imagined she loves only them. But she doesn't. She loves Flick, a bit, and possibly Ivan. But above all else, she loves Emily.'

'La Belle Dame Sans Merci. Poor Joe.'

Kate tried to talk to Emily about Joe, but Emily was airily vague, saying only that if Joe was giving up the farm to go to London, then it was his business and she was sure he was doing the right thing. Yes, she did see him from time to time, it would be odd if she didn't, him being Dan's great friend, and why did Kate think that she had any influence over him...?

They heard little from him after that. Mary told them he'd stayed with her and Clive for a short while, then found a flat-share in New Cross.

'How depressing,' said Kate, feeling depressed herself, and Mary agreed.

'I tried to persuade him to stay with us a bit longer. I liked having him around. He's so kind. But I don't think he ever felt comfortable with Clive, and to be honest, Clive didn't encourage him.'

Then, a year later, out of the blue he appeared at Watersmeet again. Dan was doing a shift in the lambing shed and didn't know Joe was there. Kate had been settling Ben, who was restless with teething, and had come down to the kitchen to find Joe at the table, his head on his hands, weeping.

She went to him. 'Joe, Joey, what is it? What are you doing here?'

He replied, in a whisper, 'I'm sorry Kate. I don't know why I came here. It's just that... I didn't know where else to go and you...and Dan... You're her sister, maybe you can explain to me... Maybe you could make her see sense.'

He smelled strongly of alcohol, but he didn't seem drunk, just profoundly upset.

'Joe, you'll have to tell me more. What's been happening to you? What's brought you to such a state? What's Emily to do with this? Joe, dear Joey, you can tell me.'

And so between tears and sighs, he told her of the fruitless year he'd just spent. He had, indeed, decided to go to London so he could be nearer to Emily. He described to Kate his lonely existence in a hovel in New Cross and how he started to hate the city, its smell, the constant barrage of noise, the grimy, yellow light at night and the lack of open space.

He told her of the hard-nosed people he met in the agro-chemical business and how he struggled to make a success of it; how the grimness of his stay in London was made worthwhile every time he saw Emily. How she was sweet and encouraging; told him he'd made the right decision and how much she admired his determination. He'd longed to sweep her away, but knew he had to have the money in place first to give her everything he wanted to give her.

After a year, however, he felt he could no longer bear to be in the city, or in his job, and begged her to go away with him anyway. Bitterly, he recounted how Emily not only rejected him, but told him he'd been deluding himself if he'd ever thought she would leave Ivan and, worse than that, she thought it'd be better for both of them if they didn't see each

203

other again.

'I love her, Kate. How can it be better for me never to see her again? I thought she loved me. I know she did.'

'How did you know, Joe? Did she say so?'

He was silent.

'Were you lovers?'

He groaned. 'No, we weren't lovers, not in the sense you mean. We kissed…' He gave a long anguished sigh. 'Magic… those kisses were magic, Kate! And she told me she loved me, but we never… She would not… Why should she say she loved me if she didn't?'

'I'm sure she did, Joe.' Kate sighed and mentally cursed her sister. 'But that's Emily; she's a passionate person. What I mean is, she thrives on love and loving. She needs it like other people need…well, sunshine. But, oh Joe, that's as far as it goes.'

But Joe wasn't satisfied and although she talked at length, sympathising, trying to explain, trying to advise him, he was not ready to hear what she was saying. Eventually he stood up and, despite her entreaties to wait for Dan's return, said he had to go.

'No, I won't wait. If he's lambing, I'd be the last person he'd want to see. I've got to go. I've been summoned for an interview with the boss tomorrow. I expect it's the chop, but I might as well hear it in person. Take care of Dan, Kate. You're both so lucky. So lucky!'

And so saying, he let himself out into the night.

Kate sighed. Seven years ago and the image of Joe's sad, lost face that night was still so clear.

William shook his head. 'Poor old Warren. He's not the first to call it a day, and he won't be the last.'

'Yes, there've been an awful lot of casualties. So far we've been very lucky here...'

No sooner were the words out of her mouth than she felt sick. How could she be so stupid? Lucky? Muriel had died of cancer and she... She had lost Dan and, for all she knew, the foot and mouth epidemic could have been the very final straw... Supposing he'd thought one of his precious herds had the disease; that he might lose the *whole* lot; the whole pedigree herd his grandfather had started, his father nurtured, and he'd inherited? That would have broken Dan.

Enough to drive him to suicide?

'Are you all right, Kate? You've gone very white.' Concerned, William leant forward and grasped her hand.

'I'm sorry. What I said...it was so stupid! About being lucky I mean. You've lost Muriel and I... Dan's dead... What was I talking about? I know his death was an accident, but there have been cases of farmers who...who... I mean, it's common knowledge that farmers are under such stress that more and more of them are...' Her voice broke; she couldn't finish.

He gave her a shrewd look. 'We all know there's been an increase in the number of farming suicides, and for a number of different reasons. Foot and mouth is just one of them. Kate, are you worrying about Dan? Is this to do with Ben, and Harry Freeman's nasty little accusation?'

She hesitated. 'Yes, I suppose it is.'

And maybe because he wasn't fussing over her, and maybe because he had an air of calm strength about him... Certainly for no other reason she could think of, either then or after he'd gone...she decided to confide in him.

'This might sound misguided, or impossible, but I've promised Ben I will prove to him Dan...that Dan did *not* commit suicide. It's very important for me, for us: Ben, Rosie and me, to *know*, not just to believe.'

205

William frowned. 'Is this wise? Don't you think you might be a bit too raw for such an undertaking? Heaven knows, it's hard enough for you as it is, but to start delving and digging, and perhaps...' His voice trailed away.

'Discover he did, in fact, kill himself? Yes, I'm prepared for that. But, honestly, however awful the truth is, it's got to be better than a permanent question mark hanging over our lives.'

21

Frank

The vixen lay stretched on the ground, wary, watching her cubs tugging away at the chicken carcass, scrambling over each other to get a better purchase on the corpse.

He watched as she lifted her keen nose to the sky. He was safely down-wind of her and if he kept still enough she could have no sense of his presence. Feathers were flying everywhere as the four little foxes made a game of their feasting. At length, their bellies full and exhausted by their play, they hurled themselves at their mother, pushing and nuzzling for her nipples. She relaxed her guard and lay on her side, the better to meet their demands.

He had her clearly in his sights. A grin creased his austere features but the smile did not reach his eyes. His finger crooked round the trigger and slowly squeezed.

Crows, magpies and pigeons erupted noisily into the sky and the brains, eyes, blood and fur of the unsuspecting mother burst in every direction. He grunted with satisfaction. Without their mother the cubs would perish very quickly.

That was the way to deal with vermin.

22

Dan

1999

Dan slammed out of the house. The yard was awash with water and mud. The rain, which had not abated all day, lashed against his face. Huddled into his Barbour, he walked moodily across the lawn, through the rain-drenched yew hedge, and down to the river. The lawn, now more mud than grass, was so waterlogged that brown footprints charted Dan's route to the point where the little stream fussed and bubbled into the rising flood. Here the willow, ash, and alder, clinging to the edge of the riverbank, were already marooned, their roots submerged under swirling, chocolate water.

'Bloody, bloody rain. Bloody, bloody day. Bloody, bloody woman!'

He stared moodily at the river; much more rain and it would burst its banks. Watersmeet had never been flooded, despite its position. The house was on a strategic rise, and although the flagstones on the ground floor oozed with damp, the floodwater had never reached it.

The farmyard, on the other side of the house, was higher still, and the risk from the brook was minimal, as it was carried through pipes under the yard, emerging in front of the garden wall by the farm's entrance. The pipes were always cleared of debris, during dry spells, to ensure there was no build-up.

One long, hot summer, when he was seven and the brook had been reduced to a trickle, Dan had found the entrance to the ducts above the farm and wriggled through them, emerging muddy and triumphant at the farm gate, and received a rare walloping from Polly.

This year, it seemed to Dan, there hadn't been any dry spells.

'This autumn has been a bloody washout,' he'd grumbled to Ted earlier, as they shovelled the slurry from the yard. 'We're going to have a shortfall in silage, and if this weather continues, we'll have to bring the cows in early… God knows what the feed bills are going to be by the spring.'

But it wasn't the rising water, or the rising financial crisis that had caused him to burst out of the house in such a mood, although both had contributed to his unenthusiastic response to Kate's proposal.

'A holiday? With the Etheridges? What on earth for?'

'Because they've invited us, that's why. You keep going on about how we need to economise… All we'd have to do is find our ferry fare and contribute to the food. Muriel's found this really nice old farmhouse in the Dordogne, with plenty of rooms and a swimming pool. The kids would love it…'

'But I wouldn't. I know Muriel's your friend, but I hardly know William, and on holiday I want to slob. I'd have to mind my manners, dress for dinner, ask permission to pour myself a drink…'

'Don't be ridiculous. You've known William all your life. It wouldn't be like that.'

'Oh wouldn't it? Apart from business, that's the only way I've ever spent any time with him. They're loaded, Kate, and if we stayed with them, we'd have to spend more money than we can afford. They'd want to go out to poncey restaurants and drink hugely expensive wine…'

'Oh don't be so melodramatic. We're not that hard up, surely?'

For a moment, Dan hesitated. Part of him longed to share with her just how bad things were becoming, just how much of a struggle he was finding it to keep cheerful, when the bills kept rolling relentlessly in and the farm's income, equally relentlessly, kept falling.

A few weeks ago he'd gone to see a financial adviser, in London, at the suggestion of his accountant. Kate had been persuaded to let Lizzie Freeman look after the children for the day and accompany him, but at the last minute she'd cried off with period pains and he'd gone alone.

In a way, he was relieved. He knew Kate needed to know all was not well with the farm, but pride made him reluctant to confide in her.

When she'd stopped work, she'd fretted about not being able to contribute to the family's finances. But the farm was prosperous and Dan had assured her, promised her, she never need worry about money: the farm could support them all, comfortably. So when the farm's income started slipping, he couldn't bring himself to tell her. He knew he'd be a lot happier if he did, but he kept on hoping, somehow, that it was a temporary blip and things would eventually improve.

He'd decided to use the trip to London to talk to her, but as she didn't go he decided to say nothing until after the trip,

210

hoping he might come back with some constructive ideas about what could be done.

The financial adviser was a guy called Steven Kelner. Quite contrary to his expectations, Dan liked him. Both his bank manger and his accountant had known his father and made him feel like an inadequate schoolboy. Steven Kelner took time to listen to Dan's own analysis of his situation; scrutinised the accountant's figures, and went into the details of all Dan's assets. At the end of the meeting it was decided that a fuller picture was needed to decide on the best way forward for the farm, and that an agricultural management company should undertake an assessment.

Reassured, Dan left Kelner's office and with time on his hands and no Kate to spend it with, he found a phone box and rang Mary. She didn't answer, so he rang Ivan. An aloof assistant was firmly putting him in his place when Ivan came on the line and arranged to meet him for a quick beer near the Houses of Parliament.

Dan was putting the phone down when a figure shuffled past, a derelict, wrapped in a blanket and clutching a bottle. There were many such wraiths on the streets of London and ordinarily Dan would have taken no notice, but there was something in the way he moved, something about the shape of his body under the thin blanket that arrested his attention.

He stepped out of the phone box and stared after the figure. 'Joe?' he called doubtfully. 'Joey?'

But the figure did not turn or falter in his shuffle and disappeared round a corner. Feeling slightly foolish, Dan hesitated for a moment, then ran to the corner.

The figure had gone.

Ivan was late and stayed only long enough to down a half pint, but he was buzzing, delighted to see Dan and full of his recent elevation from the rank of back-room boy to parliamentary candidate in an up-coming by-election.

Dan was impressed and pleased for him. 'How does Emily view the prospect of becoming the wife of an MP? Is she going to campaign at your side, turning heads wherever she goes and persuading Sharon and Kevin to abandon a lifetime of unthinking devotion to the Conservative party?'

Ivan laughed. 'If only! I think she's impressed, though, and to be quite honest, she loves the idea of the prestige she thinks she'd have if I were elected. But she's made it quite clear I go on the campaign trail alone. She's got her studio up and running and is concentrating on sculpture rather than painting, these days. Some of the stuff is rather good. Not your cup of tea, I suspect.'

'Well if it's anything like her paintings, then no.' Dan took a swig of beer, then remembering the shuffling figure, hesitated, and asked, casually, 'Has she seen anything of Joe?'

Ivan pulled a rueful face. 'Not as far as I know, not for a couple of years. She told me she'd let him know his attentions were…inappropriate, and for all I know, that was the end of it. She's got a young writer in tow at the moment. A highly successful first novel. Emily likes that touch of fame and he's as sick as a puppy whenever he sees her.'

They finished their beer and Ivan left, promising Dan and Kate a family visit when his election was over. Dan wandered off to Hamleys to buy presents for Ben and Rosie; tried phoning Mary, again with no success, and returned home a lot more cheerful than when he had left it, much to Kate's obvious relief. But he decided to wait until the farm report had been completed and he knew what it proposed before he took her into his confidence.

The visit from the advisers recommended by Steven Kelner

was not an experience he particularly enjoyed. The harvest was late, the weather was atrocious, and the farmhands viewed the consultant, a Mr Harris, with great suspicion. Even Ted was not particularly cooperative.

Dan had told Ted what he was doing and why, but only after the visit had been set up. He hadn't consulted Ted over his decision to take advice, or discussed with him the merits of a farm report.

'I think Ted feels he's been sidelined, Dan.' Polly was reproving. 'I do think, darling, you have a tendency not to share problems. Our backs are broad enough to take the rough with the smooth. You always think you can solve a problem on your own and then present the solution to the world. You mustn't exclude the possibility we might have some good ideas, too. I know you're running the farm, now, and Ted's more than happy acting as your manager, but if you don't share things with him, then you're treating him as simply one of the work force, and he's always been rather more than that, hasn't he?'

'Yes, yes, of course he is,' Dan replied testily, 'and I'm not going to make any major decisions without consulting him, so please, don't fuss about Ted.'

Polly looked offended and the conversation ended without the question being raised as to why Dan had felt the need for outside help in the first place.

He felt increasingly isolated. Kate seemed hardly to register that a major survey was taking place. Ben and Rosie both had chicken pox. Sitting with a drooping Ben on her lap, dabbing his inflamed spots with calamine while Rosie wailed miserably in her cot, she shrieked in horror when he'd suggested that they might provide the consultant with board and lodging for the three days he was on the farm.

Then, on the penultimate day of his inspection, Mr Harris

requested a visit to Woodside Farm.

Dan groaned inwardly. He prided himself that in spite of the weather and the recalcitrance of the men, Watersmeet was an efficient, professional farming enterprise and must make a good impression on anyone who knew their stuff.

Woodside Farm was another matter, and although, theoretically, the way it was farmed was not his responsibility, it was still part of the Watersmeet estate, and the poor relationship between tenant and landlord was a running sore. He knew the consultant could not go alone. Frank Leach would take no notice of any written authorisation and would immediately see him off. If he went with him, the inevitable snarl-off would be counter-productive. The only solution was to ask Ted. Frank disliked Ted, but he was also rather afraid of him, and had never worsted him in any encounter.

The visit was duly conducted. Ted reported back that Frank had been suspicious and uncooperative, but Mr Harris managed to complete his survey.

Dan breathed a sigh of relief, but Ted continued, 'You've got to do something about Woodside, though, Dan. Not only do we need to spend some money on the house, but the farm buildings are in a terrible state. To be honest, Frank is in breach of his tenancy and you could, if you've a mind to it, issue him with a notice to remedy.'

Dan laughed mirthlessly. 'His remedy would be to take a shotgun to me. He'd never let me get close enough to prove he was in breach, let alone do any work on the place.'

'Nevertheless, you can't just let it go. Or are you going to wait till he dies and the farm is in ruin?'

'It might be the simplest course. And you've always advised me to leave him well alone.'

'That's true, but I've a responsibility to the farm as your

manager, and it's clear to me that Frank's farming technique, or lack of it, is devaluing Woodside, chronically. I wouldn't be doing my job properly if I…'

'OK. But we will wait and see what Mr Harris says in his report. Thanks for that. I'll get the report to you as soon as it arrives and we'll discuss what to do about Woodside and the whole future of Watersmeet then.'

Ted looked mollified. 'I know times are tough Dan, but Watersmeet is a good operation. We'll survive.'

Dan's inclination to leave Frank Leach well alone earned him no thanks from that quarter.

A few days after Mr Harris had gone, Dan was out on the tractor, turning over the stubble in a field dry enough for ploughing. The field was high up the valley from Watersmeet, near the boundary of Woodside.

The rain had stopped the evening before, the skies had cleared and the temperature dropped. A light frost sparkled in the morning sun as it lanced low across the stubble field. Wisps of mist drifted upwards from the burnished leaves of the woods and noisy gangs of long-tailed tits flitted through the hedgerow. Attracted by the activity of the tractor, flocks of seagulls mewed, swooped and settled in his wake.

He sang lustily as he worked, undeterred by the noisiness of the tractor. It was the sort of morning he loved, the sort of morning when everything – man, machine, the earth, the sky, birds, animals, wood and river – seemed to achieve an equilibrium, a harmonious whole where no one element was more important than another. It was the sort of morning when he could believe that God was in his heaven and all was right with the world.

He'd completed nearly a quarter of the field when he saw a

man leaning on the gate watching him. The line of the furrow brought him closer to that side of the field and he recognised Frank Leach.

'Oh bugger!' he exclaimed, exasperated. He concentrated grimly on his task, hoping, if he was ignored, Frank would get bored and go away. Two more furrows and he glanced across to the gate. Frank was still there, watching him. Dan was disconcerted. Frank never normally sought him out, and these days he was rarely seen by anyone. Something was up.

Two more furrows and he was still there. Dan calculated it would take him to four o'clock to do the entire field, assuming he would stop for his sandwiches. Mulling his options over, he calculated if he didn't stop, he'd finish by 3.30… Would Frank still be waiting for him then? There was a phone in the cab so he could call Ted, but he resisted that idea. He was a grown man, for Christ sake, he couldn't be forever running to Ted whenever there was trouble. Was he afraid of Frank Leach? Of course not! Although truthfully, he admitted to himself, there was something about the man that made him uneasy.

His ploughing was bringing him nearer to the gate. He turned the furrow and looked again.

Frank wasn't there.

He was walking slowly and deliberately towards the tractor on a course the tractor must take in its furrow. Caution got the better of male pride and Dan reached for the phone and dialled Ted.

Tractor and man moved inexorably towards each other.

Ted's recorded voice invited Dan to leave a message. He'd just time to urge Ted to come up to the field, when he had to stop the tractor to avoid mowing Frank down.

Trying to keep his cool, he leaned from the cab. 'What's the idea, Frank? Not sensible to walk into the path of a tractor.'

216

Frank looked terrible. His eyes were red-rimmed and bloodshot, his pallor intensified by black stubble. His voice was slurred but his intentions were clear.

'Oi wants a word wiv' ye, Mister Maddicott...'

'Not now, Frank, I'm busy. If it's important come and see me at the house this evening, or see Ted. I'm sure he can sort out whatever the problem is.'

'Yer the problem, yer little scum bag and its no use snivellin' behind Ted Jordan's skirts. Yer the one Oi wants ter talk to and Oi'm gonna do it now. So git down out of that cab and listen ter what Oi've got to say, or are yer too much of a coward?'

'You can insult me as much as you like, Frank, but I'm not coming down, I'm not talking to you now and I want you to move out of the way so I can continue ploughing.'

Frank circled round the tractor cursing, then before Dan had time to react, he leapt, with surprising agility, at the door of the cab, wrenched it open, seized Dan's arm and pulled him out of the tractor, throwing him down hard onto the ground. Then flinging himself astride Dan, he seized his wrists and pinioned him to the ground.

Dan struggled and shouted but, strong as he was, it was to no avail. Frank had the advantage of him.

'So now yer've got to listen to Oi, so listen good. Oi knows what yer's up to, so don't say else. Yer sent that man to size up my place for sellin'. Well she ain't fur sale and Oi ain't leavin' her. D'yer hear me, Mister Madicott, Oi ain't leavin and there's nothin' yer can do ter make Oi.'

Frank was heavy on Dan's chest, his breath smelt of stale cider and as he spoke he shoved his face into Dan's so that Dan wanted to gag, but he yelled back, 'Get off me you bloody, stupid oaf. If I *was* going to sell Woodside, which I can't, even if I wanted to with you there, I'd tell you. There are other ways to get rid of you Leach, and after this, believe me I'll leave no stone unturned.'

Frank, incoherent with fury, let out a roar and momentarily loosened his hold. The two men rolled over and over, punching, kicking and yelling obscenities. They didn't notice a Land Rover come bumping up the track, nor Ted and Josh jump out and run towards them.

Ted seized hold of Frank and Josh held Dan. Bedraggled, muddied and bloodied, the two men glared at each other, too full of anger to pay any attention to Ted's sharp questioning.

Frank shook off Ted's restraint and hissed at Dan, 'Oi'm tellin' ye… Take heed, lay off my land!' And he turned and stumbled away.

Battered and shaken as he was, Dan tried to make light of the encounter, thanked them for coming to his rescue, and made them swear to say nothing of the incident to Kate.

Josh took over from him on the tractor and Ted took Dan back to his cottage to clean himself up and to concoct a plausible explanation for his cuts and bruises.

'Are you minded to report this incident to the police?' asked Ted, handing Dan a mug of tea when, stiff but clean, he came downstairs. 'After all, he assaulted you.'

Dan looked at Ted with surprise. 'Do you think I ought to? I thought we agreed to hush it up. And taking Frank to court will not improve tenant-landlord relations.'

'I suppose you're right.' Ted frowned. 'I'm just a bit concerned. I've watched Frank deteriorate over the years and I'm not sure that doing nothing is an option any more.'

'What do you mean? Surely if we leave him alone, he'll calm down. I'll just have to be doubly careful in any dealings with him. He'll die one day. He's not likely to spring any sprogs on us now, and if Woodside doesn't come back to Watersmeet in my lifetime, then it certainly will in the kids'. After all, we don't need the extra farmland and as long as the rent is paid… I can be patient, in spite of what I said to him.'

'Fair enough, it's your decision. But I repeat what I said earlier, that even if we leave Frank where he is, we've got to do something to check the rate of decay at Woodside. I shall be interested to see what your man, Harris, recommends.' Ted chuckled wryly. 'He couldn't leave the place quickly enough. Frank completely put the wind up him!'

Then yesterday, three weeks after the fight with Frank, the report had arrived. It was very thorough, full of management-speak, and very precise in its recommendations.

Like Harris himself, thought Dan savagely, as he gazed at the swirling waters of the river.

Eddies of scum had formed, reminding him for a moment of the mugs of cocoa his grandmother had insisted on making for him every night, watching him till he'd drunk every last drop. He'd hated it. Never enough sugar, the taste was bitter, and the milk, mixed with water, made it a drink far removed from the rich, creamy, hot chocolate he was given on the rare occasions he had stayed with his cousins. 'Drink it up, it's good for you.' Granny Rose was deaf to his complaints.

'This report's a bit like that cocoa,' he thought sardonically, 'good for me, but bitter.' He could see the thinking behind the report, understood the rationale. It was very sensible… Follow the proposed course of action and not only would Watersmeet survive; it could become profitable in a way that Dan had not dreamed of. But at what cost? What cost?

He had tried to tell Kate last night, when they were watching television, but he could tell she was tired and only half-listening, so he'd abandoned the attempt.

219

He had woken early, heavy-hearted, to the sound of rain lashing against the house, and he and Ted had taken time out from their main tasks to make a circuit of the farm to check the ditches, culverts and overflow pipes, as well as the stock still out in the fields.

Throughout the day he had brooded on what to do. He couldn't share the report with Ted, as he had said he would, and he knew that would become a bone of contention between them. But the report's final recommendations ruled it out. If he showed Ted the report, he would offer to resign and even if Dan refused to accept his offer, the relationship between the two men would never be the same again, particularly if the farm did founder.

Damn Harris, and Kelner, too, for having suggested the report. Dan felt helpless and resolved to talk to Kate over supper. But as soon as he'd got in, she'd started going on about France with the Etheridges and Dan, thwarted and unhappy, had allowed his antipathy to Kate's holiday plans to provoke an argument between them which had escalated to the point where he had banged out of the house.

Dan sighed deeply. It was no good standing here, getting wetter and wetter, and watching the river rising like Canute. He couldn't stop it flooding if he wanted to. Better to go back, make his peace with Kate and tell her about the report. After all, the problems with which he was wrestling were to do with their future, hers as well as Watersmeet's.

When he got back into the kitchen, she came to him and wrapped her arms around him. Wet as he was, he kissed her deeply.

'I'm sorry I stormed off like that,' he murmured, 'and I'm sorry if I was rude about the Etheridges, it's just that I...'

She stopped him, 'Don't worry about that. It was poor

220

timing on my part. It'll keep. Listen Dan, something more important... God, you're absolutely soaked to the skin. Get those things off and I'll make you a hot toddy.' She filled the kettle, a small frown creasing her brow. 'Darling, I'm worried. You'll probably think it's daft of me, but there was definitely something odd about that phone call.'

'What phone call?'

'Clive, a short while ago. He rang and asked, in the cagiest way, whether Mary was here.'

'Mary? Should she be?'

'No, of course not. The last time we spoke was probably a month ago. We agreed then we'd get together over half term or Christmas. You didn't see her when you went to London, did you?'

'No, I told you. I phoned a couple of times but she was out. Nothing odd about that, she wasn't expecting me. What did Clive say?'

'Not a lot. He was very abrupt. Just said he'd been away on business for a few days but Mary and Toby weren't at home, so he wondered whether they'd come down here and it was a plan that he'd forgotten.'

'When did he get back?'

'Yesterday. That was all I got from him before he rang off.'

Dan frowned and rubbed his wet hair with a warm towel Kate had given him. For a few minutes neither spoke. The kettle on the Aga sang and Kate poured some boiling water into a glass of honey and lemon and topped it up with a generous measure of whisky. It was black outside now, and raindrops, blown by the wind, glistened on the darkened glass of the kitchen window.

Kate shivered. 'Oh Dan, I do hope she's all right.'

Dan put his arms around her. 'There's probably a simple

221

explanation, sweetheart. I know what you're thinking, but we've absolutely no reason to think that she's run away, or that Clive has been beating her up...'

'No, and I know she's always denied anything's wrong, but we've had our suspicions, haven't we? And we've always had them, but we've done nothing about them, have we? We've never really confronted Mary, or more importantly, Clive. We're so cosy, so happy, so safe here at Watersmeet. The real world is somewhere else.'

Dan kissed the top of her head. 'We're in the real world too, Kate. We...'

But before he could say anything more, she interrupted him.

'We've got to do something, Dan. I can't just carry on cooking supper, putting the kids to bed and settling down in front of the telly not knowing where Mary is; whether she's safe somewhere, or whether she and Toby are wandering the streets, cold and wet, and too afraid to call us...'

'Us, or any one of the aunties, or Max. She's not without friends and relations in London, darling. For all you know it's as Clive said, she'd arranged to go and stay with someone and he just forgot.'

'Mary wouldn't go off on a trip with Toby in the middle of the term. She fought long and hard to get him into that unspeakable school. She wouldn't jeopardise his place there by taking him away on a jaunt. No Dan, I just know something has happened.'

It didn't matter how much Dan tried to soothe her and find explanations for Mary's absence, Kate was convinced that something was wrong. So, shelving his troubles, Dan agreed they should draw up a plan of action. This involved phoning first Clive and then all of Mary's aunts, Max, and one or two friends that Kate knew of to see if any light could be shed on

Mary's whereabouts.

Dan drew a blank with Clive. He returned to the kitchen where Kate was spooning mashed potato onto the children's plates.

'It was just the answer-phone.'

'Whose answer phone?' asked Ben, tackling a large sausage. He had recently decided to take an interest in adult conversation.

'Clive and Mary's...you remember Toby, don't you?'

'Yep, but he's a scaredy-cat. He's a year older than me an' he still sucks his thumb, like Rosie.'

'I like suckin' my fum,' said Rosie stoutly

'That's because you're a baby.'

'No I'm not. I'm fwee. I'm a little girl and you're a big bossy...'

'That's enough.' Kate intervened. 'Finish your supper, then you can watch half an hour of *Pinocchio* before your bath.'

Dan tried Clive's number several times while the children ate their food, but with no success.

'Either he's not answering or he's gone out. Anyway I've left a message to phone me. That's as much as I can do. I tried to phone Mum as well. I thought she might have some ideas, or at least she could phone one or two of the aunts and make discreet enquiries, but she's not answering her phone either. So, the aunties next.' He groaned, 'This could take some time... "Oh Dan, how lovely to hear from you... How are you...? How's Kate...? How's Ben...? How's little Rosie...? How's your mother...? We don't see enough of you...when are you coming up to London...? How the children must have grown...? What would you like for your birthday, for Christmas...?"'

In spite of herself, Kate giggled, 'That's a very good imitation of Auntie Flo. But we must be discreet, darling. Mary won't thank us if we set the whole tribe chattering.'

It was sometime later when he joined her in the bathroom, where the children were playing in the huge old iron bathtub that was long and deep enough for them to pretend to swim in. The water was full of soapsuds, plastic ducks and boats, and the brightly coloured dinosaurs that were Rosie's particular favourites. With splashes and shrieks, the children were having far too much fun to pay any attention to Kate's exasperated attempts to get them out. Dan went to her assistance.

She looked up, hopeful. 'Any luck?'

He shook his head as he scooped Ben out of the bath and wrapped him in a towel. 'Nothing. Spoke to them all. Aunt Meg said Mary, Clive and Toby had been over to Sunday lunch three weeks ago. She thought Clive was very quiet and Mary looked a bit peaky, and that it was just as well that Clive didn't have to go away again until the New Year, when he was planning to take Mary with him. But that was the only bit of information I got. You'd better try her mates, when these two are in bed.'

'I'm not going to bed yet,' said Ben indignantly. 'Rosie goes first.'

'Yes, yes.' Kate's impatience masked her concern. 'Go and flush the loo, Ben, and get into your pyjamas.'

Ben marched to the grand porcelain and mahogany affair that had been installed by one of his forebears, and yanked vigorously but ineffectively a number of times at the chain.

Kate sighed, 'We've really got to do something about this bathroom Dan. It's all very well having a gigantic bath and an antique lavatory, but the bath takes an age to fill, uses the entire tank to give a decent depth of water and you can't flush the loo until the tank has re-filled.'

Rosie giggled and started to chant, 'Ben's poo's in the loo,

224

Stinky poo in the loo...'

'That's enough, young lady.' Dan started to strip off his shirt. 'I'm just going to dive into your nice soapy water and then I'll come and read you a story. Ben can listen in if he wants.'

'Depends,' said Ben loftily, 'I've got stuff to do.'

When the children had left, Dan slid into the water. Tall as he was, he could lie lengthwise in the tub and be completely immersed.

He watched Kate picking up the children's clothes. She looked tired.

'We'll find her, Katie.' He held out a soapy hand to her. 'We'll find her. Now take your clothes off and get into this bath. The children can wait five minutes for their story and the one advantage of this monstrous piece of plumbing is we can have a bath together. We wouldn't find a modern one that'd allow us that luxury.'

She slipped out of her jeans and shirt and came to him. Her hair had lost none of that soft bouncy curl and was still as dark as ever. Her figure was trim, and her eyes... Dan was melted by them still. He loved her so much still. Desired her so much still. Despite the gathering storm clouds, he knew as long as he had her with him, nothing, in the end, would matter much. Unlike Mary, poor little Mary. He saw her frightened white face as she huddled, trembling, in the corner of the birdcage.

And he shivered.

23

Kate

2001

Kate started to write a letter to Dan almost every day. She found it comforting to write about the children, about what was happening on the farm, and to share with him the results of her explorations on the computer. After two weeks, she'd not found much specifically about him, but what it did spell out was the decline in the farm's fortunes.

Until 1996 the farm had prospered.

1996.

It all seemed to turn on that year.

It had started so promisingly. In January Kate gave birth to Rosie. Milk prices were excellent and Dan planned to extend the herds, and had even considered introducing a third by buying or leasing more land and more quota, and building another dairy.

She remembered him chortling, 'We'll have the biggest pedigree dairy operation in the West Country.'

Colin arrived to work for Polly and the market for their soft cheese began to grow.

But the business hadn't been expanded.

BSE entered the human chain. A new form of CJD had been identified, and a blight fell on the whole farming industry. Overnight the market for Watersmeet's barren cows and bull calves disappeared.

The government and their advisers dithered; nothing happened for nearly four months until, by the autumn, fields were full of stock waiting to be culled.

The following year the value of their subsidies was undermined by the strength of the pound. The Milk Marque broke up and with commercial dairies taking control, the price of milk began to fall, and fall and fall and fall.

The farm's profits dwindled and disappeared.

The computer confirmed all this.

'Dan, you must have been desperate,' whispered Kate, as she wrote. 'Why didn't you tell me?'

He'd also not told her about a huge fine he'd incurred for an error on his IACs form. That was also in 1996, and Kate noticed for the first three years of IACs, the forms did not appear on the computer, which meant that Dan must have filled them in by hand.

'Integrated Administration and Control System', like the name, they weren't user-friendly. He'd always struggled with paperwork and she recalled, with a guilty pang, she'd shown him very little sympathy. He'd complained bitterly to her about the growing number of different forms he had to fill in, usually at the busiest time of the year, with the threat of a hefty fine if he made a mistake. Why hadn't she given him more support?

'Because,' she answered her own accusation, 'I was

preoccupied with the children.'

It had led to one of their rare quarrels.

It occurred two months after Rosie was born. As a baby, she seemed to scream continuously. One night, tired out, and at the end of her tether with Ben, who'd woken and would not get back to bed, Kate had snapped at Dan, hunched over his computer.

He'd shouted back at her. 'I can't do everything, Kate. I'm not superhuman. I've been working all day, then I had to cover the milking for Matt 'cos he's got flu and Mike Rosewarm is not available; the Land Rover sprang a puncture; I've got soaked to the skin more times than I can remember, and when I do get in, you're nowhere to be seen; my dinner is a curled bit of leather at the bottom of the Aga; and I've got to get this bloody IACs form filled in tonight, because the deadline is tomorrow and if I don't send it, that's the end of our subsidy.'

Another shock, courtesy of the computer, was evidence of a hefty fine for river pollution after the floods of last year. Dan had kept that from her, too.

Just how much had he *not* told her?

He *had* told her he was going to consult an agricultural management company. She remembered someone had come to the farm, but Ben and Rosie both had chicken pox and she hadn't paid much attention, either to the visit or to any recommendations he might have made.

'That might be something to look for,' she thought, scanning the details of the last two years, 'because if they *did* recommend something different, Dan doesn't appear to have taken notice. Apart from increasing the cheese output, nothing much changed. I wonder if Ted can throw any light on that?'

The following morning she tracked Ted down in the repairs barn.

It was a miserable, wet day and Ted and Josh were standing close to the electric fire, their hands cupping steaming mugs of tea. As she joined them, Matt came in with Mike Rosewarm. Matt was out of his overalls and smartly dressed – a rare occurrence.

'Off somewhere nice, Matt?' she enquired mildly.

'I maybe,' his reply was curt, 'but that's my business.'

The unexpected rudeness of his reply shocked her; the other three looked embarrassed.

After an awkward silence, Kate replied, as evenly as she could manage. 'That's true, Matt, and I certainly didn't mean to sound as if I was prying, but it does become my business if you haven't returned for the afternoon's milking and I don't know where you are.'

'Have I ever not turned up for milking without saying anything? Have you ever had any cause for complaint?' His voice was loud and belligerent.

'*Yes! That fine for the river pollution…*' But she bit back the retort. Slurry from High Acre had been the cause, but if Matt had been at fault, then Dan would have dealt with it…

'No, but…'

'No. So why are you fussing now?'

The unfairness of his charge stung. She flushed. Mike Rosewarm smirked and Josh looked uncomfortable.

Ted made to intervene but Kate stopped him. Pathetic though this was, she'd been expecting this confrontation with Matt. Since she'd taken over the farm, he'd made it abundantly plain he resented her presence. Anything she said was treated with contempt and endless sidelong comments peppered with references to 'ignorant townies' and 'interferin' women'.

Sensing his moment, Matt went for the jugular.

'The trouble is, Kate, you won't face up to the fact this is man's work. We're all sorry about what happened to Dan, but you just can't wade in thinking you can be a farmer like him. For one thing women aren't physically built for farm labouring, so all you can do is fuss around, flapping bits of paper, talking about yields and hygiene and timekeeping, bossing us about and doing none of the graft. How can you expect us to respect a boss like that? You're not one of us.'

Although she'd been expecting an attack of this sort, part of Kate wanted to burst into tears and run away. The stress of the last few months had been immeasurable and she was working desperately hard to hold everything together. The stupidity and unfairness of his statement got under her skin...

But she was damned if she was going to let him see that. No way would she give him the satisfaction...

And she knew that it wasn't just the personal differences between her and Matt that had to be resolved, but the future of the farm, and *her* future that would depend on how she dealt with this. It was a test.

She was aware of all four men watching her.

'I'm sorry you feel like this, but I'm afraid if you want to stay on at Watersmeet, you have to accept the way things are. I can't help being a woman, but I'm the first to accept there's a lot I don't know. I'm learning, and one of the first things I've learned to appreciate is my workforce and their expertise. That's why I try to interfere as little as possible in the running of your herd. But, Matt, ultimately the farm is mine and *I'm* responsible for its success or failure. When I first told you I was taking it on, I asked for your support. I need it. That still stands. If I haven't got it, and if you feel you can't work with me, then I suppose I must accept your resignation.'

Matt started to bluster. 'There's two hundred cows in the High Acre herd. I know every single one. You couldn't manage them without me.'

'Difficult, I admit; but maybe I'd reduce the size, shut down the High Acre dairy, enlarge the size of John Potter's shed and increase his herd. It would make reasonable, economic sense at the moment.'

Matt gaped. 'You wouldn't? My herd was Dan's father's pride and joy and Dan himself expanded the dairy. You wouldn't get rid of the High Acre herd?'

'I wouldn't want to, but it depends on having a good stockman. There's no room for sentiment in farming, as you'd be the first to say. You don't have to make a decision now, but if you're going to leave, I'd like to know by the end of the month.'

She turned to leave. 'Ted,' she said crisply, 'I'd like a word when you've got a moment.'

By the time she reached the farmhouse kitchen, she was trembling from head to foot. It was in this state that Ted found her.

'Well done, Kate,' he said, putting the kettle on the hob. 'You handled that just right.'

'But supposing Matt gives in his notice? How will we cope?'

'We'll manage, as you said. Combining the herds was an option Dan once considered. But I don't think Matt will hand in his notice. Suggesting John Potter might take over some of his cows was masterly. I don't think you'll have any more trouble from him. You're the boss; you've demonstrated that by standing up to him. Now, here's your tea. Don't let it get cold, like you always do.'

He sat down and looked at her. 'So, what was it you wanted to see me about?'

Without going into any detail, Kate asked him what he

knew of the farm review, whether there had been a report, and if there had been, what the recommendations were and whether Dan had acted on them.

Ted sipped his tea and reflected, 'There *was* a report. I remember Dan saying he'd received it and I must admit I was a bit puzzled when he made no further reference to it. The agent had been on the farm for a few days and had made everything his business. Certainly made the men uneasy. We knew we needed to do something and it seemed we were in for a radical shake-up. As you know, the last few years have seen a significant drop in the farm's income. But we were busy trying to salvage what we could of a disastrous harvest and it slipped my mind until much later. I asked him about it, but he wouldn't discuss it.'

'But he always discussed everything with you. Didn't he even give it to you to read?'

'No. I suggested it but he was adamant it would be a waste of my time. The proposals were "inappropriate", that was his word. Inappropriate. It had been a waste of time and money, and that was the end of it. There was no arguing with him. You know how stubborn Dan could be.'

Kate sipped her tea, fighting back her sorrow. 'I had thought we shared everything, but I am coming to realise that Dan wasn't good at sharing problems if he thought there was nothing to be done. Maybe that's why he didn't show you the report. He certainly didn't mention it to me. Worse, he didn't tell me how bad the farm's finances were…'

'He wouldn't want to worry you, Kate.'

'So did he keep other things from me?' This particular thought had become a major preoccupation. 'We've staggered from one crisis to another… Did Dan…was there a time, last year for example, when Dan seriously thought we might lose the herds?'

Ted replied slowly, 'We had our moments…'

That evening Kate decided to tackle the piles of paper on Dan's desk. He had no particular filing system so reports, catalogues, forms, letters, invoices, magazines and newspapers were all mixed together in various teetering piles, one of which had collapsed and cascaded down the back of the desk.

She started sorting.

By the time she had cleared a couple of the worst piles it was nearly midnight, but she'd found the farm report, and a half-completed questionnaire called 'Stress in Farming'.

Too weary even to flick through them, she placed them on one side to look at when she had the time, for she had other, more pressing priorities.

The next day was Ben's birthday. He'd become listless in the days leading up to it and wouldn't enter into any discussions about what he might like to do.

'It's almost as if by looking forward to it, or enjoying his birthday, he feels he's being disloyal to Dan,' Kate told Max when he phoned to ask about Ben's present. 'We've always had a party for him and his chums. Last year they had a great game of hide-and-seek in one of the empty barns, and the party finished with Dan letting off some fireworks. This year he says he doesn't want anyone to come. I can't help feeling that doing nothing, he's going to miss Dan all the more.'

'You can't push it, Kate. If that's what he wants then keep it quiet. Why don't you promise him a rain-check and plan a treat for him nearer Christmas?'

While the children were at school, Kate baked a birthday cake in the shape of Spiderman. Putting the final touches to the icing, she heard the roar of a powerful car engine in the yard. Seconds later, Max appeared in the kitchen, carrying a brightly wrapped box.

She greeted him, amazed. 'Max, what on earth are you doing here?'

Kissing her cheek, he grinned, 'I've decided it's time to take my role as godfather seriously. I thought, if it's all right with you, I'd pick the children up from school, along with Ben's bosom buddy, Timmy whatsisname…'

'Tommy. Tommy Harrington.'

'That's the one…bring them back here for tea and then take the two boys bowling.'

'But Ben's never been bowling in his life.'

'Which is why I thought of it. Something completely different, and he's nine today; old enough to try it, although I think Rosie is too small to…'

'Don't worry about Rosie, I'll do something with her. Max, you're brilliant. He won't have time to think and he wouldn't say no to you. I'll phone Tommy's mother right now, then contact the school and let them know a stranger in an old Jag is going to sweep the children away.'

Ben returned from bowling, flushed with pride at a lucky double-strike and Kate silently blessed Max for his exuberant spontaneity.

At his suggestion, Polly put the children to bed and he took Kate out for a meal in Summerbridge.

'It's not only Ben who's in need of the occasional treat,' he said firmly. 'When did you last have one? Come on, Kate. You're going to have to learn how to play again. How can the children believe it's all right to have fun if you don't?'

So, what with one thing and another, and wary of what she

234

might learn from those particular documents, a few days passed before she returned to them.

She tackled the questionnaire first.

According to the date on an explanatory letter tucked inside the form, he'd received it in 1996. So, she reasoned, if Dan filled the form in then, it might give her some idea of his state of mind.

But Dan had completed it so patchily, it told her little: he'd ticked 'yes' against 'Do you have any financial problems', but not expanded on his answer. A tick for 'Made worse' against 'Financial situation affected by changes in agriculture policy or new legislation'; he'd ticked 'yes, have problems' to all the questions relating to paperwork. A tick for having been drenched in organophosphates; a tick for shotgun, but nothing in the section beginning with 'Is there anyone you can confide in or share your worries with?'

She struggled with this one. Did it mean Dan hadn't felt he could confide in her? Admittedly she'd not taken an active interest in the farm, but she'd listened to him, talked things over, encouraged him to share problems...hadn't she? And anyway, she wasn't the only one he could turn to... His mother shared most things with him. And Ted. Ted had always been there for Dan. Dan had told her so often enough.

Some two years ago, he'd brought the subject up. She had a clear recollection of the conversation because it had come from out of the blue...

The children asleep, they'd curled up together on the sofa to watch television. It was an indifferent murder mystery; she was half-asleep when Dan suddenly said, 'I don't know what I would do without Ted, Kate. He's as much part of this place as I am.'

She remembered the vehemence in his voice. 'Why, what's happened? Ted isn't leaving is he?'

'No, no, it's not that. It's just that… It's nothing really. I just started thinking how much I owe him. How much he's always been here for me. He was fantastic to me when I was little, Kate. And when Dad died, we could've gone to pieces. I was only nineteen and just not ready to take over. Poor old Mum was heartbroken, but Ted kept us going. He made sure I went to college, and helped Mum to set up her cheese business. And then, when I came back, all eager and cocky to show the world I'd all the answers to modern agriculture, he gave me plenty of rope, but kept a hand on it to make sure I didn't hang myself. How can anyone set a value on that?'

'Who's asking you to?' she'd asked, puzzled by his depressed air.

He'd deflected her question and the subject was dropped.

She put the questionnaire on one side, resolving to send for a copy of the survey. Although Dan had not completed it, it was possible the research's findings might be helpful.

She picked up the farm report. The name of the agricultural advisers was embossed on the cover. It was glossy, extensive, and comprehensive. A lot of time and money had gone into its compilation. Not something to be easily ignored.

When she had finished reading it, she sat and stared, unseeing, into the dark recesses of the room.

'Dan,' she whispered, 'Oh, Dan… Why didn't you tell me?'

The document was very thorough. The entire operation of the farm had been subjected to the minutest scrutiny. Seeking to secure a prosperous future for Watersmeet, its recommendations were precise and unequivocal.

The sheep should go; the upland pasture amalgamated,

ploughed, treated with chemicals to counteract the poverty of the soil, and sown with flax or oilseed rape; the cereals should be put out to tender with a contractor; Woodside Farm brought up to scratch and sold, or developed in some other way; one milking parlour to be closed, the other expanded.

Although Watersmeet was a large farm, its future prosperity was compromised by the size of its wages bill. On this, the report was emphatic.

One stockman was to be made redundant (the report recommended John Potter because his severance pay would be less).

And the remaining personnel could absorb the farm manager's role.

In other words, Ted should be made redundant.

24

Frank

They had made their nests underneath the old chicken house and were breeding fast. He knew a big female could produce up to fifty young in a year and he had spotted one or two big ones.

It was midday; the rats would be at their most somnolent. He had worked fast and had been round the building, stopping up the entrances to the burrows until, as far as he knew, there was but one way left into their underground colony.

He had given his fitchers no food for a couple of days and they were in a mean mood. He had bred them for this purpose. His ferrets would be no match for an angry rat, but these... Their teeth were razor sharp and they were very aggressive.

He lifted them, one at a time out of their boxes, holding them by the scruff of their necks, whispering to them as he set them at the hole's entrance, let them go, then picked up his spade and waited.

It wasn't long till the first rat, screaming with rage and terror, shot out and was reduced in an instant to a flattened bloody mess. Another followed and met the same fate, then another, and another. He slammed his spade down again and again with grim relish, till the rats stopped coming and the yard around him, and his body, hands and face, were spattered with blood and brown fur.

25

Dan

1999

'Yeah – cheers, Max, see ya.' Dan put down the phone and pulled a face at Kate. 'No, Mary's not with him.'

'You didn't let on that anything's wrong, did you?'

'Lord, no. I was the soul of tact. He didn't suspect a thing. Sent you and the kids his love and says he plans to come down one weekend soon and show off his latest acquisition, but he wasn't clear whether it was another old Jag or a new girlfriend.'

Dan grinned, but Kate was not amused.

'This is serious, Dan. Nobody knows where she is. I've drawn a complete blank with her friends. Most of them don't seem to have seen her for ages. She's cut herself off from everybody. Maybe Polly will get somewhere.'

But Polly had no better success, and after a few days had passed with no news, the three sat in the kitchen discussing what to do next.

'There's no help for it,' sighed Polly. 'We've got to go to the police, and the Salvation Army. They'll be discreet. They're all too used to dealing with cases like this. If Mary and Toby are in trouble, they will find her far more quickly than we can.'

Another week passed.

Dan put the farm report aside. It didn't seem so important in the present crisis. He didn't have to make any decisions immediately and he knew he wasn't going to show it to Ted.

Ted did enquire about it but he fobbed him off with some vague excuse. Ted was annoyed, he knew, but it couldn't be helped, and with Kate so worried about Mary, he didn't want to distract her with other concerns. Those could wait.

Then Max phoned.

'Where's Mary?' Max came straight to the point. 'What's going on, Dan? I thought it was a bit odd when you phoned me for no obvious reason, and wittered on about Mary. Now I've had my mother, phoning from Hong Kong, fretting because she hasn't heard from her and can't get her on the phone. I tried and got a recorded message. So I called round there this morning, early, on my way to work, and got hold of Clive. He seemed bloody furtive and muttered something about her having gone to stay with her cousins, which I took to mean you. Is she with you?'

'Er…no… No, she's not.'

'Then where the devil is she? What's going on, Dan?'

Dan floundered, but it was impossible to conceal his concern from Max.

'What do you mean she's gone missing? What the hell are you talking about? What's going on?'

'Max, I don't know, I really don't know. But Clive's not… He's not easy and I think… Mary's had a bit of trouble. She's frightened of him, Max. She's not been happy for ages, and…'

'How do you know this and not me? She's my sister, for

241

Christ sake, Dan, not yours. Why haven't you told me this before?'

By the time their conversation had progressed much further, Max was beside himself with rage, and his anger was as much directed at Dan as it was at Clive.

He tried to explain to Max that Mary had sworn him to secrecy, but it cut no ice.

Dan started to lose his patience. 'Max, it's all very well you getting on your high horse, but for the last few years she's hardly confided in me, or Kate. It could be that we're jumping to totally the wrong conclusion.

'Of course she wouldn't confide in you or Kate. It would have made things worse for her... There you both are, playing happy families, and she's had to live with that...that bastard. You should've told me. She's my sister. If I'd challenged her she'd have told *me*. I'd have sorted out that miserable, cowardly weasel once and for all...'

'That's what she was afraid of. She didn't want that. Believe me, I've tried to make her see what a nasty piece of work he is, but she would have nothing of it...'

'So you *did* nothing, just let her put up with it and didn't tell me. Too bloody busy getting on with the good life and not giving a shit about what might be happening...'

Dan finally lost his temper. The call deteriorated into a shouting match, with Max finally slamming down the phone.

'Well that's not going to help find Mary, is it?' Kate was exasperated. 'We don't want him crashing around making things worse. I know you would both leap at the chance of thumping Clive, but Mary and Toby have to come first.'

Dan, exhausted by it all, listened as she phoned Max back, calmed him down, and talked at length about what they'd done and what could be done to find his sister. When she finally put the phone down she came over to him and ruffled his hair.

'Don't be angry with Max, darling. He's as angry with himself for not having realised something was wrong, as he is with us for not having shared it with him.'

A soggy October became an even wetter November. The seasonal gales ruthlessly uprooted diseased and vulnerable trees, stripped the woods prematurely of their autumn glory, and clogged the drains and ditches with piles of blackened, moldering leaves.

During the course of one night the river flooded. From their bedroom window the following morning, Ben and Rosie gazed awestruck at a transformed landscape. A flock of terns was swimming on a lake that had been the vegetable garden. In the front of the house, the little footbridge at the garden gate had disappeared under the rushing water. The valley was under water in both directions. Only the line of willows and alders, and the parapet of the road bridge, gave any clue as to the river's course.

'Yippee, we're marooned,' shouted Ben. 'Look at all that water. I won't be able to get to school... Come on Rosie, let's put our wellies on an' see how deep it is. Look, there's Gran. She can't get across into the yard!'

Ben's excitement was not shared by his family.

Kate fretted because Muriel was going into hospital for some tests and she'd promised to lend her a particular book. Dan was anxious because, inevitably, extreme weather conditions meant trouble. And unable to cross the flood, Polly had to retreat to get her car and drive the long way round on a back lane which meant she was late for work, as was Colin. Brenda didn't put in an appearance at all. Polly was annoyed, and over lunch, grumbled about Brenda's unreliability.

243

Dan, not feeling very sympathetic, snapped, 'Well, Mum, you knew that when you took her on. If she's that bad, you should sack her and save the money we're wasting on her salary. We're not a charity. I don't know why you put yourself out for her in the first place, you get precious little thanks for it.'

'Because Dan, although we are not a charity, we can afford to be charitable.' Polly reproved. 'Brenda needs a job, if only to keep her from under Lizzie's feet, and you know how difficult it was for her to find any work around here.'

'That's because prospective employers recognised her for what she is – trouble! I know, I know…it's for Lizzie's sake. But, as I constantly tell you, Mum, she's a tricky customer, and she'll take you for a ride rather than show any gratitude.'

Getting up to put the kettle on, Kate glanced out of the kitchen window.

'There's a car coming down the hill. Perhaps Matt's told her the water's receded so she's got a lift in…'

'And pigs might fly!'

Kate cast him a look, which Dan recognised as a best-leave-him-alone-when-he's-in-a-grump look. It was true. He was short-tempered, but he couldn't help it. The weather; not being able to discuss the farm report with anyone; the prolonged silence from Mary with the resulting tension in all three of them, made it impossible for him to feel anything like his normal self.

'If only Mary would phone,' he thought for the umpteenth time. 'Where is she? She must know we've found out she's missing, and are worried sick. So why hasn't she got in touch?'

There was a light tap on the door to the yard and as it opened, he looked up, expecting Ted.

His jaw dropped. He half-rose and in his amazement he

could only squeak, 'Mary!'

Kate turned, dropped the teapot, and rushed to hug Mary with an inarticulate cry.

Polly sprang to her feet, half-sobbing, 'Mary, oh Mary, you're safe. Thank God. Thank God!'

After a lot of hugging and crying, Dan cleared the broken teapot while Kate found another and made them all tea. And then they sat and listened as Mary slowly, diffidently, her voice low and sad, told her tale.

'It's hard to know where to start… After Toby was born, everything seemed all right. We were happy. Clive was so proud of Toby and so kind and thoughtful to me. But then, after about, oh, three or four months, things seemed to change, and Clive became more and more…well…difficult. I thought at first, with the baby, he wasn't getting enough sleep, but I was just making excuses. As Toby got older, he got worse…'

'Worse? What do you mean, worse. Violent?' Dan frowned.

'No, not physically violent, Dan, but he'd have terrible moods when either he would lapse into long, cold silences, or he'd find fault with everything I did, shouting and raging at me.'

'As bad as before Toby was born?' asked Polly,

'Worse, I think. At first, he was careful not to upset Toby, but more recently, he didn't seem to care whether Toby was there or not.'

Looking at her closely, Dan could see Mary's face was drawn and thin, with dark shadows under her eyes. 'Go on,' he said gently.

'His rages were so intense, so violent; they were terrifying,' Mary continued. 'At first they followed the same pattern as before and he'd be terribly contrite afterwards. Not only would he apologise, but he'd shower me with treats and surprises. It

245

was impossible not to forgive him, or to accept his explanation that these mood swings were due to pressure of work.'

'Do you think alcohol had anything to do with it?' asked Polly. 'He drinks wine, doesn't he, as part of his job?'

'No, I really don't think so. He only drank as much wine as the job required and no more, and he didn't drink much at home.' She looked wearily at them. 'As time went by and he grew more senior in the firm, the mood swings became more frequent and more severe. I...I started to become frightened.' She hesitated. 'I thought about telling you, but I knew what you'd say. I'd tried to leave him after one particularly bad episode, but he collapsed in tears, saying me and Toby were his only reason for living. He was in such a state, I just couldn't go.'

Kate pulled a face. 'It sounds like...well, perhaps he needs help of some sort. Oh Mary, if only you'd told us!'

Dan squeezed his cousin's hand. 'So what happened? You've put up with so much, for so long, what happened to finally make you leave?'

'It was shortly after we'd been to lunch with Aunt Meg. You know he was always very impatient with my friends and relations; after this particular visit, he became cold and aggressive, and over the days that followed, his mood got worse. It got to the point where I dreaded his return home from work. Worse, Toby became tearful and started to play up about going to school.

'Then, one morning, Toby threw a tantrum and refused to leave the house. Clive... Clive smacked him hard, threw him into the car and drove him to school.' Mary broke off, swallowed hard and began again, her voice trembling. 'When I picked Toby up after school, he was pale and nervous and then I discovered my poor little boy had soiled himself. I knew

Clive was going to be late back, but that whole evening Toby clung to my side, jumping at every unexpected noise. I knew we were both waiting for the sound of Clive's key in the door.

'Seeing Toby in that state – white and frightened – I realised fully, for the first time, I wasn't the only victim, and whatever Clive said, I couldn't trust him not to hurt Toby. It was an awful moment. I decided we had to leave, then and there. I knew if I waited to tell Clive I was going, he would do everything to persuade me not to go and I might give in. I couldn't take the risk. So I packed a suitcase, took what money I could find, and went.'

'Why didn't you phone us? Why didn't you come here? We'd have looked after you.'

'I was going to, Dan. I even got as far as getting on the train.'

'Then why didn't you, darling? You knew you could trust us not to tell Clive you were here?' Polly said sadly.

'Oh Aunt Polly, I can't tell you how much I wanted to be here, safe in Watersmeet with you, but during the journey to Bath, I had time to think things through; to weigh up the consequences of what I'd done, and to decide what would be best to do next. It was painful, but I decided it would be better *not* to come to you. It would be the first place Clive would look. You'd be in an impossible position and I didn't want to risk him coming here and persuading me to go back. I realised the situation would be the same with anybody I knew, which is why I didn't want you to know where we were.'

'But we could have protected you; what the hell are families for?'

Mary gave Dan a weak smile. 'And I've got one of the best, I know that; but it was important for me to sort things out, on my own.'

'So what did you do?' asked Kate. 'Where did you go?'

'We stayed on the train until Bristol. The train got in very late and I… I wasn't thinking straight, I confess. I just didn't know what to do next. Toby was exhausted, so I found a bench and tried to settle him down to sleep. There was…there was a bit of trouble with some drunks and when the police arrived, they took me and Toby to a refuge. We've been there ever since.'

'Where's Toby now?' asked Polly. 'How is he?'

For the first time, Mary smiled. 'He's at school and then he's going to play at a friend's house. He's a changed person already, Aunt Polly. He's stopped wetting his bed, he runs around with the other kids at the refuge, he shouts and laughs and gets filthy. I didn't realise how much the quiet, neat, timid little boy was a consequence of living with Clive.'

Dan hurried across the yard to meet Ted. He was late and he hated keeping Ted waiting. The rain continued to sheet down, but he hardly noticed. Despite the enormous relief of Mary's return, he felt knackered. He would like to have crawled into bed, but that was not an option. In the repairs barn, Ted was on the phone and Dan could tell from the grim set of his mouth that all was not well.

Dan's apology and explanation were cut short. 'Good. I'm glad to hear about Mary. That'll be a weight off all your minds. Dan, we've got to get up to High Acres. The yard has flooded and from the sound of it, a fair bit of slurry's been carried down to the river.'

Dan cursed, loud and strong. The cleanliness of the dairy yard was the stockman's responsibility, but if slurry, flood or no flood, had contaminated the river, he would be the one faced with a hefty fine.

The relentless rainfall had given birth to a new spring above

High Acre. This had bubbled its way across the yard to join the river and taken with it a load of farmyard detritus. It didn't help that Matt had fallen behind with his routine and an angry exchange of words took place between the three men, fighting up to their knees in the mucky flood to minimise the damage, secure the slurry pit, and divert the new stream.

It was very late when he got back to the house, filthy and hungry. The children were in bed and Kate was asleep on the sofa. His dinner, left to keep warm in the bottom of the oven, had dried and shrivelled. He gloomily stepped out of his filthy overalls, made himself a cheese sandwich and went to his study.

The report lay on his desk, glossy, expensive, reproachful. He slumped in his chair, picked it up and flicked through the pages. No easy answers there. He touched his computer and it sprang to life. He had one email, from Steven Kelner:

Hi Dan, you should have had a chance to read the report by now. Any thoughts? Give me a ring and we can discuss a course of action.

'Oh no, we bloody well won't,' said Dan aloud. '*I've* got to sort this one out… Me, not you, not anyone else.' And he pushed the report out of sight, under a pile of papers at the back of the desk.

He had never known such weariness. He slumped forward onto the desk and closed his eyes. Thoughts jostled in his over-tired brain: here he was at the age of 34, lovely wife, lovely kids, beautiful old home, everything he had ever dreamed of and everything he thought would be his, safe and secure for all time. But it wasn't. Nothing was really safe and secure.

He thought of Mary and her flight into the night, and felt a great sense of shame. He hadn't really believed she was in

249

danger, but as the days had lengthened into weeks without any word from her, he had become increasingly concerned, and after his spat with Max, feelings of guilt had set in. He couldn't help thinking he should have done more for Mary. They'd always been close, but when they'd both got married, he'd allowed that relationship to slip. He'd been so preoccupied with Kate, his children, and the farm, it had been convenient for him to take her version of life with Clive at face value. He'd let her down. Without thinking about it, he had let her down.

And wasn't he letting down everyone who depended on him? He'd always believed he was a good farmer. It was something he did naturally, without thinking too deeply about it. But perhaps he was deceiving himself. After all, the proof of the pudding... Under his care, the farm was beginning to struggle. They might even go bankrupt. His father had left him a healthy enterprise. Now...

He couldn't see his way forward. He wasn't going to abandon his principles and sack Ted and John Potter, or turn the farm into an agro-chemical business. If only there was someone he could share this with, someone not involved but who would understand where he was coming from. Steven Kelner had his uses, but he was not a farmer so he could never really understand the layers of history, the loyalties, the traditions that made Watersmeet so much more than just a business.

For the first time in ages he really missed Joe, and the image of that shuffling figure flitted across his mind. Could Joe really have sunk that low? And if that could happen to Joe, and if Mary could end up homeless in a refuge, then what might Fate have in store for him?

He couldn't bear the thought of losing Watersmeet, or Kate, or the children. But he might be helpless to do anything to prevent such disasters. The things he held dear, his very existence at Watersmeet, all seemed so vulnerable. And it was up to him. All up to him.

He switched off the lamp and slumped back in his chair. Flurries of raindrops threw themselves against the window-pane, coursing down in rapid, uneven rivulets.

He'd never questioned his strength to plough on, his ability to find solutions to most problems. But now... Now his confidence had been shaken and looking into the future, he felt afraid.

26

Kate

2001

Kate brooded over the farm report for several days before she slowly, reluctantly, came to the conclusion that its recommendations were not unreasonable. The farm could not continue operating as it had done. Even with the injection of capital it had been given after Dan's death, she knew they were only buying time. If she wasn't going to find herself in the same position as Dan in a few years, things had to change. But repelled by the report's solutions, she decided there had to be other ways of meeting the challenge.

She presented the problem to Polly and Ted at their weekly meeting.

'So what are you proposing?' Ted's expression was neutral. 'I don't wish to be a damp squib, Girlie, but you haven't been at the helm for very long. Wouldn't it be better to wait until you've had a bit more experience on the job?'

'I'm not proposing changing anything right now, Ted, but

we've got to start thinking about the future and thinking about it in perhaps…well, perhaps in a more creative way. If, for example, we decided to go organic, that's going to take time, but we could start checking it out now, couldn't we? It would be such a big change we'd need to look at all the implications. But from what I understand, organic farming does seem to be the only area that's growing in a dwindling marketplace. We'd be daft not to consider it. And there are other things we might do.'

'Like what?'

'Well, like putting our milk into producing our own products instead of selling it on. Look how well Polly's cheese is doing… but it's so small-scale. We could produce more varieties. We could sell butter, cream, yoghurt, ice cream…'

Polly smiled, 'But I want to retire, Kate. Are *you* going to take this on?'

'If that's what we decide, then I would. But I'm not going to impose anything on either of you. Why don't we think about it and perhaps come up with other ideas. What about Woodside, for example?'

'What about Woodside?'

'You've said often enough, Ted, that we've got to do something to stop it going to ruin. I know Dan tacitly allowed Frank to be left alone, but he could live for another forty years…'

'Surely you not thinking of evicting Frank, Kate?' Polly looked startled.

'I'm not ruling anything out,' Kate replied. 'I just think we need to make the best of *all* our assets, otherwise those assets will trickle away before we realise it. That was the prospect Dan was facing.' She faltered. 'His death has given the farm a second chance. I don't want to let him down.'

There was a moment's silence.

Ted cleared his throat. 'Happen you're right. Diversify to survive, that's what we're told, isn't it? It won't be the be-all-and-end-all, mind, but you've got a point, we mustn't be too stuck in our ways. Let's think on it.'

Kate knew she was adding to the pressure of their workload. She worried constantly that, without Dan, they all had to do so much more to cover everything. She was doing her best, but she was the first to admit that, as an apprentice, she was not much of an asset.

To her great relief, Matt told her he was staying, saying he 'owed it to Dan, and to Dan's dad', to take care of the herd they had so carefully nurtured. However he did not welcome her presence in his parlour and by common consent, John Potter undertook to teach her about the dairy side of the business.

One cold November morning, she went out with Ted to walk the boundary of the farm's estate, looking at the fields and checking the fences and hedgerows.

It was not a prepossessing morning. The cloud was low and sullen, and visibility was limited. The trees and hedges loomed out of the mist, garlanded with spiders' webs strung with droplets. The ground was heavy with damp and Kate's boots quickly clogged up with mud, making it hard for her to keep pace with Ted's long stride.

As they walked, he pointed out the damage done by deer, rabbits, moles, and the birds, of which the main culprits were pigeons, rooks, crows and magpies. He talked about game-keeping and showed her the cover laid at the edge of the fields and woods for pheasants; pointed out badger sets, rabbit warrens, and the runs in hedges used by small animals. On one such run they found a snare carefully concealed in the hedgerow.

Ted was angry. 'Cruel things, these, Kate. Any animal putting its head in this noose suffers badly. But come to think of it, there's little about a poacher's craft that isn't vicious.'

'Do we have a lot of trouble with poachers?'

'It's a running sore for everyone. Got so bad last summer that we had Ken Snook on to us; he was losing that many birds it was getting out of control.'

'Ken Snook?'

'William Etheridge's game-keeper. He's a good man, if a little slow. You know Mr Etheridge pays us for the shooting rights over Sparrows Woods, don't you? Any pheasants are his. He pays us to put in this ground cover and we maintain the woodland.'

'Why don't we have our own game-keeper? Surely there's enough work for one?'

'Maybe. Dan's father was not interested in shooting. Josh's father was the gamekeeper here when I arrived, but he died shortly after. I had no skills in that direction at all. It was a question of getting a new keeper and giving me my cards, or doing without one. Mr Maddicott decided he could do without a keeper. The old Mr Etheridge was a keen 'huntin-n-shootin' man and pleased to be able to extend his fiefdom. It suits us the way it is at the moment. Ken helps us keep the rabbit population under control and shoots the odd pesky deer, which helps offset expenses.'

'I suppose if poachers confined themselves to rabbit and deer, you wouldn't object to them so much?'

'I don't like poachers. They're thieves by another name, and the animals and birds they steal and sell for profit, on the whole, have bad deaths.'

'So what happened last summer, when Ken Snook

255

complained?'

'Dan said he'd deal with it; it was his responsibility. And I guess he did, because the poaching appeared to stop.' He looked grimly at the snare in his hands. 'Looks like he's up to his old tricks again.'

'Who is "he"?'

Ted sighed, his breath hanging heavily on the air. 'Why, none other than your favourite tenant, Frank Leach.'

'Him! Why does he always turn up like the proverbial bad penny?'

Ted merely grunted and they walked on. He pointed out the features of the fields and described their use; which crops were going where, and the land to be used for pasture or earmarked for set-aside. Kate listened attentively, but when he fell silent, her thoughts returned to her tenant.

A few days later, she paid a visit to the family solicitors, Crouch and Lovell.

The firm had been the Maddicotts' solicitors since the dawn of time and there was very little that David Lovell, the senior partner, didn't know about the affairs of Watersmeet. She was disappointed, therefore, to discover he had retired shortly after Dan's death and that her appointment was with his son.

Nicholas Lovell was just a little older than she was, the only surviving member of the Lovell-Crouch dynasty. Dan had liked him and had told Kate he much preferred to deal with him rather than his more formal father.

Kate had only ever met Nicholas at her wedding. He was a short, thin man dressed in the ubiquitous grey suit, brightened by a dark cherry-red felt waistcoat. His hair was receding and he affected a pair of half glasses perched on the end of his nose, which gave him a faintly quizzical expression. He'd inherited his father's office and the room was full of books, papers, files, and heavy old furniture. On his desk were large cheerful photographs of his wife and two children, the only splash of colour and modernity in the Dickensian gloom.

He was pleasant and helpful but it was apparent he'd seen little of Dan in the last few years. Their business concluded, she was about to take her leave when he put his hand on her arm and said with warmth, 'Anything I can do to help, Kate... please, just ask.'

She was touched. 'There is something, Nick. It's this: we know Dan was under a lot of financial pressure before he died; so what puzzles me is the whole business of Woodside Farm. The farm's been going to rack and ruin for a long time, but he wouldn't give Frank notice to remedy, let alone to quit. If he had, then the farm could have been sold, or developed in some way, which would have helped relieve our finances, surely? Can you tell me what exactly is the nature of that tenancy? Dan never really talked about it, and Polly doesn't seem to know. But if it's possible after all this time, *I'd* like to know.'

'I'll do my best to find out for you. We're in the process of computerising all our clients' files and I'll have to do some delving in dusty boxes for this. It might take a little time, so I'll give you a ring when I've found the answer. I know the old story of course, but not the actual detail. It will be interesting to find out. Anything else while I'm opening the archives?'

'No, I can't think of anything immediately... Oh, yes. It's rather trivial, but Dan once told me his grandmother, Rose Maddicott, wrote in her will that he was to read certain of her diaries. I'd love to know which ones they were.'

Kate's curiosity about these diaries had been re-awakened one evening when, too tired to write much to Dan, she'd idly picked one of the diaries off the shelf.

The handwriting was fine but firm and after some concentration, Kate had become absorbed in the daily grind of a young farmer's wife in the Nineteen-Thirties. After that first taste, she started to dip into them regularly. They fascinated her. Full of minutiae, opinions, happenings both big and small, and tantalising references to members of Dan's family who had only existed for her before in photographs and odd memories. It was an extraordinary record, but the thought of Dan struggling to read them amused her. All the domestic detail, interesting though it was, would hardly make a riveting read for a busy farmer.

He had never told her which particular journals Rose had been so anxious for him to read. If she could read them herself, she thought, it might be one little mystery she could clear up.

It would also provide a welcome diversion from the difficulties she was facing elsewhere.

Richard Burbage, their accountant, was much less helpful than Nicholas. A tall, thin man, in his late forties, with an impatient manner, he had a rather dismissive way of talking to her.

He didn't know that Dan had taken out that particular life insurance policy. Why should he? Yes, the farm had not been doing too well, but that was to do with market prices and all farmers were going through tough times, so why should Watersmeet be different? Yes, it was feasible for Watersmeet to survive if their operations continued as before, but yes it would be better if they broadened their output and put more into producing, but no, he hadn't discussed this with Dan...

Dispirited, Kate returned home to face her next ordeal: a party being given by Joe's parents, Pete and Janet Warren, to celebrate the sale of Ashcroft Farm and their retirement.

258

Kate had initially decided not to go. She was very fond of the Warrens and sad to see them go, but she found it hard to accept invitations. She hated crying in front of people and found sympathy, almost inevitably, brought on the tears.

It was Ted who changed her mind. He never normally discussed her domestic arrangements or social life, so he took her completely by surprise when he offered to look after Ben and Rosie the night of the party.

'But I've decided not to go, Ted. It's very sweet of you to offer, but... Anyway, I thought you'd been invited too?'

'So I have, but if you'll forgive me for poking my nose in, Girlie, I think it would do the children good if you went. It's hard, I know, but life's got to carry on. If you don't allow yourself to have any fun, what are you saying to them?'

'You sound like Polly.'

'She talks a lot of sense. I know she wants to go to the party and I think it would do her a lot of good. But if you don't, then happen she will find reason not to herself. I know it won't be easy, but you're a brave person. If it's not for yourself, then go for her sake and for the children's.'

But it was with a sinking heart she went upstairs to get ready. Lizzie had arrived to babysit; Ted was waiting to escort her and Polly.

She stared at herself in the mirror. What on earth should she wear? She froze with indecision; the choice of dress became critical. If only she could pull on the pair of old jeans and shirt that had become her comfortable, not-having-to-bother clothes.

Dan had loved her to dress up. Last year they had gone to a huge New Year's Eve party to celebrate the Millennium and he had splashed out on a dress of soft red wool.

As she unhitched it from its hanger, she said softly to his

photograph on her dressing table, 'I'll wear this for you, Dan. You'll always be with me, be part of me. I love you.'

Downstairs, she found Ben absorbed in a Spiderman video that Lizzie had bought over, and Rosie in floods of tears. When the little girl saw her, she wept even more loudly and clung to Kate's leg.

Kate was alarmed. 'What's wrong?

'She don't want you to go to the party. She's just makin' a fuss,' replied Ben, his eyes glued to the screen.

'Perhaps I shouldn't go, I can't leave her like this.'

But Polly and Lizzie were firm, and so was Ben.

'No. You go, Mum. We'll be fine. Lizzie's promised to make us popcorn later. Don't take no notice of Rosie. She's pathetic!'

At which point, Rosie stopped wailing and started to pummel him. Reassured, Kate made a quick exit.

The party was well underway when they arrived. It appeared the whole neighbourhood had turned out to give the Warrens a good send off. Polly, a solicitous Ted at her elbow, was soon in the centre of an animated group. Kate was put at ease by the kindly warmth that greeted her, and plied with offers of drink, food, and conversation. Suddenly exhausted, she made her way to an emptier room. She found William there.

He was very quiet and seemed in low spirits. They chatted in a desultory fashion, but when she told him about her unhelpful conversation with Dan's accountant, he looked surprised. 'Didn't he at least give you the name of that financial adviser Dan went to see?'

Kate looked at him blankly. 'Financial adviser? I didn't know he had one. Wouldn't that be his accountant?'

'Those days are long gone. Accountants, these days, do the books, charge a fortune, and advise you to go to a financial adviser for everything else. Dan mentioned to me, the last time you came to dinner, that he was going to London on his accountant's recommendation, to see some fellow for financial advice. I was under the impression that you were going with him?'

A dim memory stirred. 'Now that you mention it… I didn't go, though, and Dan never really talked about it. He came back more excited about Ivan becoming a parliamentary candidate. But I know the farm report followed shortly after that…'

'Then get his name off Burbage; follow it up… There must have been some correspondence or emails between them.'

'Dan seems to have deleted his emails, but you're right, he must have discussed his situation with this man… I'm so stupid,' Kate frowned, annoyed with herself, 'how could I have completely forgotten about Dan going to London while *you* remember a chance conversation?'

'The day Muriel told me about her cancer, every little thing was thrown into sharp relief. I could probably recount, word for word, everything anyone said that evening.'

Kate stared, shocked. 'You mean we came to dinner the day she told you?'

'Yes. But you knew Muriel: she wasn't going to let a little thing like a death sentence put her off a dinner party. That's partly why I'm here tonight. Couldn't bear the thought of her ghost scolding me for choosing to stay at home.'

'Of course… She died two years ago today, didn't she, William? I'm so sorry. How could I have forgotten that?'

'Because, my dear Kate,' said William firmly, taking her empty glass, 'you've more than enough of your own sorrows to cope with. We're in danger of drowning in misery here and we can be sure neither of our partners would've approved. Come on, let's re-join the party and I'll find you another glass of wine.'

A week later Kate found herself sitting in a deep leather armchair in Steven Kelner's office.

He was as unlike a financial adviser as she could have imagined. Instead of a city whiz kid in a designer suit, a man in his early fifties, with a slightly military bearing, greeted her. His hair was thin, spread over his pate and held in place with a liberal smear of Brylcreem. He sported a thick, neatly trimmed, salt and pepper moustache, and wore a brass-buttoned blazer, with pressed grey flannels and a tie that looked as if it had originated from somewhere in the services. He was a plump man, with a florid face and gleaming brown button eyes. The scent of his aftershave, while not unpleasant, was prominent. His gestures were elegant and on his left hand he wore a heavy gold signet ring.

'He wouldn't be out of place in the men's department of John Lewis,' Kate thought. 'What on earth was Dan doing, consulting him?'

He'd not heard of Dan's death and was sensitively sympathetic.

It was a useful afternoon. Whatever Steven Kelner might have looked like, he had a shrewd mind.

He told her about Dan's first visit. 'He was concerned, but in my opinion, not unduly depressed, and it was a constructive meeting. There are a lot of assets tied up with the Watersmeet estate… A number of possible avenues suggested themselves, I made one or two recommendations and he left.'

'Was it you who suggested the farm report?'

'Yes. It seemed a good first step.'

'How did Dan react to the results?'

Steven Kelner pursed his lips and blew gently across the tips of his fingers. 'I don't think he liked the bulk of the report's recommendations; he told me later it had been a complete waste of time and money."

'Was it?'

Steven Kelner was unembarrassed. 'Not really. If he'd been a different sort of farmer, it might have been spot-on. As it was, it threw up one or two useful ideas Dan might have pursued. In the event, he didn't contact me for months after the report was completed. This is quite common though, Kate. The report hadn't delivered the solutions he wanted and he lost confidence in it, in me, and quite possibly in his ability to do anything to change the situation.'

Kate grappled with the implications of what he was saying.

'But he did contact you again? You said he consulted you a couple of times?'

'Yes, he did. Well into the year 2000, about May I think, but I can look it up on my file, if you like. I understand the dairy was beleaguered by further falls in milk prices and Dan felt that inaction on his part was no longer an option.'

'So what did you suggest?'

Steven Kelner rose to refer to his computer. He looked up from the screen. 'We divided the whole enterprise into three parts: the parts that Dan was prepared to change; those where he was doubtful; and those where, categorically, there would be no action. We had a long discussion and he left, saying he'd get back to me.'

'And did he?'

'Not immediately. But then I wasn't expecting him to. He made it clear he was entering a very busy phase and I'd asked him to collect together various bits and pieces of information relating to any pension plans, insurance, loans, mortgage, tenancies, that sort of thing. We finally had another meeting, our last in fact, at the end of October last year. In the New Year I wrote to him, outlining one or two ideas, but then I didn't hear from him until the early summer, by which time, I think, you were in the thick of this foot and mouth epidemic.'

Kate took a deep breath. 'This is difficult, I know, because you didn't really know Dan well, but…how did he seem?'

'Seem?'

'Yes. At the first meeting with you, you said he seemed concerned but not worried. Was he like that the second and third time, or more concerned? Did he seem…depressed to you?'

Steven Kelner gave her a keen look.

'Depressed? Yes, the last time I saw him, I think he was. The situation with the whole farming industry was getting him down. He said as much, and he told me that he felt it was becoming a struggle to survive.'

Kate felt the colour drain from her face and she shivered. This was too raw. But she knew she had to press on. And she had to be prepared for the worst…

Kelner leant forward and patted her hand.

'However, my dear, I don't think he was clinically depressed, if that's what you mean. I think the whole scenario at the time was getting him down. But you would know better than I… I didn't think he was the sort of person to lie down and give up. When we spoke again, in the late spring, he'd decided to pursue one or two ideas, which would have eased any pressing debt.'

'Was the life insurance your idea?'

'Yes. I know we were looking to cut costs, but it worried me he had neither a life insurance nor any pension plans in place. The business's major asset is the estate itself. To put it crudely, the house alone is worth a small fortune. One solution to the farm's financial problems would be to make that asset do a bit of work. But if he raised money by mortgaging Watersmeet, he needed to ensure that if anything happened to him, the house would be safe for you and the children.'

'I see,' said Kate slowly. 'But he didn't mortgage Watersmeet, and yet he took out the life insurance policy…'

'Yes, he did. I had urged him that it was in the family's best interests for that policy to exist, whether or not he mortgaged Watersmeet. Sensibly he took my advice. He didn't want to mortgage, so to fund the policy *and* to relieve the farm's financial difficulties, he decided to do something entirely different. This was why he phoned me last May. Quite frankly, I was surprised. It was something I'd suggested from the outset, but he'd always refused to consider. I'd been expecting him to get back to me when things had been set in motion.' He cleared his throat delicately. 'When did he take out the life insurance?'

'A month before he died, in June. He'd paid one premium.'

Steven Kelner pressed his fingers together and pursed his lips, his brow furrowed as he digested this piece of information.

Kate swallowed hard; she could see he was thrown. The conclusion seemed inescapable. Unless…unless the life insurance was part of a greater plan, interrupted by his premature death… She grasped this straw.

'What was it he was planning to do? What had you advised him to do that he had been so unwilling to consider earlier?'

'Get rid of your remaining tenant and develop or sell Woodside Farm. It's a valuable asset, not realising anything like its worth at the moment. The farm report highlighted that fact. Woodland, farmland, river frontage, farm buildings… there's a lot there. The level at which the rent is set is unrealistic. If he *had* sold, the money invested would have provided a useful income…funded a pension scheme…bailed out the farm. In my opinion it was the best solution, in spite of the difficulties he might expect from his tenant…'

Kate stared at him. 'Frank Leach? Dan was going to get rid of Frank Leach? Are you sure?'

'Certainly. He couldn't have been clearer. He wanted Frank Leach off his land before the end of the year.'

27

Frank

The feral cat screamed and spat at him, twisting this way and that in an effort to release his paw from the trap. The steel had bitten into his leg, now a mess of fur, bone and blood, but the pain, far from subduing the animal, seemed to aggravate his furious defiance.

His enemy lowered the shotgun and viewed the angry cat through narrowed eyes. 'Thee'se given Oi a lot of grief,' he said softly, 'so Oi's got a better plan for thee'.

With a swift, deft movement, he took the snarling creature by the scruff of its neck, released its mangled leg from the teeth of the trap and stuffed it into his leather poacher's bag.

The polecats' hutches had been built around a central run and the four fitches in their individual cages were restless, hungry and angry.

He emptied the snarling cat out of the bag into the middle of the exercise run, pulled up each of the hatches and watched as the four deadly foes, lethally territorial, rushed out to attack each other.

Finding an intruder, their line of attack changed and united they turned on it.

He crouched on the ground and watched, his face impassive.

The noise was bloodcurdling, the fight prolonged and furious. It wasn't one-sided. The feral cat put up a valiant fight, slashing and biting, inflicting some wounds on his opponents. But the four creatures had been bred as killers and the cat, outnumbered, eventually slumped, his eyes turned glassy and with one final mew, as he might have given as a kitten entering the world, he left it.

28

Dan

2000-1

'You'll be sorry you asked, Ivan,' Dan said mockingly. 'But since you have, I can tell you it's been one of the worst years I can remember.'

'Oh? That's bad news, Dan. In what way?'

The Dinsdale family, with Ivan, had come to Watersmeet for Christmas. He and Ivan were tackling the washing up after lunch on Boxing Day, when the rain clouds had parted long enough to make the idea of fresh air and exercise seem attractive.

Dan had chosen to stay behind and clear the dishes on the grounds that he'd had plenty of both already.

Ivan had offered to help, jumping at the chance of a few minutes' respite from the incessant chatter of Mrs Dinsdale. It gave Dan a golden opportunity to share his fears with a member of the family who would listen and understand.

Stacking plates in the dishwasher, he tried not to sound too desperate.

'This continuous rain, for one thing. The fields are waterlogged, we've had to re-sow the barley, and the silage yield is so poor we're going to have to buy in. It's the same for farmers everywhere… You can't do anything about the weather, but you've got to do something to help us, Ivan, the industry is nearly on its knees.'

'The weather is pulling everyone down. This year has…'

'Not only is the weather filthy,' Dan hurried on, wanting Ivan to hear the worst, 'but we're still suffering from the effects of BSE. We've had swine fever. And the price of milk has gone into freefall. D'you know I get 8p less for a litre of milk than we did six years ago, and we're talking high-quality here?'

Ivan looked sympathetic, but was silent.

Dan finished filling the dishwasher and turned on the taps in the sink. 'We'll have to wash these pans. Here, use this cloth to dry.'

He resumed his litany. 'Can you explain, Ivan, why it is we're paid our subsidies in euros? The pound's so strong it means they are worth less to us than to the Europeans, and yet we're all in the same marketplace. And to rub salt into the wound, I spend more time on paperwork than I do farming.' He chipped away at a burnt pan, then said, trying to keep his voice light, 'Sorry to go on about it, but quite frankly, any more disasters and I could go to the wall.'

But Ivan, drying the saucepan he'd picked up more thoroughly than he'd ever dried anything in his life, did not appear to hear the note of desperation in Dan's voice.

'I sympathise, Dan, I really do. I said when I first met you that I don't know why you do it and I still don't. The government won't *let* the farmers go to the wall, I'm sure of it. It's just that we're playing in a world market now and we can't afford to be sentimental. We can't cling on to traditional ways of doing things. It's harsh for those that do fail, but you once told me a strong wind brings down mainly old and diseased trees.'

He flapped his tea towel. 'I never understood why dishwashers are fine for plates and the easy stuff, but useless dealing with crusty pots and pans. A bit like us politicians, I suppose.' He gave a short, hesitant laugh, 'I don't know, Dan. I'm only a backbencher, and a very new one at that, but I've faith in the direction the government is going *and* its commitment to ordinary people. We won't ditch the farmers, like Thatcher did the miners. You'll survive, I'm sure of it.'

Dan stared at him for a moment then turned back to the sink. 'I hope you're right.'

He was so disappointed.

Despite their different backgrounds and temperaments, they had become good friends over the ten years since they met. When Ivan stood as a candidate in a by-election, Dan had taken the night off and gone with Kate, to lend moral support during the long night of the count. He had been so excited when Ivan was elected, and although he knew it was incredibly naïve, he felt, somehow, he'd been given a direct line to Westminster.

He was not alone. When the locals heard that Dan's brother-in-law had been elected as an MP, albeit for the 'wrong' party, Dan had received quite a few requests for help. He'd passed them on and Ivan, ever courteous, promised to see what he could do, but little if anything happened.

There was a growing rift, a disconnection, between town and country. Dan was increasingly aware of it. It went deeper than the age-old arguments over blood sports. It was a sense of powerlessness, of not being heard, of not being valued any longer.

He had hoped to be able to share some of this with Ivan, hoping Ivan would bring this state of affairs to the attention of his political masters. But after his election, Ivan had become even busier and they met infrequently.

Hearing that he and Emily were coming for Christmas, Dan had been pleased. Over the years he found Kate's mother increasingly difficult to stomach and he'd been dreading the prolonged contact of Christmas. Ivan being there to share the burden was a great consolation. But more important had been the thought he'd be able to confide in him; but the moment had come and gone and it just hadn't happened.

He looked much the same, however, Dan, inspecting him more closely, saw that the startling pallor of his skin had an unhealthy luminous tinge, silver streaks were evident in his black hair, and the burning intensity of his gaze seemed dulled.

'I suppose it must seem as if we farmers are always grumbling,' he said lightly. 'Goes with the job. How are things with you, Ivan?'

'Exciting. Exhausting. Frustrating. Demanding. Never a moment to myself; a bit like you in a way, Dan. When I first thought of standing, I was so excited... So driven by what I was going to do... Fired by what the party could achieve in power, and how *I* could make a contribution to that...'

'And now?'

'Oh I'm still fired, still driven; but it's like I've got to learn to walk all over again and I fall over myself with impatience. There is so much red tape, so much protocol... So many people resistant to change, *real* change: who can't see, won't see the best way forward. It's terribly frustrating, Dan. But I'm learning patience. We'll probably have an election this year and I'm determined to increase my majority and once that happens,' his eyes flashed, 'then I'll make sure I'm not ignored. I want a

272

government post, and I'll do battle for it.'

'And how is Emily coping with all this excitement?'

The animation faded from Ivan's face. 'Oh you know Emily,' he said casually. 'She's her own person. When she does make an appearance the attention is very gratifying. But she's busy with her gallery, her commissions, and her slaves. You've no idea how honoured you are that she's here, but she's insisting we go back tomorrow. I tell you, Dan, it's almost got to a point where even Flick has to make an appointment to see her.'

'And how does Flick fit in with your busy lives?'

'Fortunately she's very adaptable. Never makes a fuss. But I think she spends too much time on her own and that concerns me. It's good seeing her with your two. I know they're much younger, but she's having great fun with them.'

'And they think she's the bee's knees. You should send her here for some of the holidays, Ivan. My mother used to worry about *me* being on my own. She would import cousins to keep me entertained. It's what cousins are for! Send her to us.'

Ivan smiled. 'I must say I think she'd prefer to be here than in Canterbury, which is where Emily tends to leave her.'

Dan patted him on the shoulder. 'It's sorted then, I'll talk to Kate and she can fix it with Emily.'

They were interrupted by the clatter of the walkers returning, muddy and soaked through from a sudden downpour.

'Of course, it's so much wetter in the West Country isn't it, darling?'

Dan heard Margaret Dinsdale even before she arrived in the kitchen, and whichever 'darling' she was addressing didn't have a chance to reply.

'I don't think it's stopped raining since we got here, although of course it's nothing like as bad as it has been. All those floods. I'm sure it's due to global warming, whatever they say... All

273

those people, losing their homes – it's terrible… Though why people live in caravan parks, I really don't know… And you, so close to the river… If you only knew how my heart stops every time they report flooding. And it must make farming so difficult… All that mud everywhere and having to keep the cows in all the time. I don't think I realised how much they smelled, a sort of sweet, sickly smell, isn't it? But I suppose you get used to it, living with it. I think we deserve a bit of sunshine now, don't you…? All this heavy cloud quite dampens the spirits. Do you know, Katherine, your Father and I haven't been here in the winter before? It makes the place look quite different… I'd always thought how golden and warm the stone looked… Cotswold stone I suppose… Though we're nowhere near the Cotswolds, are we… But in fact it's quite grey… But then, nowhere looks its best in winter does it? Oh Dan, is that kettle on for tea? I'm dying for a cup. Polly, I must give you my scone recipe, it's so simple even little Rosie could follow it, and what is teatime without scones and homemade jam?'

There was a gleam in Polly's eye as she went to help Dan, but she merely smiled. 'We're usually too busy for tea in that sense, Margaret, but if you'd like to show Ben and Rosie how to make them, I'm sure we'd all enjoy them.'

Kate, helping the children pull off gumboots and raincoats, caught Dan's eye and grinned.

While maintaining the veneer of civility, the two older women had disliked each other from the beginning.

Although Margaret Dinsdale had gone to university and Polly had not, Polly was better-read, she shared Roger's enthusiasm for books and his quiet, dry humour. In her company it was noticeable how his manner and conversation became more animated, and it was obvious to Dan and Kate that Margaret resented this. Her dislike was further compounded,

Kate explained to Dan, because Polly disapproved of Emily, particularly after the Tom affair.

'My mother thinks that Emily can do no wrong, so anyone who is at all critical of her must be seen off. But actually, Polly has never liked my mother very much, has she? And I'm sure my mother has picked up on that. Whatever else, she's not stupid.'

Polly had absented herself more than was usual over the holiday period but, Dan observed, this hadn't deterred Margaret from finding every opportunity to make little sarcastic comments all in the guise of innocent surprise.

Polly's absence would be remarked on: 'I thought Polly always had lunch with you. I do hope us all being here hasn't driven her away?'

Likewise her presence: 'Poor soul, she must get lonely, but do you two ever get any time to yourself?'

Polly's cooking was a prime source of point scoring: 'Some people are naturally good cooks, aren't they Polly, and some people just don't seem to have any idea. I hold the mothers responsible. After all, if you don't teach your children to cook then you are depriving them of a life skill. My mother taught me, I taught Kate and I know you agree, Polly, she's wonderful in the kitchen! Did your mother teach you, Polly?'

But Polly could score points, too: 'My Mother didn't know how to cook, Margaret, she never had to.'

Margaret resented the easy way Ben and Rosie hugged and kissed Polly, or cuddled up to her when she read to them, and implicitly accepted her authority over them.

So Polly was criticised for being 'too easy' with them or 'too strict'. And in her presence, Margaret would woo them with sweets and little bits of pocket money, which would cause Polly to purse her lips with disapproval.

Then Margaret would say, 'Dear little things, it's such a pity they don't live nearer to me. We would become such great friends. You're lucky to have the time to devote to them, Polly. You mustn't begrudge me treating them, when I see them so rarely.'

Or more subtly and more effectively, she would make unfavourable comparisons between Ben and, more often, Rosie, and her other grandchild.

In her eyes, Flick was perfection. Margaret would call upon Polly to admire Flick's prettiness, her daintiness, her long dark curls, her dancing, her singing, her academic achievements... On and on she would go until Dan knew she had Polly silently screaming, and he or Kate would be driven to defend Rosie's right, at the age of four, to be loud and boisterous, to be untidy, to argue with Ben, and to have a runny nose and muddy hands and face.

After the Boxing Day walk, Margaret found a new line of attack.

She had arrived back from the expedition thoroughly out of sorts because Roger and Polly had spent the entire walk absorbed in comparing notes on the Whitbread shortlist. Kate laughed as she recounted this to Dan. 'Not only was she unable to join in the discussion, but Dad ignored all her hints about walking by *her* side, helping her over stiles, or taking her arm for the muddy bits. He just nodded at the children whenever she complained and told them to "look after their granny". She was not pleased.'

'So you and Emily had to jolly her along. That must have been fun. You're right, Ivan and I had the better deal washing up.'

'Oh no, Emily sheared off early on to make a telephone call. It was left to me to keep her company. I was so glad when the rain set in again and we had an excuse to return home. So I hope you and Ivan did all the dishes because you certainly had the easier option. Mum was breathing fire by the time we got in. Didn't you notice? Poor old Polly is going to be in for it. Mum's on the warpath for sure!'

'I'm sure my mum can look after herself. Come on, I'll give you a hand with supper since Emily hasn't offered. Mum has volunteered to help Ted with the milking, so I am free and willing. Emily and Ivan can bath the kids and we can persuade your parents the best thing they can do is sink in front of the telly with a glass of sherry. It'll be nice to have you to myself, if only for half an hour.'

He'd just finished laying the table when Margaret drifted in.

'Where's Polly?' she asked, just a shade too casually, Dan thought.

'She's doing my shift in the milking shed,' he replied. 'She's helping Ted.'

'How very kind of her.' There was a slight pause. 'Does she do that often?'

'What, help in the milking shed? From time to time. Obviously Ted's in charge, but she's very experienced.'

'I see, so she helps Ted,' there was another pause.

Dan poured her a glass of sherry and suggested she might take a glass through to Roger. She stood instead at the table and looked at the place settings. Dan and Kate exchanged glances and waited.

'Is Flick having supper with us after all?' was her next line.

'No,' replied Kate, 'she ate with the other two, earlier. She was hungry and they all want to watch a movie together.'

'Then, Dan, you've laid one place too many. There are eight places set and only seven of us.'

'That's right. Dan has set for eight. Seven of us and Ted.'

'Ted? But he ate with us yesterday, didn't he? Does he share all your meals?'

'No, but since it's Christmas and he's no family around… Do you have any objection?' Dan couldn't quite keep a belligerent note out of his voice.

Margaret smiled sweetly. 'Don't be silly, Dan. It's your house. You must obviously invite whoever you like. I just wondered, that's all… I mean, he's not family, is he? Although I know he's been with you for a long time… He does seem to be here rather a lot. Still I'm sure it gives Polly pleasure… They are much the same age, aren't they…? And it is good to be able make up the numbers. I have such difficulty finding suitable partners for those girlfriends of mine who are on their own now… I'll just take this sherry through to Roger… Mustn't neglect him, must I? Give me a shout Katherine, if you want any help.'

Emily and Ivan left the following morning and Flick was left in the charge of her grandmother. Without her favourite daughter to fuss over, or her awesome son-in-law to flatter, Margaret turned her attention to Polly and Ted, enmeshing them in a web of innuendo.

She was too canny to spell out precisely what she was suggesting and Dan, at first, was amused. But after two days of significant looks and arch comments, he was no longer entertained. In some indefinable way, her hints seemed as much directed at him as Polly. She would pore over old photographs of his parents and any early photographs in which Ted featured, as if she was willing them to yield up some sort of secret. Then, in a saccharine, arch manner, she would cross-question Polly about being a woman in the 'macho' world of farming, and tease her about marrying again.

Polly, disconcerted and perplexed by Margaret's behaviour, bore it with her customary composure.

Late one afternoon Margaret went to meet her as she finished in the cheese shed and insisted on being shown around the farmyard. In one of the barns they found Ted and Dan mixing feedstuffs. The two men broke off to greet them.

Margaret, her eyes bright, turned to Polly and laughed, girlishly, 'Polly, I've had a wonderful idea... Call me a silly romantic, but I think you should marry Ted.'

Too startled for words by this extraordinary statement, Dan saw his mother go white, then scarlet with embarrassment. Ted froze at his side.

Undeterred, his mother-in-law carried on. 'You've been on your own far too long. You're still an attractive woman, and Ted here, would make an ideal husband – he's so close to you and Dan, it would be cementing a bond that already exists.' She tittered. 'You'll forgive me for speaking my mind, won't you Ted...? I'm afraid its one of my besetting sins. Roger tells me it will get me into trouble one day... But I'm so fond of Polly and I hate to think of her dwindling into old age, all alone... I'm so lucky I've got Roger to look after me. I don't know what I'd do without him. We all need someone, and you've worn those widow's weeds for too long, Polly...'

Polly's distress was evident and Ted looked tortured.

Margaret Dinsdale's behaviour, borne with patience by all of them for so long, was suddenly too much for Dan. He jumped down from the trailer and exploded.

'You stupid, interfering old woman. What are you talking about? How my mother chooses to spend her life is her affair, and how Ted chooses to spend his, is his. What do you mean by sticking your nose in? I'm sick and tired of listening to your endless rubbish, and your snide little comments about everybody. You're an absolute pain in the arse! If it wasn't for Kate, I'd send you packing right now!'

279

And trembling with rage, he charged out of the barn.

Margaret burst into tears and ran off, leaving a stunned Polly and Ted alone to sort out their embarrassment.

It was some time after milking had finished and the evening was well-advanced when a mutinous Dan opened the kitchen door to the farmhouse, expecting to be greeted by a host of accusing eyes. But the kitchen was empty, and the table was bare.

He stood in the middle of the room, straining to hear the sound of human activity. The house was so silent it accentuated the burbling of the Aga, the ticking of the clock, and the nervous rasping of his breath. An irrational fear gripped him. Had they all gone? Kate and the children as well? He'd been so angry he couldn't really remember what he'd said, but he could imagine Mrs Dinsdale would paint it in the worst possible light.

There was the sound of light footsteps, the kitchen door opened and Kate walked in. She smiled with relief when she saw him and slipped her arms around him. He held her tight and for a moment they didn't speak. Then she said gently, 'I was worried about you. It's getting late.'

'Yes, I know, I'm sorry. I thought it best if I didn't… I went up to check on the ewes after milking… It's just that I… I'm sorry, Kate. But only because she's your mother. I probably shouldn't have said what I did. But she… Are they in the sitting room? The house seems very quiet.'

'They've gone.'

'Gone?' He gaped at her.

'Yes. Sit down and I'll tell you while I get your supper. You must be starving, you poor thing.'

Assembling his food, she described how her mother had burst into the kitchen and collapsed into a kitchen chair, screaming for Roger and insisting they had to leave immediately.

'We could get little sense out of her except that you'd been exceedingly rude to her and that it was completely unprovoked. I was to go and pack her bags. And she said if I had any sense, I would pack mine, and the children's as well. The children, of course, were fascinated by all this, but that didn't stop her hysterics. In fact she became even more dramatic, saying she would never see her little darlings again and ordered Flick to go and get her things!'

Kate giggled. 'It was quite a performance. Dad and I tried to calm her down but she was having nothing of it. Then Polly came in and Mum burst into tears. Polly was really good with her. She apologised to her for your over-reaction; said you were just being protective but had gone over the top. She said she knew Margaret hadn't intended any harm by her remarks, and she was not offended. I could tell from Dad's face he was mortified. He's not stupid. He knew she must have said something awful to cause you to erupt like that, so when she continued to insist on leaving, he didn't put up any opposition. I made them some tea, they wouldn't stay for supper, and then they went. Mum put up a bit of a fight about Flick, but Dad agreed with me that she should stay here until Emily wants her back in London.'

'Did my mother tell you what happened, Kate?'

'After they'd gone, I prised it out of her. My mother's a monster, Dan. I'm not surprised you flipped. If it had been me, I would probably have grabbed the nearest pitchfork and skewered her. How deeply embarrassing she is. Your mother was fantastic though. She helped me feed the kids and then went back to her place, saying you and I could do with an evening alone together.'

She wrapped her arms around him. 'I'm so glad you came back before bedtime!'

Without their guests, they spent a quiet New Year, and life at Watersmeet settled back into its usual patterns.

The weather continued to be bad, and since they had been forced to bring the cows in early, food supplies were running low. But the milk yield continued to be good and Polly reported increased interest in their cheese, and suggested they might expand to produce a soft blue.

Dan was pleased, particularly as this was a development he'd discussed with Kelner the last time they'd met.

Whenever he thought of Steven Kelner, Dan mentally blushed. The man was so patient, and hadn't give up on him even when, after months of refusing to respond to his calls, Dan had, unequivocally, thrown the farm report back in his face.

He'd persuaded Dan to pay him another visit and had systematically gone through all the options, accepting and listening to Dan's objections. He then made a number of suggestions that had solved Dan's immediate cash-flow crisis. It was a bit like going to see some sort of therapist, Dan thought, unlike going to see his accountant who always made him feel worse.

On his last visit to Kelner's office they had sat and talked through the long-term prospects of the farm, and he admitted to feeling very depressed at the state of his business, and its future.

'We're just tinkering at the edges, Steven. It's like patching hedges with straw. The next wind blows it away and we have to start all over again.'

'Then mend those hedges with something more substantial, Dan, you have the means. I understand you feel there's a principle at stake; it's very honourable of you. But would your tenant behave the same way towards you if he was in a similar situation?'

'No, he wouldn't, but that is not the point, is it? He's entitled to be there and I'm not going to be the Maddicott who evicts him.' Dan was emphatic.

But Steven persisted. 'If you took back Woodside Farm you could use the capital to relieve the situation with your business, long-term. You could expand the cheese operations without a bank loan, *and* sort out your personal insurance situation, Dan, which is critical.'

A slight frown creased his brows and the tips of his elegant fingers played against each other. 'If anything happened to you tomorrow, God forbid, where would your wife find the wherewithal to sort this out? The Maddicotts might well lose Watersmeet. If you didn't want to sell, then you could get a business loan and develop that land in some other way. Giving him notice to quit because you need the land for non-agricultural development is perfectly legitimate. Had you thought of that?'

No, he hadn't and nor was he going to. He knew that neither Steven Kelner, nor anyone else, not even Kate, quite understood his reluctance to do anything about Frank Leach at Woodside. Even Ted, while respecting his decision, occasionally voiced his exasperation at the state of affairs. But Steven's comments about his life insurance, or lack of it, rattled him.

'I must do something about that. I must, I must, I must!' He would chant like a mantra whenever he thought about it, which was usually when he was busy doing something else.

29

Kate

2001

'You're very quiet Kate. Something on your mind you want to share?' Max poured her a glass of wine and sat back looking at her, his eyebrows raised.

They had arranged to meet in an Italian restaurant in Floral Street, just off Covent Garden. It had been one of Kate's favourite haunts when she lived in London. It held no strong memories of Dan for her and was a good neutral place, therefore, to meet Max after leaving Steven Kelner's office.

Unusually for him he was there before her, and she was glad of that. During the brief period they'd dated, she'd disliked being the one to arrive first at any agreed rendezvous. She hated sitting alone in a bar or restaurant, so she would make herself arrive a bit late and then dart in, peer round, then retreat for a walk round the block if he wasn't there.

She felt tired and drained after her visit to Steven Kelner, and was glad to see Max ensconced, waiting for her with a chilled bottle of white wine. And so she told him about her trip, and a little of what Kelner had told her, and of the question that was nagging at the back of her brain.

'I've asked Nick Lovell to see if he can find out the original conditions of the tenancy of Woodside farm; but I don't understand, and I never *have* understood, why Dan was so reluctant to do anything about Frank Leach. Dan was a funny mixture of the pragmatic and the romantic, and although he could be compassionate, he was not sentimental. And there was nothing about Frank Leach to excite compassion; quite the reverse, in fact.'

'Yes, but dear old Dan had a strong sense of responsibility, didn't he? And not only did he feel responsible for Frank because he was his tenant, but I think, in a way, by letting Frank be, he was trying to assuage his feelings of guilt.'

'Guilt? Dan?'

'Yes. You know the story of Mary and the birdcage and of Dan throwing the chicken shit over Frank's head?'

'Surely you're not suggesting he feels…felt guilty for that?'

'No, but he told me that shortly afterwards the farm was raided, the birds were removed, and Jem was taken to court and prosecuted. I don't think he received any great penalty, but it would seem the publicity surrounding the court appearance, and more particularly, the loss of his birds, knocked the stuffing out of him. He died within a year, and Frank, for one, held Dan responsible for his death.'

'But that's ridiculous. Jem *was* a horrible old man and got what was coming to him. He was lucky not to have been prosecuted for what he did to Mary.'

'True, but nevertheless Dan felt responsible. After all, we were trespassing that day. Jem was a horrible old man, and a recluse, and it sounds as if Frank takes after his dad. I haven't

285

seen him since that day…'

'No? Actually, I've not seen him more than a couple of times in my entire time at Watersmeet…'

'I think Dan believed, at the very least, that Frank should be left alone. I'm very surprised to hear that he'd had a change of heart and was going to oust him. Doesn't sound very likely to me. Things must have been desperate.'

'Yes,' said Kate wretchedly. 'And I wasn't aware of it. What sort of wife does that make me?'

'Dan was never good at sharing his problems, Katie. If he didn't tell you, it's because he didn't want to. Don't start feeling guilty, or that you were responsible for Dan's death. You were a bloody good wife to him and he knew it.'

Putting her on the train later, he gave her an unexpectedly warm hug. 'Look after yourself, Kate, for all our sakes. I'll see you soon. I'm planning to come down and take Ben and Rosie off to the pantomime as a Christmas treat if that's all right with you?'

Kate thought long and hard after her visit to Steven Kelner, and then she phoned Nick Lovell.

'Nick, it's about Frank Leach…'

'I haven't got information on the tenancy for you yet, Kate…'

'No, it's not that. I think the time has come to do something about Woodside Farm. According to a report Dan had drawn up, it's in a terrible state and I don't think we should let things slide any further.'

'Really? Are you sure?'

'Yes, I am sure. Very sure.'

'Well, good, I think you're doing the sensible thing. I suggest, in the first instance, you write to him and put it all on a formal footing. You don't have to be too aggressive about it, but be firm and tell him it's his first warning: that the dilapidation of the farm buildings would put him in breach of his lease and that your letter will be followed by a second warning and then a notice to repair, if he takes no action. I'll fax you the wording if you like.'

When Kate had sent the letter, she told Ted.

He raised his eyebrows and said impassively, 'Yes? Don't tell me he's responded?'

'No, he hasn't, but…'

'He's more likely to tear it up than read it.'

'Yes, which is why I think it's time I paid him a visit. If he hasn't read the letter, then I can spell it out for him, and if he has read it, then I can tell him I mean business. It will also be an opportunity to see if things are as bad as they appeared to be the last time we were there.'

Ted frowned. 'You don't have to go, Kate. That's something I can do.'

'I know you can, but I think it's something I *ought* to do. Ultimately he is my responsibility and I've hardly met the man. The only time I've ever spoken to him was when Ben went missing. And anyway, I've been thinking of what he might do if we do get him to leave. I know it's pretty derelict, but I thought we could restore Keeper's Cottage and let him have it for a nominal rent. It's too small and remote for many to want to live there, but he might be interested. I want to put that to him.'

Still expressing misgivings, Ted agreed that she should go, on condition that he went with her.

Frank, however, eluded all attempts to arrange a meeting. November had slid into December when finally, exasperated by their lack of success, Kate proposed they pay a visit to Woodside Farm unannounced.

The place was empty when they arrived, and after hanging about for a while and shouting for him, Ted and Kate started to inspect the condition of the house and outbuildings. They were just about to go into the barn when an inarticulate roar followed by a stream of obscenities stopped them. Kate turned to see Frank striding across the yard from the edge of the woods, a shotgun under his arm. Despite the fact she had every right to be there, Kate shivered, very glad that she hadn't come alone.

Ted cut across the other man's angry invective. 'That'll do, Frank. I've been trying to arrange a meeting with you for the last couple of weeks. If you'd bothered to reply to my note, we wouldn't have taken you by surprise like this.'

'Oi don't need no meeting with you, Ted Jordan. Ged outa here and take her with you. Snoopin' where you not wanted. Oi knows what yer up to, you and the widder. This is my farm and you is trespassin'…'

'Frank,' Kate began, trying to keep calm, 'as your landlord, I need to check the state of the farm; you know that. I should have been before, but…'

'You clear off,' he growled. 'Pokin' yer nose in. It ain't no business of yourn, this is *my* farm…'

'It is our business, Frank,' said Ted. 'This level of deterioration makes it very much our business and, believe me, it will be in your best interests to cooperate.'

'What Oi does with *my* farm is *my* business, Mister, an' Oi'll thank ye to clear off and take that there widder with thee. Oi've nothin' more to say so bugger orff…'

He turned, as if to walk away.

Kate, determined not to lose the opportunity, ran in front of him to block his way. 'Listen Frank, you've read my letter. You know that if you fail to do the basic maintenance and repair to

288

the buildings, I can re-possess. But I...'

Her efforts to him inform him of his rights of action were met with a barrage of further abuse. The question of Keeper's Cottage was not even broached.

Then backing away from them, looking wildly at Kate and Ted, he cocked his shotgun.

'Time to go, Kate,' Ted muttered. 'Put up your shotgun, Frank,' his voice was stern. 'If you start waving that about so freely, the next visit you'll have will be from the police.'

Kate was frustrated by their lack of progress with Frank, but they had seen enough, in their brief visit, to convince them that the degree of dilapidation was worrying, and at the next farm meeting, Ted produced a rudimentary survey he and Josh had made of the state of Woodside's fields, hedges and ditches.

'The time has come,' Kate told Polly, 'when it would be negligent of us not to take this further. I'm going to get Nick Lovell to write to Frank, giving him a formal notice.'

Ted's support for Kate's proposal left Polly with no alternative but to reluctantly agree.

Nick phoned back a few days later. 'I sent Leach his notice to repair as soon as you phoned, Kate. He should have got it a couple of days ago. I've got the information you wanted on his tenancy... The will wasn't so easy to locate, and, I'm afraid, it's mainly irrelevant, since the law on which it was based has been superseded by more recent legislation, which means the legality of the provisions of this will would be called into question these days.'

'What were they, anyway?'

'Well, to put it simply, it was a form of entail. The Maddicotts agreed that the tenancy of Woodside Farm would pass unhindered from father to a 'legitimate son of his blood';

289

and the rent would be re-negotiated only when the tenancy passed to the heir and then subject to no further increase during the lifetime of that tenant. That provision is still in force apparently, so Frank Leach is renting Woodside for peanuts.'

'Was that standard practice?'

'It's unusual within the farming community. And all the more surprising as there was obviously no love lost between the two families. You see, without this agreement the Leaches, would have had no statutory right to tenancy. Within three months of the death of the incumbent tenant, the Maddicotts could have whipped in a notice to quit. But as it happens, Frank now has security of tenure because of subsequent changes in the law in 1976. The only way you can get him out is if you decide you are going to use the farm for non-agricultural use, or if, as you say is the case, he causes the farm to fall into disrepair, or he fails to pay his rent.'

'Thanks, Nick. I guess Dan knew all this. Nick, did Dan plan to take the same course of action as me, to go down the 'terrible tenant' route, and send him notice?'

'If he did, he didn't talk to me about it.'

'So as far as you were aware, Dan had no plans for Woodside Farm?'

'No, none that I knew of. But it's possible he spoke to my dad about it. He's off on a cruise at the moment but you could check with him when he gets back. There's nothing on the file, though.'

Kate felt so deflated she could hardly bring herself to thank him, but before she could ring off, he continued, 'You wanted to know about Granny Rose's bequest?'

'Oh, yes?'

'It's interesting, Kate. She was an eccentric old woman,

that's clear from her will. Anyway, she specified five diaries she wanted him to read, covering the period from 1945 to 1949. She'd added a codicil, later, saying she realised he might not have the time to read them all, but she was insistent that he should read some particular entries. If you've got a pen handy, I can give you the dates.'

That night, in her letter to Dan, Kate wrote: 'So I've finally taken action against Frank Leach. The farm is in a terrible state and Ted agrees inaction is no longer an option. I know you always defended his right to live at Woodside, but Steven Kelner told me you'd changed your mind. I know you would never have abandoned him, so I will look after him, don't worry about that…'

When she finally turned the computer off, she reached across to the bookshelf and ran her finger along the dates scratched on the covers of Rose Maddicott's diaries until she found 1945. She pulled it out and took it with her to bed.

30

Rose

1945

Rose Maddicott's bicycle bumped along the rutted track that wound its way through the trees and undergrowth to Woodside Farm. Her mouth felt dry and her heart was thumping faster than the energy demanded by her exercise.

When she had volunteered her services, she had not expected to feel quite so apprehensive. She had seen it as her duty to go. After all, the Leaches were their tenants. It was, quite simply, the ridiculous antagonism between them that had prevented her from fulfilling her obligations.

Samuel had told her not to get involved but she felt, keenly, that she had failed in her Christian duty not to have gone to Woodside Farm when the child was first born. There had been one or two attempts by the ladies in the village to deliver parcels of food supplements and baby clothes, but all attempts to meet the young mother and admire the baby had been fiercely repelled by the formidable old Mrs Leach.

Now word had come through the village network that the old lady was gravely ill and not expected to live much longer. The Village Action Committee had got together, led by the vicar's wife, and they had decided they would be failing as good Christian women if they didn't hold out a hand of friendship and support to the young Mrs Leach. She was, by all accounts, a frail creature after what had, again according to village gossip, been a difficult birth.

The bundle of toddler's clothes that had once belonged to Rose's young son Jack, along with the jar of calf's foot jelly and the other items that would give the dying woman nourishment, bounced in Rose's capacious bicycle basket.

She had not told her husband, Samuel, of her mission. He was content to let her have her way in most things but she knew he would not approve of her going to see the Leaches. Not that he would expressly forbid her to go. He knew better than that. She might stand only five feet in her highest-heeled shoes, but she had a will of iron that more than compensated for her lack of height. She was thirty-five; she had survived the birth of two still-born babies, and just when she had abandoned hope of ever giving Samuel a child, Jack had arrived. He, now a healthy five-year-old, was the apple of her eye, though the child would never have guessed it.

The war years had been difficult for most, and although the war was over, living in post-war Britain had become harder. But Watersmeet was a prosperous farm, they had done relatively well out of the war years, and with judicious management, they would continue to flourish. All the more reason, she argued to herself, to overcome the barriers set up by this prolonged estrangement and show a little charity to those who not only might need it but had the right to expect it from her, as their landlord.

Her bicycle wobbled over the last rut and through the gate. The yard was empty and silent. She leaned the bike against the wall of the barn and lifting off her basket of parcels, she looked around her.

The yard was much like most of the farmyards she knew: shabby and full of decaying farm paraphernalia. The hayrick in one corner of the yard was nearly depleted, the residue of hay scattered wide around its base; a small milking parlour in another corner was a stone island in a sea of cracked brown dung; the freshly raked midden heap, next to it, steamed and stank. Brown hens scratched in the dust at the entrance to the barn, and a new tractor was visible in the dark interior. A border of hollyhocks and larkspur brightened the appearance of the farmhouse, but on a field-gate close to the house the stiffened corpses of a crow, a weasel and a stoat dangled on a line. One side opened out on to farmland; the woods closed round on the other three. The birds were silent with the summer's afternoon heat and the trees seemed dark and oppressive.

Despite the warmth, Rose shivered. Resolutely she turned to the house and stared up at the windows. The house stared blankly back. Its front door was shut and the wisps of weed and grass invading the porch suggested it was rarely used.

She walked briskly around the side of the milking parlour to the back door, and knocked tentatively. Silence. With more determination she knocked again and listened.

She had been told that old Mrs Leach was at death's door. There must be someone in the house… She was sure she could hear the rustle of movement and whispering, so she knocked again. After a few minutes the door opened just wide enough for a small, white, heart-shaped face to peer round.

'There's nobbut me here,' quavered the girl. 'What d'yer want, please?'

Rose had her speech prepared. 'I've come to see how old Mrs Leach is doing, and to bring one or two things for her to eat that the district nurse thought would be good for her.' As the girl hesitated, she added, more warmly, 'And I have brought you one or two things for your little boy. He must be nearly eighteen months by now and they grow so quickly at that age, don't they? My boy, Jack, is five, and shooting up so fast. He really can't wear these things any more so I thought they might be of use to you. It's so difficult to get clothes these days, isn't it, even with the ration books?'

With some reluctance the door was opened a bit more and Rose could see that the young woman was carrying a toddler on her hips. What struck her immediately about the little boy was the pallor of his skin. He stared at her with pale green eyes; his hair was so dark, it was almost black. He had a long face and a long nose, and an air of great sadness that struck Rose as piteous in such a small child. She looked at the pale, frightened face of his mother and realised, with shocked concern, that she was little more than a child herself.

'May I come in, Mrs Leach,' she said gently. 'I won't stay long, but I so wanted to meet you and your little boy.'

The girl flushed and was about to say something, but changed her mind. She glanced nervously about her then opened the door to let Rose in.

'I'm so sorry about the mess,' she said hurriedly. 'I've got a bit behind with my chores today.' She looked anxiously up the stairs. 'We must keep our voices down; the old lady, she don't like...'

'Strangers, yes I know. Don't worry I'll be very quiet. Is your husband out harvesting?'

'Jem?' Again she hesitated. 'Yes. He won't be back for his tea for some while yet.'

The conversation that followed was a very one-sided one. The girl was almost monosyllabic, and apart from the fact that she was an orphan and that her name was Susan, Rose learned very little about her history or about her life at Woodside Farm. She was a bit more expansive when talking about her little boy and so they spent some half hour of whispered conversation, during which Susan unbent sufficiently to offer Rose tea and some biscuits, warm out of the oven.

'You're a wonderful housekeeper,' whispered Rose admiringly. 'These biscuits are quite delicious, and your kitchen… I don't think I have ever seen a farm kitchen quite so shiny and clean. How do you do it, with the baby and Mrs Leach to look after as well?'

Susan glowed. Apart from Franklin, in all her life, no one had ever paid her a compliment before. She'd never had a conversation about babies with anyone, and she was enjoying it so much, she was almost tongue-tied. She found herself relaxing; she warmed to this formidable little woman, and didn't want the visit to come to an end.

But end it had to, and abruptly. There came a loud thumping on the ceiling and Susan looked up, instantly terrified. She jumped up, and telling Rose to wait a moment, fled up the stairs, leaving the little boy sitting on the floor, staring at the stranger. Rose talked gently to him, but he remained unresponsive until she held out her hand to stroke his cheek. He bit her hard. The pain and unexpectedness of it caught her by surprise and she yelped. There was a moment's silence upstairs and then a breathless and white-faced Susan came running down the stairs, clutching an envelope in her hand.

'You must go… I'm so sorry when you've been so kind… The old lady heard summat.'

'My fault. The baby bit me! I do hope you won't be in too much trouble. May I call again?'

Susan was inarticulate with conflicting emotions. The half hour she had spent with this lady had been the nicest thing that had happened to her for so long, but she was going to have to deal with a tyrannous cross-examination from the old witch upstairs. More significantly, she was worried about Jem's reaction if he discovered she'd had a visitor.

After the birth of little Frank, he had taken her to register the child. When she emerged from the Registry Office with the birth certificate, he had taken it from her and told her that he was going to hold onto it as an 'insurance'.

'What d'ya mean, Jem?' she asked. She had never really recovered from the difficulties of Frank's birth and her spirit had been broken, comprehensively, by Jem and his mother.

'Insurance 'gainst yer doin'summat yer'd be sorry for, that's what Oi mean. We'ave 'ere the babby's birth certificate, which shows the world he's a bastard and yer a whore. Now Oi've no son and yer've no home to go to, save wot Mother and Oi 'ave kindly given ye. Keep yer trap shut, look after the house and Mother and Oi, and yer liddle babby will 'ave a name and if ye keeps yer nose clean, by and by the farm will belong to he. But I'm warnin' you missee, say a word to anybody and ye'll be out and yer babby will be taken from ye.'

He had her trapped and they both knew it.

And so it was until Mrs Leach's last stroke. Along with her son, she had contrived to prevent Susan having anything but the most fleeting contact with the wider world. When his mother was felled by the stroke, Jem had reminded Susan of his warning.

'She might not be able to keep an eye on yer, but do as Oi say an' Oi'll not say owt. An' Oi don't want you talking to no strangers, not now, not ever. They're not welcome 'ere.'

Shortly after Frank's birth, the wretched Susan had found pencil and paper and had written a desperate letter to Franklin. She told him of her misfortunes and begged him to come and rescue her and his little son. She was watched so closely, however, she had no means of smuggling the letter out of the house, or of passing it on to someone who might post it for her, and so it had lain concealed under her mattress for over a year.

It was this letter that she clutched in her hand when she rushed downstairs to tell Rose that she must leave. She pressed it into Rose's hand and begged her to send it. A puzzled Rose had barely agreed and placed the letter in her empty basket, when the kitchen door opened and Jem walked in.

31

Dan

2001

Shortly after the New Year, they had a visit from Mary and Toby. Mary had been to see them a number of times over the year since she'd fled, and in spite of the fact that Clive had continued to give her a hard time, he'd kept his distance and she was growing in confidence, looking younger, prettier, and much more relaxed than she had for years. Toby had changed too – bright, happy, and much more confident.

Ben and Rosie were delighted when they heard he was coming to stay the night.

'He's really good at sword fights, Dad. We're gonna play pirates and have sword fights in the sittin' room. He has one sofa and I has the other; they're our ships, see, and we fight for our ships and the floor is the sea an' if we touch the floor, we drown!'

'What can be my ship?' Rosie wailed. 'I wanna a ship too, I wanna fight too. I'm old enuff…'

'No you're not,' retorted Ben. 'You cry and won't die when you get killed.'

'Yes I will. Just see if I don't.'

When the children, exhausted by their games, finally fell asleep, the three adults sat around the kitchen table, catching up with each other's news.

Then Mary said, quite out of the blue, 'Can I give you some news about Joe?'

Dan was startled. 'Joe? I haven't heard anything from him for years. We've completely lost touch.'

'Have you seen him?' asked Kate. 'How is he? He just disappeared from our lives.'

'I think he tried to disappear from everybody's lives, including his own,' said Mary. 'And actually, if I hadn't left Clive when I did and ended up in Bristol, he would probably have succeeded…'

'So how did you come across him? Where's he been all this time?' Dan had missed Joe acutely over the years, but was all too aware he'd done very little to find out what had happened to him.

'It was that night, when Toby and I arrived at Bristol Temple Meads station. I was in pieces and not thinking straight and I tried to settle Toby and myself down for the night on a bench, but we attracted the attention of a bunch of drunken down and outs. I think I told you about this. One of them demanded money and when I said no, he became quite threatening. The rest of the group came to join him, but then one of them pushed the others away, telling them to leave me alone. A fight broke out, the police came and the drunks were hustled away. But I recognised the one who'd come to my rescue. It was Joe.'

'Joe! *What?*' Dan stared at Mary, shocked.

'A down and out? Joe? No!' Kate stared at Mary.

'I know, it sounds so unlikely, but I was convinced it was him. I couldn't do much for ages, 'cos I was too busy fighting Clive and trying to sort myself out. But when I finally left the refuge, I went looking for Joe. I couldn't forget his face, you see; I couldn't not try to find him.'

'But you didn't say anything to us, about it? Why not? We might have been able to help you?

'You're always so busy, Dan. And I didn't know how Joe would react if he knew people were looking for him. I know that when I went to the refuge, I didn't want anyone to know what had happened to me. I thought there wasn't much lower I could sink. I'd ruined my life. But I was lucky. Down and outs, tramps, drunks, call them what you will, they were all part of somebody's family once, and they end up being treated with less dignity than dogs.

'It was the Salvation Army who helped me find him in the end. It took ages to persuade him even to talk to me, but I was not going to give up. Eventually he told me what had brought him so low, and how he'd lost his job in London. Having quarrelled with his dad, he couldn't come home. Then he got chucked out of his flat, by which time he'd started drinking heavily. It was an awful spiral and he was so depressed because… well, he couldn't pull himself out of it. He drank to anaesthetise himself – from his depression at first, and then from the awful state he'd got into. And believe me, when I found him he was in a terrible state. I think it was only because he'd been so fit from working on the farm that he wasn't dead.'

Dan swallowed hard, a painful lump in his throat. 'Where is he now?'

'He's got a room in Bristol and he's trying to get work. Oh, Dan, he's so much better. It's nearly a year since I found him; he's stopped drinking altogether and he is trying hard to rebuild his life. I told him I was coming to see you this weekend and I knew that he really wanted to come, too, although he didn't say anything. Please, Dan, can he come and see you? It would mean so much to him. And to me.'

'Of course he can come.' Kate spoke without hesitation. 'Why shouldn't we want to see him?'

'Dan?'

Dan felt confused. Part of him longed to see Joe, but he felt odd – a mix of hurt and anger. He'd needed Joe and Joe had been nowhere to be seen. So things had gone badly for him, but in this he wasn't alone. And he, Dan, could have helped him get back on track. Friendship was a two-way thing, wasn't it? So why had he turned his back on his life-long friend?

'Yes. Fine. Why not?'

He was aware of a puzzled look from Kate before she jumped up to get the calendar. 'How are you fixed next weekend? Come and have supper on Saturday and stay overnight…'

'I got the impression that you weren't particularly overwhelmed at the thought of seeing Joe again?'

He and Kate were cuddled together on the sofa, watching the last embers glow and fade in the fireplace.

Dan shook his head. 'No, that's not true. It's just that… Why hasn't he been before? It must be nearly a year since she found him. So why the great secrecy? Why didn't she tell us earlier? He was my great mate. Why didn't he get in touch with *me*?'

Joe supplied the answer when he found Dan in the dairy the following Saturday afternoon. The visitors had been expected to arrive early in the evening and Dan was completing his milking shift. Absorbed in his work, he didn't notice Joe till a familiar voice behind him drawled quietly, 'Still singing to

302

your cows, boy?'

It had been a standing joke among his friends when they were young that Dan sang while he milked, and he'd been called 'the singing cowboy'. He'd not been teased about it for years.

He swung round and saw his old friend standing there. Much thinner, much paler, his hair thinning and with an uncertainty about him that was new to Dan, but it was, unmistakably, Joe.

Dan dropped the cluster he had just taken off and shouting a spontaneous and joyous 'Joey!' flung his arms around his friend.

Joe felt thin and frail, but his hug was strong and responsive and from that moment, until his departure the following afternoon, the two friends were almost inseparable.

'I know I should have been in touch. Believe me there were many times when I couldn't believe how much I'd thrown away but I couldn't see past what I'd become, how far I'd sunk… And then my previous life became a blur, a dream world, and it seemed to me I'd always been a drunken bum. When I started drinking, I was so angry. Angry with myself, angry with my parents – I really wasn't rational – and angry with you, too, Dan.'

'Me! Why?'

'Oh, for all sorts of reasons. Because I felt you hadn't taken me seriously. You had everything I wanted, and I convinced myself that it was you who prevented Emily from going off with me.'

Dan stared at him. 'How did I do that?'

'It was your friendship with Ivan. I was jealous, I guess. I persuaded myself that you warned him that I was…I was in love with Emily, and you brought family pressure to bear on her to turn me down.'

'Oh Joe, I didn't, believe me…'

'Of course you didn't. I know that. Look, I wasn't rational.

I wanted to explain why I didn't turn to you for help. I think I went a little mad. I realise now that actually I wasn't ever really in love with Emily. I was infatuated and that infatuation worked on me like some sort of poison. It was all my own fault. I jumped in at a deep end without checking whether I could swim, and if it hadn't been for Mary, I would have drowned. It's Mary, Dan, who's taught me the difference between love and infatuation.'

Startled, Dan stared at Joe.

He flushed. 'I haven't said anything to her, so don't you say a word. She's no idea. She's had an awful time with that shit, Clive, and the best I can do, for the moment, is to be a good friend to her and make no demands. So, please Dan, don't say anything!

'No, no I won't. Don't worry. But I do wish you'd come here before. I would have helped you, gladly. You know that.'

'Thanks, yes, I do. But it was a pride thing. I wanted to take control of my life again. And now I've got a roof over my head, and I've got a job. I'm only on trial; I've got to prove to them that I'm no longer the useless bum who's drunk away the last six years of his life. I guess it's no great shakes, but it's a job I'll enjoy, and it'll bring in some cash, so wish me luck, Dan, old pal…'

The kitchen was a hive of culinary activity when they rejoined Kate and Mary. Dan looked around him in some surprise. 'Blimey, Kate, this is taking the fatted calf a bit far; you're cooking up a storm…'

Mary was contrite. 'I'm sorry, Dan, it's my fault. I told Max we were coming here this weekend and he's just phoned Kate to ask if she minded if he came too. He was away over Christmas and New Year and thought it would be a good opportunity to catch up on us all. I hope you don't mind?'

'Of course I don't, if Kate doesn't. We've room for one more, I'm sure. It'll be fun.'

But it wasn't just one more. When Max's car roared into the yard an hour later, he was accompanied by the most beautiful girl Dan had ever seen. She was tall and willowy, and moved with a sinuous grace.

'This is Sonia,' explained Max, looking with great satisfaction at the effect his companion was having on the assembled company. 'I hope you don't mind my bringing her, Kate, but she was originally booked on some modelling assignment this weekend and it fell through at the last moment. Rather than leave her bereft in London, I thought I'd bring her to meet my nearest and dearest. I've told her all about you and Watersmeet and she's dying to meet you.'

But if Sonia was dying to meet them, it didn't show. She proffered each a cool elegant hand, surveyed them in turn with great green eyes that lingered longest on Dan, then tossing her blond hair back with a casual flick, demanded Max take her in out of the cold. She looked faintly appalled when she met the children and disappeared as quickly as she could to 'freshen up'.

Her presence and lack of interest in anything drained the evening. She was the silent spectre at the feast, saying very little and eating even less. The conversation became stilted and instead of relaxing over the meal, Dan could see the others were becoming increasingly uncomfortable.

All Kate's efforts to draw her out met with hardly more than a bored, monosyllabic response.

After an initial effort, Mary gave up on her and concentrated on Joe and Kate.

Dan felt completely fed up, and just wished she'd go to bed

and leave them to get on with the evening. He drank more quickly than normal and opened another bottle of wine.

Only Max seemed completely unaffected, flirting lightly with Kate, teasing the children when they made the odd appearance, quizzing Mary over her new job, questioning Joe about his, and reminiscing with Dan about the adventures they'd had on the farm as children. He made almost no attempt to include Sonia, and when Dan's prayers were answered and she languidly rose from the dinner table saying she needed an early night, he casually flapped a hand in her direction saying he would be up later.

At that she stopped. For a moment her poise crumbled and Dan saw tears start to her eyes. 'Max,' she said, and there was no mistaking the pleading in her voice.

'Don't be a drag, Sonia,' he said coldly. 'I told you, I'll be up later.'

After she had left the room there was an uncomfortable silence. Dan poured himself another glass of wine.

'Sorry about that,' said Max lightly, reaching across for the bottle. 'She's become rather a bore. Shame really, she was great fun when we first met.'

'Well I don't know why you had to inflict her on us,' said Mary crossly. 'I was really looking forward to this evening. It's the first time we've been together since Ben's christening. Why did you have to bring her?'

'Good question, little sister, and the answer is not for your ears. Sufficient to say she's got a lovely body…'

'She's certainly got that…' Dan chipped in, slurring his words slightly, 'but that's not enough, is it?' He waved his hand at Kate. 'What I mean to say is, Kate's got a lovely body, but she's not boring. She's got a lovely mind too, and a brain, an' conversation… Your girlfriend… She didn't hardly speak, that's no good to man nor beast.'

Kate grinned. 'Perhaps she didn't like us, sweetheart. People don't have to, you know.'

'Rubbish, everyone likes you Katie. You're just… And you can cook! That dinner was lovely an' she didn't eat a thing.' He turned to Max. 'You need someone like Kate, Max. It's time you settled down with a lovely wife, not lovely like her… whatsername…but lovely like Kate. That's what you need.'

Mary laughed and Kate, grinning, removed Dan's glass. 'You're going to have a horrible hangover tomorrow, Danny, and don't you have to be up at five for the cows?'

That was a cue for Joe to push back his chair. 'Yep, and I've promised to help, so if you show me where the dishwasher is, Kate, I'll start to load it. That was a fantastic meal, Danny's very lucky!'

The others also started the move towards clearing up, but Max poured himself another glass of wine and drank deep. Dan's words appeared to have touched a nerve and for a moment he sat scowling at his glass. Then he looked up and with an attempt at lightness, replied, 'You might well be right, Dan, someone like Kate is certainly what I need. Trouble is, there is no one quite like Kate so I make do with the Sonias of this world. I rely on you…' he encompassed them all with a rueful grin, 'to make sure I don't make the mistake of marrying one of them.'

Mary was indignant, 'Max, you're horrible. You treat women like you do your cars. You buy these old wrecks, lavish money and attention on them and when they look perfect, you get rid of them. Only with women, it's the other way round. You meet someone beautiful and independent, decide you want her and when she's succumbed to your charms and her independence is gone, you're bored and get rid of her.'

307

'The trouble is,' Kate said sleepily to Dan, as they curled up on the sofa to watch television the following night, 'Mary's right about Max and women. I think it stems from never having had to make an effort to get anything he wanted.'

'How do you mean?'

'Your cousin's very good-looking. He is now; he was when I was an adolescent. Not only that, but he has a very engaging personality. Haven't you noticed? He only has to ask for something, grin in that lazy way, and he gets given it straightaway. The end result must be that he doesn't really value anything...'

'Unless he can't have it...'

'When I suspect he sets a disproportionate value on it. Don't misunderstand me, I love Max. He's great fun and one of our oldest friends, but I don't always like him and I didn't this weekend, and I think it was a shame he had to muscle in on your reunion with Joe.'

32

Kate

2001

Kate shivered. It was cold in the cellar and the air smelt musty. The flagstones were sticky black with damp and flecked with little patches of distemper that had flaked off the walls.

She rarely came down here. It was full of mouldering Maddicott history: old wellies, cracked riding boots, discarded waterproofs, broken pieces of china waiting in vain to be mended. Pictures that had fallen out of favour were stacked against a wall. Black polythene bags stuffed with discarded clothing, waiting to be consigned to the next jumble sale, were dumped on top of boxes bulging with unwanted toys, china and books. Garden furniture was stashed alongside a large plastic paddling pool. A rickety bookcase housed myriad bottles and jars containing anything from turpentine to screws to unidentifiable pickles and jams of indeterminate age.

Alongside the tall, sleek, grey metal gun cabinet installed by Dan's father, a battered wooden cupboard contained spare bulbs, spare bags for the vacuum cleaner, spare keys for every lock in the house, a big box of wrapping paper wilting slightly with the damp, and boxes of Christmas decorations, some dating back to the mid-nineteenth century as the Maddicotts never threw anything away that might have some use. It was these that Kate was looking for.

The question of Christmas had been nagging for some time. Dreading the thought of it, she had pushed it to the back of her mind, throwing herself into the farm and the children, and devoting any spare time to the question of Dan.

Christmas! She sighed deeply, and crouching on the damp floor of the cellar began pulling out the boxes of glass baubles that she and Dan had so carefully packed away last year. There were carrier bags full of tinsel; a box of decorations made by the children and collected since they were tiny; the old rosewood nativity scene that had been part of the Maddicott Christmas for as long as anyone could remember; a wooden roundabout that whizzed round at amazing speed when its candles were lit; and a box of assorted angels and fairies of different ages and glamour, all of whom had graced the top of the tree at some point in their history.

The family took it in turns to choose which one was to have that particular honour. Last year Ben had chosen a small pink, plump, plastic fairy with frizzy blond hair and a wobbly arm, at least forty years old. They had all shrieked at his choice but he had remained firm.

'I feel sorry for her. She never gets chosen an' she's got a nice face. She looks like that lady who teaches us swimmin'.'

She and the children had decorated the tree during the day last year, as a surprise for Dan and Polly.

It was going to be so different, so difficult this Christmas. Her heart sank every time she thought about it. It didn't

310

matter what they did, they would all be thinking about last year. It would be so much easier if they could go away – take a holiday somewhere. She knew that was what William had done when Muriel died. He went again last year and was going away again this Christmas. But she had Polly to think of, quite apart from the cost.

Then her mother had phoned and raised the subject. The conversation Kate had been dreading had followed an entirely predictable course:

'Katherine, darling, Daddy and I have been talking about Christmas…'

'Yes, I…'

'It's extraordinary how quickly the year has gone… I can't believe it's nearly that time again, although of course the shops have been full of Christmas gifts since September, even before that in some places… Did you know there's a Christmas shop in Canterbury now so you can buy Christmassy things all year round? Though why anyone should want to buy Christmas decorations in the middle of July…'

'No, I…'

'Mrs Marsh, you remember Mrs Marsh, darling? My bridge partner, such a sweet woman, although her bidding is not one of her strong points… She told me it has become fashionable for some firms to have their Christmas parties in the summer, so I suppose there is some demand… It takes all sorts…'

'Mum, I don't…'

'Now darling, we've been giving the matter some thought… We do appreciate how difficult it's going to be for you this year, you poor, poor thing…'

'But I don't want…'

'You've been so brave, it breaks my heart… So we think a change of scene would do you the world of good…

'But I can't…'

'And the children, poor little things… They've always enjoyed their trips to us, and as we came to you last year, we think it would be a good idea if you were to come here…

'Mum, I don't think…'

'You haven't been back here for Christmas since you got married, have you…? Not that I blamed Dan, or Polly, but it's very hard to lose a daughter like that… Christmas is just not the same when one of the family is missing…

'Mum!'

'I grant you we were all together last year at Watersmeet… It was wonderful Emily and Ivan came as well, wasn't it? They're such busy people… Do you know that Ivan hasn't had a chance to visit us this year at all, and I have a whole host of people dying to meet him? Well, Emily has just phoned to say they *will* come, just for a couple of days, so I thought we could have a big Christmas party… But your father said, and I quite agree with him, that you shouldn't be on your own this year, so we think it would be much the best thing if you came here. You could come as soon as the children break up from school and stay till New Year… That way you wouldn't have to worry about a Christmas tree or anything… And Flick will be here for the whole of the holiday, which will be fun for your two little ones… Emily is busy with her new exhibition so she is dropping Flick off as soon as she finishes school… It's going very well, she says, and she is getting such a lot of attention… so gratifying. Well, darling, do say you'll come?'

Kate took a deep breath. There were times during a call from her mother when she was tempted to put down the phone and cut off the remorseless flow. Dan had taught her to stand back and not to be so affected by her mother's crass insensitivity, even to joke about it.

On this occasion however, anger and disgust in equal measure, threatened to overwhelm filial nicety. She was too raw for the luxury of indulgence and her sense of the ridiculous had deserted her. The thought of spending even ten minutes listening to her mother made her feel weak.

'It's very nice of you to invite us, Mum, but I couldn't leave Polly.'

There was a pause.

'Polly would be very welcome to join us, darling. I do have my PGs of course, right over the Christmas period this year… I couldn't say no, they were so insistent…and with you and the children, and of course, Emily, Ivan and Flick, we will be a teensy bit squeezed for space, but I'm sure we could fit Polly in, somewhere.'

It was no good. Just then Kate hated her mother. She had to ring off before she said anything she'd later regret.

With a promise to think about the invitation, she did so, but not before her mother had wailed down the line, 'But darling, if you don't come to us, then we'll have to come to you. Roger is adamant, and I agree with him, it's at times like these you need your family… But if we are to come to you, what will happen to my Christmas party? Everyone is so looking forward to it… And Ivan is only able to have a couple of days away… And Emily so wants to be here for Christmas…'

For twenty-four hours Kate had simmered with anger, unable to share her shame with anyone, unable to see a way out that would not upset her father and offend her mother, or leave Polly in the lurch and herself utterly miserable.

Then Mary phoned and asked about her plans for Christmas. Kate had bared her soul.

'I don't want to go there, Mary, I really don't. But I don't

313

see how I can get out of it. And I certainly don't want them to come here. I don't want to keep making comparisons with last year, and with them here I would, and it will be unbearable.'

'Kate, you're a grown-up. You don't have to do anything you don't want to, certainly nothing that's going to make you more miserable. Just say no, you've made other arrangements.'

'Like what?' Kate sighed. 'If only it were that simple.'

'Come and stay with us. That's why I'm phoning. Toby and I would love it if you all came. The house is a bit small, I know, but we'd manage – and that would be half the fun – you could share my bedroom with Polly, the children would all go into together and I'd sleep downstairs. Joe hopes to be able to join us for some of the time, and is looking forward to having three children to play with. Do say yes. It would be lovely to have you to myself for a while.'

Kate was touched. Both Mary and Joe in their separate ways, had been to hell and back. Mary was modest about the role she played in Joe's rehabilitation, but Joe told Kate that without Mary's fierce determination to save him, he would have drunk himself to a miserable death in the gutter. In turn, Mary was adamant that without Joe's support she wouldn't have had the strength to stand up to Clive, and would probably have given in to return to a living hell.

'The truth is,' Kate had said to Dan as they had lain in bed one night discussing Mary and Joe, 'their weaknesses gave the other strength. Mary was so affected by Joe's state it brought out the fight in her, and Joe was so affected by Mary's plight, it brought out the fight in him.'

'So all's well that ends well,' Dan had replied, sleepily. 'Actually, it sounds like one of those Victorian melodramas, and now Joe will sign the Pledge and, twirling his bow-tie, will see off the evil Clive. I wonder if his dad will have him back at Ashcroft. It would be great to have him around again. I've missed him'.

But there'd been no grand reconciliation. Joe's father was too badly hurt by his son's desertion and subsequent disappearance, and did not encourage him to return home. Joe got work on the far side of Bristol and Kate had not seen him since Dan's funeral.

Mary had borrowed money from her parents to buy a house in the Bedminster area of Bristol. It was small, and while she loved her dearly, Kate quailed at the thought of sharing a bedroom with Polly for more than one night.

So she hesitated. 'Mary, I can think of no one I'd rather spend Christmas with, but would you and Toby consider coming here instead?'

It was Mary's turn to hesitate. 'I'd love that, Kate, you know I would; Watersmeet has always been my second home. But… won't your family want to come and stay if you are there? It's just that I don't want…'

'There's no danger of my family being here if I can reassure them I'm not going to be on my own. Emily and Ivan have only got a couple of days off, so they've arranged to go to Canterbury. Mum wants to show off her MP son-in-law and has planned a big Christmas bash. I'd be an embarrassment in my widow's weeds. You'd be doing them and me a favour by coming here; the relief of guilt all round!'

So it was settled. The children were pleased at the thought of having Toby to stay. Joe was going to join them on Christmas Eve, Polly invited Ted to join them, and Max phoned to suggest he might make up one of the party.

'Nicola is going to Kenya for the festive season, but I thought

I'd rather catch up with my family. Mary tells me she is coming to you, so please Kate, may I come too?'

Kate laughed at his pleading tone and felt quite glad that Nicola, whoever she was, was taking herself off and wouldn't expect to be invited too. Max's presence would lighten the whole occasion.

Now, on her knees in the cellar, sorting out Christmas decorations, she found herself thinking about Mary and Joe, each struggling to put their lives together, both a lot happier than they had been for years. She and Dan had thought themselves so fortunate, so lucky by comparison. And here she was, struggling to put *her* life back together.

For a moment, surrounded by the memorabilia of happy times, she felt overwhelmed by her loss.

Dan was dead. There would be no happy ending. She hadn't even been able to say goodbye to him. She'd been asleep when he left the bedroom.

Had he kissed her goodbye?

If he was going out to shoot himself, had he kissed her goodbye?

She would never know, and it was so important.

The damp of the cellar floor seeped through the knees of her jeans, but her discomfort suited her mood and she wept into the glittering strands of tinsel she had been sorting.

'Kate? Kate?' It was a man's voice, calling from the kitchen. William Etheridge.

Kate wiped her runny nose on the back of her hand, got to her feet and, with her arms full of decorations, made her way to the kitchen.

'Hello William,' she said brightly, dumping the decorations on the kitchen table and concentrating on them, hoping her tearful countenance was not too much in evidence. 'Cup of tea?'

'No thanks, Kate,' he said gently, 'I'm off to pick the kids up. We're going to spend the night with the grandparents before we fly out. I just wanted to drop these off.'

To her surprise, he produced three brightly wrapped parcels. 'Just little things,' he said awkwardly, 'for you and the children, something to put under the tree. It will be tough, Kate, but you'll have the comfort of knowing it'll never be quite so tough again.' He kissed her lightly on the cheek. 'I'll see you in the New Year.'

Stuttering her thanks, she accompanied him to his car.

Splash, thinking it was time to go and meet the children from school, danced excitedly at her heels. William laughed and tickled the back of his ears. 'How's the little fellah getting on? They can be very demanding at his age.'

'He's doing brilliantly,' Kate replied warmly. 'And he's such a good guard dog. It's thanks to him we weren't fried in our beds last night.'

William turned, concerned, 'What? What do you mean?'

'I'm surprised you haven't heard, I would've thought it'd be all over the county by now. We had a fire in the outhouse at the back of the kitchen last night.'

Kate's dreams had taken on a nightmarish quality. She had set out across familiar fields to take Dan his sandwiches, but then she found herself walking through woods she didn't recognise, and in the distance she heard the howling of dogs. She tried to run, tripped over a root and got caught in a bramble bush that hooked her hair, her clothes; and as she struggled, the sound of the dogs got closer and closer. 'Dan!' she screamed soundlessly and woke up.

317

The bedclothes were tangled round her body and she was covered in perspiration. As she lay there still shaking from the dream, she realised that she could still hear the sound of the dogs. Except that it was just the one dog – Splash. He was barking, loudly, urgently.

She lay listening, waiting for him to stop, assuming that he'd been disturbed by a fox or badger coming too close to the house, but he carried on barking, so she got up and pulling on one of Dan's sloppy sweaters, went to investigate.

Despite huge opposition from the children, she'd insisted Splash spend the nights in his basket in the kitchen and not on their beds. He was still barking when she reached the kitchen and turned on the light.

'Splash, what is it boy, what's up?'

At first she thought her vision was blurred with sleep, but there was no mistaking the acrid smell. The kitchen was filling with smoke.

Unable to see where the smoke was coming from, she grabbed the phone.

'Ted, it's Kate, I'm so sorry to wake you, but something's on fire here.'

'Where are you, Kate?'

'I'm in the kitchen and it's filling with smoke, but I can't see a fire anywhere…'

'Right. Get the children up and get out of the house. I'll phone the Fire Brigade and get on down to you. It's probably nothing to worry about, but get yourselves out as quickly as you can…'

The sound of Splash's barking had already woken Ben, and within minutes, the dog at his side, he was following Kate, carrying a sleepy Rosie, out into the yard. Ted joined them and almost immediately the first of three fire tenders arrived. By this time, flames were licking round the kitchen door.

In a remarkably short space of time the fire was doused. It was established that the blaze had started in an outhouse built on the yard wall of the kitchen.

'They think it might be due to faulty wiring,' Ted reported later. He and the senior officer had spent some time in conversation as the men had raked through the outhouse, checking that the fire was out and trying to establish its cause.

'Lucky you noticed the smoke before the fire really got a hold. He said it could have been very nasty.'

Kate shivered. 'Faulty wiring? I thought we had the wiring regularly inspected by Stan Binding?'

'We do. I'll have to double-check with him that he does do the outhouses…'

Kate stroked Splash's silky ears and smiled up at William. 'So you see, William, I've a lot to be grateful to Splash for. He's the hero of the hour.'

William looked grave. 'That's bad. You were lucky the fire didn't get a hold. I thought I could smell something acrid. Are the children OK?'

'Absolutely fine. They were very excited by the fire engines, of course, and they're so proud of Splash. He's a brilliant watchdog. Thank goodness he woke me up.'

33

Frank

He put out his hand and touched her hair. It was so silky, so soft, so unlike anything he ever remembered touching. A luxuriant waterfall that tumbled, dark and curly over her shoulders, dancing with her every movement.

Timidly he began to stroke it and the action took him way, way back into his childhood. A time when he was very small and She had brought him a little black kitten. She had found it in the barn, She said. It could be his to keep, She said. He remembered touching the little thing, so tiny he could feel its bones under its soft, black, downy fur. Its eyes were bright blue, almost as blue as this girl's. A tiny rough tongue had tickled his hand. You must feed it, She said. Give it some milk, it must be hungry. Is it really mine, he had said, mine forever? Yes She had said, yours forever. You must love it, like I love you, She said. But She was wrong. She was always wrong.

Vermin, his Dad had said, and you know what we do with

vermin, don't you boy? Yes Dad, he had said and he had put the little kitten in a sack, filled it with stones, and flung it far into the river. Good, his father had said, now you're not a baby any more, you must come and work with me on our farm.

'That's enough,' said the girl with dignity. 'You'll make my hair dirty if you carry on stroking it like that. Sit down here,' she patted a mossy mound, 'and we shall have our picnic.'

Obediently he sat and, mesmerised, watched the two girls as they unpacked a basket. They chatted to each other as they unpacked, the older girl, with the long dark curls, issued orders and the other, younger child, carefully put out three tiny plastic plates decorated with rosebuds, three even smaller matching cups and saucers, a plastic teapot and a small bowl. Orange squash had been poured into the teapot, three sugar lumps filled the small bowl and a chocolate biscuit dwarfed each tiny plate.

The orange was poured into the miniature cup. 'Sugar?' asked the girl. He nodded humbly, and she dropped a sugar lump into the squash, displacing most of the liquid.

She handed it to him. 'You'll have to eat the sugar lump first, then I'll give you some more tea. Biscuit?' She handed him a plate.

He hadn't met creatures like this before. Tiny, dainty little things. Like sprites from some long-forgotten story that he might have heard at school, before school had become a place of torment and hatred. Or from something She might have told him when he was little.

She was forever telling him stories of people and places far away, and how one day they would go there. But they never did, and now it was inconceivable to him that he should ever leave, or that he should want to. He felt threatened by people, disliked and unwelcome. He didn't care. He had his farm and *while he had that, he was safe.*

He knew he had to watch over his land and in return his land would keep him. It was a lesson his dad had beaten into him. But it was a struggle – had been a struggle always – and one he was losing. He had no time for farm animals and got rid of the last of the stock when his dad died. The chickens had kept him going for a while, but now they had gone. Their huts falling in, overrun with rats and the other vermin, which he struggled to keep at bay. And the land, too, was being invaded by colonising tendrils of bramble, and squadrons of nettles relentlessly encroaching everywhere, accompanied by huge pervasive clumps of rusty dock.

So he had turned to the woods and here he was comfortable. The animals and birds provided him with all the meat he could eat and with enough left over to sell and provide for his other needs. There was not a creature in the woods safe from his traps and snares, and he moved through the thickets and trees with consummate stealth.

Thus it was he had come across these little girls the day before. He had watched as they ran into the woods; watched as they started to play hide-and-seek; watched as the dark-haired one had lightly shinned up a tree and lay concealed on a branch; watched as the younger one hunted, called, and wailed.

Why he had left his hiding place, he wasn't sure – he normally would have slid away unseen. They were so...so different. Apart from when he was a child at school, he had never spent any time with children, or indeed, had ever really watched any at close quarters. He was fascinated.

All night long he thought about them. They had shown no fear of him; asked him lots of questions he hadn't known how to answer; told him they would be his friends... He'd never had a friend before, had never wanted one; and they had invited him

322

to join them the following day for their picnic. He didn't know what a picnic was, or what to expect. All he knew was that the two little girls excited strange unfamiliar emotions in him, and he wanted to see them again.

When the picnic was over and packed away, dark hair tossed her curls and suggested a game of hide-and-seek. 'You can play,' she told him. 'It'll be more fun with three. I'll be the seeker first. I'll count to twenty.' She put her hands over her eyes and started counting. The other child ran off immediately, but he remained where he was, staring.

She stopped counting and was astonished to see him still standing there. 'What are you doing? You should be hiding. Don't you know how to play hide-and-seek? You go and hide, and I try and find you. Go on, I'll count again.'

He lay in the long grass, in the shadow of a wych elm. Hiding was something he was good at, but not something he had ever associated with 'fun', nor had 'play' been part of his life, except when he was very small and She was still around. He struggled to understand why he was doing this. Here he was, lying still in the wet grass for no other purpose than for a little girl to jump on him. It was daft, but the sensations inside him, unheralded, unknown, and powerful beyond his understanding, kept him from slipping away.

They had been playing the game for some time, but he gave no thought to that. He thought instead of the two little creatures, so different, so fascinating. The younger one, with her short curly hair, the colour of ripe wheat, intense round blue eyes and rosy, plump cheeks. She was completely trusting, held his hand and called him 'my fwend'. He found he liked that.

The older one was much more wary, alert to everything, like the deer when they knew he was pursuing them. If he believed in such things as enchantresses, then she was one, and he had

323

fallen under her spell.

Something thumped him in the middle of his back and alarmed, caught off-guard, he snarled and rolled quickly over grabbing the assailant as he went. She put up no resistance, but lay, pinned by his body, her blue eyes staring at him, her face white, her black curls spread out on the grass. For a moment he lay there, looking down at her then lifted a hand and gently stroked her face.

She said, her voice cold, 'Would you please get off me. You're squashing me. I can't breathe and I'm getting very wet.'

Reluctantly he rolled off and slowly got up. She was on her feet and inspecting her clothes. 'I'm really muddy,' she said. 'It's time we were going.' And turning on her heel, she walked away without a backward look.

He made no attempt to follow, but stood there, watching her leave, with a desolation that echoed back down the years, to a time when he had returned to the empty house, after he had watched them bury Her.

34

Dan

2001

'OK. I'll phone you back if there's a problem, but I'm sure it'll be fine. Bye.'

Kate put the phone down just as Dan entered the kitchen, rubbing his damp hair with a towel.

'Who was that?'

'Emily.' Kate replied, taking the towel off him as he sat down at the table. 'Here, let me.' And she proceeded to vigorously rub his head.

'Ow, careful. I don't want to become prematurely bald.'

'No danger of that,' she dropped a kiss on his thick mop of hair. 'Mmm, you smell nice. Breakfast is nearly ready.'

She walked back to the Aga, where she'd been frying sausages when the phone rang.

'Shall I call the kids?'

'No, they had theirs earlier. ''Cos it's half term, they're awake with the light and raring to play... Would you mind pouring out the coffee?'

'Love to.' Dan picked up the coffee jug and poured out two cups, then settled at the kitchen table with the newspaper.

'What did Emily want? Very rare for her to phone you unless she wants something.'

Kate laughed. 'You're horrible, Dan Maddicott, but as it happens, you're right.'

Dan smirked and drank his coffee. 'So – what *does* she want?'

'She wants to come and stay for a few days.'

Dan groaned. 'What? When?'

'Today. She can get away later this afternoon.'

'With Ivan?'

'No, apparently not. She says he's very busy – got something on… Oh, and there's a dinner that he wants her to attend but she doesn't want to; says she's too hassled by it all. All she wants is some peace and quiet, so can she come down and do some painting. She'll bring Flick. Apparently it's her half term too.'

Dan sighed, said nothing and looked down at his paper.

Kate turned back to the pan and cracked in an egg. 'I couldn't say no, Dan. She's never asked before. I know you don't like her that much, but she is my sister and I hardly saw her at Christmas…'

'She didn't exactly make an effort, Kate.'

'No, but I think something's troubling her and it will be good to have her here by herself.'

'And Flick.'

'Yes, and Flick. The children will be pleased. They both thought she was wonderful, and you yourself said we should invite her down here more often. She had such a good time with us at Christmas. It's only for a few days.'

'Still, I wish Ivan was coming. Emily on her own spells

326

trouble.'

An article in the paper caught his attention and he whistled under his breath. 'That's not good. That's not good at all...'

'What isn't?'

'It was on the radio, yesterday. Now it's confirmed: foot and mouth at an abattoir in Essex...'

'But that's the other side of the country. They'll contain it quickly enough. Why should we worry?'

'Because,' replied Dan, his face grim, 'it might be the other side of the country, but so many local abattoirs have closed; people now send their stock all over the country for slaughter. Those infected animals could have come from anywhere.'

It was a rebellious-looking Flick who trailed in after her mother that evening. She barely responded to Dan's greeting or Kate's warm hug; nodded indifferently at the two children who danced around her; walked through to the sitting room, and rejecting all offers of food or drink, threw herself in a chair and switched on the television.

Emily appeared quite unconcerned by her daughter's behaviour: 'Oh she's in a burr because I wanted her to come here with me and she didn't want to... She had a party to go to tomorrow night and can't understand why I wouldn't leave her to her own devices. She said she'd arranged a sleep over with some friends, but Ivan wouldn't hear of it... The last time she went, we found out they'd been smoking and drinking... At eleven years of age, it's appalling! Although it was only the dregs from wine bottles the girl's parents had left behind after a party... Anyway Ivan hit the roof and said there were to be no more sleepovers... Though it's easy for him to lay down the law like that... He's hardly ever home and it's me that has to make all the babysitting arrangements, and anyway Flick refuses to have a babysitter now. She says at eleven she's too old and she'd be humiliated if her friends found out. She has a point... But what was I to do? Ivan wanted me to go to this awful fundraising dinner in his constituency... I'd have had to listen to some boring old fart, eat their ghastly food, drink water then collect Flick at some unearthly hour. I wouldn't wish a night like that on my worst enemy! So much nicer to come and see you.'

Not for the first time, Dan was struck by Emily's similarity to her mother.

'So Ivan has to go to his dinner alone and poor old Flick has to give up her party...'

Emily tossed her black curls, her eyes flashing at the critical tone of Dan's voice. 'Believe me, Dan, Ivan is better off not having me to worry about, and Flick will get over it. She told me what a brilliant time she had here last holiday, and it will be good for her not to spend the week hanging around that particular bunch of friends.'

If Kate thought the next few days would be spent in cosy intimacy with her sister, she was mistaken. When Dan came in from the morning milking, Kate was giving the children breakfast; of Emily there was no sign.

'She doesn't often get up for breakfast,' said Flick, airily. 'She's too tired. May I have another piece of bacon, please, Auntie Kate? We *never* have cooked breakfasts at home, this is yummy.'

She had quite recovered from her ill-humour and gave him a sweet smile. 'Uncle Dan, the best thing... Auntie Kate has arranged for me to go riding today, with a girl who's got *two* ponies, lucky thing. My friends will be sick!'

When Dan returned for lunch, Emily had just emerged,

announcing that as it had stopped raining she was going to take her sketchbook and go for a walk.

Her departure was interrupted by an unfamiliar shiny black sports car arriving in the yard.

Dan, followed by Emily, went out to meet the visitor. She stopped in her tracks when she saw the car and the young man who got out of it. Dan was convinced she swore under her breath, but the pleasure with which she greeted the newcomer suggested his presence was an essential ingredient of her happiness.

'Jamie, how wonderful! How on earth did you track me down?'

Jamie, Dan reckoned from the youthfulness of his skin, was in his late twenties. He was almost bald on top, with a high, domed forehead fringed with tufts of brown hair falling thickly over his collar. With a black velvet suit and white linen shirt, he was more suited for some literary soirée than the farmyard. He stood there, pale and shivering, in the early February sunshine.

When he first got out of the car, Dan thought he looked haggard, but at the sight of Emily, his face lightened then flushed like an adolescent. 'Don't be cross with me. I had to see you…'

Emily turned to Dan. 'This is my friend, Jamie Goldsmith, Dan. He's a writer. This is my brother-in-law, Dan Maddicott, Jamie. Don't worry, he won't have heard of you, he doesn't read books.'

Dan found himself shaking a damp, flaccid hand. 'Pleased to meet you, Jamie. Emily, why don't you take your pal into the kitchen. He looks half-frozen. I've got work to do, I'll catch up with you later.'

When he returned for a cup of tea in the late afternoon, he

found Kate alone. With gusto she filled him in.

'It's second nature for Emily to flirt with anyone, whether she's pleased to see them or not. They have to be completely enslaved before she drops the act, so it was some time before I realised she wasn't pleased to see Jamie. Not at all! I was cross because it was clear from the start he was angling to stay and I thought it was a put-up job between them. Apparently he's a writer whose first book was a bestseller. He's onto his second but he's suffering from 'writer's block'; so the story goes he's looking for a farm where he can stay and research his book, because it's set on a farm. Emily told him about Watersmeet, so when he heard she was coming here, on impulse he leapt in his car, and came to find her, and us. That's his story anyway.'

'But you didn't believe it?'

'I think parts are true. He is a writer. I believe the bit about writer's block. I don't believe the bit about looking for a farm to stay on. He's here because Emily's here, and Emily is here because…'

'Yes, why is Emily here?' Dan put his mug down, suddenly very fed up with his sister-in-law. 'It wasn't just because she wanted to avoid that dinner with Ivan was it? Or because she thought the country air would do Flick good?'

'No, of course not. I don't know, darling, I can only guess… Jamie's obviously hopelessly infatuated with her and equally obviously she's no longer enjoying his attentions. Perhaps she came down here to get away from him, which is why she was so pissed off when he turned up…'

'Another Joe, eh? Poor sod.' Although he had no particular sympathy for the unfortunate Jamie, Dan felt disgusted.

'As you say, poor sod. Anyway, I made him a cup of tea and a sandwich. As soon as she reasonably could, Emily said she didn't want to lose any more daylight and she was going off to sketch. Jamie immediately leapt to his feet and said he'd go with her. She was really cross, but I lent him a pair of gum boots and a coat, so off they've gone.'

Dan, snorting with displeasure, went to join Josh in the milking parlour.

Just as Josh was fixing the clusters, Emily appeared, Jamie in tow. Josh hadn't seen Emily for years and grinned engagingly at her as he straightened up from his work to greet her.

Now thirty, he was big and beautiful, his skin only slightly coarsened by continuous exposure to the elements. His blue overalls flattered his broad shoulders and long legs; his face was ruddy with the cold, and a warm glow emanated from him as a result of his physical exertions.

The contrast between him and Jamie couldn't have been more marked.

Jamie, frozen with the cold, stood huddled into his coat, his shoulders drooping with misery, his face a patchwork of blue, white and red. His hair, damp as the air, hung limply over his collar and the overhead strip-lighting accentuated the gleaming baldness of his pate.

'I could have sworn a gleam came into Emily's eyes when she saw Josh,' Dan told Kate, later.

Kate laughed, 'It would have done, Jamie or no Jamie. Don't you remember how outrageously she and Josh flirted with each other the very first time she came down here with Ivan. But I bet you the moment she clapped eyes on him, she saw him as a way to get rid of poor, lovesick Jamie.'

'She's unscrupulous!'

Kate, feeling sorry for a thoroughly dejected Jamie, offered him supper and a bed for the night. Despite receiving absolutely no encouragement from Emily, who'd arranged to meet Josh for a drink later, he accepted.

His morale was further deflated by Flick's reaction on seeing him when she returned from riding. 'What are *you* doing here?' she said with evident distaste, and turning to her mother, demanded imperiously, 'Did *you* invite him, Emily?'

Emily didn't even bother to look up from the sketch she was finishing. 'No of course not, darling. Don't be absurd. Jamie's master of his own destiny.'

Supper was a tortured mix of polite conversation and awkward pauses, and Dan was greatly relieved when Emily finally went to the pub, an anxious Jamie in tow.

They could only guess at what happened but they were about to go to bed when Jamie returned, alone, a seething mixture of resentment, misery, anger and despair. He glared at them as if he resented their presence and held them responsible for whatever humiliations had been his that evening.

'I'm just returning the coat you lent me. Look… I've got to go back to London. I want to leave Emily a note. Have you got some paper I could use?'

His manner discouraged further conversation, but Kate tried to persuade him to stay.

'No thanks. The sooner I put some distance between myself and…that fellow…the better. And Emily has made it quite clear that…that…' He swallowed and savagely bit his lip. 'I've got to go. Could you see that she gets my note? Thanks.' And he was gone, slamming the kitchen door behind him.

For a moment they both stood, listening to the sound of the car growling away up the hill. Then Dan stretched and yawned.

'Come along, Katie. I need my bed and unless you want to wait up for that errant sister of yours, I fancy a kiss or two before I crash out…'

Early the following morning Josh was working in the lambing

sheds at High Acre, and Dan, who was going to give him a hand, took the children along to admire the first flush of new lambs. The children then ran off to play in the woods nearby.

Kate had instructed him to find out from Josh what had happened the night before, but apart from asking him outright, he couldn't think of a way to raise the matter. Josh appeared as cheerful and as unconcerned as he always was, and Dan's greater concern, that Josh, too, might fatally succumb to Emily's charms, seemed groundless.

The unexpected arrival of Emily in the lambing shed confirmed this. She told them she'd decided not to waste the morning in bed and had come to find the children.

Dan told her where they were playing, but she showed no inclination to go and look for them. Instead she hung over the bars, admiring the new-born lambs and subjecting Josh to a series of artless questions. He answered her good-naturedly enough, but paid more attention to his sheep.

'Josh never feels very deeply about anything or anybody,' Kate reflected later, as they lay in bed mulling over the day. 'And he takes it for granted that he doesn't have to make much effort to get what he wants. Bit like Max, in a way. But what's different about Josh is that he doesn't mind if he doesn't get what he wants, or if people don't fall at his feet. Unlike Emily, who'll work at it till everyone is under her thrall, he couldn't be bothered to make the effort. He's the ultimate laissez-faire merchant. Are you still awake?'

'Yep. And with you, so far. Carry on.'

'I know Josh isn't Emily's usual fare. He's not exactly an intellectual – he's a farm labourer with no ambition; but you've got to admit he's physically *very* desirable. I bet you Emily saw Josh as a way of getting rid of the unfortunate Jamie, flirted with him like mad in the pub, and when Jamie left, continued to flirt, rather liking him and his attention. So much more flattering to have a hunky male hanging on your every whim than a washed-out, balding, ineffectual intellectual!'

Although amused by her analysis, Dan felt uncomfortable. 'I really like Ivan. I'd hate to see him brought down by any of this.'

'Oh,' Kate yawned, 'it will fizzle out. There is no way Josh would go to London, and Emily hates the country. And I wouldn't worry about Ivan, Dan. I think he's got the measure of Emily. It's Flick I'm thinking of. She must have wondered at her mother's sudden interest in new-born lambs.'

Dan chuckled in the dark and putting further thoughts of his troublesome sister-in-law to one side, gathered his wife in his arms.

'Now Mrs Maddicott, I have a serious question to put to you. You've suggested my employee is irresistible to women. How irresistible do you find him, eh?'

'*All* movement of livestock?' Dan stared at Ted. 'You're kidding?'

'I wish I were,' said Ted. 'It's as bad as we feared, and might get worse. Since Tuesday, forty-two farms at least have been identified. No one near us yet, thank God. But it can only be a matter of time.'

Dan wiped his brow with the back of his hand, leaving a long muddy streak. It was a cold February day. The countryside, beset by what seemed like a continuous rainfall since the previous autumn, had been teased earlier in the week by a glimpse of spring, with blue skies and dancing clumps of snowdrops. But it hadn't lasted: the clouds gathered and formed a low, dull blanket of bleak winter grey. A wind, picking up from the east, had resulted in a drop in temperature and the flight of Emily and Flick to the relative warmth of the city.

Dan, arrested in the task of scraping the yard, didn't notice the cold. He climbed out of the tractor. 'Then we'd better get cracking. Get everyone over to the house. Give me half an hour. I'll get onto the NFU and find out the latest.'

'We've been holding our breath since Tuesday,' he thought, trudging towards the house. 'I can't believe it. How much more are we going to have to take? It's one bloody thing after another.'

The kitchen was empty. It was mid-afternoon and Kate had gone off somewhere with the children. He pulled off his overalls, filled the kettle and pushed it, hissing and popping, onto the hob, then padded out of the kitchen to the study.

'It's like a war!' He found the notification that had arrived that morning from the Ministry of Agriculture. 'After years of attrition, we're now under siege, with heavy casualties predicted. I hope to God Watersmeet won't be among them!'

When he returned to the kitchen he found his workforce had assembled. Josh, in from the lambing shed, had taken advantage of the unexpected break to eat his sandwiches; John Potter was helping Polly make tea, and Ted, Matt, Brenda and Colin sat round the table, quiet and expectant.

Polly was just pouring the tea when Kate walked in.

Startled at the sight of their entire workforce gathered in her kitchen, she turned to Dan, 'What is it? What's wrong?'

He tried to give her a reassuring smile. 'Nothing to worry about, yet, Kate. It's foot and mouth; the latest news is not good and so we're pulling everyone in to decide on our next move. Where're Ben and Rosie?'

'I've just taken them over to the Harringtons'. They're going swimming. Move over. I think I should be in on this, too.'

Dan explained to the assembled workforce that although there appeared to be no immediate threat in their area, the rapid development of the disease in other parts of the country, away from its place of origin in Northumberland, meant no chances should be taken. He and Ted set out their plans. The farm was to be placed under a regime of no-go areas and restricted movement.

All the stock was to be examined twice a day, and since the disease was more difficult to detect in sheep, all contact between the sheep and the dairy cattle had to be stopped. This meant Josh was not to go near the cattle and to have no contact with Matt or John Potter.

Dan and Ted, who worked across all aspects of the farm, divided their labours between the sheep and arable work, which Ted took on, and the dairy herds and farmyard, which Dan took on. Matt would milk with Mike Rosewarn, Dan with John Potter.

The cheese makers were to be restricted to the cheese shed, with no access to the rest of the farmyard. Kate and the children were not to use the kitchen entrance to the yard, but to enter the house by the main door, and were to have no contact with the livestock. The yard was now out of bounds to them for the duration of the crisis. Disinfected pads were to be laid at all yard and field entrances, with footbaths for pedestrians.

The arrangements were received in silence, but Dan could tell from their long faces that they were not welcome, and the little shrieks of incredulity from Brenda spelt resistance from that quarter.

'I know these measures seem draconian,' he said, feeling weary, 'and you might think I'm over-reacting, but the first we heard of the outbreak was three days ago, by which time forty-two farms had already been infected. The latest update says the

336

number is approaching eighty, and what is more, these farms are not confined to the North – a farm in Devon has been hit.'

Intakes of breath and worried murmurings rumbled round the table. Dan felt Kate take his hand and squeeze it.

Ted took over. 'I know I don't need to spell it out, but that is a doubling of numbers in three days, and why, folks, until we get the all clear from MAFF, we keep our heads down and do everything by the book. Fortunately for us the cows are still in, and will be until mid-April if this weather continues, and the ewes have almost finished lambing.' He looked round the table. 'I don't have to emphasise how infectious this disease is, so it's really important you observe the conditions we've set. And, I'm afraid, no contact with other farms.'

There was a stunned silence at this, then Brenda piped up, 'How long are we going to have to put up with this?'

'I really don't know, Brenda.' Dan replied. 'I hope it won't be too long. The last major outbreak was in 1967 and I think that went on for a few months.'

'A few months!' she shrieked her dismay.

'But as a result of that experience, the government should get it under control more quickly this time…'

But time passed and the disease spread so rapidly and so extensively, Dan began to feel increasingly pessimistic.

It was with a certain amount of relief that he greeted the 'Countryside is closed' message from the government, and they were able to put up closure notices on all the footpaths that crossed their land. However the measure served to exacerbate the sense of siege, and Dan's state of mind was not helped by the fact that he was working twice as hard.

Every morning was marked by the checking of each cow for any tell-tale blisters, and when he came in from the milking, he would spend a troubled half hour on the computer checking on the geographical distribution of the latest outbreaks and the latest advice from MAFF or the NFU. He would then confer with Ted on the phone, before he could be persuaded to sit down for breakfast.

'What worries me,' he said to Ted one morning, 'is the contiguous culling policy. For all the precautions we've taken here, if one of our neighbours develops the disease, then our beasts are dead meat. My grandfather built up these herds, and my father doubled the size of them. Am I going to lose the lot?'

And nothing Ted could say would console him.

Then, with immaculate timing, a letter arrived from the bank, asking Dan to make an appointment with David Morgan, the manager.

The meeting was as sticky as he'd expected. He was bumping along against the limit of his overdraft, and while Mr Morgan expressed sympathy and talked about temporarily increasing the limit, he was insistent that Dan should start to reduce his debt.

Dan sat in his study, gloomily gazing out of the window as the first stars appeared in the clear twilight sky.

'At least the evenings are getting lighter,' he murmured, as if it were some sort of compensation for the financial cloud looming over his horizon. In the distance, he could hear the scampering feet of the children on some last escapade before Kate drove them to bed. In spite of his mood, he grinned to himself. They were great kids. He and Kate were so lucky.

He sighed, pulled the farm report out of a pile of papers and flicked through it. If he were to do anything at all, it would have to be something drastic. He would phone Steven Kelner in the morning, if he had a chance. He knew what he would say – get rid of Frank Leach. Sell Woodside Farm.

Dan's jaw set. The farm had been through bad times before, but they had not sold off any land. The estate was more or less the same size as it had been for a hundred years or more, and he was determined he should hand it on to Ben and Rosie intact. That was their right, their birthright, as it had been his.

More than that, much as he disliked Frank Leach, Dan was adamant he was not going to be the one to dispossess the Leaches, whatever he might threaten to the contrary. He couldn't fully explain it. Not only were there elements of pride and paternalism involved in his stand, but also there was the niggling responsibility he'd always felt for Jem Leach's untimely death. The least he could do was to let Frank stay where, as far as Dan was concerned, he was entitled to be.

He mulled over the other possibilities as he had done before, countless times.

Watersmeet House was worth a substantial amount these days. 'Make your assets work for you,' Steven Kelner's voice echoed in his brain. He could raise a sufficient mortgage on the house, meet his debts and then keep his fingers crossed for a change in the farm's fortunes. But, if he did that, he would have to do something about life insurance, because if, God forbid, anything should happen to him, Kate would be in a dire situation.

The more he thought about it, the better this course of action seemed to be. 'After all,' he reasoned, 'if anything does go drastically wrong, I've always got Woodside Farm to fall back on. But first, before I do anything else, I must get that life insurance sorted. I must, I must...'

He stood up, stretched and yawned, and feeling more positive, if only because he had made some sort of decision, he went to join in with the children's bedtime story.

35

Kate

2001

'Oh no!' Kate wailed when she saw the car. The windows were completely frosted up. 'We're late enough already! Come on children, give me a hand. I knew I should have put the car in the barn last night.'

The clear skies of the night before had resulted in the temperature plummeting. The frosted rim of every leaf on the yew hedge glittered in the weak rays of the early morning sun. The lawn sparkled, stiff and white. The leafless branches of the trees were framed in ice, and late roses expired on frozen briars. Trailing wisps of mist hung on the surface of the river, and clouds of steam from the cowshed hung in the morning air. The yard glistened, black and hard, patch-worked with grey frozen puddles.

'Yippee, look at me... I'm an ice skater!' yelled Ben, slithering across one the size of a small pond.

'Me too, me too!' Rosie joined her brother, skidding and

sliding on the slippery surface with shouts of joy. Splash tried to join in, barking his enthusiasm for this new sport in which his paws went in every direction except forward.

Ted came round the side of the cowshed and grinned at them as he went to help Kate de-ice her car.

'The gritting lorries were out early this morning,' he told her, 'so the roads should be OK. Just watch Rooks Hill when you come back. At this time of year it doesn't get the sun, so the frost lingers.'

'I'll be fine,' she smiled at him. 'It's not like you to worry, Ted.'

'No,' he hesitated. 'Can you drop by the feed store when you get back, Kate. There's something I need to talk over with you.'

She looked at him closely. 'Is everything all right, Ted?'

'Yes, yes. Nothing to worry about. Just when you've got a moment... Time you were off. Start the car and I'll gather those three up for you.'

The countryside was stunning, crisp and sparkling, and on the way to school the children excitedly chattered about whether it might snow or not, and whether they might have a white Christmas.

'Wot's a "white" Christmas?' Rosie asked. 'How can Christmas be white, it's lots of colours.'

'It's when it snows, silly. It snows on Christmas day. I hope it does. I love snow.'

'I've never seen snow, 'cept on television, in *Bambi* and *Thomas the Tank Engine*.'

'That's because you're only little,' said Ben, not unkindly for once. 'I've seen lots. It's great fun. If it snows, I'll help you make a snowman just like Dad made for me when I was little.'

Kate dropped the children off at school and stopped on her

way back, to walk Splash across the fields for a vigorous half hour's exercise.

The frost was thick on the ground here, and her spirits lifted to see the dog run so exuberantly across the field, his ears flapping, his tongue lolling with excitement, and leaving little bright green paw prints in his wake. The frosted grass was a new experience, and he went into a long slide, rolling on his back, wriggling and waving all four paws in the air in such ecstatic abandonment that she laughed and the dull, depressed feeling that had settled on her after her conversation with the insurance agent, lifted.

She had, with some difficulty, tracked him down and persuaded him to meet her. He was polite, but seemed guarded and embarrassed by her questioning. He could remember little of the actual conversation that he'd had with Dan. He'd tried to persuade him to choose a package that involved a pension plan as well as a lump- sum pay-out, but Dan had told him, categorically, he wasn't interested in planning a pension. And that was it.

She didn't know what she had expected but she'd gone into a deep gloom.

It didn't help that the research document she'd sent for, *Suicide and Stress in Farming* arrived the day before, and although Dan didn't fit the mould, the report was unequivocal in its findings: financial stress, long hours of work, increasingly complex forms and regulations, and events like BSE, had resulted in farmers becoming a high suicide risk.

Walking across the fields with Splash, she mulled over everything she had learned so far.

On the one hand she hadn't noticed anything amiss with Dan before his death. She'd gone over and over the events of the day before and nothing struck an odd note. Nor had

342

anybody else close to him mentioned anything. If he *meant* to do something so...so extreme...he *would* have behaved differently. There was no guile about Dan, of that she was sure.

But then, on the other hand, he *had* kept from her all his financial worries, all his concerns for the future of the farm, and he hadn't told her about the life insurance. She sighed. She felt she was no further forward. No, she corrected herself, it was worse than that. Everything so far seemed to be pointing in one direction. But she could not, would not, accept that conclusion.

She turned back towards the car, calling the dog. 'Come on Splash, time to go back and see what Ted wants.'

The frost was beginning to melt where the sun's rays touched it, but was still thick and white in the shadows. The roads had been gritted, as Ted had said, and didn't seem unduly slippery, but she proceeded with caution, the road from Great Missenwall being a winding, narrow one. Polly's cottage was on a bend at the top of Rooks Hill, and marked the beginning of a steep descent down to Watersmeet House and the river.

Passing Polly's house, Kate started down the hill. The car was in third gear and she put her foot on the brake, pressing the clutch to change down to second. Her foot on the brake went straight to the floor. She couldn't believe it.

She tried again.

Nothing.

Frantically she pumped at it.

Nothing.

The car gathered speed.

She screamed.

Her insides seemed to liquify.

'Don't panic! Keep calm! Think!' A small voice in her brain took over.

343

She put her foot on the clutch and the car seemed to go even faster.

She jammed the gear into second.

The engine screamed and juddered and she pulled as hard as she could on the hand brake.

The car went into a sideways skid.

One side of the lane was flanked by an old wall, on the other side a ditch and a high-banked hedge. In an uncannily detached state, as if she had all the time in the world, Kate considered how to bring the car to a halt. One solution would be to crash into the stream and possibly the garden wall of Watersmeet at the bottom of the hill, or maybe she could turn the car into the farmyard gate…

But fate took a hand. The car started to spin as it skidded, turned upside down, rolled over and over, and came to a halt in the ditch.

The noise of the car's engine, the sound of the crash, and the hysterical barking of the terrified dog brought Polly, Colin, and Brenda running from the cheese shed, John Potter and Josh from the milking parlour, and Ted out of the repairs barn. But Kate lay still, quite unaware.

'Kate! Katie darling, are you all right?' It was Dan's voice, loving, concerned.

Kate groaned and opened her eyes.

Dan was kneeling beside her, stroking her face, holding her hand. 'Oh thank goodness. You gave me such a fright. Are you all right?'

'Dan? Dan?' She struggled to get up, but couldn't move. She hurt all over.

'Sssh. Don't move. I'll go and get help. You've knocked yourself out. Don't move. I won't be long.'

344

She struggled to grasp his hand, hold him back, but it was no good, all movement seemed impossible. Tears started to roll helplessly down her face.

'Dan, don't go. Don't leave me.'

'I must. Don't cry, sweetheart.' He leant over her and kissed her. She felt his lips firm on hers, the brush of his cheek against her face. 'I love you, Katie.'

'Don't go,' she sobbed. 'Please, please don't go...'

But he was gone.

She remained unconscious as the fire brigade extracted her from the wreckage of the car, and an ambulance took her and Polly in a dash across country to the A&E unit in Bath. The examination and tests were thorough, and as Kate finally scrambled back into consciousness, the general consensus was that she'd had a remarkably lucky escape and that her injuries were comparatively slight.

'A broken wrist, a broken nose, two cracked ribs, two black eyes and a headache; you got off lightly. The car was a complete wreck, but as Ted said, those old Volvos are built like tanks and the fact that the roof didn't cave in saved you.' Polly couldn't quite stop her smile from wobbling.

Kate didn't feel as if she'd got off lightly. Her head ached, her whole body felt as if it had been beaten black and blue, and her eyes and nose were so swollen she could hardly breathe or see.

But they were not going to let her out for at least for a couple of days. Not only had she been unconscious for some time, but her spinal cord had been badly bruised, resulting in temporary paralysis, and they needed to keep her under observation.

When she was finally settled in a ward, she drifted into a painful semi-doze, trying desperately to recapture those few moments when Dan had been with her.

Ted arrived to collect Polly.

His voice was gruff. 'My god, Kate, you had a lucky escape. The car's a complete write-off. You must have hit a patch of black ice. The police said there were a lot of accidents on account of the ice this morning…'

Wearily Kate shook her head, 'I don't remember the detail, Ted. The car skidded I think, but the brakes didn't work. I kept on jabbing at them and there was nothing there…' A terrible thought then struck her and her voice shook with fear. 'Splash – is he all right? It's bad enough I'm here, but the children will be beside themselves if anything's happened to him.'

Ted looked drawn, but his eyes and voice were warm. 'Don't fret, Girlie, he got off more lightly than you. He jumped out of the car as soon as the firemen prised open the door, apparently none the worse for wear. I've had him checked over by Jeff Babbington.'

'Oh, thank goodness!' Tears sprang to Kate's eyes. 'But what shall I do about the children? I can't let them see me like this…'

'But if you don't let them see you, they will imagine the worst,' Polly said gently. 'I think you should let them come. It'll be a shock, but they're resilient and once they know you're going to get better, they'll deal with it. Lizzie is picking them up from school and Ted is going to take me over there now. I'll put together some things you might need, and the children can come back in with me. Honestly dear, if you feel up to a visit from them, the sooner the better, I think.'

Polly was right. The children were shocked at the sight of their mother unable to move, her face cut and bruised, and her wrist in bandages. But they recovered rapidly and their visit did all three of them a great deal of good.

As she left, Rosie had confided to her mother that Ben had

bet her a whole Mars bar that she would cry during the visit. 'An' I didn't, did I, Mummy, so now he's gonna sulk 'cos he's gotta buy me one.'

But Ben didn't sulk. He just looked rather stricken at leaving his mother behind, which had cut her to the quick, and Maggie Potter, who arrived shortly after the children had left, found her in floods of tears.

'I can't stay here, Maggie. I can't – I've got to get home as quickly as I can. Quite apart from the fact the children break up from school in a couple of days, it's Christmas next week!'

'Yes it is, Katie, and you can be sure they will push you out of here as soon as they can,' Maggie replied, 'so there's no point in fretting. We'll all rally round.'

And of course they did. Polly told Kate that the phone never seemed to stop ringing with offers of help and inquiries after her progress. Even William Etheridge had phoned all the way from the Seychelles.

'He apparently heard about the accident from his manager, Jim Evans. He was very concerned, Kate. I didn't realise he had become such a friend, but of course you and Muriel were close, weren't you? He's a nice man.'

Margaret Dinsdale surpassed herself. She telephoned Kate, wore her out with a long, rambling speech of self-justification for her own inaction, finishing with a gentle grumble: 'I'm sure Polly didn't think when she told me you'd had a bad accident, darling. She can't have imagined how I must have felt… For a moment I thought you'd been badly injured, and it's only superficial after all. Are you sure you won't change your mind and come here for Christmas? It's going to be a spectacular party, on Boxing Day, you know, and you could be very helpful with the catering, darling…'

Her father walked into the ward the day after she'd been admitted and sat by her bedside the whole day, reading while she slept, and talking to her when she wanted to talk. His company was soothing and in his presence, Kate found the almost overwhelming desire to cry, slowly recede. When he finally stood up to go, the love they shared, inarticulate, often swamped by events and other peoples' demands, was stronger than ever. She held his hand tightly.

'Dad, I'm so glad you came. I've missed you.'

He understood and gently stroked her face. 'And I've missed you, darling. When the call came through, I thought I'd lost you, and all the way here, I felt so angry with myself.'

'Why, Dad?'

'Because I've allowed your mother to dictate the pace. It's not her fault at all, it's mine; I've found it easier to go along with whatever she organises and it's not good for any of us. I'm my own person and I'm suffering from an overdose of inertia. So, sweetheart, since you're my number-one priority, I warn you I shall be knocking at your door, begging a bed as often as I can get away. I've a student who can look after the bookshop at weekends, and your mother doesn't need me to help with her B&B. You don't have to push the boat out for me, I shall be happy to slot in as one of the family.'

'Oh Dad,' Kate whispered, overcome. 'I'd love that, I'd really love that.'

She was kept in for four days until, stiff and painful though it was, her battered body was able to carry her as far as the bathroom and back. She had packed her belongings and was waiting for Polly when Max walked into the ward, accompanied by two very excited children.

'Mum, Mum, look who's here! We've come to take you

home…'

'An' we've got a big surprise for you, you'll never guess what it is…an' I helped, I did!'

'Max! What are *you* doing here?'

'I've come to collect you, silly. Since I'm coming for Christmas, I thought I'd finish work early and then come down to help look after you all. I've spoken to Mary and she's doing the same, so she'll be here tomorrow.'

He picked up her bag. 'Christmas starts with your return home. My God, Kate, I've never seen eyes that colour. They're spectacular. Has anyone taken a photograph yet?'

'We've been counting the colours of Mum's bruises every day. Black, blue, purple, green, yellow…' said Ben gleefully.

'They're much better than yours, Uncle Max,' observed Rosie.

Max touched a bruise on his forehead and grinned. 'I'm sure they are, but I didn't set a car rolling over and over down a hill to get mine.'

'How did you get it, then?' asked Ben, curious.

Max laughed. 'It was a parting present from an ex-girlfriend. She broke my cafetière over my head.'

Polly had made up a bed for Kate in the sitting room. The surprise was a Christmas tree, decorated with every ornament, glittering object and scrap of tinsel the children could find space for.

'We put it in the window in here, so you could see it,' Ben explained. 'Uncle Max said it wouldn't be no good for you in the hall. Do you like your surprise?'

'It's a wonderful surprise. I think it's the loveliest tree I've ever seen.'

'So do I,' agreed Rosie. 'I chose the fairy. I think she's

349

the best thing, and Uncle Max has bought lots of chocolate decorations. We're gonna put them on when Toby gets here.'

Mary arrived with Toby the next day, and with mounting excitement, the cousins roared around the house; Polly handed over the kitchen to Mary, and Max took over the role of chief entertainment officer. A warm, merry atmosphere prevailed: so different from the one Kate had dreaded.

Ensconced comfortably on her sofa, unable to do much, she asked Polly to bring her the five Rose Maddicott diaries that Nick Lovell had specified, then settled down to carry on reading where she had left off.

Polly was curious. 'Why are you so interested in old Rose's journals, dear? Surely I can get you something more enjoyable to read?'

'It's a bit of detective work, Polly. Do you remember Rose's bequest to Dan?'

'Vaguely. I know she wanted him to read her diaries, which I thought was very unrealistic of her. Dan's reading material rarely stretched beyond *Farmer's Weekly*. I don't know when she thought he'd make the time to read her jottings.'

'You're right, but I became intrigued, so I got Nick Lovell to look out exactly what she'd asked him to read. Now I have the time, I thought I'd see if I can get to the bottom of the mystery, if there is a mystery, that is.'

The following day, at Ted's suggestion, they had the weekly farm meeting. Discussing farm business did a lot for Kate, distracting her mind from the aches and pains of her body and the lurking aftermath of shock. When the meeting finished, Polly went off to make tea and Kate and Ted sat in companionable silence as the light faded from the sky and the sitting room was illuminated by the flashing of brightly coloured tree lights.

'Ted,' – in the comfortable peace of the sitting room Kate felt secure enough to finally give voice to a nagging disquiet – 'please don't think I'm being hysterical, but…' She paused.

'Hysterical is not a word I associate with you, Girlie. What is it?'

'It's just that – I know everyone thinks the accident was caused by ice, but I keep going over and over it in my mind,' she shuddered. 'And what I remember is putting my foot on the brake and it going straight to the floor. The brakes weren't working. They weren't working, Ted. I didn't imagine it. If they had been, there would have been some resistance, wouldn't there?'

Ted frowned and rubbed the side of his nose, thoughtfully.

'Shock can play funny games with the memory, Kate…'

'I know, but I'm sure, Ted.'

Ted was silent for a moment, his thin craggy face silhouetted in the brightness of a large log burning in the fireplace, making his expression hard to read.

'Well I tell you what,' his voice was calm and reassuring. 'The car's been taken over to Vince's garage, to wait for the insurance assessor. Vince says nothing's going to happen till after New Year, but I'll have a word with him and see if, in the meantime, he can give it the once-over. The car's wrecked, but he might be able to find out if there was something wrong with the brakes.'

'Thanks, Ted.'

They were interrupted by the children's shouts from the kitchen. They had returned from a private shopping expedition with Mary and Max.

Kate put out a hand. 'Ted, please, don't say anything about this, will you, particularly not to Polly? You're probably right and it's my imagination playing overtime. It's going to be

351

difficult enough for her as it is and I don't want to cast any more of a shadow over Christmas… Christmas!' Kate repeated faintly, as the children burst in, full of excitement about their secret purchases.

Joe arrived on Christmas Eve, a week after the accident, and it was the first occasion that Kate, hating being an invalid and determined not to be out of action longer than necessary, joined them for dinner.

As it was Christmas Eve, the children stayed up to eat with them. The conversation around the table was animated. Toby and Ben swapped school stories with Joe. Rosie was chattering to Ted and Polly about Father Christmas and the growing pile of brightly coloured parcels under the tree. And Mary and Max engaged in sibling banter about Nicola, Max's absent girlfriend. It was such a good-humoured, relaxed occasion, Kate felt full of warmth and gratitude towards them all.

'I haven't forgotten you're not here,' she addressed Dan silently, 'but they're making as it good as it can be without you, and I love them for it.'

'How are you getting on with Rose's diaries, dear?' Polly turned to Kate, 'Uncovered anything interesting?'

Kate laughed. 'It's labour-intensive! Her handwriting is so tiny I have to concentrate hard, but it's fascinating stuff – an extraordinary picture of country life at the end of the war. But she wrote so much, I've decided not to read them all, for the moment, it would take too long. I'm concentrating on those entries she really wanted Dan to read. The one curious thing so far, Polly, is that they're all to do with Woodside Farm. I haven't got to the end of them yet, but they mainly describe the friendship between Rose, and Susan Leach, Frank's mother. Did you know they were friends?'

By now everyone, except for the children, who'd slipped away, was listening with interest.

'No. I don't think Rose ever mentioned her. In fact she'd forbidden any discussion about the Leaches in her presence, even before I came. I just thought she was carrying the family feud business a bit too far. Actually, I'm ashamed to say I don't think I ever knew the name of Frank's mother. Did you, Ted?'

'I'm not sure I did. People gossip whenever anything unusual goes on. They gossip if it don't! I think folks found it surprising Jem had got himself a bride, and thought it a great good fortune for the Leach family when she presented him with a son. But she was long dead and rarely, if ever, talked of when I arrived at Watersmeet.'

'And Rose never mentioned her, or said anything about the Leaches to you?'

Ted scratched his head. 'Not that I can remember. Apart from that time...you'll remember it, you two...that time Jem locked young Mary in the bird cage...'

Mary shuddered. 'How could I forget? I used to have such terrible nightmares after then. And when things got bad with Clive, I had the nightmares all over again, except that Clive was Jem...' Joe reached for her hand. 'But what had that to do with Granny Rose?'

'She ticked us off fiercely for having gone there, I remember that much,' Max interjected. 'She was a formidable old lady, although she was only about six inches tall. She terrified me!'

'Yes,' Polly smiled. 'She terrified me. But go on Ted, you were saying...?'

'Well, the day after all that happened, she stopped me in the yard, fixed me with those beady eyes of hers and made me tell her, in every tiny detail, exactly what had happened and what was said. The birdcage affair shook her up, I do remember that… She knew of it, for sure, which took me by surprise: as far as I knew, she'd never been to Woodside. She kept muttering, 'the birdcage, not the birdcage!' Then she grabbed me by the arm and said I wasn't to let Dan go anywhere near Woodside again. She held onto me until I promised, then she went stomping off back across the yard to the house and nothing more was ever said. To be honest, our paths didn't cross very much, and I thought by that time, she was…well…was getting quite eccentric. So maybe this obsession of hers with her diaries is no more than that, Kate…something and nothing.'

'It might be,' agreed Polly. 'But I remember it was soon after that happened she made me drive her into town to see the solicitor.'

'And she didn't tell you why she wanted to see him?' Max asked.

Polly shook her head. 'Rose didn't confide in me.'

'I'd like to know more about this Susan,' mused Kate. 'Who was she? Where did she come from? Was she local? How old was she? When did she die? She was the wife of our tenant, for goodness sake! There must be some way of finding out.'

'The parish register might tell us something,' Polly suggested. 'Presumably she and Jem married in church. I know you could get married by special licence in the war, but we're dealing with country folk here, and they wouldn't have thought that a proper wedding. Once we've got her maiden name, we can find out if she was born locally. In any case, we're sure to find her death registered. Once Christmas is over, Kate, I'll check that, if you like.'

'In the meantime,' Mary rose to her feet and started to collect the dishes, 'Christmas is nearly here, and we've a huge amount to do. Max, Kate is looking wiped out, give her your arm and take her back to the sitting room. Joey, round up those

354

children, who, I swear, are getting noisier by the minute, and throw them into the bath…'

Max and Joe had undertaken to fulfill the Father Christmas role, and Mary and Polly prevailed upon the children to go to bed earlier than they wanted to. Ted saw Polly home, and the four friends rounded off the evening by opening a bottle of champagne and toasting Dan.

Much later, lying on her truckle bed, Kate heard the grandfather clock in the hall chime midnight.

In past years, she and Dan would still be up at this hour, tired out but still wrapping presents, drinking wine, and stuffing the children's stockings and willing them to go to sleep so that they too could go to bed.

'Dan,' she whispered, 'Dan. It's Christmas.'

Her only answer was a spit and crackle of flame from the log Max had thrown onto the fire before he went to bed. The room was full of the distinctive sweet scent of pine, mingled with the burning apple-wood log and the slightly claustrophobic smell of recently snuffed candles. Stabs of firelight sent deep shadows dancing throughout the room and setting the tinsel and glass baubles on the tree afire with reflected light.

Kate had intended to move back into her own room that night but at the last moment, the thought of waking up without Dan made her quail and she decided to stay where she was, in this room so full of Christmas Present.

36

Rose

1949

The winding track from the lane to Woodside Farm was sufficiently long to make Rose uneasy whenever she came to call on Susan. Not that she was afraid of Jem. Far from it. But in spite of herself, the moment she turned off the lane she felt furtive. The clandestine nature of her visits made her feel uncomfortable, and on that long, rattling approach to the farm she could not rid herself of the feeling that malignant eyes in the undergrowth watched her, and the harsh calls of the crows were summoning up Jem to confront her round the next bend.

She didn't come often. Quite apart from the silent disapproval of Samuel, she was busy all year round. She had to supervise the dairy and the production of butter, cream and cheese. She was responsible for the hens, the ducks and the bees. She made honey, bottled the fruit from the kitchen garden and the orchards, made jams and preserves and chutneys, baked bread daily, and supervised the feeding of the farm workers as well as running the house for Samuel and young Jack. What spare time she had was spent in sewing and mending, and writing her daily journal.

But she still made time when she could for Susan, and not out of a sense of duty, although that had driven her on the first occasion, but because she liked her and because the poor girl had an air of desolation about her which left Rose for the first time in her life, feeling helpless.

She had never known such a concentration of despair. She sensed something was very wrong but didn't know what she could do about it. Susan was not forthcoming about her past, and while she was touchingly grateful for Rose's visits, she avoided all conversation that concerned her life with Jem. She went out of her way to ensure he and Rose never met, and Rose was complicit in this. Susan had told her of the beating she'd got from him after that first visit to Woodside farm and Rose was well aware that if Jem found out about her visits, Susan would bear the brunt of his anger.

It wasn't too difficult for the two women to arrange the visits without attracting attention. Farming has very definite routines, and particularly in the summer months, the farmer would be expected to be out of the house for most of the day.

Rose had taken a gamble on her second visit and had avoided discovery. After that, Susan would tie a ribbon to a bush where the track emerged onto the lane, if it was convenient for Rose to visit, and Rose would arrange to pass by that spot during the third week of every month.

So far they had been undetected, but Rose was getting uneasy about the child, Frank. He'd turned five and would be starting school in September, which would make her visits easier to arrange. In the meantime she was afraid he would tell his father about his mother's visitor. Try as she could, she didn't like the little boy, even though Susan plainly adored him. He didn't appear to reciprocate that love, and never seemed to give her all the little cuddles and caresses that Rose had received from Jack when he was a toddler. He was a silent child and whenever she visited, would stare and stare at her, never smiling, hardly responding to her when she tried to talk to him.

To her relief, he hadn't been present the last two times she had visited, and Susan told her that although he was barely five years old, Jem had decided he was no longer a baby and the time had come for him to work on the farm.

Today's visit was the first Rose had managed to make for a couple of months. She had cycled along the lane yesterday and there was the pre-arranged signal. That was fortuitous because Rose wanted to see Susan for a particular reason – she wanted to find out about the mysterious American.

As a ploy to check for Susan's signal, she had used the pretext of needing darning wool to cycle to Great Missenwall. While she was in the village shop, a young man, a stranger, walked in and spoke to the post mistress, in an American accent.

''Scuse me, ma'am, I'm a stranger hereabouts and I am looking for directions to Woodside Farm. Can you oblige?'

The postmistress peered across her desk at him. 'I am not sure that I can divulge that information, young man. I am a servant of His Majesty's Government and we have been at war. Whom do you wish to see?'

The young man looked a little uncertain. 'Sure ma'am, and I was part of that war. I was over here, on your side, but that was five years ago. I have a friend I wish to look up…'

'Friend? Jem Leach? There must be some mistake. Are you

sure you've got the right place?'

As the young man hesitated further, Rose stepped forward. 'Excuse me, perhaps I can help. I'm Mrs Maddicott and Woodside Farm belongs to my husband, as part of his estate. The Leaches are our tenants.'

The American turned to her gratefully and repeated his request for directions. Under the pretext of showing him which road to take out of Great Missenwall, she drew him outside, away from eavesdropping ears.

'Forgive me for prying,' she said, 'but is it Susan Leach you wish to see? I only ask because her husband is not an easy man, and doesn't welcome visitors. He makes it very difficult for poor Susan...'

'Does he?' replied the American, grim-faced. 'Well, ma'am, I'm a match for any one. Yep, you're right, it's Susan I've come to see. Although I didn't know she was married. That changes things a bit, but you could say we've some unfinished business which I aim to see through.'

'Again, please excuse me for being nosey, but some years ago, I posted a letter for Susan. It was addressed to an American regiment that had been based in Shepton Mallet. They'd left some considerable time ago, but the Embassy, in London, very kindly undertook to send it on. I happened to notice the letter was addressed to a Mr Franklin Driver. Is that you?'

'Yes, ma'am. Franklin Driver at your service. I'm much obliged to you for forwarding the letter. I'm only sorry it has taken me so long to get here. I've been on active duty overseas ever since I left Britain, and only recently been demobbed.'

Although there were a number of questions she was burning to ask him, she felt it would be too impertinent, so she confined herself to giving him directions, with a warning to proceed with caution.

The last sight she had of him, the young man was striding confidently off in the direction of Woodside Farm, whistling cheerfully, a kit bag thrown over his shoulders. Although she knew her neighbours in the shop would be waiting for her return, ready to indulge in some juicy gossip-mongering, she chose to disappoint them and cycled straight home. She liked Susan too much to attach any whiff of scandal to her name, and she so wanted Susan's story to have a happy ending, without quite knowing what that ending might be.

She reached the farmhouse unchallenged and, parking her bike, looked up at the curtains of the bedroom window overlooking the yard. They were drawn back.

It was a further safety precaution she and Susan had devised – if there was a change of plan and Jem was about, one of the curtains would be half-closed.

The yard, as usual, was empty of life apart from the group of dusty brown hens. She walked around the side of the house, expecting to find Susan baking in the kitchen. She always baked the day Rose visited, trying out recipes that Rose had brought her and making a little extra that would not be missed.

Rose knocked on the door and waited. There was no response of any kind and she could hear no sound of movement in the kitchen, nothing. Puzzled, she knocked again. Again, nothing. She tried the door handle. The door was not locked so she peered round into the kitchen and called softly. There was no sign of Susan, and no sign that any baking had taken place. The residue of some sort of meal was still on the table, which in itself was unusual, since Susan was a meticulous housekeeper.

She went to the foot of the stairs and called up in case Susan was incapacitated and lying down. No answer. Emboldened by her concern, she slipped up the stairs to check. She'd never

360

been up here before and found that the farmhouse had three bedrooms, one larger than the others, which she assumed to belong to Susan and Jem.

There was plenty of evidence of Jem there, but nothing, not even a hairbrush, of Susan's.

The next bedroom in size was clearly the little boy's room and the tiny room at the back, under the eaves, was where she found Susan's things, but no sign of Susan herself. Unlike the beds in the other two rooms, Susan's bed was neatly made.

Rose stood there, her heart thumping. She was not normally given to wild flights of fancy, but as she stood there, trying to work out the significance of the separate rooms and what might account for her friend's absence, a wild hope caught her imagination.

Could the mysterious American have whisked Susan away? Was the poor girl now somewhere far away from the brutal clutches of Jem Leach and their awful child? But as soon as the thought had taken shape, she knew that whatever might have happened, Susan would never go anywhere without her little Frank, and the evidence of the dirty dishes and the unmade beds suggested he was still around. But something must have happened, and happened since Susan had put the signal in place.

Rose slipped down the stairs again and checked the only other room she hadn't been into. A sitting room, the room most country folk only ever used for laying out their dead. That was empty too.

Concerned, her heart thumping, she went outside into the yard. She daren't call out, so she quietly walked around the side of the house to the corner of the barn and looked about her, listening intently.

She thought she heard a slight noise, a noise distinct from

the sounds of the yard and the woods. A hissing, followed by a plaintive mewing, so soft she could have imagined it. But no, it came again and was quickly suppressed. A strange, high-pitched, rather unearthly mew. It came from the barn.

It took a little while for her eyes to become accustomed to the gloom. Her attention was drawn to a large wire cage in one corner. It was a large birdcage occupied by a number of fiercesome birds of prey, each attached to their perches by leather thongs. One, an owl unlike anything she'd seen before, huge, with golden feathers, great tufts like horns and wicked, angry eyes, was clearly disturbed, flapping its wings, hissing and spitting and trying to reach something on the ground. She drew closer, and there, huddled up, on freshly churned soil, was her friend.

Horrified, Rose tried the door to the cage, but it was padlocked. She dropped to her knees. 'Susan,' she called softly, 'Susan, it's me, Rose…'

The bundle stirred and a barely recognisable Susan lifted her head. Her face and hands were covered in dried blood and earth, as if she had been trying to bury her head in the ground to get away from the birds, and behind the dirt, her face was swollen with tears and bruises. She had a black eye that was virtually closed; her lip was split and caked with dried blood, which also ran down from a cut on her nose. At her movement, the angry bird hissed and tried to claw her, but it wasn't the bird that the wretched girl shrank from. As soon as she saw Rose, a look of horror distorted her features still more.

'Rose, go away. Go away!'

'I can't leave you like this. Don't be absurd. I've got to get you out of here. You poor, poor, creature…'

'Leave me alone, leave me alone. For pity's sake, go away.'

'I won't. I'm going to get you out of here if it's the last thing

I do. Who did this to you? Jem? He's no right to treat you like this. Susan, I've got to open this door. Where does he keep the key?'

'You don't understand…' Susan started to cry. A weird, soft wailing that unnerved Rose.

'Susan, don't cry. I'll get you out and take you away. We'll tell the police; Jem won't get away with this, I'll see to that… Just tell me where to find…'

'NO!' Susan screeched with such force and venom Rose was momentarily stunned.

The birds shrieked and spread their wings, straining at their leashes to peck and claw, but Susan took no notice. She hissed at Rose through the wire, 'You don't understand a thing. I don't want you to do nothing. I don't want to go with you. I don't want no police. Get it?'

'But Susan, Jem can't…'

'Yes he can and I don't care… You dare bring the police here… You're an interferin' old busybody, stickin' yer nose in where it ain't wanted. I don't care if I die in this cage. I don't care!' Huge sobs racked her frail body, but still she continued with her diatribe. 'You think you're my friend – well yer ain't and I don't want you comin' round here any more, so fuck off, you miserable old cow and go and do good to some other poor bitch, but leave me alone!'

Rose was appalled. 'Susan, I can't leave you like…'

Susan, with all the strength she could summon, screamed back at her, 'Yes you can. Once and for all, fuck off and don't come here ever again. If you don't go, I shall scream and scream till Jem comes. He can throw you out an' he won't be gentle about it, tenant or no tenant. And it will serve you right, you stuck-up bitch…'

The invective grew worse. The birds screeched, flapped

their wings and strained at their leashes. Her one visible eye was wild in her face as she spitted and clawed at the wire. Whatever emotion drove Susan, de-humanised her. In the face of such a ferocious outpouring, Rose could only retreat.

Shocked by what she had witnessed; hurt, and deeply depressed by the absolute rejection of her friendship, for days and weeks she brooded, not able to share the events of that afternoon with anybody, or do anything to help her friend. Susan had made it clear the last thing she wanted was any sort of intervention by her or by the police.

A month later she cycled past the track to Woodside Farm but there was no sign of a token. She made discreet enquiries about Susan and heard that she was occasionally seen going about her business. When young Frank started school in September, Susan completely ignored Rose's attempts to speak to her and Rose finally had to accept, that whatever else had happened on that day, her friendship with Susan had ended.

Of the American and his whereabouts, she never heard another word.

37

Dan

2001

Spring finally settled on the countryside. The hedgerows fluoresced with bright leaf buds and snowy-white blackthorn; daffodils gave way to primroses, celandines, violets and lady's smock.

Still the foot and mouth disease spread. The number of animals slaughtered passed the million mark and continued to rise. The weather remained wet and Dan kept his cows in despite the increasing cost of the feedstuff he was forced to buy, and the difficulties faced in its delivery.

In mid-April the children broke up for the Easter holidays and Kate reminded Dan that they had promised Flick she should come and stay with them. Dan demurred, but Kate was firm.

'The children have been extremely patient with the restrictions, darling. Flick will be a welcome distraction for them. Besides, having her staying here will be easier for us to manage than friends coming round for the odd day.'

So Flick came, and after an initial sulk about not being able to go riding with Tilly Etheridge, she settled into her role as favourite cousin with great gusto. The children had a gloriously wet and muddy time racing across the empty fields, playing hide-and-seek in Sparrows Woods, and if the weather was too bad, exploring the remoter regions of the old house about which Flick invented such wild stories of ghosts and witches that Kate had to intervene, as Rosie became too terrified to go to bed.

By the end of April, the news was more optimistic, the number of confirmed cases seemed to be declining, the weather brightened, and Dan and Ted decided it was time to release the cows from their long confinement. Watching even the most mature matron gambol in the fresh green field, brought a smile to Dan's face and he felt the awful strain of the last few crisis-laden months start to ease.

When he got home that evening, however, he found Kate badly upset. She rarely cried, so seeing her with eyes red and swollen, he was filled with alarm. He went straight to her and folded her in his arms. She clung to him, weeping onto his chest.

'Oh Dan, Dan, it's so horrible… It's hit me how bad it is… When's it going to end? I can't bear to think of what you've been going through…'

Dan felt his gut turn to water; he had never felt so afraid. 'What is it, Kate? Has Ted phoned through? Are the sheep infected? Have you heard something from Matt? What is it sweetheart?'

'No, no…it's not us. It's the Warrens. It was on the TV just now; on the news. Joe's father; you could see he was trying to

366

put a brave face on it, but he was fighting back tears... They showed pictures of gunmen in white boiler suits... And they said the sows tried to attack them, but they were only trying to defend their piglets.'

For a moment she was incoherent with sobs, then she lifted her tear-stained face to look at him. 'All gone, Dan; all his pigs. But the worst thing was, they didn't have the disease. It was a farm on the other side of them, closer to Devizes. How can such slaughter be justified, Dan? I just don't understand why we can't vaccinate. Poor, poor Mr Warren, it's going to destroy him.'

Dan said nothing, but remembering his joyful cows, he felt numb.

'Does that put us in the front line now?' Kate asked, her voice small and fearful.

Dan stirred and kissed her.

'No, no. There's a good fifteen miles between us and Ashcroft Farm and while it might not count for that much, Watersmeet lies to the west of the farm and the prevailing winds at this time of the year tend not to be easterly. We're safe, for the moment, but it's a reminder that the fight is not over yet and we will not be able to relax until there are no more reported cases, anywhere. Oh Kate, I am so tired of all this!'

But they struggled on, and apart from occasional small alarms, the disease did not strike and then, slowly at first, the number of fresh cases began to fall.

Halfway through May, Rosie had an invitation to her best friend's birthday party. Difficult though it was, Dan and Kate had struggled to ensure that the children did not miss any school, but they had not encouraged any other social activity, which the children felt very keenly. Faced with his daughter's woebegone face as she showed him the invitation, and knowing the disease was now in sharp decline, Dan agreed that she could go to the party. As Kate was poorly with flu he would both take and collect her.

Just as he was about to leave, Ted hailed him from across the yard. He looked worried.

Automatically Dan tensed. 'What is it, Ted, what's wrong?'

'I've had a call from the home my mother's in, Dan. She's had a fall. They think she's broken her leg. She's been taken to hospital.'

Dan was conscious of an overwhelming sense of relief and immediately felt contrite. 'Oh, I'm sorry to hear that. What do you want to do?'

'I need to go, I'm sorry. It's not the best time of the year...'

'No, but we'll manage. How long do you think you'll be away? Where is she?'

'Sandwich, the other side of the bloody country. I've tried to get her to move closer, but she's as stubborn as old boots.'

'So that's where you get it from,' Dan grinned. 'Don't worry about us. I'll pull Mike in, if necessary, and there's always old Sammy, itching to get back into the milking parlour. Just let me know when I can expect you back.'

Ted patted Dan's shoulder. 'Thanks, I'll give you a ring as soon as I know the score.'

Rosie was bubbling with excitement when he picked her up, her face sticky with chocolate and clutching a party bag containing assorted sweets, balloons and a sickly smelling rubber with matching 'gel' pen. As they drove home she insisted on recounting every detail of the party, but in the middle of describing a particular game, she broke off and shouted, 'Oh look, Daddy, look! It's my fwend!'

They had just past a small, battered tractor. At his daughter's shout, he peered into the rear-view mirror and saw, with a shock, that the driver was Frank Leach. He tried to keep his voice steady.

'Your friend, Rosie?'

'Yes. We met him in the woods, Flick and me.'

'In the woods? What were you doing there?'

'We was playin' hide 'n' seek an' I couldn't find Flick. I shouted and shouted, but I couldn't find her and then my fwend come and said she was over there and she was.'

'What did you do then, darling?'

'We talked to him an' Flick asked him lots of questions an' he said he lived all alone, an' Flick asked him if he was lonely and he said no, he liked it and Flick asked him if he had any fwends and he said no, so Flick said she and me would be his fwends and then we heard Ben callin' for us so we said it would be our secret, he would be our secret fwend, and then we come home and had our tea.'

Dan swallowed hard, scarcely able to breathe. 'Did you see him again, your friend?'

'Yes, Daddy. He came to our picnic.'

'Your picnic?'

'I took my dolly's tea set and Flick got some biscuits and some juice from Mummy and we had a picnic in the woods.'

'Why was your friend there?'

"Cos we asked him, silly. 'Cos he was lonely and Flick said we should and he said yes so he did.'

'What happened after your picnic?'

Watching her in the rear-view mirror he could see her wrinkling up her little nose, trying to remember. 'Nuffin'. I think we played hide-'n'-seek a bit and then we had to come home. I didn't want to but Flick said we had to and then she said she didn't want to be fwends wiv him any more.'

'Did you see him again?'

'No, Daddy. Flick didn't want to, so we didn't go to the woods no more.'

Dan tried to act normally, responding to his daughter's cheerful chatter as she passed onto other subjects of more immediate interest to her, but his thoughts were in a turmoil. Probably nothing had happened in the woods, but could he be sure of that? Rosie seemed totally unaffected by the encounters, but was she? And what of Flick? What had changed her mind about Frank? To meet the girls once by accident was one thing, to meet them by arrangement was entirely another. What could have been in his mind? Did he, oh dear God forbid... Could he have molested them? Frank loathed him, no question, but enough to harm his little girl?

They arrived home and as he was undoing her seat belt, he ruffled her curls. 'The man we saw today, Rosie, Flick was right. He wouldn't be a very nice friend. Please don't go to the woods by yourself, will you? And tell Daddy if you see him again. Promise me?'

He made a cup of tea and took it to Kate. She was flushed and feverish so he confined himself to a description of Rosie's enthusiastic enjoyment of the party then left her to try and get some sleep.

He called Emily on her mobile, got a recording so left a message to phone back. Polly came in to get the children their supper, but he was late for the evening's milking so he didn't have time to stop and share his anxieties with her. He brooded throughout the milking, his mind flickering over what might have happened, and what might happen if he didn't do something.

Emily phoned shortly after he got back in and he briefly

recounted what Rosie had told him, and expressed his fears. Emily sounded unconcerned but she said she would talk to Flick. She phoned back shortly after he had got the children to bed.

'I don't think it's nearly as bad as you think, Dan. Flick could hardly remember meeting this man. She said they bumped into someone in the woods the first time they went there. She was hiding, Rosie started to panic because she couldn't find Flick and started bellowing, this man appeared and told her where she was, and that was that. She was very surprised to hear that Rosie said they played with him or that they arranged to meet him again, let alone be friends. She said he was a creepy-crawly and smelt and she couldn't wait to get away from him. That sounds a lot more likely to me… Doesn't it to you? I think Rosie must have made it up… You know how children are at her age… I remember Kate having an imaginary friend when she was six…wouldn't let me play with her because she had her 'friend' to play with… I wouldn't worry about it, Dan.'

But Dan did worry about it. He didn't altogether believe Flick's version of events. Rosie was not a particularly imaginative child, much more down to earth and practical than Ben, and without any guile in her dealings with people. He had never known her to make things up in this way.

He settled Kate down for the night and took himself off to the spare room, where he lay and brooded till the early hours.

The following morning he phoned Steven Kelner. After a long discussion with him, he phoned the insurance company Steven Kelner had recommended, and made an appointment for an agent to visit him at the farm.

He then phoned his solicitor and friend, Nicholas Lovell. Nick was out, so he spoke instead to his father, David Lovell, and asked his advice on the re-possession of Woodside Farm, and the termination of two hundred years of Leach tenancy.

If David Lovell was surprised at this unexpected turn of events, he gave no indication but carefully set out for Dan what had to be done. 'I'll draw up the notice, Dan, and let you have a copy at the same time I send it to Leach.'

'No, thanks all the same, Mr Lovell. I'd rather write it myself – you've told me everything that has to be included. Thing is, if you sent it, I can't guarantee that Frank would read it, so I'll write this myself and take it to him. I'm determined he knows I mean it. He's got to go.'

38

Kate

2001

On Boxing Day, Kate endured a long complaining call from Emily, trapped by her mother's ambitious party plans and resentful that Kate was not with her to share the load. Kate thought she could detect some other concern. A worry half-hinted but not articulated, its existence denied as soon as she encouraged Emily to confide in her. Of her own dramas, there was little or no discussion.

After supper, still too fragile to help with children or dishes, Kate picked up Rose Maddicott's diary for 1949 and settled down to read the last of the entries on Rose's list: July 22nd.

The others joined her in the sitting room just as she finished, closing the journal with a shocked gasp.

'Well? Don't keep us in suspense… What does she write about? What's it all about? What's the mystery?' Max pulled up a stool and sat beside her.

'Mystery? I'm not sure about that... That's not explained. Not yet, anyway. But Mary, you weren't the first person to be locked in the birdcage; Jem Leach appears to have made a habit of it. In this entry Rose describes how she found his wife, Susan, imprisoned in the cage, half-demented, covered with blood.'

She frowned, 'It's quite horrible, but if you can bear it, I'll read it to you.'

The contrast between the cosy atmosphere of the sitting room, the twinkling lights of the tree and the warm, friendly glow of the crackling fire, and the horror of Rose's account of Susan's situation, couldn't have been greater.

When Kate finished reading there was an uncomfortable silence, finally broken by Polly.

'I don't understand, what has all this got to do with Dan?' she fretted. 'It's really nasty, but why did she want him to read about it?'

'What do you think, Kate?' asked Max. 'You've read all the entries now, what do you make of it?'

Kate replied thoughtfully. 'You know, I honestly think there *is* something behind all this. All the entries have described her visits to Woodside Farm, which Rose keeps secret even from Samuel, Dan's grandfather. Then, out of the blue, this American guy arrives to see Susan...'

'What American guy?' Mary asked.

'Rose mentions him in the previous entry, the day before she finds Susan in the birdcage, on 21st July 1949.'

She turned back the pages of the diary.

'She describes how she meets him in Great Missenwall. He's looking for Susan. He tells Rose his name is Franklin Driver. Rose tells him where he will find Susan and the last she sees of him, he's heading off for Woodside Farm.'

She looked up, excited. 'Rose is clearly dying to know more

because he's already made an appearance in the story. The first time she meets Susan, the very first entry Rose wanted Dan to read in August, 1945, Susan asked her to post a letter, and Rose wrote that it was addressed to a Mr Franklin Driver. This is the American, who now turns up four years later!'

Polly shook her head in bewilderment. 'Now I *am* confused. What *has* this to do with Dan? With anything?'

Kate shrugged. 'I don't know. I don't know. But Rose thought it was important. She and Susan were friends. Susan asks her to send a letter addressed to an American, which Rose does. Then, years later, the American appears and disappears, and Susan, bashed and brutalised, ends up a prisoner in the hen house. She sends Rose away and they never see each other again. There is something about this that's *so* important she believes Dan should know about it.'

'Have you read all the entries she mentioned?' demanded Max. 'Surely she gave Dan some explanation, somewhere?'

Kate consulted her list. 'That's it; 1949 was the last one…'

Frustrated, she opened the journal again, and ran her finger firmly down the centre-fold, then noticed for the first time, a tiny pencil jotting in the central margin.

'Wait, look here, in the margin, she's written a date: 14th March, 1951.'

'1951. Right, I'll go and get it. Where are the journals kept?' Max leapt to his feet.

'In Dan's…in the study, on the long shelf, on the right-hand side of the desk. The years are written on the spines.'

Max was not gone long before he returned with the journal and gave it to Kate. Joe threw a log on the fire, and the spitting of the fresh tinder was the loudest sound in the room as she turned the pages to find the entry.

She looked up in surprise. 'How odd: there's hardly anything for the 14th. Not at all like Rose; she normally writes reams. I'll read what it says:

'*Susan Leach is dead. The Doctor gave me a letter from her to be read by me alone. He made me promise not to divulge the contents to anyone. I have just read it and I have never felt so much in need of God's guidance. Indeed, there's no-one else I can turn to, not even Samuel, least of all, Samuel. My poor, dear friend. I will go to Church tomorrow and pray for her. In life, I failed her; in death, dear God, I fear I might have to fail her again.*'

Kate put the diary down. 'And that's all. One paragraph, when normally she would write pages and pages.'

'Wow,' murmured Joe. 'Pretty heavy stuff!'

Mary shivered. 'It's rather spooky – like a ghost story, but for real. What does she mean, "in death I fear I might have to fail her again"?'

'Perhaps she was afraid she wouldn't be able to keep her promise to Susan; that she might be tempted to divulge the contents of her letter?' suggested Polly.

'Did she never say anything to you, Polly?'

Polly shook her head. 'No, Max, as I told you before, I didn't even know she knew Susan Leach. But is there nothing else, Kate? Nothing to give us any further clue? Having brought Dan this far, it seems strange to break off without telling him everything.'

'The rest of the page is blank. Perhaps she says something after her visit to the church the next day.' Kate turned the page and let out a whoop. 'Yes! Here we are, a slip of paper tucked in the crease. It's been written much later. It's dated July 29th 1977 and addressed to Dan...'

'That's when Jem locked me in the birdcage.' Mary's eyes were round with horror.

Kate read out the note.

'Susan's letter is now with Crouch and Lovell. You have to ask for it, Dan, I have told them not to give it to you otherwise. God forgive me if by keeping it secret I have caused further trouble, but I promised Susan I would share her terrible story with no one. God bless you, my dear boy, Grandma Rose.'

'Poor Rose. She adored Dan. How grieved she would have been if she had known...' Polly's voice trailed away.

'I just don't understand why Rose did nothing,' Mary burst out. 'I find her behaviour incredible. If it'd been me and I found a friend, beaten and crazed and imprisoned in a cage, I'd call the police at once. She didn't tell anyone. Why not?'

'You forget how long ago this was,' Polly replied. 'Attitudes towards domestic violence have only started to change in my lifetime. At the end of the war, I don't suppose there'd be a policeman in Britain who'd come between a man and his wife.'

'And Rose says that Susan categorically refused all offers of help...' Kate pointed out.

'Now that I find bizarre,' snorted Max. 'Rose is offering her a way out and she sends her off with a flea in her ear.'

The rest of the evening was spent in fruitless speculation as to what had happened and what it meant. It was unlikely the solicitor's office would be open the next day, which was frustrating, but Kate promised she would get hold of the letter at the earliest opportunity.

The following morning they were up early. Joe and Max had accepted an invitation from Jim Evans, William Etheridge's farm manager, to join him and Ted in a shoot, and Mary and Kate were going to spend the day in preparation for the farm's Christmas party, the following evening. Polly and Mary had tried to persuade her to postpone it, but Kate insisted it go ahead.

'We've always had a party for everyone over Christmas. Dan would be ashamed of me if I called it off because of a few bruises.'

In truth, she needed to keep herself as busy as the stiffness of her bones would allow. Her enforced inactivity meant she had more time than she liked to brood on her narrow escape, and she yearned painfully and hopelessly for Dan.

The nightmares returned. In the depths of the previous night she'd woken in the grip of a terrible dream and lain awake for what seemed hours, afraid to go to sleep again in case she should find herself back in the same nightmare. So, feeling weary, body and soul, she helped Mary and Polly prepare the food for the party.

The phone seemed to ring continuously – friends and neighbours asking after her, and offering help. Finally, after yet another call from a well-wisher, Mary intervened. 'I'll answer the phone from now on, Kate. You look exhausted.'

Before Kate had time to object, the phone rang again.

Mary pounced. 'Oh, Nicola – hi – yes, thanks, and Happy Christmas to you too… No, Max isn't here at the moment… Yes, I'll get him to phone you… He hasn't? Oh, I'm sorry… I can't think… Where are you phoning from…? London…? But I thought you'd gone to Switzerland, skiing? No…? All right, I'll tell him… Bye.'

She put the phone down, grinning, but before she had time to share the joke with Kate, there was an interruption from Polly at the kitchen window.

'A police car's driven into the yard – how very strange. What on earth do they want?'

'Maybe it's about the accident?' Mary joined her.

Kate shook her head. 'Ted said they weren't interested, and it's hardly likely they'd call round the day after Boxing Day, just to see how I am…'

There was a knock at the door and Kate opened it to a young uniformed officer. He nodded in greeting. 'Sorry to trouble you, is the farmer, Mr Maddicott, at home?'

'No,' Kate struggled to keep her voice even. 'I'm Mrs Maddicott and I'm the farmer.'

Startled, he stared at her. 'You're the farmer? I don't mean to be rude, ma'am, but I was expecting to see…um … There's no Mr Maddicott?'

Kate swallowed her indignation at the hopeful tone of his voice. 'No, I'm a widow. My husband's dead. How can I help you?'

Thrown, the policeman consulted his notebook. 'Er, is Mr Jordan about?

'Ted Jordan is my manager, and no, he's not here at the moment.' Kate opened the door wider. 'Why don't you come in and see if I can help you. If it's farm business you're on, then I should be the first to know.'

'Sorry, ma'am,' he mumbled as he entered the kitchen. 'It's just that you took me by surprise… You don't look much like a farmer, if you don't mind me saying so.'

At that Kate had to laugh, and having introduced Polly and Mary, led him through to her study. As she lowered herself stiffly into her chair, he surveyed her critically, 'You look as if you've had some sort of accident?'

'Yes, my car skidded on some black ice. I had a lucky escape. Now, what can I do for you?'

379

'It's about the fire you had before Christmas, Mrs Maddicott.'

It was Kate's turn to stare. 'I'd forgotten all about that. What about it?'

'Well, to come straight to the point, the fire chief at the incident was not too happy about the cause of the fire. He took away one or two samples, and we've had the forensic report passed onto us. It seems the fire might not have been an accident…'

Kate felt the colour drain from her face. 'You're saying the fire might have been started deliberately?' Her voice sounded hoarse. 'Someone tried to set fire to the house? With us in it? Why would anyone want to do that?'

'I'm afraid, Mrs Maddicott, these days arson is not that uncommon on farms. Sometimes it's the farmers themselves, desperate for ready cash and hoping for an insurance pay-out. Sometimes it's a tramp; sometimes it's malice. It's for us to try and find out which it is…'

When the men returned from their day's shooting, they found a sombre trio putting the finishing touches to the party preparations.

Kate filled them in.

'After he'd finished putting the wind up me, he went and poked round the outhouse, then left without saying very much more other than he might be back to talk to you, Ted, and that we should all be vigilant.'

'That goes without saying!' Max looked at Kate with concern. 'You look very pale, Kate, are you OK?'

'I feel terrible,' Kate replied. 'We all do. Ever since he left, we've been going over what might have happened if Splash hadn't barked.'

'But who would do such a thing? It's just so sick!' Mary burst

380

out.

Ted frowned. 'Do the police have any ideas, Kate?'

'I don't think so. At first he implied it might have been me...'

'You?' Max's jaw dropped. 'How did PC Plod figure that out?'

'He said it's not that unusual for a farmer, faced with mounting debts, to set fire to a barn and claim the insurance. He accepted that it was not very likely in this case. I don't think he has much idea. He asked if I could think of anyone who would want to hurt us; anyone with a grudge...' She shrugged her shoulders. 'But quite honestly, I can't think of anyone, certainly no one who would...well, want to harm us.' She shuddered, clasping her hands tightly to try to stop them shaking.

'Have there been any other fires in the neighbourhood recently?' Joe turned to Ted. 'D'ye remember that part-time fire fighter who used to set fire to barns because he loved putting them out...'

'Not that I know of... Although you're right, there are spates of arson from time to time – mainly bored teenagers getting a taste for bonfires. But it's usually the more remote buildings or haystacks...'

'Perhaps a tramp took shelter in the outhouse, lit a fire to keep warm and it got out of hand?' Polly brought a tray of tea over to the table and pushed a steaming mug into Kate's hand. 'I think that's got to be the most likely explanation. Now drink that while it's hot. You need it.'

'You're right, Polly, and it's no good speculating about grudges and attempted murder, as if that were at all likely! This is Great Missenwall, remember,' replied Kate with a firmness she was far from feeling. 'Now, how about some Christmas cake? You must be starving. How was the shooting?'

The children arrived in the kitchen shortly afterwards and the subject of the fire was not referred to again until after supper.

Although she had put a brave face on it, Kate was very shaken by the policeman's visit. As the evening progressed she felt increasingly vulnerable. The more she thought about it, the more she realised she was dreading the moment when everyone had gone and she'd be alone. In the absence of Dan, their presence had made a great difference, and until this latest blip, she had started to feel almost cheerful again.

'You're very quiet, Kate,' commented Max as the four friends settled in the sitting room after Polly and Ted had left. 'Are you all right?'

'Yes, yes. I'm fine. Just...'

'You're not brooding about the fire, are you?' Mary looked closely at Kate. 'Honestly, Kate, I think Polly was right: it was probably a tramp...'

Kate's smile was wan. 'Yes, I know. I'm just being silly. Maybe it's because I still fell a bit shaken up after the accident. It's just that...well, I'm going to miss you lot...'

There was a moment's silence.

'I've got to go to work tomorrow,' said Joe, 'but I could be back for New Year...'

'And I'm not going back to Bristol until after New Year...' Mary's eyes widened suddenly, 'but Max is meant to go back to London, right now!'

Max looked at her in some surprise. 'What do you mean?'

'I forgot in all the excitement... Nicola phoned this afternoon and said, in no uncertain terms, that it was one thing you choosing not to spend Christmas with her because of your family commitments, but New Year was quite another. She wants you back in London for some party or other this

382

weekend. She sounded really cheesed off. She's been trying to get you on your mobile.'

Max looked put out.

'Don't worry, Max. You must go. I'll be fine. I've got Polly and Ted to look out for us. I've been lucky that you've all managed to be here for so long. I can't tell you what a fantastic difference having you here has made...'

'There are more important things than partying at the moment. Nicola will have to wait. And anyway,' Max stretched and yawned, 'you and I are taking the three terrors to the panto on Saturday.'

Mary took Kate's hand, 'Katie, come and stay with us. The kids would love it. At least till the end of the holidays. I've arranged for a student to look after Toby until he goes back to school, but if you were there, I wouldn't have to, so you'd be doing us a favour. I can't bear the thought of leaving you here.'

Kate was tempted. 'Thanks Mary, I might just take you up on the offer, or at least send the children and we'll share the cost of the child-minder. But I honestly think the best thing I can do is throw myself into work as soon as I can.' She attempted a laugh. 'All this lying around does wonders for the imagination and very little for common-sense.'

The following day was given over to the farm party, and in spite of Dan's absence, or maybe because of it, with everyone making an effort it was a terrific success.

Colin brought his fiancée; Josh brought his mother, who, as the last gamekeeper's widow, saw her attendance as her right and her duty. Sammy Godwin, retired, but now helping out John Potter, came with his wife; Mike Rosewarn came with his Nancy, a dour-faced woman who nevertheless managed to wish Kate 'all the best, considering'. Matt and Lizzie Freeman came with their three offspring, including their eldest son,

Kevin, who was back from university. He had been a regular babysitter for the Maddicotts, so when the children saw him, they fell upon him with cries of pleasure. The Potter boys were also greeted with whoops of delight, and young Harry Freeman, emboldened by his brother's presence, abandoned his mother's side and joined the youngsters roaring around in a party of their own upstairs.

Brenda surprised Kate by producing a bunch of flowers for her. Kate's obvious pleasure resulted in a faint blush lightening Brenda's habitual sulky countenance. Released from the confines of her dairy uniform, Brenda's natural prettiness shone. She had come alone and before long she was engaged in a flirty conversation with Josh, which he seemed to enjoy as much as she did.

At one point, looking round the room at all those familiar faces and listening to their animated chatter, Kate felt a great surge of affection towards them all. She felt safe with them; *they* were her extended family. The panic she had felt at the prospect of losing Mary, Max and Joe started to ebb.

'Penny for them.' Max handed her a glass. 'You're looking very serious. Not brooding, I hope?'

'On the contrary,' she smiled. 'I was just thinking how lucky I am. We might have our ups and downs, but these people are all my friends. They won't let anything nasty happen if they can help it. I can't keep you or Mary any longer. You've got to get on with your own lives. I've loved you being here, but you need to get back to London, to work and to Nicola…'

'Ah, Nicola… Come on, Katie, Josh has put on some reggae. Let's get those stiff old bones of yours working!'

The trip to the pantomime was great fun. The two boys laughed so much, they slid off their seats; Rosie, completely confused by the cross-dressing, shouted louder than all of them, and the adults joined in with as much gusto as the children.

It was late when they returned. Mary put the excited children to bed and went herself, leaving Kate and Max in the kitchen, she with a cup of tea and he drinking deeply from a bottle of wine he'd opened.

Without warning, Max broke off from a lighthearted post-mortem of *Babes in the Wood* and took hold of her hand.

'Listen Kate,' he said with an urgency that took her by surprise. 'You don't have to stay here, you know. Come back with me. I'll look after you. You belong in London; the kids will adapt; they're bright little beggars…'

She looked at him, amazed. 'I don't believe I'm hearing this. Are you really suggesting I sell Watersmeet and turn my back on everything I've put into it over the last six months, everything that was Dan's entire life?'

'And cost him his life. Nothing is worth that, Katie. You're not safe here.'

'What do you mean? This is my life. I belong here, whether you like it or not. All my friends are here…'

'Is it because of old whatsisname?' His voice was slurred, and an ugly flush transformed his features. She stared at him.

'What are you talking about?'

'That fellow – the widower – the guy who wanted to buy you out… Is he the reason you're refusing to see sense and come back with me?'

She was furious. 'You're talking nonsense! What are you on about? William Etheridge has got nothing whatsoever to do with my decisions. I don't know what you're suggesting…'

Max banged his fist on the table. 'I lost you once before, to Dan. I'm damned if I'm going to lose you again to some other farming oick!'

Her fury turned to ice. 'I'm not yours to lose. I never was. I've seen the way you treat women and nothing would persuade me to become your next victim. You must be very drunk otherwise you wouldn't talk such rubbish. You've been a brilliant friend, but if that's to continue, you must understand I'm *not* in the marketplace. Not for you, not for William Etheridge, not for anyone. I love Dan, and that is the beginning and end of it.'

Max left on Sunday after lunch. He was very contrite all morning and not only did Kate forgive him his outburst, but she suddenly felt very weepy at his departure. She tried not to let it show, feeling cross with herself for this unusual display of weakness.

He put his arms around her as he left and hugged her tight.

'I know you'll take care, Katie,' he said gruffly, 'but I don't like leaving. If anything worries you, anything at all, just give me a call and I'll be here in a flash. In any event, I shall be down again very soon. You won't be able to keep me away.'

'I wouldn't try. Please, come back soon. And bring Nicola, if she'd like to come.'

He smiled but said nothing and climbing into his old Jaguar, roared off up the hill, the children jumping and waving after him until he was out of sight.

It was quiet that evening, with just Kate and Mary left at Watersmeet. Talking over the immediate future, they decided Mary and Joe should take all three children to Bristol on New Year's Day, and Kate would join them at the weekend, bringing the children back to Watersmeet in time for the new school term.

The following morning, Mary and the children went off for a swim, leaving Kate alone in the house for the first time for nearly two weeks. She was starting to move more easily and

386

the prospect of getting back to work cheered her.

'I haven't written my letter to Dan for ages,' she thought as she settled in the study. Her elbow caught a small pile of papers on the edge of the desk, scattering them over the floor.

'Oh bother!'

She bent down to pick them up, but her mobility still being impaired, she couldn't bend down far enough and had to slither out of her chair onto her knees to gather them. Thus it was she caught sight of a wedge of papers that had fallen down the back of the desk and were trapped between the desk and the wall. The desk was deep and she was about to crawl through the kneehole to reach them when she heard Ted calling her from the kitchen. She pulled herself out and went to find him.

He was standing staring out through the kitchen window and did not immediately turn round when she came into the kitchen.

'Ted, you wanted me for something?' she prompted.

He turned. The expression on his face was impenetrable and no smile returned her own.

'Ted, what's wrong?'

'I'm not sure, but we need to talk this through.' He came over to the table and sat down. She sat opposite, trying to read his face.

'What is it? What's happened?'

'Vince from the garage phoned this morning. They've run a check on your car...'

Kate held her breath.

'Thing is, Kate, they're not sure and I don't want us leaping to any conclusions. You've had some nasty shocks and it would be all too easy to assume the worst scenario...'

'What did they say? What did they find?'

'Vince's not happy with the brakes. It's true the car is

pretty mangled, but he says the brake fluid, which shouldn't have been affected by the damage, has drained out pretty comprehensively. If that had occurred before you skidded, then that was why the brakes behaved the way you said they did.'

Kate tried to sound normal. 'How could that have happened?'

Ted sighed. 'He says the leakage was from the brake cables. If they were really old and neglected, I supposed they might have perished. The only other explanation is for them to have been tampered with in some way.'

'What does Vince think?'

'Well, at the moment, that's what Vince is thinking, but he hasn't got the equipment to prove that any slits or cuts aren't a result of the accident. He's not happy though, and he'll point it out to the insurance assessor when he turns up.'

'What good will that do?'

'Well, I suppose, if the insurance guy agrees with him, it becomes a police matter and then, presumably, the forensic boys 'll have a look.'

'When will they do that?'

'Goodness only knows. It's still the holiday for lots of people. I don't suppose the insurance lot are going to be in a hurry to send someone out to look at a wrecked car.'

'Why don't we go to the police, ourselves?'

'With what? A suspicion? I think they might pat us on the head and send us home.'

Kate leaned towards him, her face tense and white. 'Ted, you do realise we are talking about two, not one, but two possible attempts on my life. And you are saying the police might not take us seriously?'

He looked anguished. 'Yes, I know. The same thought occurred to me. You're right, we have to tell them; but we've nothing concrete to go on. It could just be coincidence. But yes, we have to tell them. In the meantime, if you can bear it, I think we should go over everything ourselves. See if we can make any sense of it.'

Kate got up. 'I'll put the kettle on. This could take some time. Have you told anyone else?'

'No. Polly's busy in the cheese shed, and anyway, I wanted to talk to you first.'

She sighed. 'I'd like not to have to tell her. God knows how she'd take it, she's been through so much already.'

'I agree with you there, but it might be better not to exclude her. We've always shared everything, and she'd be very hurt if we left her out of this one because we wanted to protect her.'

Kate returned to the table with two mugs of tea. 'So how do you propose we thrash this out? Draw up a list of people who might want to kill me? And not just me, remember – the children, Ben and Rosie, were in the house the night of the fire. And…' she shivered, 'I took them to school in the car the morning of the accident.'

Ted took her hand. 'Kate, we don't have to go through with this. I just thought it might be helpful. We don't know how the police will react and so anything we can do, anything we can think of, which will persuade them to take us seriously… But then, maybe there is nothing in it at all and I'm behaving like a hysterical old woman…'

'No, I don't believe that.' She looked at him. He'd always shouldered everything, without hesitation. She had to stop leaning on him; it wasn't fair. She drew a deep breath.

'So where do we start? Inexplicable accidents? Then we should start with Dan's death, shouldn't we? Because in spite of all my attempts to find out if he killed himself, or whether it was an accident, I'm no closer to an explanation.'

He cocked his head, startled, and she found herself

389

explaining to him about her promise to Ben and what she'd uncovered about the farm.

'And have you reached any conclusions?' he asked her gently.

She took time to reply. 'On the day of the car crash, I was very low. The evidence seemed so stacked in favour of the suicide verdict. Everything, that is, except Dan himself. Lying in bed and thinking it over and over, I've come to the conclusion that Steven Kelner was right. Dan was depressed by the state of the farm's finances, much more than any of us realised, but you know as well as I do, he was a fighter, and from what Steven Kelner said, he was starting to fight back. I... I thought because he'd taken out life insurance, he'd decided suicide was the only way out of our financial difficulties. But that is such a cliché! I don't believe anybody really would do such a thing and I'm ashamed, so ashamed I ever thought it a possibility.'

Tears started in her eyes and rolled freely down her cheeks. 'I'm ashamed of lots of things, actually, Ted. Dan didn't confide in me enough, and if he did, I didn't really listen. But I think the life insurance was probably the first step Dan took to re-establish control over the future, and deciding to give Frank Leach notice was part of a plan for the farm he intended to see through.'

'Did he give Frank notice? He never mentioned it to me.'

'I don't know. I don't think so. I can't find any evidence he did, so I suppose, although he told Steven Kelner he was going to, he either hadn't got round to it, or he'd changed his mind and decided to take no action. That seems more likely.'

'Yes, it does. Do you know when Dan had that conversation with Mr Kelner about Frank?'

'I think he said it was towards the end of May, but I've made

390

a note so I can check.'

'The end of May? Maybe that's why he didn't say anything to me. It was about that time I had to go over to Sandwich, to sort my mum out. He'd probably changed his mind and decided to take no action before I got back.'

He thought for a moment and then said, firmly, 'But I agree with you. We can rule out suicide. That really would not be Dan's way. So we are left with one of two options. Either it was an accident, which is what the coroner found, and we have to give a lot of weight to his findings, or it was…'

'Murder? An attempt that succeeded? And so we come to the fire in the outhouse and the car… Were they accidents, or were they attempts at something more?'

'Assuming, for the moment, they were all deliberate acts… who on earth would you put in the frame, Kate?'

She looked at him, agonised. 'The only person who really disliked Dan, and by association, me and the children, is Frank Leach.'

'But he's *always* disliked him. It was just one of those things; the Leaches and Maddicotts *never* got on. But they've never resorted to killing each other. We're talking about rural Somerset here, not the streets of New York.'

'Yes, I know, but I can't think of anyone else, I really can't.'

'But we've absolutely no evidence at all, have we? And are you ready to go to the police with such an accusation?'

Kate drooped. 'No, you're right, of course not. But what can I do? Wait, like a sitting duck, until he has another go, which might be more successful?'

'Don't lose sight of the fact that this is only suspicion. Even if you are right, it might not be Frank at all. I think we must pull Polly and Mary in on this and decide how to go from here.'

At that point, Splash jumped from his basket, ears pricked,

and rushed to the door to greet the children, who were returning from their swimming trip.

Ted gave a faint smile. 'I'm glad you've got him. He's a good guard dog. He barked the night of the fire. If he barks again at night, don't ignore him. But don't do anything yourself, please. Phone me.'

'And phone me,' said Max when he phoned later that evening. 'You must keep me in touch, Kate, promise you will. I feel out on a limb here.'

Splash didn't bark that night, but he did the following night, New Year's Eve.

Joe, who had returned, was up and out in a flash. The only evidence there might have been an intruder was the yard gate open and swinging on its hinges.

On New Year's Day, they straggled down for a late breakfast. Mary and Joe, with all the children, were to leave for Bristol after lunch, and Polly and Ted were going to move into the farmhouse.

Apparently unaware of the tension among the adults, Rosie and Ben were bubbling with excitement at the prospect of their trip to the city.

'Auntie Mary says we can go on a boat across the water and see a big iron ship…'

'She says we can go to the zoo…'

'We can go to this place where you can do all sort of experiments. It's near where my mum works. And there's a place where you can see plants and insects and things…'

'Can we take Splash, Mum?' asked Ben. 'He'd love to see the city an' I'll look after him, promise.'

'Splash is better off here, darling. He can look after me. Now, why don't you let him out to have a pee? He must be bursting, we're so late down.'

Ben opened the kitchen door and Splash disappeared out into the yard. Pulling on his boots, Ben followed the dog outside.

Moments later they heard him shouting. 'Splash, leave that alone! Leave it! Come here! Splash – you naughty dog! Come here!'

He appeared in the doorway, bothered. 'Mum, Splash has found something in the yard and he won't leave it. It looks like a bone, and when I tried to get it off him, he growled at me. Splash has never growled at me before…'

'It's a dog's instinct,' said Joe, ruffling Ben's hair. 'Never come between a dog and his bone, Ben, even if you are his best friend.'

'If you've been handling bones, you'd better go and wash your hands, immediately,' chipped in Mary.

'Bone!' Kate's voice was sharp. 'We don't give Splash bones. He's too young. Where's it come from?'

Joe didn't hesitate. Barefooted, he ran out into the yard and seconds later, he shouted for Kate to get straight onto the vet.

'But it's New Year's Day. He won't be at his surgery…'

'Then phone his mobile. Get him here as quick as you can and tell him…' His voice was urgent. 'Splash has been poisoned. Tell the vet the dog has been poisoned.'

39

Frank

It was completely dark outside when he woke. He didn't need a clock. He knew what hour it was. The screech of the owls called him, taunted him. 'Now is the time. Why are you waiting? Hunter, start hunting.'

He didn't need to dress. He had lain on his bed fully clothed. That was what he did, these nights. In the dark he knew where to find his boots, then silently (superstitiously so, for there was no one to hear him and call out; had been no one, for years) he crept down the stairs. The kitchen was pitch black and cold, but he didn't put on the light. He went to the hearth where his coat was hanging, put it on, slung a canvas satchel over his shoulders and went to the kitchen door. The bolt drew silently back and he let himself out into the chill of the night.

The icy rawness did not touch him, nor did he register his breath, hanging heavy on the night air. He sniffed about him and listened before he moved off in the direction of the woods.

The moon sailed high in a star-struck sky and illuminated the yard in a glimmering grey light. The brightness of the moon might have betrayed him to a watcher, but he had no reason to fear anyone would be watching. He had a way to go, but he knew his way, knew his prey, and he moved swiftly and silently across the silver-drenched farmyard and melted into the dark fringes of the wood.

After the brightness of the yard, the wood was black. The brilliance of the moonlight did not penetrate the tree canopy and, suddenly blind, he felt for the path he was to follow. He cursed silently, willing his night vision to adjust. The absolute dark always took him by surprise, and in his blindness he felt every pebble, every unevenness of the ground underfoot. He tripped over a straggling tree root and swore. Some way off, a vixen shrieked. He stopped, breathed in hard and closed his eyes. When he opened them, he could dimly make out the grey snake of the path ahead.

In the heart of the woods, he relaxed. This was his territory. He had trod this way by moonlight so many times, the twist and turns of the path, the shapes of the trees, the roots and rocks that might trip an unwary man, were familiar features to him. Here he was at home, a hunter hunting. By the moonlight, he should have been able to make out the plump shapes of any pheasants perched on branches above his head. There was just enough light to see and not be seen – a good night for taking the birds. But the birds were not there.

Something had disturbed them and he knew what it was. He stood quite still and listened, his own harsh breath loud in his ears. It was not silent in the woods, the owls called and answered, and, periodically, there came odd screeches and cries as some creature met its demise.

Not far off a twig snapped, a sharp crack in the darkness, and the undergrowth faintly rustled. A faint smile flickered across his face and he melted through the trees in the direction of the sound.

Almost invisible in the shadow of an old oak, the movement of a gun caught the moonlight. Intent on bagging a pheasant roosting nearby, the hard thrust of iron in the small of his back took the poacher by surprise. He froze, his gun slowly lowered and, almost rigid with terror, he turned his head.

'Why Frank,' he babbled. 'You gave Oi a turn. Thought it was ol' Snook...'

He was rewarded by a sharp jab in his back. 'These are my woods, Billy Rogers...my birds... You'se on my patch...'

'But Frank, there's plenty enough for us both...'

'These woods are mine. If Oi catch yer here again, yer dead meat. Geddit?'

Still keeping his gun trained on the quivering poacher, he picked up a canvas bag half-full of pheasant. 'Oi'll take these...'

'But, Frank...'

'And Oi'll count to ten. If you ain't gone by the time Oi've finished countin', Ken Snook will 'ave a noice little surprise waitin' for him in the mornin'...'

'You fuckin' bastard, you wouldn't...'

'One...'

For a moment he stood there and listened to the fleeing poacher crashing away through the undergrowth. If Ken Snook were patrolling the woods tonight, he'd be here within minutes. Slinging the bag over his shoulder, he returned to the shadows.

40

Dan

2001

'Yer wanter no whose pochin Sparrers Wood. Arsk Frank
Leech. Hes ther tomorrer afor dawnlite'

Dan frowned at the note. It was written on a greasy piece
of lined paper, probably torn from an exercise book. The
envelope, addressed to him, was also grubby and well-creased.

Josh had given it to him that morning. He'd stuffed it in his
pocket and forgotten about it until, changing out of his work
clothes, he'd emptied his pockets.

Josh had told him he'd been given it at the pub the night
before and he'd promised to see that Dan got it. He didn't know
the name of the man who'd pushed the note into his hand, but
he looked familiar, possibly someone from the coterie of cider
drinkers and poachers who frequented the public bar.

Yes, Dan did want to know who was responsible for the latest
round of poaching. It had got so bad he'd had Ken Snook on

the phone complaining bitterly about the level of devastation among the pre-season pheasants.

Frank Leach was always Snook's prime suspect, but he was elusive, skilled at vanishing into the undergrowth undetected. He probably knew the woods better than Ken Snook himself, so it was almost impossible to confront him or charge him with anything concrete.

Dan suspected Snook was right in his suspicions. As far as Dan could tell from the state of Woodside Farm, Frank, not being the farmer his father, Jem, was, would have to supplement his income in some other way to survive.

Dan had sent him the notice to repair, but Frank had not responded. He'd subsequently gone over to the farm on a couple of occasions, taking Josh with him as a precaution, but there was never any sign of Frank. The last time he'd gone he pinned a note to Frank's door, warning him that he was going to be issued with a notice to quit, but still there had been no response.

This note looked as if it might be from someone settling a score. Why else would Dan have been sent it? If he acted upon the note it would solve two problems at once – he would have the opportunity to confront Frank about the poaching, as well as ensuring that he knew, once and for all, he was to leave Woodside Farm by the end of the year.

Dan thought about telling Ted of his planned expedition, but decided against it. Ted had returned from his trip to Kent, grey with fatigue; they were busy with the harvest, and both Ted and Josh needed all the sleep they could get. Ted would have already gone home for the evening and if Dan was to be at Sparrows Wood before dawn, he would have to leave by 4.30 am.

He could deal with Frank Leach by himself.

He went down the stairs to join Kate in the kitchen with the note in his hand. He had been intending to show it to her, but decided against it. He turned to the study instead and put it under his mug, on a shelf by the desk. She might worry about him going off by himself on such an errand, and so he decided instead to make up some story about shooting a few rabbits before the morning milking. Heavens knew that was what he should be doing. The pesky things had burrowed a large warren on the edge of the fields up there.

'Dan,' Kate stood at the door. 'We're waiting for you. Everything's ready.' She laughed at the blank look on his face. 'The funeral. Have you forgotten?'

He had. 'Sorry, sweetheart. It completely slipped my mind. How's Rosie?'

'Oh, she's fine. She's been living off the drama all day at school; she's terribly excited about the funeral. Ben has made the coffin from an old shoe box, and she has picked some flowers; so if you're ready, we can lay the poor little beasts to rest.'

That morning Rosie had found the headless corpses of two of her three pet guinea pigs in an upturned run. Of the third, there was no sign, and Dan had to break it to a heartbroken Rosie that, in all probability, Miss Mischief had become breakfast for Mister Fox and his family.

'Why?' she'd wailed. 'Why did he kill all of them if he only wanted Miss Mischief to eat? Why?'

'It's the way they're made,' he'd replied. 'They just like killing, it's their nature…'

Dan put his arm around Kate's shoulders and gave her a squeeze.

'I'll go and get a spade. We can bury them in the flowerbed under the yew hedge. Why the foxes are bothering taking guinea pigs when the rabbits are flourishing in ever greater numbers, beats me.'

'Perhaps they like a little variety in their diet. If we get any more pets, we should make the children shut them up at night.'

'Yep. But I've got to do something about the rabbits. I think I'll get up before milking, tomorrow morning, and pot a few.'

And, he thought, when he presented Ken Snook with his poacher, he would ask him as a return favour to do something about the rabbits.

41

Kate

2002

Ben was hysterical by the time Splash was taken off to the vet's surgery. Tom managed to make the dog sick and the terrible heaving of his flanks abated. But nothing would convince Ben that his pet wasn't going to die until the vet eventually phoned back to say all was well, but that the puppy would need to be kept under observation for a few days.

It was with great difficulty Kate persuaded her children to stick to their plan to accompany Toby to Bristol.

'Just think how awful it will be for you here at Watersmeet without him. He's safe with Mr Babbington and will be home before you. I promise I will go and see him every day and tell you how he is…'

Eventually, late into the evening, they left and Kate, exhausted by the trauma of the day, excused herself from supper with Ted and Polly and went to bed to wrestle with nightmares, and to brood.

The fire had started after she sent Frank the first letter; the brakes failed after she had paid him a visit; Splash was poisoned after she had told Nick Lovell to send him the second letter. Had Dan sent him a similar notice? But she didn't know that, and she didn't know, for sure, that Dan's death was not an accident.

The next couple of days were uneventful, but she was on her guard the whole time she was out of the house.

'It's probably paranoia,' she finally confessed to Polly, 'but I feel as if I'm being watched all the time; I feel eyes on my back, following me wherever I go, whatever I do. It sets my skin tingling and my nerves jangling, but I never see anybody. There's nobody there.'

'Possibly it's because you're still recovering from the accident, dear, and Christmas is hardly a restful time, is it? But all the same, don't you think – if only to set your mind at rest – maybe it's time we went to the police?'

'I don't know, I just don't know. I can't see beyond going into the police station and saying, "Er…excuse me, I think someone is trying to kill me." And then what? I've no proof of that; no proof of anything: a fire that may or may not have been started deliberately; a car that may or may not have had its brakes tampered with, and a dog who ate a poisoned bone. Not much to go on, is it? Not much to base an accusation on…'

'Perhaps not, but I'm worried that we're doing nothing. Look, Kate, I know you plan to go and see Nick to collect Rose's letter. Promise me you'll consult him, and if he advises you to go to the police, then you'll go.'

Polly spoke to Ted about Kate's fear and they decided, without being explicit about their suspicions, to involve the workforce.

'I just want you all to be watchful,' he told them. 'We might be wrong, but the police tell us they think the fire was started deliberately and then the pup was poisoned. Farm sabotage has to be taken seriously. So if you see anyone who has no business here, tell me, or Kate, or Polly, immediately.'

'Sabotage! That's goin' over the top a bit, ain't it?' snorted Matt to John Potter, as they walked out of the barn.

'Well, I suppose if the police are taking it seriously...' replied John Potter. 'They're not going to waste their time, are they? And if you think of barns being torched just for the hell of it...if someone has a thing about Watersmeet, they could do an awful lot of damage. I'm thinking of my cows, Matt – stuck inside as they are at the moment, they'd be a sitting target for anybody with a mind to mischief!'

Inevitably, there was much discussion among them, but it was clear nobody had seen anything of any significance. Their general mood reflected the January weather: gloomy and overcast.

Needing a distraction, Polly kept her word and searched for any mention of Susan Leach in the parish register. She shared her findings with Kate and Ted over supper.

'I found her death recorded. Poor little thing, she was only twenty-three when she died. But as to her history, there isn't a clue. No maiden name, place of birth, nothing. There's no record of the marriage to Jem, either, which I find odd. So I suppose Jem met her and married her out of the district. No mention of Frank's baptism, either, which is also a bit strange. I went to have a look for her gravestone to see if there was anything on that, but I couldn't find one. Jem's there all right, so are his parents, but no sign of Susan. If it wasn't for the presence of Frank, one might think she never existed.'

'Talking of Frank, I've been thinking, maybe I should go and see him.' Ted was thoughtful. 'For all sorts of reasons, it seems like a good idea. I can confirm that we expect him to leave the farm and spell out Kate's offer of Keeper's cottage, but also I'll check out how he is. I've not seen him for over a month and he was in a bad shape then.'

'I think that's a good idea,' Polly said warmly. 'I know it's silly, but I've been worrying about him. Supposing our conjectures about him are completely wrong? He's such a recluse, a visit from the police might completely unhinge him, and they wouldn't be gentle with him, one can be sure of that. He might lash out and then he *would* be in trouble which, indirectly, would be of our making.'

Kate, remembering her last visit, frowned. 'You know best, Ted. But I think you should take Josh with you – supposing he went for you?'

'He's never done that before; I'm not worried. But I will take Josh.'

'You'll be lucky to find him – remember the problems we had before Christmas?'

'Don't worry, a poacher has to sleep sometime. Josh and I will be up very early tomorrow morning.'

The following morning Kate waited for Ted to return, but he still hadn't appeared by the time she had to leave for her appointment with the solicitor.

'I have to admit I'm curious,' said Nick Lovell, handing her a large brown envelope addressed to Dan. 'Rose left strict instructions the letter should not be handed over unless it was specifically asked for, and more than that: on no account should any reference be made by us to indicate its existence.'

Kate smiled. 'Polly thinks it's Rose, enjoying a wild goose

404

chase, but I don't know... Perhaps all will become clear when I read this.' She hesitated and then, mindful of her promise to Polly, told him what had taken place over Christmas.

'I don't want to sound paranoid, but there are just one too many coincidences, and coupled with the uncertainty over Dan's death, my imagination is working overtime.'

'How do you mean, "uncertainty over Dan's death"? The inquest said it was an accident. Do you have any reason, any reason at all, to think otherwise?'

Having nerved herself to confide in him, Kate was instantly deflated. 'No, not exactly, but if there is someone who is conducting a vendetta against us, then surely that raises a question mark?'

'So,' he persisted, 'you're saying Dan might have been killed by someone? That he was murdered?'

She looked at him, wretchedly. 'It sounds so melodramatic, I know. But yes, yes I am.'

He tapped his fingers on the desk. 'And you think Frank Leach is behind all these attacks on you...'

'If they are attacks and not accidents, yes.'

'And so you think Frank might have killed Dan?'

Kate groaned, 'Oh I don't know, I don't know, Nick. But I can't think of anyone else who hates us enough, or who might have a motive.'

'The motive being?'

'Dan was thinking of giving Frank notice to quit. Whether he did or not, I don't know. But now I have, and I've told him so.'

There was a long silence. Kate, waiting for Nick to speak, was miserable. His cross-questioning had highlighted the very reasons why she'd not gone to the police in the first place, but it had done nothing to remove her unease.

He gave her a slight smile. 'Well, all things considered, I think it is not unreasonable to go to the police and tell them what has happened over Christmas, and of your concerns. If you like, I'll come with you...'

'Oh Nick, I would be so grateful. Thank you.'

'But I'm worried about you fingering anyone without better proof. You can't connect him with any of the accidents, from Dan's death – which I think we should only mention in passing – to the poisoning of the dog. If you identify him, the police will undoubtedly pay him a visit, but they've nothing with which to hold him.'

Kate, remembering Polly's concern, nodded. 'You're right. So perhaps I shouldn't mention him?'

'If they ask you if you've any suspicions, which I may say, they are almost bound to, then you should tell them. That's reasonable, Kate. We just have to make it clear that you have absolutely no proof.'

Nick was tied up with appointments for the rest of the day, so they settled he and Kate would go to the police station the following afternoon.

Having left his office, she dropped in at the vet's surgery. Jeff Babbington had called her earlier to say Splash was more than ready to come home.

'It's only cats that are meant to have nine lives,' he observed wryly, handing over the frisky, excited dog. 'First the car crash, then strychnine poisoning... He's a lucky little fellow. Not many animals would have survived eating that stuff. It was lucky Joe Warren was about.'

'But how,' she thought, as she thanked him, 'how can I keep him safe? The children would never forgive me if anything else happened to him.'

This question preoccupied her all the way home.

A familiar Land Rover was parked in the yard, and with a sense of real pleasure she hurried into the kitchen to greet William Etheridge.

William hugged her, clearly as pleased to see her. He was so warm and calm, she found herself telling him as much as she could of the dramas of the last three weeks.

'I've heard part of the story already, from Jim. It would have been hard to keep it quiet. As far as I can gather the good folk of Great Missenwall are waiting, with bated breath, to see what disaster will befall Watersmeet next. I sincerely hope they're going to be disappointed!'

She laughed. 'So do I, but I can't take any chances with Splash. I've decided he'd better go into kennels for the time being.'

'He'd hate that. He can come home with me. He'll be safe with us, and he can come back here whenever you want.' He looked at her, concerned. 'But Kate, I'm really glad you're going to the police. I think you've taken an unnecessary risk by being so scrupulous. Put it in their hands. But in the meantime, don't take any more chances, will you? And phone me if there's anything – and I mean anything – I can do.'

After he'd gone, she made herself a cup of coffee and went to the study. The car accident, followed by Christmas, had left her behind with the monthly accounts and when she'd woken that morning, she'd resolved to get on with her life.

The castor of her chair had caught in a small tear in the rug and as she knelt to release it, she remembered the sheaf of papers she'd spotted earlier behind the desk.

They were dusty and stained. She sat and sifted through them. They were all copies of letters that Dan had sent. Mostly printed, but one or two were photocopies of handwritten notes, including one to Frank Leach giving him notice to repair and spelling out, in no uncertain terms, that unless he responded satisfactorily within a given time, he would be given notice to quit.

Then she remembered Rose's package containing the letter from Susan.

42

Rose

1951

Rose stared at the letter the doctor had given her. The envelope was grubby and creased, the handwriting shaky but clearly addressed to 'Mrs Rose Maddicott', with 'Private' heavily underlined.

'Poor soul,' he said. 'She was very near her end but would not settle until I had promised her I would put the letter into your hands and say not a word of it to anyone else. Then she made me promise to make a similar request of you – that you should read this letter, but not say anything about its contents to anyone. She was most insistent: it was for your eyes only.'

'She could only have been about twenty-four.' In spite of having heard nothing from Susan for two years, Rose was upset. 'What did she die from, Doctor Whittaker?'

'Ostensibly it was pneumonia, but sometimes, Rose, patients just lose the will to live, and when that happens it could be anything that finishes them off.'

'Oh, the poor little thing.'

'Yes,' he said gruffly. 'If they had called me sooner, I could have whipped her into the cottage hospital. Done something for her. I don't like losing patients unnecessarily. Between you and me, Rose, your tenant is a brutish clod and his son looks as though he takes after his father.'

'Susan adored Frank.'

The Doctor looked at her with curiosity. 'You knew her, then? I did wonder about the letter…?'

'Yes, I knew her. We were friends, but it was difficult to maintain our friendship in the face of…well, you're aware of our situation.'

'Yes, of course. Poor soul, I don't suppose she had another friend in the world. Whatever induced her to marry Jem Leach… Well, take your letter, Rose, and please respect her last wishes. Not a word to anyone.'

That evening, with Jack fast asleep and Samuel pouring over stock breeding manuals in his study, Rose sat at the kitchen table, ostensibly to write her journal. She opened the letter.

Dear Rose,

My heart is so full I don't know where to begin. I am going to die soon, but before I do, I want to make things right with you and me so please, Rose, read this letter and I hope you will find it in your heart to forgive me for all the terrible things I said to you on that day. You were my friend and I treated you so bad, but I had to, as you will learn when you read this. Rose, I am going to tell you some terrible things, but I want to die having shared them with you. You are wise and clever and will know what to do with what I am going to tell you, but please promise me, if you read on, you will do nothing to hurt Frank. He is all I have had to love in the world. The only other

410

person I care about is you. We cannot be friends and Frank does everything that Jem tells him, so I have nothing left to live for, so don't feel sorry for me when I am gone. I shall be very glad to die, even if God punishes me for it.

Her heart full, Rose read on.

Thus she read of the events that landed Susan in the unmarried mothers' home, of her escape, of being picked up by Jem Leach, of her effective imprisonment by the Leaches until the birth of her son, of her constant fear of her baby being taken from her, and of the offer that Jem had made to her concerning the baby.

Rose exclaimed out loud, she couldn't help it. The villainy, the absolute, ruthless villainy of the Leaches! And to pass off Susan's child as Jem's own and so prevent Samuel from rightfully reclaiming the farm… She was going to find it very hard not to take this straight to her husband.

She read on.

Susan told her how soon after his birth she had written to Frank's father, begging him to come and rescue her. She had held onto the letter for nearly eighteen months before chance, in the shape of Rose, gave her the opportunity to send it.

She wrote glowingly of the pleasure that Rose's visits gave her, and poignantly of the growing alienation of her darling little boy once Jem started to take an interest in him. How he was encouraged to ignore her, treat her like a servant, disobey her, even hit her, so that by the time he was five, she felt she had lost control of him. Her only consolation was that Jem appeared to reciprocate the affection Frank showed him and she slowly came to believe, in spite of the threats he made to her, he would not harm the little boy, or allow him to be taken away.

411

She then came to the events that surrounded the day Rose found her locked in the birdcage.

I had just been up the track to tie on the ribbon for you and it being nearer tea time than I had thought, hurried back in the kitchen to set out their food. I heard a whistling and looking out the window saw something that I have dreamed of every night since I came to this godforsaken place. My Franklin walking down the track towards the yard. I stood there, frozen. I thought I was dreaming. I closed my eyes and opened them again and there he was, entering the yard as large as life. I could hardly breathe from excitement, but before I could call or run out to him, Jem appeared round the corner of the barn followed by little Frank. They must have finished cutting the grass up at Top Meadow and had come back early for their tea.

Rose, it was like a horrible dream. Jem immediately started shouting at Franklin, asking him what his business was and telling him to leave. I thought that maybe if I went out, it would make Jem worse, so all I could do was stand there and watch.

It was horrible.

When Jem heard Franklin's voice asking for me, he sort of went mad and started pushing him. Franklin pushed him back, and then before I knew, they were on the ground rolling over and over, punching and shouting. Franklin was obviously getting the better of it. He was much younger and looked very fit, and for all Jem's strength, he ended on the ground with Franklin sitting astride him, knocking him about.

Then, and I can hardly bear to tell you this next bit, Rose, but you must remember he was only little and he thought Jem was his Dad and there was this strange man beating his Dad

412

up... I saw Frank pick up a spade that was leaning against the barn. It was heavy, but he was a strong lad for five. Dear God, the horror of it. I saw him strike Franklin over the head with that spade. At that I ran out and shouted at him to stop, but he took no notice of me and carried on hitting, and hitting, and hitting. Franklin slumped to the ground, his head a bloody mess. I ran to him, but it was no use. I could see he was dead.

My son had killed his father. It doesn't bear thinking about, even now. I must have fainted or something, because when I came to, they were dragging the body to the barn. I followed. They opened the door to that terrible birdcage and buried poor Franklin in there. God knows what I said, but when they had buried him, Jem gave me a thorough beating and threw me in the cage too, 'to spend a little time with my boyfriend,' he said. He then warned me that if I said a word to anyone, not only would I lose Frank, but that he would be imprisoned until he was old enough to be hung as a murderer. They then left me and I spent the night there, half out of my mind. I convinced myself that Franklin might still be alive, so I tried to scrabble up the earth with my bare hands. Every time I made too much movement, those awful birds would scream and attack. But Franklin was dead. After all that time, he had come to find me and now he was dead. So I wanted to die too and tried to bury myself with him, so at least we could lie together in death. But God wouldn't let me die.

Then you came, and all I could think was that if you got me out of the cage or sent for help, then Franklin's body would be found and the whole horrible story would come out, and who knows what they would have done with little Frank. I couldn't take that chance, so I had to drive you away. Kind, dear, Rose, screaming at you like that I was no better than them. I knew I wouldn't see you again, couldn't see you again because

I would have to explain, and I couldn't.

So that is it, Rose. God forgive me, but I shall be glad to die. I just hope that you will not continue to despise me, as you have had every right. And please, Rose, please don't do anything to hurt my little boy. I know I place a great burden on you by this request and will just say that if at any time he should become a threat to you and yours, then you can use what I have told you, otherwise, let him be in peace, for my sake.

Your grateful friend,
Susan

Rose sat for a long time. Eventually she got up and went to her bureau, on which her journals were stacked and pulled out the one for 1949. Turning to her entry for the 22nd July, she wrote a note in the margin, then neatly folding Susan's letter, tucked it into the fresh pages of her journal for that day, accompanied by a very short entry. The following morning, without a word to Samuel, she went to church and spent a long time on her knees in tearful prayer.

She did not open those journals again until 1977. Jem had locked Mary in the birdcage, and her grandson, Dan, had been in a terrible fight with Frank. Against the entry for 22nd July 1949, she made a further note, turned to her entry for 1951, and removing Susan's letter, left a note addressed to Dan tucked into the page. The following day she went to see her solicitor in Summerbridge.

43

Kate

2002

Kate put Susan's letter to Rose on one side and stared blankly out of the study window into the garden. The letter and its implications were almost too much for her to take in.

Why hadn't Rose Maddicott said anything when she was alive? *Why?* Slowly, reluctantly, dreading further revelations but needing some sort of explanation, she opened a note to Dan from Rose, enclosed with Susan Leach's letter.

> *My dear Dan,*
>
> *By the time you read this, I will be dead. Perhaps you will never read it and in a way, that is what I hope, because then I will not have broken the promise I gave to Susan Leach.*
>
> *Dear boy, do not dismiss my letter as the foolish ramblings of an old woman. What I have to recount should be taken seriously.*
>
> *By now you will have read the pertinent entries in my*

journals. You may well have wondered why I selected those particular ones and what the point of it all was. I think the enclosed letter, the one I received from Susan Leach after she had died, will make everything clear but I wanted to prepare you for it first. I believe, in order to understand everything, including the way I have acted, you first needed to understand how my friendship with Susan grew and under what circumstances.

I still blame myself for not having gone back to her after I found her that day. Terrible though her secret was, I am sure if she had shared it with me sooner, I could have helped. Though, truthfully, I do not quite know how, but at least she wouldn't have died alone, utterly without friends. So all I could do for her in the end was carry the burden of her secret.

But I am running ahead of the story. When you have read her letter, you will understand better, although I have no doubt that part of you will blame me for not having told your grandfather, or your father. But understand, Dan, the secret was hers, not mine , and I was honour-bound not to tell anyone unless the safety of my family was at stake ,and until now, my family's safety has not been threatened. But today you and your cousins have come back from Woodside with Ted Jordan. He has told me of everything that passed.

Jem Leach! The very mention of his name makes me shudder, and at the thought of that poor little girl being locked up in the birdcage, I felt faint. He told me, too, of the threat Frank made to you, Dan. Ted Jordan made light of it, but I know how seriously it should be taken.

I do not wish to do anything to deliberately bring misfortune or harm to Susan's family, and while I am alive I will be vigilant in protecting you from any possible trouble from that direction. However I do realise that Susan's story is too

416

important to Watersmeet to die with me, which is why I am passing it on to you, my dear Dan.

I know Frank is not actually Jem's son and therefore is not legally entitled to inherit the lease of Woodside, but it is unlikely that Frank will have children and you will one day take possession. The two families have co-existed for years and there is no reason why they shouldn't continue to do so.

We have so much at Watersmeet and the Leaches have so little. I know you won't use the information I am giving you unwisely. You're a kind, sensitive boy and I am proud to be your grandmother.

Rose Maddicott
Watersmeet
June 29th 1977

44

Frank

The moon was no more than a nail's paring, but for all that, it was a bright night and in the woods the shadows were deep. The dew was heavy and the ground underfoot was slippery.

The path he followed wound steeply downhill. Tree roots, sinewy trip wires, twisted across the way. Loose stones, wrapped in a thin film of ice, made the descent more treacherous and minuscule stone avalanches cascaded down the path in front of him as he dislodged the rubble beneath his feet. The path descended the hillside alongside a small stream that rushed downwards over moss-covered rocks, under fallen branches and through tunnels of brambles.

Nature was intent on dawn and already the air was full of birdsong, the dark sky giving way to an ever-brightening grey veil. Through the branches of the trees, the last reluctant stars glimmered distantly.

He was nearly at his destination but his breathing did not

alter, nor his heart beat faster, nor his pace change, save to prevent himself from skidding down the precipitous slope. He arrived at the stile, part of the boundary between the woods and the fields, and stopped.

This was the place.

A fox, slinking along the far perimeter of the field, froze in its tracks, glanced at him as he shifted the gun in his grasp and slipped away into the hedgerow. Cocking his gun, he concealed himself in the undergrowth adjacent to the stile, at the side of a substantial beech tree.

The wind, such as it was, was in his favour and it was not long before he saw the doe, her youngster at her side, step delicately out of the trees and start to nibble the grass.

He raised his gun.

45

Dan

2001

Dan shot out a hand to turn off the alarm before it woke Kate. It was still dark outside and he groaned inwardly at the thought of having to get up so early. Part of him wanted to drift back into sleep and get up at the normal hour. It was tempting. His encounters with Frank Leach had never been pleasant and this was likely to be the stickiest yet. But he needed to make sure that Frank understood his tenancy was at an end. He wanted that man off his land and nowhere near his daughter.

He dressed quickly and quietly; kissed Kate in her sleep and murmured 'Rabbits' into her ear. He slipped downstairs, went down to the cellar to collect his shotgun and slung the cartridge bag over his shoulders. He was going to take the opportunity, while he was up on the edge of the woods, to bag a few rabbits after he'd confronted Frank.

The little stream that busied past the front of the house had its origins high on the line of hills above Watersmeet. It began life as a swampy spread of green marshland rather than a romantic spring bursting from rocky outcrop, staining the meadow in which it emerged in a wide band of electric green bog, trapping the unwary walker in a glutinous morass of red mud.

By the time it entered Sparrows Wood, the terrain had ordered its course and shape, and the brook splashed and fell down a well-defined gully shaped over hundreds of years. Where it re-joined the farmland, Dan's ancestors had taken a hand and it obediently followed a course determined by them, creating a watery boundary around a number of fields before disappearing underground into the conduit that eventually brought it out again in front of the Watersmeet farmhouse.

As a child he had traced the stream from the point of stasis where it met the greater force of the river, up to its green, weedy genesis. He had dammed it, paddled it, fished it, built waterfalls, created lakes, and sailed small craft down it.

On that darkling moment before dawn, he paused at the confluence of the river and stream and experienced, as he had done ever since he was a child, a moment of calm, an acceptance of his place and his fate in the order of everything.

He turned, and following the course of the stream, slowly climbed the fields away from the house, away from those he loved most in the world, up to the stile into the woods.

Here, one leg over the top, his eye was caught by a slight movement on the far side of the field. A dog fox with something in its mouth was slinking along the hedge line. His eyes narrowed, remembering his daughter's tearful face the morning before. It was an opportunity too good to miss.

Astride the stile, he cocked his gun and had the fox in his sights when the fox, with uncanny instinct, suddenly stopped and disappeared into the hedgerow. Disappointed, Dan lowered his gun and turned to complete the manoeuvre over the stile. The wood was wet with dew and his foot slipped.

To the accompaniment of the glorious symphony of a dawn chorus, a light went out. Blood mingled with the water of the brook and bubbled downwards over the fields, through the conduit, past the sleeping house and into the river.

46

Frank

'Whad'yer doin' here? Yer trespassin…yer've no right to be here. Clear off before oi bloody make yer…'

He should have known she wouldn't give up, the Queen Bitch. She'd sent her creatures and they'd caught him off guard. The first streaks of dawn light were barely in the eastern sky when he'd walked into his kitchen to find Ted Jordan sitting in his chair, and the young farmhand standing next to him, waiting for him, filling the room, tainting the place.

'Get out of my house!' he shouted.

Seeing them there, where they'd no right, his insides hurt with the anger of it. He'd left his gun in the barn along with the birds he'd bagged an hour back, otherwise he'd have turned it on them.

'Bugger off – you bloody better bugger off!'

'Be quiet, Frank, and listen to what I've got to say.'

Ted Jordan was speaking, cold as flint. How he hated

Jordan, *always had, but he was afraid of him, too. He was the Maddicott's hard man, their hit man; he had no fear in him, he was the enemy as much as the widow.*

'What d'yer want?' he growled.

He had no choice. A hunter taken by surprise has to tread softly, warily, watch and wait. He knew the game, the trap they were going to spring.

'I've come to see you, Frank, because there've been a number of accidents at Watersmeet...'

'What's that to Oi?'

He sneered, wanting them to go, wanting them to leave him be, wanting them to stop talking.

'Because the police are now involved. They want to know who's behind these accidents, and whether there's any connection with Dan Maddicott's death.'

'It weren't Oi. You can't blame Oi, Ted Jordan...'

His voice sounded hoarse.

He could hear the old man's voice whispering in his ear, 'They hang murderers, little Frank, that's what they do. They puts this rope around they necks...' He found his voice and shouted as loud as he could,

'You can't pin that on Oi, Ted Jordan, much as you and those Maddicotts would like...'

'I don't want to, Frank. But how do we know you didn't?'

'Well Oi didn't.'

The sound of the gunshot had reverberated round the woods. Clouds of nervy pigeons had risen into the sky; the air was filled with the alarums of a thousand birds. The doe he'd been stalking bolted, and after one quivering moment, so did he.

'Oi was in Sparrow Woods when Oi heard a shot and do you know what Oi did? Oi scarpered, that's what. If Oi'd know it was he, Oi'd have gone and looked, just to check the bugger

424

was dead. But Oi didn't kill 'im.'

Ted Jordan looked so angry he thought he was going to lash out. He froze, tense, waiting. No one had hit him for a long time. The last time the old man had tried, the last time he'd taken off his leather belt, he, Frank, had seized it off him and larruped him back, good and proper.

'What about the attacks on Mrs Maddicott? What do you know about those?'

He wasn't going to hit him. The moment had passed. But he must remain alert, on guard, see them off.

'They stand 'em on this trap-door, boy, and then it suddenly opens and crack, yer neck's broken...' *The old man's voice again, filling his head, filling his brain. He could feel the perspiration break out all over his body.*

'What d'yer mean?' he growled. 'Why should Oi be bothered with the likes of her? And anyways, who d'yer think yer are, askin' Oi these questions?'

'Well if you won't answer me, I'm sure the police will be more persuasive.' He held out a letter. 'Before I go, Frank, Mrs Maddicott has asked me to make sure you see this. She would like to know you understand what it says, so would you read it out to me please.'

It was a trap. He was not walking into it. He looked down at the paper.

'Women are deadly,' *the old man had said.* 'Soft and slippery, they won't stop till they gets what they want.' *And he was right.* 'Don't you trust 'em' *he'd said.* 'Yer've got to show them who's boss, otherwise they'll get yer, they'll get yer, mark Oi...'

'Do you understand what it says?'

The words dripped, ice cold, into his brain.

'Oi understand what it says, right enough, and you can tell her Oi ain't leaving. This place is mine and no one, no one, yer hear, is goin' to take it from Oi...'

No one, no one. He'd had enough, too many words, buzzing round his brain, dancing in front of his eyes like a cloud of biting insects. He wanted them to go away, now, now.

He turned and crashed out of the kitchen, away from the farmhouse, away from them, running, running through the woods till he felt safe, in his den, well out of their reach.

In the heart of the woods was an old stone quarry. It was over a hundred and fifty years since anyone had hacked into the hillside, and the artificially created cliff, pitted with small caves and overhanging rocks, had long been softened with creepers, moss, and ferns. Ash, oak, sycamore and rowan had rooted in the crevices, and undisturbed, strong and vigorous, thrust towards the light, their tangle of branches concealing the presence of the quarry from above. Around and over the mutilated ground, a tenacious mantle of bramble had grown, through which ran a myriad of tunnels, the highways and byways of the small creatures of the woods. It was a dark and secret place, and inaccessible.

He sat in the shelter of a cave, staring into his thoughts. He was a creature of these woods. They sheltered him, protected him, fed him, and had always done so from when he was a small boy and needed to escape from harsh words and beatings.

He'd learned the lessons of the woods, of the animals and birds that occupied them. There was no kindness here, no softness. The bigger creatures preyed on the smaller, who preyed in turn on the smaller still, and they all fought to defend what was theirs.

He was part of that chain. He would fight to protect what was his. He was a hunter. It was time to start hunting. No one would see him. Stealth, cunning, watchfulness, he had learned all these things. He would get his prey.

47

Kate

2002

Kate stood up, shaking off the trance that had enveloped her since reading the letters of Susan and Rose. She needed to clear her head, detach herself from it all, weigh up the implications, and think of the next move.

Above all she needed to share her thoughts with Dan.

But his presence was no longer in the study. Sentimentally, she had tried to disturb as little as possible to try and keep him there but, she realised, all she was preserving was the dust and decay of memory. Nothing symbolised that so much as his fossilised coffee mug. She picked it up, and the note on which it had been sitting came away with it.

It provided her with final confirmation, if confirmation were needed: Dan had been murdered and Frank was his killer.

She felt desperate. Suppressing the instinct that warned she would be better not to go out alone, she wrote Polly a brief note, left it on the kitchen table, and slipped her mobile into her jacket pocket.

Mindful of the danger, aware that if Frank were stalking her she would not see him, she climbed out of a side window of the house, slipped through the yew hedge, which would conceal her both from the front of the house and the farmyard, and made her way along the riverbank to the point where the little stream joined the river. She leapt over the stream and shielded by a thick tangle of blackthorn and sloe, she skirted the river to the bridge.

If he were going to spot her, she would be most visible crossing the bridge.

But she could see no one.

Passing swiftly over the bridge, she climbed into the meadow and took the footpath that led up across the fields for some two miles to the little church.

It was a steep climb, the ground was slippery underfoot and it was hard going. Her rasping breath hung heavily on the air, her mouth was dry, her heart thumped, but she didn't notice. Her entire attention was absorbed by her thoughts.

Frank! Frank Leach killed Dan! How could they have all been so blind? She had been so determined, from the first, that if it hadn't been an accident then it must have been suicide. How could her brain have been so addled she could think that Dan, her darling, beloved Dan, would have taken his own life? Now this…this revelation. Murder? Murders belonged to another world, not to them. They were ordinary people. They could understand accidents, encompass suicides at a pinch, but murder?

It was almost more painful than anything. So wanton, so cruel, so obscenely unnecessary. How would she explain that to the children? How would they cope with the knowledge that their father's life had been taken by someone else? How would that affect the rest of their lives? Unanswerable questions.

If only she didn't have to tell them.

Why? They would want to know. Why?

Why? Her brain moved restlessly over the accumulated facts. Frank wasn't Jem's son – was he afraid if Dan found out he would evict him? Or that Rose knew about the murder of his real father and had told Dan? It wasn't rational, none of it was. But maybe that act of terrible violence, at such an early age, set him on the path of madness…or maybe he was already mad and that was what Susan was worried about?

Woodside Farm was all Frank had and Dan gave him notice, just as she had done. The note she had found stuck to the bottom of the mug was a ploy, probably from Frank himself, to lure Dan into the woods. And now he was after her.

The wicket gate creaked quietly as she let herself into the churchyard. In January it had a desolate air. The grass was sodden and dead with winter's cold, the bare branches of the trees shivering in a bitter north wind; the paths between the graves were streaked with mud, and the few flowers that lay on them were forlorn and waterlogged, wilting with the cold.

She stood by Dan's grave and spoke softly. 'Dan, I know it all now, all that matters. You loved us and we love you still, and always will. Nothing can take that away. Dan, I'm in such pain. I don't know what to say, what to do…' The tears flowed. 'I can hardly bring myself to speak about it, but I've got to, haven't I? I promised Ben and Rosie I would find out the truth, no matter how painful. Now I know. And I didn't realise how bitter that knowledge would be. It's so awful, I can't bear it! Help me, darling. Please, help me…'

She didn't hear the creak of the wicket gate or the soft footfalls coming towards her. It was a sudden impulse to kiss the turf on Dan's grave that saved her, for at that precise moment Frank Leach, his poacher's snare taut between his hands, pounced to catch her round her throat.

Her unexpected movement left Frank lunging at the air and, off-balance, he fell half on top off her.

In her nightmares, fleeing from the pursuing figure, Kate's limbs had always turned to lead. Awake now, her terror gave her the strength to pull herself away and she ran screaming across the graves, straight into Ted's arms.

Josh, immediately behind him, leaped past and made a grab for Frank, but he was too slow, and the last Kate saw of Frank Leach he was leaping over the wall and disappearing out of sight.

48

Kate

2002

'There, it's all there, all the proof we need that Frank killed Dan.' Kate was still shivering, in spite of the blanket that Polly had wrapped round her and the huge mug of tea Ted had pressed into her hand.

The three of them were in the kitchen, waiting for the police to arrive. Polly and Ted were reading the documents Kate had pressed upon them.

'Frank killed his father, that's what Rose wanted Dan to know, and he wasn't entitled to Woodside Farm. Dan sent notice to Frank and so Frank lured Dan up to Sparrow Woods. Then, when I gave him notice, he turned his attentions on me. It's as clear as day!'

Ted looked up. 'No it's not, Kate.' His voice was sympathetic, but firm.

'What do you mean?' She could hear her voice shrill with disbelief. 'I must stay calm,' she thought.' I mustn't get hysterical, not now. Not when I'm going to have to face the police.'

'What I mean is I don't think Frank killed Dan.'

'What?' Kate stared at him.

Polly was equally startled. 'But Ted, why on earth not? It couldn't be clearer…'

Ted spread the papers out on the table. 'Susan's letter is strong stuff; we've no reason not to believe her, but you know not being Jem's son wouldn't make any difference to his right to the tenancy, not these days. We know, now, that Dan sent him notice, but Kate, Frank never read the letter; he didn't know that Dan planned to get rid of him and he certainly didn't write that note luring Dan up to the woods.'

Kate felt completely confused.

'How do you know all this?' Polly demanded.

'Because he's totally illiterate. He can neither read nor write. I'm amazed we never discovered this before, but then, I suppose, we didn't have an awful lot to do with him and I guess he'd learned sufficient to scrawl a signature when it was required…'

'But he knew I was giving him notice,' Kate protested, unwilling to let go. 'And he tried to kill me. He read my letter. The same as Dan…'

'No it's not the same. He knew you wanted him to leave because you told him so, face to face. He never even opened your letter. And Dan never saw him; Josh told me. They'd gone up to Woodside so Dan could deliver the notice personally. But although they waited ages, they didn't see Frank, so they pinned the letter to the door and left.'

'But how do you know he's illiterate?' Kate demanded. 'What makes you so sure?'

'Josh and I went to Woodside Farm early this morning,

before dawn. I was determined to talk to him, but there was no sign of him so we went inside the house to wait for his return. The place was a shambles, hadn't been cleaned for years I reckon, and while we were waiting we had a bit of a look round. In the sitting room there was an old wooden bureau, the top of which was half open. I pulled the lid back and found it stuffed full of unopened letters and circulars, dating back at least twenty years. He'd thrown nothing away but, oddly, nothing was opened. I sifted through them as best I could and found your letter, Kate, and eventually one from Dan. Again, both unopened. It was so strange it set me thinking and I looked round the place again. Now, in any farmhouse, even the most impoverished, you'd expect to find stock magazines, farming manuals of some sort, tabloid newspapers perhaps, the odd book even, invoices, notepaper – almost certainly, a biro or two, pencils, perhaps. There was nothing.'

'But that note, luring Dan up to the woods...' Kate's voice trailed away.

'I really don't think he wrote it. Yes, I think it was what took Dan up there that morning, but I'm inclined to think it was from some disgruntled poacher. There was no love lost between Frank and the rest of that godforsaken fraternity.'

'But do you have any *real* proof, apart from the stuff you found, that he's illiterate?'

'When he returned, I told him that you wanted to be sure he knew he was under notice. I gave him a letter I had picked out, at random, from his bureau. I told him it was from you and asked him to tell me what it said.'

'What did he do with it?' Polly asked.

'He opened it, stared at it, said he understood it right enough, that you wanted him to leave but that he wasn't going and nothing you could do would make him give up Woodside.'

Ted shook his head. 'He was blustering. He'd no idea what was in that letter.'

'So you don't think he killed Dan?'

'No, I don't. When Frank found us in his house, he had a fit. I told him we'd come because of the attacks on you and that the police were re-thinking Dan's death. Kate, he was adamant he didn't have anything to do with it. He said he was in the woods when he heard a gun shot and he scarpered.'

'And you believe him?'

Ted took Kate's hands in his and said gently, 'Yes, yes I do. For one thing, his manner when I talked about the attacks on you was completely different.'

'I see.' Kate sighed deeply and slumped back in her chair. 'But everything pointed to him…but if… So what happened when you left?'

Ted grimaced. 'He left before us. He became very agitated after the business with the letter and suddenly rushed out. We followed, but he'd disappeared. So we came back here. John Potter was shouting for help, so I delayed coming to tell you what had happened.' Ted pursed his lips, looking grave. 'It was stupid of me. Unforgivable. It wasn't until Brenda gave the alarm that I realised the danger you were in. If I'd come to you as soon as I got back…' His voice choked. 'I'm so sorry, Kate.'

'Oh Ted, there's nothing to be sorry about…' She squeezed his hand. 'It was very frightening, but at least it's all out in the open now, isn't it? I have to believe you're right – he didn't murder Dan, and, you know, that is such a relief. I just didn't know how I was going to tell the children… It was just too horrible… And I know, I *know* Dan didn't commit suicide. It was an accident, as the coroner said in the beginning.' She gave him a woebegone smile. 'The children and I can now move on, and that's thanks to you.'

But Ted was not comforted. 'But I exposed you to real danger, Kate. If Brenda hadn't spotted him…'

'I never thought I'd owe my life to Brenda!' said Kate, lightly, attempting to cheer him up.

The fortuitous arrival of Ted and Josh in the churchyard, it transpired, was due to Brenda. She had been standing outside the cheese shed, having a quick fag, and had watched as Kate walked up over the field. Then she noticed a man appear from under the bridge and climb into the field. She had finished her cigarette, gone back inside and casually mentioned what she'd seen to Colin. He immediately told Polly, who rang Ted and then rushed to the house. That was when she found the note telling her where Kate had gone.

'We tried phoning you, to warn you,' Polly shook her head, 'but your mobile was switched off. Oh Kate, I had a few nasty moments!'

The sound of a car arriving in the yard interrupted them.

Ted stood up. 'Looks like the police have finally arrived. Are you feeling strong enough for this, Kate?'

She sighed. She was not looking forward to it, not at all. She attempted a smile. 'Bring them on in. Oh Ted, just to satisfy my curiosity, the letter you gave Frank to read, pretending it was from me. What did it actually say?'

A slight smile flickered across his features. 'It was a letter from The Friends of St Mary's, asking for a donation to help restore the church tower.'

49

Frank

He knew they were looking for him. His home was being watched. He knew it wasn't safe to be seen, but he was a hunter and he knew how to remain invisible. They made so much noise, thrashing and crashing about. They were everywhere. But they would go, in time; they did not have the patience to sit and watch and wait.

Not like him.

The moon had risen clear and full on the cold, star-filled night when he saw the last of the cars leave.

He slipped down to the house, wary, watchful. It was dark, quiet. There was no-one about, but it was clear they had been here, had touched everything. Nothing was as he'd left it, as if some animal had urinated on everything, despoiling his space, staking a claim.

He went from room to room. It was the same, everywhere. Both his room and the old man's room: the beds had been stripped, cupboard emptied, drawers upturned.

He had not been in the old man's room since he had watched him die, screaming with the pain of it. He'd started to die from the day he'd locked that girl in the birdcage. They'd had a bad fight after that and for the first time, he, Frank, had taken the old man's belt off him.

That was when the old man had told him who the corpse was in the birdcage and had mocked him. He shouldn't have done that. He shouldn't have done lots of things, but he shouldn't have done that. It took nearly two years, but, bit by little bit, the tiny doses of arsenic ate into his gut and he died.

They'd even been in Her room and not bothered to put it back the way he always kept it, for Her. He stood in the doorway looking at the wreckage, and somewhere, deep in the heart of him, a great sob formed. They would not take it from him. They would not.

He turned and slipped down the stairs, out of the house and went to the barn.

It did not take him long. Soon everything was in place. Standing for the last time at the kitchen door, he struck a match.

The fire in the farmhouse was sufficiently bright to illuminate his passage through the dark of the barn, his tall silhouette throwing a long shadow across the floor to the twisted remains of the birdcage. He climbed in, sat on the earth, and scrabbled in the soil until he felt something hard. Then he relaxed and lit another match.

437

50

Kate

2002

The fire had taken a firm hold before it was spotted. By the time the fire engines arrived, it had almost burned itself out. All that was left of the farmhouse and the outbuildings were piles of ash and rubble.

Raking through the embers of the barn they came across the burned-out body of Frank and a half-exposed skeleton.

The atmosphere at Watersmeet was sombre as they digested the news.

Polly was particularly upset. 'Poor Frank, what a horrible way to die.'

Ted, unusually demonstrative, put his arm around her. 'Yes, but think of it Pol, what would have happened to him if the police had caught up with him? Do you think Frank, who was a half wild creature, could have survived any form of imprisonment? It would have been a slow, torturous death for him. Better this way, however horrible it might seem.'

'And he took Woodside Farm with him. That must have given him great satisfaction,' Kate added.

That afternoon she drove over to Bristol to collect her children, and after their return, she and Ben walked up to Dan's grave.

On the way, she told him a little of the events of the last few days and, more particularly, of her search to find the truth behind his dad's death so that she could fulfil her promise to him.

'It *was* an accident, Ben. An accident. Why he climbed the stile with a cocked gun, we will never know. But he had such ideas for the future of the farm and for saving Watersmeet. He was full of life and hope.'

Ben struggled, confused and upset. 'And that man, Frank, didn't kill him? You're sure? He tried to kill you…' He shivered, close to tears.

'No, darling, he didn't kill Dad. We're sure. There's nothing now to fear, Ben. Frank's gone and I'm here. I'm safe.'

At the graveside, she knelt down and took her son in her arms. 'Listen to me, Ben, I want to tell you something, something very precious. Nothing we can say or do will bring Daddy back, but nothing can take away what he gave us, and what we have still, and that is his love for us. He might not be with us, physically, but I know he's with us, watching us, loving us. It's difficult to explain, but I'm sure, darling, that the thought that made me bend down just as Frank tried to…tried to attack me, that thought came from Dad. I'm sure of it. He saved me. Oh darling, there'll be times when we'll miss him so much it'll be unbearable. But the fact is, we – you, Rosie and me – have known his love; we have shared something precious and nothing can take that from us.'

*

439

Night had fallen. Ted had gone off to help with the evening's milking. Polly was upstairs reading to the children, and Kate was in the kitchen, peeling vegetables for the evening's supper.

She had expected to feel relief but instead she felt numb. She had reached the end of a journey. She had achieved... What? There was no feeling of elation, but no comfort either. No sense of...well, something life-enhancing; something she could feel joyful about. For the truth, the irreversible truth was that Dan was still dead and there was nothing she could do about it.

She turned, leaning against the sink, and looked around her. The kitchen, warm, untidy, was the same as it had been before he died. He could have just left the room, gone out of that door... She closed her eyes.

'Life goes on, Katie,' Dan's voice whispered. 'I'm not far away.'

She froze. She knew instinctively she was not alone. Her skin prickled. 'Dan,' she said hoarsely, 'Dan...' The tears sprang to her eyes. 'Please, Dan... Please... I'm listening, Dan, say something... I love you...'

But he'd gone and she was alone, with the comforting, whispering sounds of the kitchen.

She groped for a tissue. 'How different,' she thought, blowing her nose, 'my life has been compared to Susan Leach. Poor, wretched creature: no one to love her. What a sodding, horrible life. No one but Rose cared. Dan loved me. And he loves me still. He gave me so much. So much! And what did Susan have? From anybody? Nothing! Whatever else,' she said aloud, 'I'll find your grave, Susan, however difficult that may be. And when I find it, I'll put up a headstone for you.'

A tap on the kitchen door interrupted her, and before she'd had a chance to wipe her eyes, Splash bounced in, barking

440

excitedly. William followed, a bottle of wine in one hand, a bunch of flowers in the other.

'Splash heard Ben and Rosie are home and doesn't want to be parted from them any longer. And hearing about your narrow escape, Kate, I thought a glass of wine would be a good idea. But,' he added, looking more closely at her and putting the wine and flowers down. 'At this particular moment I think what you are more in need of is this...'

And so saying, he put his arms around her.

No-one had hugged her like this since Dan. Warm, strong, undemanding. She melted into the hug and was comforted.

A few moments later, he let her go.

'Ready for that glass of wine?'

'Thank you, William, thank you so much...'

Before anything more could be said, the roar of an engine entering the yard interrupted them. Moments later Max burst into the kitchen, a bottle of champagne in one hand and a large bunch of flowers in the other.

'Katie, I just heard; I came as soon as I could, I...' The expression on his face when he saw William was comical.

Kate, laughing, hugged him. 'Oh Max, it's lovely to see you. You're just in time to join us for supper...'

The telephone rang and leaving William and Max to sort themselves out, she went to answer it. It was her mother.

'Katherine, darling, I'm glad you're there. You haven't spoken to the Press have you?'

'No, not ...'

'Such dreadful people... Making something out of nothing... making everything up and so persistent. Won't take no for an answer...'

'But why...'

'I can't count the number of calls today...and they've even

441

come to the house… They won't go away… There's one outside now. I understand why they call it door-stepping…'

'Mum, I don't know why…'

'It's outrageous, there should be a law about it. I've told them, I'll call the police, but they take no notice. They're just waiting for us to go out… We're virtually prisoners… You're to say nothing to them, Katherine, nothing at all, do you understand, and tell Polly too, we must be absolutely discreet.'

Kate was completely bewildered. 'We will, Mum, don't worry. I don't know why you've been bothered. The inspector in charge of the case said that there *will* be press interest, but the police are going to advise us how to handle that…'

Her mother cut her off sharply. 'Police, how are they involved? This has got nothing to do with them… Is it worse than I thought? Is Emily in more trouble than she's told us? Katherine, you'd better tell me everything you know. That dreadful man! He took advantage of her… I wish she'd never met him… Writing about her in such a way… Everyone is talking. The scandal! Think of the scandal. Poor Ivan. I knew things weren't right. He hardly spoke to anyone at my Christmas party and then he left early. Such a disappointment… Everyone had so wanted to meet him…'

'Emily?' Kate interrupted. 'Is this to do with Emily?'

'Yes of course it is. Who else would it be about? Really Katherine, I know you've had your troubles, but there *are* others in the family who need our support…'

'I'll talk to you later, Mum. I've got to go, I've got guests…' And for the first time in her life, Kate put the phone down on her mother.

For a moment, numb no longer, she stared at the phone and then, to the amazement of both Max and William, collapsed into a chair, helpless with laughter.

A Letter to Dan

It's Rosie's birthday tomorrow, my darling. Do you remember the day she was born you brought me a bunch of early snowdrops? This morning, I went for a walk along the river to the great old ash tree. You took me there once, on a freezing January day, and showed me the first snowdrops of the year, growing in the shelter of the tree roots. They were there this morning and I picked a bunch to put on your grave.

Rosie is very excited about her birthday. She is going to have a small party. Ben gave her a hard time at first.

'How can you have a party without Dad?' he demanded. 'Who's gonna do the games?' But when she grew upset, not only did he relent, but he offered to organise the games himself. Eight little girls – a bit of a tall order I suggested, even for a superior nine-year-old – but he insisted and so Toby is coming over to help him. I'll tell you tomorrow how they get on.

Ben doesn't seem so angry. He still asks me questions about the Leaches and about what might have happened, and I try to be as honest with him as I can be. He's being very protective of Rosie, but I've encouraged them to talk about everything as much as they need to.

We are going to discuss what to do with the ruins of Woodside Farm at today's farm meeting. I am against re-building. There was so much unhappiness in that house. Better, I think, to put it to some other use. Ted has suggested turning the woods into some sort of a wildlife sanctuary and building a visitor's centre on the site.

I have thought a lot about Frank and his poor mother. I know you will understand when I say 'poor Frank', and that I am glad, for his sake, it's all over. You and I had so much, Dan. So much love, so much laughter – they had absolutely nothing.

It feels like I've reached the end of a major chapter in my life. It's time to move on, but my dearest, dearest Dan, I know I am not leaving you behind. I carry your love inside me. It will always be part of who I am.

Acknowledgements

My heartfelt thanks to those of my friends who read *A Long Shadow*, sometimes more than once, providing me with invaluable advice and very welcome support.

And a particular thanks to Scott Pack without whom this book would have languished, unread, unseen, on my desk top.